In the Company of Strangers

This is a work of fiction. Names, characters, places and incidents are products of the author's imagination or are used fictitiously. Any resemblance to actual events or locales or persons, living or dead, is entirely coincidental.

To order additional copies, please contact us.
BookSurge, LLC
www.booksurge.com
1-866-308-6235
orders@booksurge.com

P.D. LaFLEUR

IN THE
COMPANY OF
STRANGERS

In the Company of Strangers

Beware of entrance to a quarrel; but being in,
Bear't that the opposed may beware of thee.
Polonius to Laertes
Hamlet, William Shakespeare

To Suzanne, Marc And Lauren

CHAPTER ONE

Near Bayou La Batre, Alabama

THE ALUMINUM CREW boat bobbed like a cork in the Gulf, still dangerously close to the mammoth steel cargo ship to which it had been tied. Its cargo loaded, the crew of three was pleased to be on its way. The captain shoved off and set his course northwest. The twin engines growled and the bow raised its nose. Minutes later, they approached the cove and the captain aimed the bow towards the wooden dock. This was an unusually cool afternoon for a summer day in Alabama, but the dock's owner stood alone, dressed in a tee shirt, shorts and sandals, and patiently waited for the crew boat to slow and tie up. Wordlessly, the crew unloaded the five crates and placed them on the bed of a pickup truck. The captain approached the dock's owner and accepted an envelope that he knew held a wad of bills, a fine payday for light duty, and a full week's pay for each crew member for just a few hours' work. They exchanged nods. No words were said.

The owner of the dock climbed into the cab of the pickup and drove slowly, deliberately, to a large metal building that served as a garage and warehouse. When he had driven inside, he shut off the engines and slid the double doors closed. He scanned the five crates of cargo. They were only six feet long, two feet wide and three feet tall, but they possessed a power unknown less than a century ago. Spray-painted on the sides were a series of numbers and the forbidding symbol—three triangles in a circle warning of nuclear materials. Inside them, he was assured, were sufficient arms to eradicate a small city. Not that he'd ever use them. But one never knew when they might be needed. And he wanted to be prepared. And be on the winning side if and when that moment ever came.

The Mozambique Channel

THE SEA BELOW was calm and visibility was crystal clear. Just ahead lay Madagascar. Clearing a ridge over rugged foothills near Morondava, the cargo plane circled twice before it began its final descent. The pilot lined the nose of the plane even with the single runway and almost skimmed the tops of the palms and mangroves as he trimmed the craft and reduced engine speed. The tires met the pavement and he gently brought the plane to a halt. In seconds, two large delivery vans, white and unmarked, appeared from the edge of the rainforest and pulled within feet of the cargo door. Sixteen minutes later, the cargo was offloaded and the captain pointed the nose into the wind to begin his takeoff, his task accomplished. The seven crates, each bearing the distinctive symbol of nuclear materials, were on their way to a destination unknown to him. He had no interest in knowing the specifics. He was just relieved to have the crates off his plane.

The pilot knew that a packet would be waiting for him in a locker at the Durban airport when he arrived, and that it would contain a thick stack of South African rands. The procedure was always the same. The new wealth he enjoyed from being chartered by the peculiar man whose name he never knew was welcomed. He had his own plans for his future, and they did not include ferrying horrific cargo over dangerous waters in an aged aircraft. For now, he was simply glad that the cargo was gone. He had no desire to be vaporized into the next world.

Off Stewart Island, New Zealand

THE TRIP WAS made in the calmest of waters at midday. The craft, a forty-six foot Chris Craft trawler, was lumbering towards the small private harbor nestled along the southwestern tip of the island. The boat's owner, ruddy from the sun and wearing only swimming trunks and a canvas cap, smiled to himself as he slowed the engines and prepared to angle the cruiser towards the dock. He was alone on this trip. It was a relatively small shipment this time, certainly smaller than the last shipment he received. He'd have no trouble muscling the three cartons by himself. They weighed less than one hundred pounds each, and he was in excellent physical shape.

He shut the engines down and coasted gently to the dock. In two minutes, the ropes were secured to the cleats, and he turned his attention to the three cartons. He hoisted them from the deck of the boat and placed them side-by-side on the surface of the dock. In a few minutes, he'd place them in the rear of his aging Jeep, a relic from the American GIs in World War II, and drive them to his small warehouse. But for now, he'd remain on board his boat, enjoy a cigar, and consider his good fortune. The cargo had cost him less than three million American dollars. The money was nothing to him; he had hundreds of millions at his disposal. But in return, he was now the owner of six handheld rocket launchers, each armed with a small nuclear warhead.

Whether or not he'd ever have to put them to their intended use, he could not predict. But as an observer of world affairs, he sensed growing unrest in all corners. An uprising in East Timor. A riot in Cincinnati. The Islamic Jihad spreading out from the Mideast. Al-Qaida. Who knows what band of crazies would be the next big threat. Getting arms of superior quality and firepower was becoming easier than ever, and he envisioned frightful possibilities as they increasingly fell into the wrong hands. He wanted arms in the right hands, especially nuclear arms. His arms. His hands.

CHAPTER TWO

Boston

CAPTAIN HENRY OATES eased the Navy-issued, dark blue Ford sedan into the right-hand lane of the Central Artery, out of the line of traffic and down the ramp. The exit sign was barely readable in the developing dusk of this November afternoon: "South Station-Kneeland Street," but he was not unfamiliar with the terrain; his travels had taken him to Boston often during his career. At the end of the ramp, he turned left and wove slowly through the tangle of trucks and cars and the pedestrian swarm of Kneeland Street on the seedy fringe of Chinatown. The pace was impatient, the traffic signals in this section of the city but a suggestion. He was unruffled by the noise and the motion as he managed his way through the congestion and came to the Park Plaza Hotel. He turned left and waited for the light to change. Ahead of him lay the less frantic triangle of Park Square. If his memory served him correctly, and it invariably did, when he reached the square, he should turn right onto Columbus Avenue, turn right again at Dartmouth, then left at Copley Square. As a matter of course, Captain Henry Oates trusted his memory and his instincts, and he was rarely disappointed.

He glanced at his watch, the new Tag Heuer he had recently received from his wife for his forty-eighth birthday. Ten past four. He would reach the Prudential Center, park in the underground garage, eat a light dinner alone, and be well rested and fully prepared for his meeting with the senator at seven thirty.

This was not to be a social call. When he received the call from the senator two days ago asking him to take time from the weeklong conference at the Newport Naval War College in Rhode Island for a few hours and come to Boston, he knew the meeting would be all business. From the tone of the Senator's voice, Oates could tell that the senator would take the opportunity of the meeting to raise the issue once again of discontinuing their "arrangement." In the senator's sanitized words, "An amicable disaffiliation." The meeting could prove to be a real ballbuster, Oates speculated, but it was his intention that they would not be his balls that would be busted. No sir. A seasoned officer with a position of immense importance in the Pentagon, Oates was accustomed to facing obstacles, and he knew well how to deal with them: They could be stepped around, jumped over, or blown up. At this moment, Oates didn't particularly care how he might deal with this evening's obstacles, but he was absolutely certain he would emerge with his testicles intact. He had worked too hard, too long. He had taken too many risks to have his arrangement with the senator, and his life's careful plans, cut short on someone else's whim. It was too soon. Maybe in a year, maybe even a little less, the prospect of going their separate ways would make sense. After all, this was not a lifelong endeavor. Their arrangement had a limited useful life in the very best of circumstances. But he needed another year before calling it quits, before he cashed in and cleared out. He'd just have to talk some sense to the senator at the meeting and make his point eminently clear—the arrangement was not to be terminated. Not yet. Period. Paragraph.

It was precisely 4:30 when Oates turned the sedan onto the entry ramp of the Prudential Center underground parking garage. He took his parking receipt from the dispenser, found a space against a wall in the far corner, and pulled in. Shutting off the engine, Oates placed the keys and the parking receipt in the pocket of his dress blue jacket. He had purposely chosen his dress blues for this evening's meeting. The uniform, pressed to a knife crease, shimmering with four stripes up, four stripes down, and bearing a blaze of medals, would carry its own deliberate message to the senator. Especially when it was worn by someone with the physical presence of Captain Henry Howell Oates. *Don't screw with me. Don't even think about it.*

Oates angled his frame from the seat and slipped the jacket on. He flexed his shoulders and caught his reflection in the car's window. He smiled, and with studied ease, walked slowly, hatless, to the garage stairs and rose to face the fifty-two stories of the Prudential office building, the central feature of a sprawling, upscale sub-metropolis known less formally as "The Pru," with its residential high-rises, retail marketplace, and a score of restaurants. He paused, deliberated, and then opted to walk to the plaza's south entry. Oates was casually aware of the glances he drew as he entered the full light of the Prudential Center's enclosed shopping mall, and he usually enjoyed this sort of attention more than he might have admitted. He was tall, with a lean, athletic build, stately good looks, and flecks of gray at the temples. On another day, or at another time in his life, he might have returned the glance of an attractive young lady with one of his own. But tonight he paid little attention; his mind was gearing up for the meeting. Another quick glance at his watch. Plenty of time to decide upon a restaurant, select a quiet table, eat a light supper, relax, and consider his strategy for the evening.

***

IN BRIGHTON, THREE miles away, an uneasy Senator John Munroe approached the tollbooth at the Massachusetts Turnpike. He fumbled in his pocket for some change and a fistful of loose coins spilled across the gray leather seat of his Eldorado.

"Hello there, senator!"

The senator looked up abruptly. The toll collector recognized Munroe, who returned the greeting with an automatic smile and a mechanical wave that belied the knot in his stomach. Munroe handed the collector two quarters, mumbled thanks, and drove off. He ran his fingers through his trademark blond waves and daubed his forehead with a handkerchief. It was late November, but he was perspiring heavily. His starched white shirt was damp and clammy against his skin. He was not looking forward to his meeting with Henry Oates, but there was no way to avoid it. Munroe had been given his instructions: Their "arrangement," however well hidden from public scrutiny it may have been so far, and however profitable it had proved, must come to an end. At once. The schedule had been moved up. The gears of Munroe's political machine were being put in motion, the funding already in place, and this ongoing arrangement with Oates presented a potential and considerable barrier. Munroe's mentor, the architect of his political career, had insisted. Next year was the year. THE year. The situation was exceptionally ripe, and the resources were ready and waiting to be put to use. The biggest campaign of Munroe's life would be ready to launch soon, and he could ill afford to have any hint of his transactions with Oates see the light of day.

The nation had proved its capacity to abide scandalous presidents, to be sure, testing, but rarely fracturing the ability of the masses to suffer depravity in its leaders. But most of those scandals concerned sex, money, the misuse of authority, or sordid bits and pieces of all three. Munroe's association with Oates certainly involved enormous sums of money, but it was founded on the force of power, a terrible power. Arms, missiles, even nuclear devices, secretly, explicitly illegally, and very profitably parceled out to a short list of selected firms and individuals around the globe. This was a thriving arrangement taking maximum illicit advantage of Oates' position in the Pentagon and Munroe's standing in the United States Senate. Even an electorate inured to the perverse appetites of thieves, liars, and satyrs at the highest levels of its government would be repulsed if they detected the malodorous machinations of the Oates-Munroe connection. Detection was out of the question; a hint would be fatal to Munroe's chances.

The meeting tonight would be at Munroe's Boston office on the forty-fifth floor of the Prudential office building. The only staff member in Munroe's office today was Meredith McCarthy, the administrative assistant for his Boston office for twelve years, and she left the office at precisely 4:30 every day. She knew nothing of this evening's meeting, and Munroe felt certain of Oates' discretion. So he and Oates would have time to talk through the issues before them in private and on Munroe's turf, which was fine with Munroe.

The issues before them were not meant for public consumption. Not at all.

Munroe's nerves were taut, and he approached the meeting with dread. He detested confrontation, in spite of his growing reputation as one of his party's freshest and fiercest pit bulls. But this was different. In the Senate, his moves could be choreographed, his words scored and rehearsed to achieve their precise intended effect. Like an actor entering the stage, Munroe prepared himself well for his very public Beltway battles and knew his lines before the plays began. Tonight, though, he feared he would face a loose cannon in Henry Oates. Rehearsals might be helpful, and Munroe had practiced his delivery well. But Henry Oates, he predicted, would likely have his own script. Munroe would need to counter with his best performance.

As he drove Munroe tried to play the meeting through his mind, anticipating Oates' opposition. *It will be important to present my position carefully, argue rationally, and respond calmly,* he thought. Oates will listen and come to understand that their arrangement, however well it had served the needs of its participants for the past three years, must be brought to a quiet, immediate close. This was the ideal outcome, but Munroe admitted it was idle, wishful thinking. As he entered the turnpike tunnel and approached his exit, Munroe dismissed this scene, much more certain, instead, that Oates would resist the proposal fiercely and deny Munroe any hope of an easy victory.

He pulled into the parking ramp beneath the Prudential building and approached the ticket dispenser. From the visor, he pulled his parking card and inserted it into the slot reserved for VIP tenants of the building. Munroe, like most of the executive tenants, had parking rights built into his lease. That way, he wouldn't have to pay each time he used the garage. For one flat rate, Munroe only had to tape a monthly parking sticker to his windshield and slide a special plastic card with its encoded magnetic stripe into a slot. He removed his card and the gate opened immediately. He wheeled the Eldorado into his reserved spot near the end of the first row and stopped the engine.

A glance at his watch told him it was nearing 5 o'clock. He sighed deeply and opened the door of his car with a sense of resignation. As he slipped on his gray suit jacket tailored at Louis', as were all his clothes, Munroe hoped that by 8 o'clock, the meeting with Oates would be over.

It would be. Unceremoniously over.

He shook his head. *This is crazy*, he thought. The deals with Oates were never meant to go on forever. At least in Munroe's mind they were not; at first he was appalled at the concept. It was only at his mentor's insistence and assurances that the clandestine arms shipments were in the best interests of the nation that the idea took shape and became a reality. And now, with the senator's plans being laid out for the coming year—huge plans, enormous plans—the understanding with Oates would have to end. It had to stop. So be it. Munroe knew the marching orders. He accepted them. And it was his job to convince Oates of the same.

The garage elevator took him to the office building's lobby. When he stepped off and made his way to the central elevator bank that would take him to his floor, he was only mildly aware of the nods and stares he drew from passersby. A frequent subject of local and national news broadcasts, John Munroe, United States Senator, was recognized by nearly everyone. He was on autopilot now, acknowledging the attention with mindless hellos and occasional oblivious smiles. He was grateful that he was the sole passenger in the elevator for the ride to the forty-fifth floor. He took a deep breath and exhaled slowly. He needed strength.

Munroe stepped off the elevator and made his way down the hallway to his office. He used his key to open the oversized oak door and entered the empty anteroom. As expected, Meredith was gone for the day. He entered his private office and noted a stack of messages next to his phone. He ignored them and walked, instead, to the window, which faced east. The skies were unusually clear and Munroe's eye was caught by the juxtaposition of stars glittering in the darkened eastern sky and the faint remaining pink edge of the western horizon reflecting off the mirrored facade of the John Hancock office tower a few blocks away and in front of him. He yearned momentarily for the tranquility the scene implied.

Turning back to his desk, he walked around the back and sat in the heavy leather swivel chair. The chair had sentimental significance for Munroe, for his parents had presented it to him when he was first elected to the Massachusetts legislature some fifteen years earlier. A man of such importance, his mother told him then with a prideful smile, should have such a large and comfortable chair in which to think great thoughts. He was reminded of her words when he reached inside the top drawer for a pad of paper and a pen. *They are not to be great thoughts tonight, dear mother,* he mused with deepening guilt. Munroe began to organize his thoughts for one final dress rehearsal.

He set to work by placing key words in an outline on the pad before him. He jotted down recollected remarks from the conversation he'd had with his mentor, the architect of his career, his "Chairman," as Munroe referred to him, two days ago. It was then he had received his very specific orders: Call Oates and terminate the arrangement at once. Munroe truly sensed some relief at the prospect of extracting himself from his compact with Captain Henry Oates. He had no quarrel with the outcome; it was the process of achieving it that disturbed him deeply and instilled in his gut a hollow, acid fear.

Recording snippets of recalled conversation, Munroe occasionally strung the words together and mouthed them to test their strength and effectiveness. Once in a while he'd stand at his desk and recite a sentence or two, with appropriate gestures to enhance the scene; he needed the confidence a dress rehearsal could provide. The oversized U.S. flag on the wall behind his desk would, he hoped, lend him some added credibility and endow his words with some greater authority than he actually felt at the moment.

Munroe checked his watch frequently with futile foreboding. He wanted 7:30 to come, and he wanted it to forever remain in the distance.

While he worked diligently and desperately hoped he would prevail upon Oates, Senator John Munroe had yet no way of knowing that this evening's meeting with Captain Henry Oates would not only bring an end to the arrangement, it would do so in a sudden, horrifying fashion that would forever change his life and the lives of many people he'd never meet and never know.

CHAPTER THREE

MATTHEW KEYES KNEW that November weather in Boston was chancy. It could be harsh with the promise of an arctic winter, or balmy with the sweet spices of fall. This evening was windless and still mild from the day's just departed sun. At 5:30, the sky was as clear as crystal and already at its darkest.

Keyes had arrived earlier in the day and began a solitary reacquaintance with the city with a lazy stroll though the streets of Back Bay. It was a comfortable day for admiring the brownstone buildings and the tree-lined boulevards of the area. But now, the sidewalks were clogging with office workers moving briskly to their buses, subways, cabs, and vanpools. Automobile traffic had thickened and was anxious to move north, west, and south. Impatient horns and the sudden squeals of brakes punctuated the rush hour crush. Pedestrians darted, determined and unafraid, across streets close to the cars, everyone eager to be someplace else.

Standing near the corner of Dartmouth and Boylston streets, Keyes felt isolated amid the throng. Although Boston was his favorite city and was once his home, he'd been living in northern Vermont for several years, and this day amounted to just a brief visit for him. Unlike those around him, Keyes was not poised to move in any particular direction. Instead, he ambled slowly, absorbing the congested scene around him. People parted to pass him by. To them, he was just an ordinary man dressed in jeans and a common blue parka, a momentary non-threatening impediment to this evening's migration.

Had anyone paused and genuinely and seriously considered, though, Matthew Keyes would still appear unremarkable. Certainly he did not look like someone poised on the threshold of his life's greatest adventure. Even to himself, he felt, well...average. That was the word. To him, it was an indictment. Or more precisely, the owner of an indifferent life. Tomorrow morning, with his scheduled departure from Logan Airport, this would finally begin to change. Matthew Keyes truly felt poised to make, in his own personal way, a difference.

He stopped at a corner news dealer and bought a copy of the *Boston Herald*, supposing that he may wish to occupy himself later on. But his mind was fully occupied at the moment with thoughts of passing this evening in this city, indeed, what would be his last evening in this country, for the next ten months. The anticipation of soon embarking upon a long held dream consumed the largest zone of his brain. He expected he would enjoy a pleasant, solitary stroll through the familiar streets of Boston before relaxing in his hotel room with stories of the Celtics, the Bruins, and the latest political scandal in this scandal-hungry place. He considered his immediate options and decided that he'd begin with seeking out a single stool at the end of a quiet bar and drink a draft beer or two, perhaps even eat a modest meal, and to this end, he aimed generally east. The venerable Parker House at the far edge of Boston Common, specifically its dark, walnut-clad pub room in the basement, if it had not changed, would provide the atmosphere he sought, and Keyes unhurriedly headed there.

He crossed Dartmouth Street and made his way along the broad sidewalks of Boylston Street towards the center of the city. Slowing occasionally to glance at the window displays in the small shops along the way, he was only faintly aware of workers continuing to pass him by. Keyes was not a man to turn heads or draw attention. Average height, glasses, thinning hair turning from brown to gray. Maybe a little thicker around the middle than he'd prefer. Approaching midlife—maybe *lunging* toward midlife. Positively unremarkable. His fellow pedestrians were oblivious to him and impatient to get to their homes, to get somewhere at least comfortably distant from the buildings in which they found themselves confined for the past eight hours or more. He knew how they felt, for he had once worked in this very neighborhood.

"Matt!" He was momentarily startled from his anonymity when heard his name. He turned in the direction from which he thought the call had come, adjusting his glasses and squinting, unable to determine the precise source, and didn't spy a single familiar face in the crowd. He dismissed the shout, acknowledging that there were probably dozens of Matts within hailing distance, and idly continued on his way.

"Matt Keyes!" He heard his name again, his full name this time, defining him with certainty. This time the voice was closer. Matt eventually saw one body break the flow of the crowd's movement and make its way towards him. Some moments passed before he recognized her features, clad as she was with a scarf loosely draped around the collar of her long wool coat. A spray of freckles and the fiery glow of her burnt-copper hair gave her identity away.

"Joanne!" he acknowledged with a sudden smile. "Hi! I didn't think anyone would remember me here."

She gave Keyes the quick, solid hug of a close friend and stepped back, smiling, appraising him from head to foot and back up again. "Let me get a look at you, Matt. It's been …what …eight years?"

"All of that," he answered. "I moved to Burlington almost ten years ago." He studied her face for a moment and smiled. "Joanne, I can't believe it. You look terrific."

She did, too. Dimpled cheeks bordered a broad, easy smile. Oval face framed in silky hair aflame with reflections even in the low light.

"Well, I might have gained a pound or ten since I saw you last, but I haven't grown entirely gray and wrinkled yet, and hair color works wonders. But you don't look so bad yourself. How have you been?"

"As usual, Joanne. I'm sitting up and taking nourishment." Matt smiled when he said the words which had once been a source of amusement between them. "My gut is a little bigger. And I'm a little more nearsighted. How are you doing?"

The people walking past Matt and Joanne were forced to go left and right around the pair. Inevitably, they received an occasional intolerant jostle.

"Let's get out of here, Matt. Let's find a place where we can sit and talk for a while. You got time?" She slung her purse strap over her shoulder and took his hand, tugging firmly as she moved them into the walking flow. She didn't wait for his answer.

Matt recalled in a rapid rush how much he had been attracted to Joanne Stowe when he'd been a young engineer in Boston on the Crane & Stewart staff. Joanne had been the clerk/administrative assistant/gopher for the civil engineering unit to which he was assigned. Joanne was the lively, bright, and attractive young woman who had most closely tempted Matt's aimless and unwritten resolve to never marry, never commit to anything long-term. In a moment, memories of those same feelings resurfaced. Matt wondered for not the first time if she was not the single, driving reason why he left the firm and Boston for another opportunity three hundred miles away in Burlington. He tried to dismiss the thoughts as he followed Joanne's purposeful movements.

She talked loud enough to overcome the ambient noises of the crowds around them. And she talked quickly, as he knew she would. "We can get a cup of coffee around the corner on Clarendon. I want to sit down for a while and talk, find out what you've been doing." Matt recalled that there had been a small café at end of the block. She appeared nearly unchanged by the years except for a wiser look, tempered a bit by time and experience. He noted her guarded eyes, however, which betrayed the smile, as if she'd been injured somehow since he last saw her.

"Look, Joanne, if you're on your way home, don't let me hold you up."

"Yes, I'm on my way home, and no, you're not holding me up." She took his arm in hers, still firm and resolute. "I don't have to be right home. My mother is watching home and hearth tonight.

Anyway, I want to find out what you're doing back in Boston. What have you been doing since you left? How long are you going to be around?" Rapid-fire.

"Not long, really," Matt said. They emerged from a knot of people and walked slower and together now, side-by-side. "I'm only staying the night. Tomorrow, I'm off to live in the jungle." Joanne flashed him a wide-eyed look of surprise. They arrived at the café, and he held the door for her. As she passed in front of him, he remembered how diminutive she was.

Joanne read his mind: "Still five-two with heels on. Built low to the ground for speed and balance." She moved to an empty booth, removed her scarf and coat, and sat. "So, tell me about this jungle, Matt. Are we talking 'jungle' as in pythons, lizards, and killer fish that devour wading hippos in seconds? Or are we talking 'jungle' like in New York or Philadelphia?"

Matt was clearing the fog from his glasses with a napkin from the dispenser on the table, one of the hazards of moving to a warm interior from the cooler outside air. "Tomorrow, at 10:30, I'm flying to Miami. Then, I fly to South America. In two days, I'll be a couple thousand miles up the Amazon, heading up part of a project team that's doing research in the rain forest, trying to reverse some of the damage."

"That's terrific, Matt." She meant it. She looked at him earnestly. "How did you land that job?"

"The firm I'm with in Burlington won a contract sponsored by the Brazilian government and the United Nations to do some work in the interior. I convinced my boss to let me put the proposal together. It's part of a multinational project, and I put my name in the hat to be the on-site project leader. I won the drawing, so I'm on my way. Course, there weren't a lot of names in the hat."

"Why not, Matt? It sounds like a great opportunity."

He was about to answer when a waiter appeared. They both asked for black coffee as the waiter swabbed their soiled and sticky table with an equally soiled and shredded wet cloth. Matt and Joanne, in silent unison, watched the dampness evaporate before deciding the table was dry enough to rest their elbows.

"The firm I'm with isn't very big, and there aren't any other engineers there with the background you need for this particular job."

"You still working with subsurface conditions, soils, and things like that?" Joanne asked.

"Soils, geology, movement of subsurface water; I'm still getting paid to goof off in the dirt." Joanne acknowledged Matt's self-deprecation with a smile, reminded of the days when they worked together at Crane & Stewart; of all the engineers on staff, Matt Keyes had an affinity for projects requiring the dirtiest underground work. He was never one for three-piece suits or long meetings in the boardroom. Matt continued, "Also the job means a ten-month commitment, and that's a long time away from the wife and kids, neither of which is an issue in my case." Joanne paid attention, but didn't respond. "The pay is pretty good, but you've got to get used to living in a remote area that was described to me as primitive at best. It means living in a sixty-four-square-foot hut without plumbing. The nearest village of any size is Canutama, and that's barely a dot on most maps. Maybe once in a while I'll get to Manaus, which has at least some of the trappings of civilization. But this isn't the kind of job a lot of my pampered colleagues are looking for."

Joanne could tell that, for all Matt's belittling remarks about this project and its difficulties, he was plainly exhilarated about it. She smiled as she said, "Most of the people I work with think that a weekend camping in a state park is roughing it. So here you are, Matt, ready to tackle the pythons."

"No one told me about any killer fish, Joanne, so maybe I'll have second thoughts now that I've talked with you."

Joanne said with sincerity, "Matt, I can tell you're excited about this project, and I'll bet you end up loving every minute. This sounds like the kind of project you were meant to take on." There was a wry tone to her voice when she went on. "But you called it a ten-month commitment. I didn't think I'd ever hear Matthew Keyes say the 'C' word." Joanne looked him straight in the eyes, and Matt knew she was only half joking. Their conversations in the past, at least on this particular subject, did not elicit smiles from Joanne Stowe. "Ten months in a jungle; that's a long time by anyone's standards. Will you be able to get back home at all during that time? For holidays, or to see your family?"

"The only one left is my sister, and she's got her own family to keep her busy. So it's really not so bad."

There was concern in her voice when she asked, "Do you still go to New Hampshire on weekends every so often, Matt? Does your mother still live there?"

The waiter reappeared with their coffees and set them down on the table.

"My mother died a few years ago."

"I'm sorry, Matt. Your mother was a delight, and I liked her a lot." That was true, Matt reflected. Joanne enjoyed his mother's company, and his mother similarly held a warm corner in her heart for Joanne.

Matt sipped from his cup and the coffee burned his lips. It was still steaming. Joanne was calmly drinking her coffee, which he presumed was as hot as his. *How can she stand it?* he wondered. He looked up and studied her. Fine laugh lines had appeared at the edges of her mouth and at the corners of her eyes since he had last seen her. Waves of freckles still danced recklessly across her face. *She's so attractive, so alive and aware, and ...she hasn't said one word about her own life yet.* "Enough about me for a while. What about you? What's going on in your life? Where are you working?"

"I'm still with old Crane & Stewart. Now they call me the administrative coordinator, and they pay me a little better, but basically I'm tending to the needs of a fourteen-person engineering group which considers itself so able, so talented, and still so underpaid. Some things never change, Matt. But Joanne O'Byrne just keeps rolling along as chief babysitter of these post-pubescent civil engineers."

Matt was caught off guard. "Joanne O'Byrne? What happened to Joanne Stowe? When did that happen?" Matt was genuinely amazed. "Wait a minute, you didn't marry Alan O'Byrne, did you?"

Alan had been another engineer with Crane & Stewart, joining the firm at around the same time as Keyes. He remembered him as a more sober sort, even a little standoffish when it came to after-hours get-togethers, which were staple fare for Matt and his colleagues who were mostly single, fresh from college, and eager to take on the world ...albeit a world compromised by the grim reality of planning gravel roadbeds and expansion joints. Matt remembered Alan as one colleague who seemed to take it ('it' being himself, his engineering career, the world at large, even life itself) seriously.

"Did too, Matt. Seven years ago." She wore a broad Cheshire grin. "Now ask me if I'm divorced from said Alan O'Byrne, and the answer is yes again." Joanne saw that Matt's mouth remained a bit ajar, as if he was getting ready to ask a question but just couldn't spit out the right one. Joanne raised her hand from the table and waved off his attempts at a question or comment.

"It's a long story, Matthew. So you see," she said with sudden seriousness, "you probably did the right thing by leaving Boston and going to Vermont when you did. You weren't ready. Who knows ...if it had been you and I, instead of Alan and I, I might be the former Mrs. Keyes by now."

Matt took the words in and tried to process them fast enough to respond with something appropriate. All he could manage, though, was a mumbled, "I didn't know." He studied her face intently as he spoke. "I guess I really lost track of everyone back here. Married to Alan O'Byrne? Divorced?"

Matt was genuinely intrigued that such events could occur in what he perceived to be a relatively brief period of time. After all, he'd been more serious about Joanne Stowe than he had been about any woman, before or since. To think that enough time had passed for a courtship, assuming it wasn't a whirlwind romance (and Matt could not conceive of Alan O'Byrne conducting anything on that basis), a marriage, and a divorce and everything in between was a blow to Matt's sense of time.

With all these impressions floating about in his mind, Matt made a connection. "Joanne, you said that your mother is at home tonight. How is she? Does she live with you now?"

"She doesn't live with me, actually. It's the other way around since Alan I separated. That was a year and a half ago. Mom's doing great, and she's been terrific as a babysitter."

"Hold on, does that mean that there's a little Alan or Joanne?"

Joanne's brow furrowed at the suggestion. "He's not a miniature Alan or anyone else," she insisted testily. "His name is Joshua O'Byrne, and he's his very own person. And, I'm proud to say, he's an adorable human being who happens to be the best thing that ever entered my life." She was proud, that was clear, and she realized that she was sounding more than a little emphatic. She added with a laugh, "It may have been a lousy marriage, but Joshua was worth every bit of it."

Matt was struck by Joanne's high-spirited report. The subtle signs of pain that he saw in her eyes earlier could now be more easily explained. But she was every bit as quick as he remembered. He hoped that Joshua inherited most of his genes from the Stowe side of the family.

"Where is 'home' for you and Joshua?"

"My mom still lives in Melrose. Same place I grew up. When Alan and I split, I moved back home with Joshua and he stayed in our house in Belmont for a while. Then we sold the house, and Alan moved to San Diego. He was basically an uninvolved father anyway, so three miles is as good as three thousand. My mother's house is really too big for one person, and she was glad to see us move in. At least, she's seemed happy since we've been there. It's not a permanent thing, but it's been fine so far. How about you? Are you staying in town tonight?"

Matt took a breath. He was still digesting the basic facts. "I'm staying at the Copley Plaza," he answered. "It's my one last taste of the finer things in life before I begin my lizard diet for the next ten months."

Joanne watched Matt's eyes as he spoke. Matt knew that his mouth was doing the talking, but Joanne's eyes were doing the real communicating. There was a pause after he finished speaking while

Joanne held her gaze. He hoped he was hearing her silent words correctly as he prepared to speak again.

"Look, Joanne, since this is my last night in the country for quite a while, how about doing a little celebrating? You could call your mother and tell her you'll be home late, and we could go out to dinner together. Sort of a reunion. After all, it's not exactly every day that we see each other."

Matt waited hopefully for an answer and simultaneously considered the alternative: a few beers, the *Herald* and CNN in his hotel room.

Joanne brightened at the suggestion and stood. "I know just the place for dinner, Matt. I'll make a phone call and make sure everything's OK. Be right back."

As she made her way to the pay phone near the coffee shop entrance, Matt picked up the check, left a tip on the table, and made his way to the register. By the time he'd settled the bill and turned around, Joanne was by his side. Her long coat was buttoned and her scarf wrapped around her collar. She was ready to leave.

***

THREE BLOCKS AWAY in the Cranberry Café at the Prudential Center, Captain Henry Oates jotted down some notes on a napkin. He had eaten all he was going to eat of a grilled chicken Caesar salad, and he pushed his plate aside. This was the quietest restaurant in the mall, and he'd specifically requested an out-of-the-way table. He sipped from a glass of iced tea and studied his checklist. It bore eleven entries, destinations, all designated by Senator John Munroe for illicit arms and materials shipments for Oates to arrange. *The good senator from Massachusetts ought to be reminded about this list,* Oates thought. He ought to be reminded, too, that three of the shipments were still pending delivery. What in hell did Munroe think Oates would do with three highly illegal caches of weapons that were already in some phase of delivery if the arrangement were to cease?

Oates made some mental notes before he carefully tore the

incriminating napkin into a hundred tiny pieces. Not that the napkin represented the single existing record of the shipments. Indeed, Oates would be certain to remind Munroe at the right time tonight that there existed a formidable record of every transaction, every date, every destination, and the contents of every shipment. That revelation itself should be sufficiently powerful to convince Munroe that their arrangement would not, could not, cease. The dance wasn't over. Not now. Not yet.

CHAPTER FOUR

J OANNE HAD CHOSEN Caffè Sardinia in the North End for dinner, having recalled it as one of Matt's favorites from years ago. They entered the dark and smoky tavern near the corner of Salem Street and walked past the bar to the separate dining area, a collection of mismatched tables and chairs in the back near the kitchen. The rich aromas of garlic, onions, and oregano filled their senses. The hour was early for dinner, and all but two of the tables were empty. Matt suggested one along the back wall and asked for a bottle of the house red wine as they took their seats. They lingered over the blackboard menu as they sipped their wine, each bringing the other up-to-date with the events of the past several years.

Matt had not kept in contact with Joanne or anyone else in Boston since moving to Vermont. His professional life for the past ten years, he said, consisted of the usual unremarkable happenings one might expect of a civil engineer. Design work for canals, drainage systems, roadbeds, and the like. Engineering, he went on with a note of resignation, is not necessarily the career choice of those seeking high drama.

Joanne heard the excitement in his voice when he spoke about the Canutama Project, though, and recognized it as a welcomed injection of stimulation into his life. Matt agreed. "It is, Joanne. I didn't choose a career in engineering unconsciously, at least not at first. But the mundane part of the job gradually swallowed me up as it walked by, and I accepted it without thinking. Maybe I even sold out, in a sense. I'm not getting any younger, and now I have an opportunity to do something different. And worthwhile. I've seen a lot of photographs and videos of the devastation to the area where I'll be working. The blasting and the burning for the past twenty or thirty years have been terrible. It's tragic, and I think can help turn it around in some small way."

Joanne studied his face as he talked. Matt had gained some maturity since she'd last seen him, and he sounded to her like a man coming to grips with his mortality. *Perhaps a bit early for a midlife crisis,* she thought, *but a personal crisis of some sort.* She wouldn't have used the words "sold out"; she recalled him more kindly than he recalled himself. He'd been preoccupied, careful, Mr. Steady. He had certainly accepted a lesser role for himself than she might have chosen, but she'd been prejudiced. She'd been in love with him.

His glasses, as usual, occasionally slipped down his nose a bit, and pushing them back up was a trademark habit of his. *He was never the Clark Kent-type,* she thought, *but his large eyes and easy smile were endearing. His hair was thinner now, but he'd let it grow a little longer, streaks of silver appearing among his otherwise dark brown waves.* "Any special woman in your life, Matt?"

Matt put on a crooked look of nonchalance. It wasn't artificial. He didn't answer right away, but stared at Joanne directly when he spoke. "I've gone out with a few women in Burlington since I've been there, but nothing serious."

There was creeping resignation once more. Matt Keyes, she could see, was not an especially happy human being. *This introspection is new for him,* she concluded, *and he might not like what he's seeing.*

"There was someone a couple of years ago who wanted a real long-term relationship," he went on. "Over the course of six weeks, she gradually left a few things at my condo every time she came over." A wrinkled smile appeared as he continued. "It started with a pair of tennis shoes, then some clothes another time, then she left some compact discs, and her makeup, and after a while she was using one of the drawers in my bureau for her stuff. When we broke off, it took three trunk loads to move her stuff back to her place. Now if a woman comes to my place, she's not allowed to bring in anything she can't carry in her pockets."

They both chuckled at his story.

There was a prolonged, but not uncomfortable silence between them, and Matt swirled his wine around in his glass as Joanne watched him. The waiter appeared, and they ordered their dinners and another bottle of wine.

After devouring his dinner of clams and fish in a spicy tomato sauce, a preparation Matt remembered as cioppino, he studied Joanne's plate and paid particular attention to the sizable portion of eggplant left uneaten. In a gesture reserved for closest friends, Joanne inched her plate towards Matt. With her eyes and a nod, she told Matt it was acceptable to take from her plate whatever he wished, which he did.

"Wonderful." Matt savored the taste and texture of the eggplant, cheese, and tomatoes. "I'm told that I'll have to learn to love all kinds of strange delicacies in South America. The people who briefed me described some of the local dishes, and they probably won't find their way to the menus of most restaurants in the U.S."

Joanne was expansive as she gestured to the tabletop, "Enjoy while you can, Matthew, for tomorrow you leave all this behind."

Matt pushed his seat back from the table and sat back in his chair. Patting his stomach gently, he said, "Now, I am prepared to die."

During their dinner they talked mainly of the people they both knew from Crane & Stewart. Who, since Matt's departure, had left of their own accord? Who were banished from the firm in disgrace? Who had been promoted to higher positions within the firm against all laws of nature and common sense? Matt wasn't surprised that many of the names he remembered were now someplace else. Moving from one firm to the next was not uncommon in his field, Matt knew, and was almost expected of one who was building a career in engineering.

The people he remembered from C & S who were still associated with the firm were the more senior people, the principals, and the old guard, and Joanne stimulated a flood of memories for Matt when she simply mentioned their names.

"Mel Kennedy is still around," commented Joanne. "And he's

still a bear for every single detail. Neurotic that man is. I guess if we had an organization chart, he'd be the one I report to."

"Mel seemed like a nice enough guy, but he always struck me as an absentminded professor. Sort of stuck somewhere in another time and place."

"That's him exactly. And he hasn't changed."

"How about that crusty old guy in charge of Structural? Is he still there?"

"You're being kind. He's a miserable S.O.B., and he's alive and still kicking up a storm," Joanne answered. "That's Trygve Jensen you're talking about. It probably won't surprise you to learn that he still has trouble stringing five civil words together in a single sentence. He's old enough to retire, but unfortunately, he's in great physical shape, and he'll probably be there for at least another five or ten years or until he drops dead. He's a partner, so he can stay about as long as he wants."

"You used to say that he must have been a school yard bully as a kid, and I always thought you were right."

"Believe me, when anybody gets a call to go to Trygve Jensen's office, it's time to advertise for the position. He must take some perverse sort of pleasure in delivering bad news, like, 'Hey, you over there—you're fired! And don't let the door slam you in the ass!' Jensen is one very difficult man."

Joanne wasn't smiling as she talked of Trygve Jensen, and Matt could understand why. During Matt's years at C & S, he found Jensen to be hypercritical and overbearing. His coarse manner made him merely rude, but the engineers in the Structural Unit were convinced of his downright meanness. Matt considered it his good fortune that Jensen and he had not worked closely on any projects. He recalled more than a few bright engineers who resigned positions at C & S solely due to Trygve Jensen.

Joanne brightened when she continued. "But the oldest of the old timers at C & S is Mr. Banks."

Matt sat upright at the mention of his name. "Mr. Banks is still there? Marshall Townshend Banks? My God, I figured he'd be retired by now."

"Actually, he turned seventy-six last month, and he's doing just fine, thank you. He is still one of the most charming gentlemen on the planet. He comes in to the office at least three days a week, still stays involved, and still buys all his clothes from Brooks Brothers. Bow tie, suspenders, and all."

"Imagine a man with all his money, and he still shows up at the office. If I was as well-heeled as Mr. Banks, I would like to think that I'd retire to a life of leisure. Maybe have a place on Cape Cod, another place in the Bahamas. Nice boat, all the trimmings. Does he ever mention retiring?"

"If he does, it's not to me. I figure he must be good for a few million, but he still says hello to everyone at work, with a smile. Crane & Stewart is like his child, and I don't think he'll ever give it up entirely." She paused for a moment and looked at Matt straight on. "As I remember, Mr. Banks really took a liking to you, didn't he?"

Marshall Townshend Banks. The name still evoked fond memories for Keyes. "He was more like a kindly uncle than a boss in a lot of ways. He really paid attention to us, I remember, and I used to think that a man with all his money and prestige could have dismissed us as irrelevant, and nobody would have thought anything about it. I was what, twenty-three when I started there? And he was part of the old Boston society. But he'd ask me questions about why I chose to design something a certain way, and he'd actually listen to my answer. In fact, he loved to chat about what life was like for him when he was just starting out. You know his wife was Crane's daughter, didn't you?"

Joanne nodded. She had never met the late Caroline Crane Banks, but she knew the story about Mr. Banks having been a struggling young surveyor before having been blessed with the good fortune of marrying the boss's daughter.

"Once," Matt related, "I remember him telling us about what Boston was like when he was young. How he'd catch a burlesque show in Scollay Square during lunch or see a Red Sox game when Ted Williams was still young. When you see him, please tell him that I was asking about him."

"Certainly, Matt. He'll like that."

Their conversation and their desserts came to a simultaneous end, and they both placed their dinner napkins on the table and moved to rise. Joanne spoke.

"What do you say about heading back with me to my car? It's in a lot on Stanhope Street."

They walked towards the city's center, enjoying the sights and smells of a deserted Haymarket Square, where the days were filled with pushcarts and hawkers yelling prices and customers elbowing their way through the crowd to pick out their fruit and vegetables. They passed by the sounds and lights of Faneuil Hall and Quincy Market and entered the ocean of red brick surrounding the cold, angular concrete of City Hall. They were approaching the Government Center subway entrance when Joanne pointed to a building across the street. "Do you see that crescent building there?" Matt nodded. "There's a plaque on the wall over there at the exact site of the Old Howard Theater when this was all part of Scollay Square."

Scollay Square was once the designated epicenter of sin in the city of Boston, housing a garish collection of taverns, cheap hotels, tattoo parlors, vaudeville stages, and strip clubs. When Boston was an active naval base, sailors would flock to its gaudy lights and loud noises, and the lively business of extracting cold cash from the pockets of fresh-faced innocents thrived. It was a seedy, but amiable place.

In the fifties when the Navy base closed, the square took on the look of an aging, heavily rouged wench. Scollay Square eventually died a quiet and lonely death. In a Puritan frenzy of urban renewal, on its grave were erected a half score of faceless, bloodless facades to house the thousands of municipal, state, and federal bureaucrats who worked there. In the 1960s, Scollay Square ceased to exist, except in memories.

Joanne mused as they walked, "It's hard to imagine that this same spot was filled with dance halls and gin mills. It's too civilized now, don't you think?"

"I'm trying to picture old Marshall Banks as a young man down here," Matt answered. "It must have been quite a place back then."

They made their way down the stairs of Government Center Station and boarded the subway. In ten minutes, they exited Copley Station, very near the same spot where Joanne had called his name a few hours earlier. It was 8 o'clock now, and the evening had grown colder and the winds were far stronger now. Matt put his arm around Joanne's shoulder to shield her.

"As long as we're here, you ought to see the city from the top of the John Hancock Tower before you leave. It's a clear night, and it should be a great view." Matt agreed, and they walked briskly across the street to the plaza in front of the heavy rose and brownstone Trinity Church. Dodging a swerving car along the way, Matt recalled just how much of an adventure was crossing a Boston street, where traffic lights are rarely taken at face value. What a contrast with the generally affable and polite drivers of Burlington. Nevertheless, Matt excused Boston's drivers, whose streets were, quite literally, laid out to a large extent by meandering cows making their ways back to their stables at the end of each day from their grazing ground of Boston Common in the seventeenth century.

They crossed one more street to reach the entrance to the black steel and mirrored glass John Hancock Tower. The polished gray granite lobby of Boston's tallest building echoed the chill and severity they had just left outdoors. They made their way to the elevators, and thirty seconds after the doors closed, arrived at the sixtieth floor. Matt had been here once before, but that had been during the day and it was crowded then with children and tourists. Tonight they had the floor nearly to themselves, and he was struck by the relative silence and subdued lighting of the observatory this evening.

From a height of eight hundred feet, the lights of the city below formed angles and patterns that made landmarks easy to distinguish. Except for one section of Back Bay, Boston had no grid of planned blocks and avenues. This absence of right angles gave Boston its own personality, and Matt enjoyed the view.

"It's absolutely beautiful, Joanne."

"I think it looks better because you can't see the litter from this high up, and it puts a whole new perspective on things."

Matt smiled as he panned to his right and a telescope caught his attention. "How about a close-up view?" he asked as he walked towards it. He reached into his pocket for some coins and dropped a quarter in the slot. "You first."

Joanne stood on her toes to reach the eyepiece. "They make these things for normal people." But she was taking in the entire city.

"I'll go down to the next one," Matt whispered.

"OK, but why are you whispering?" Joanne spoke, without interrupting her viewing of the streets and sites below.

"Feels like I'm in church. It must be the low lights."

They shared the observatory with only a handful of others. A young couple was evidently interested in Cambridge to the north as they pointed out various landmarks to each other. Another small knot of what appeared to be businessmen were huddled in the northeast corner, probably looking at the Hatch Music Shell or Mass General Hospital, from what Matt could tell.

As he walked by, he overheard one describe the John Hancock building as "the one with all the falling glass." True, he knew. When the sixty-story John Hancock Tower was first erected some thirty years earlier, the huge panes of reflective glass that made up the entire exterior of the building would randomly shatter without warning and drop summarily to the ground. It was a very public embarrassment for the company and a distinct hazard to pedestrians, who used the sidewalks in the area. After months of testing, a new type of glass was found more suitable, and over ten thousand panes, literally acres of glass, were systematically removed and replaced.

Matt reached the next telescope, but the coin slot was taped over and a sign affixed to the lens: "Out of Order." He looked around the corner and spotted another telescope. No tape. No sign either. "I feel like such a kid," Matt thought as his coin dropped in the slot and the viewer opened up.

"Not the greatest view from this side," Matt muttered to himself as he aimed his telescope first to the left and then slowly to the right. "Roxbury, some apartments, Copley Place, a condo project, the Prudential Tower ..."

The view to the west was not an especially interesting one. Its largest feature was the Prudential Tower, an uninspired monolith and among the less attractive large buildings in the city. Matt contented himself with scanning the fifty or so floors. A restaurant sits at the very top. Just below is an observatory not unlike the one he was currently in. Many of the office floors were lit up, despite the late hour. Matt picked out what appeared to be a cleaning lady in one office. He felt like a spy, invading the private spaces of the unsuspecting. In another office, Matt could see a cluster of workers at CRT screens. *Probably one of those twenty-four hour customer service units,* he thought. Most of the offices were empty, though, their occupants having been among those he had seen surrounding him on the sidewalk earlier in the evening.

Matt tilted the telescope a little further, and what caught his eye was an animated discussion...maybe "discussion" was too gentle a word...between two men. It was more than animated; it was intense. Matt felt as if he was eavesdropping on a very loud and heated argument. The men were toe-to-toe.

"What's got you so wrapped up, Matt?"

***

SENATOR JACK MUNROE sought to portray himself as a "man in control," but any control he might have had over the current situation in his office was vanishing quickly. Ironically, it was Munroe who called for the meeting. He would firmly, simply, and privately communicate to Oates that a decision had been reached. He fully expected resistance, but he would be insistent, and he would prevail. The word had been passed to him by the "Chairman," a force who brooked no complaint.

So Munroe was less prepared for Oates' flat and outright refusal to accept the decision, and for the smoldering rage the decision had obviously inflamed. The meeting had begun well enough, with a few pleasantries exchanged, but now, only a few minutes into the meeting, Munroe's sense of order had disappeared in the face of Oates' quiet anger.

"That's absurd, Henry," Munroe said in yet another attempt at rebuttal. Munroe had lost his place in the script, and both he and Oates knew it. "And you are a fool if you really believe what you're saying!" Munroe was trying to maintain a voice steady and strong. He was grasping for some authority against Oates, but the attempt to sound self-assured came across instead laden with dread.

Henry Oates, on the other hand, not only presumed himself to be a man in control, but he knew at this particular moment that he was, in fact, in absolute and full control of this situation. Henry Oates spoke in a low and evenly contained smolder. "I'm telling you the honest truth, senator, and I can't change the truth no matter what you and your people might think."

Henry Oates, naval Captain Henry Howell Oates, had honed his skills as a "man in control" during a long and distinguished career with the United States Navy. First at Annapolis, where he took highest honors in two sciences and led the defensive squad in Navy football. Fast rising officer after graduation. A series of ambitious appointments leading to assistant to the chief of Naval Operations. Passed over for a major sea command, but promoted to a position of extraordinary power in the Pentagon. Renowned expert in highly technical weapon systems. And responsible for hundreds of millions of dollars of specialized arms and equipment purchases by the U.S. Navy annually.

On the other hand, Senator John Bennett Munroe, all-American wonder boy, prep school, Ivy League, and spoiled rotten, was simply no match for the captain.

At the moment, Munroe was unfortunately inclined to agree with that assessment. He was unsettled by Oates' measured wrath. "For three years, Henry, for three solid years I've been working with you." Munroe pointed his finger and punched the air in a gesture of insistence. It came across as weak, pious, and he knew it. With a growing sense of imminent defeat, he went on, "I'm not out to hurt you, for Chrisakes." He would try to placate Oates. "This is just a business decision, Henry. The time has come. Listen to reason. We both knew perfectly well from the start that this arrangement wouldn't be permanent."

Henry Oates, his uniform trousers still holding its press to a blade's edge, appeared to cool, his anger abated. He leaned back and enjoyed the comfort of the overstuffed wing chair. His eyes casually roamed the room, ignoring the senator and letting the silence hang. *Munroe may not have balls,* he thought, *but the bastard's got taste. Or his decorator does.* He returned his stare to Munroe, who was now standing next to his massive oak desk, and smiled a slow smile. Or smirked. To Jack Munroe, it looked like the smirk of a madman. "Jack, Jack, Jack, you're getting all wound up over something you could take care of with a simple phone call. Then I leave. A happy man. Both of us happy. Lord knows, this deal was never going to be permanent. But it's too soon, Jack. That's all. Just too soon. Now, my friend ...and, to be precise, it's been thirty-three months, Jack, not three years ...are we still in business or not?"

A frustrated, cold-sweating Jack Munroe gestured, jabbing the air again to punctuate his words, "Henry, I'm trying to tell you we can't do it. It's all done. Finis!" His voice pleading, "There's no more need to funnel money through our deal! It's over! I've been trying to get through to you that the risk is just too great. Accept that, Henry; face facts!"

The smirk never left the captain's face. In a flat voice, he responded, "You don't understand the situation, Jack. In fact, you haven't understood anything I've said to you at all. This is not over. Not over by any means. Too many wheels are in motion now to simply stop. This is a flourishing operation that we have, Jack. A business that develops its own momentum and goes through its normal business cycles. Very businesslike. I even keep very complete business records, if you're interested." He caught Munroe off guard with that revelation, and he knew it. "Very careful records. You understand, don't you, Jack?"

Now the smirk vanished, and Oates' features hardened. "I'm here, Jack, because I am running this business. I didn't drive here from Newport just for a goddamned cup of tea, Jack. I've done very well for you in this business. And I've got my butt on the big fat line. All the time. Every day. Not like you. You get to play it safe. Why, you can't even take a shit without first getting permission from your board of directors, can you, Jack? And even then, the Chairman will send a nanny to make sure you wiped yourself.

"Wake up, Munroe. Senator Jack Munroe," he said with emphasis and a sneer. "This is a cash business, and I intend to keep collecting the cash." Oates never ceased his icy stare as he continued. "Goods have been shipped. They are on their way to their destinations. And you are the one who called in the order, Jack. You. In my business, you, my good man, are technically a 'receivable,' and I don't need any more receivables. Cash, Jack. That's not so hard to understand, is it, Jack?"

Now Oates stood, a larger man and a powerful presence. He knew how to use that presence, and it was having its effects on Jack Munroe. Oates took slow steps towards Munroe until he was inches from him. He cocked his head to one side and assessed Munroe as a boot camp instructor would assess the lowest recruit. Munroe, rising star in his party and point man for several controversial initiatives, was not accustomed to this position, and he did not enjoy it one bit. Oates kept his voice low and strong as he spoke, just inches from the senator: "Munroe, you just sit here in your fancy fucking high-rise office, or in your goddamned senate office suite, insulated from the dirty world by your staff, and your involvement is clean. You don't know what it's like to put your ass on the line every single day. I mean, really on the line. Not you. Not the people behind you. You just 'invest.' Is that the right word, Munroe? Invest?"

Munroe tried to stand his ground, but leaned back against his desk. Oates continued staring square at Munroe, now nose to nose. Munroe leaned back further and grabbed the edge of the desk to keep from falling backwards.

Oates continued his growling tirade. "Meanwhile, who's

running the shop? Whose ass is fucking exposed? It's your money, senator, but it's my ass! And if the show closes, Munroe, you just lose your fucking money. Me? I stand to lose my fucking ass."

Every word found its mark. Munroe took the verbal blows like an overmatched prizefighter with his back to the ropes and nowhere to run and hide. *I told them Oates was crazy,* Munroe thought, frantic. *I warned them he wouldn't accept the decision without a fight.*

The arrangement had been made three years ago ...no, thirty-three months ago ...between Senator Jack Munroe and Captain Henry Oates. In his position at the Pentagon, Oates had the necessary access to several outlets involving arms and equipment of all types. Some of these outlets had official sanction. Foreign governments routinely sent representatives to Washington to purchase military goods, and Henry Oates was on every visitor's "must-see" list. But other prospective buyers were either entirely unofficial, or unofficial segments of otherwise official outlets. In any case, Oates had access with a capital A.

"Having" anything in Washington, especially access to outlets involving particularly dear commodities like high-tech weaponry, can put a person in an enviable position. Oates knew that his access allowed him to trade for the things he really wanted to have, like money and all the luxuries that money could buy. Like prestige of the type he could not attain since he was passed over in favor of a stinking sonnavabitch with connections to the new chief of Naval Operations. True, his Pentagon job was one of great responsibility and authority, but the acrid taste of seeing his command slip out from under him was never erased.

Now, Oates' lucrative and unofficial client wanted to cease their arrangement, and Oates wasn't ready for this just yet. In another year, maybe less, he'd be sufficiently empowered to do what he wished with his business and his life without the benefit of Senator Jack Munroe or the people who backed him. For that matter, he'd be in a position to simply retire comfortably and far away, and finally be rid of all the struggles and the risk. His retirement homes were already bought and paid for. And conveniently offshore, just in case someone happened to stick his nose someplace where it didn't belong. But he was not ready to retire just yet. Not now. Not yet.

Munroe's telephone call to him two days ago prompted this Boston trip from Newport. Munroe knew that Oates would be in Newport, a key player in planning a major, multinational exercise involving all branches of the military. The Newport Naval War College would host dozens of the world's leading military strategists, and Oates would be among them. Munroe wanted to visit with Oates personally to advise him that their arrangement would cease. *Amicable disaffiliation, my ass,* thought Oates. *It's too early and too sudden.*

Already on its way to a buyer in South Africa were several crates of missile components. Munroe had brokered the order and Oates had followed through. In another seven days, a similar shipment would be off-loaded in New Zealand. These two arrangements alone were worth nine hundred thousand dollars to Oates' personal account in Zurich.

Where did they ever dig up this Jack Munroe anyway? Oates mused. *A pretty boy, all the right schools, all the right clubs, fancy law firm, and U.S. senator for the last four years. But simply not tough enough. I've broken plenty of bigger and better men than this little weasel. Look at him. Eyeball to eyeball, and he's caving in. You don't even have to lay a finger on him, and he's getting ready to babble like a baby.* Oates decided to turn up the heat.

"You make me sick, Munroe. Sick. You haven't got anything at all that wasn't handed to you. Not a damned thing. I had to fight for everything I've got. Fight! And do you know what's funny about that, Munroe? At least I know why I'm doing what I do. At least I know why I'm up to my eyeballs in this business. Greed, sure. And revenge. Deep, dark, old friend, Mr. Revenge." He continued with a twisted smile, "And I'm winning the goddamned game, Munroe, based on the highest traditions of greed and revenge. I've had plenty of time to think about it, and that's where it comes from. But you? You're a spoiled, little rich kid, Munroe. Got everything he wanted on a goddamned platter. So what drives you, Munroe? Greed?

Maybe. But I think it's fear, good old-fashioned fear. Underneath the shine is nothing but a big, sad sack of fear, Munroe, and now you're going to tell me that we're going to have an amicable disaffiliation? What a way to put it! Do you know what that sounds like? Coming from you?"

Oates was nearly on top of Munroe now, shouting directly in his face. Munroe was leaning back over his desk, propping himself up with both hands. He was perspiring heavily. Papers fell to the floor. A ceramic vase tumbled to the carpet and split into several pieces. Munroe was slipping, and he knew he'd slump to the floor himself unless he gained some purchase.

My God, he thought, *Oates is a crazy man.*

Finally he felt something solid behind him. The brass elephant, a gift from a colleague who had traveled to India last year. It was solid and heavy. If he held on, at least he wouldn't slide any further.

He's screaming at me. In my face. The decision to get into the arrangement wasn't mine in the first place. But did Oates honestly give this arrangement a life of its own? That it would go on and on forever?

"Get back, Oates. Get off of me." It was a most feeble attempt to exert himself, and Munroe knew it would fail.

"You disgust me, Munroe." Oates was relentless. "You and your backers, whoever they are. Who are they, anyway, Munroe? Would they like the whole world to know their names? How would they feel if they knew that Senator John Munroe was ready to cave-in? And you'd sell their names in a split second, Munroe. Cause if I go down, if my ass gets nailed to a tree, I'm writing a book, and you'll be the main character. Receipts, invoices, dummy companies, names, places, dates, times, Munroe. Would you like that? Would your backers like that? That would help your political career a lot, wouldn't it? If the rumors are true, Munroe, and you decide to go for the brass ring next year, my little black book will be a best seller, won't it? And you'll be washed up on the beach."

Munroe had held his position. No more slipping backwards. He had a strong hold on the elephant, and it gave him a spark of confidence.

"Off, Oates. Back off. Now!"

Oates held eye contact with Munroe, looking deep into his eyes, searching. Suddenly Oates straightened up and looked away in disgust.

With Oates turning aside and backing off, Munroe took a deep breath. For a reason he couldn't understand, he maintained his grip on the brass elephant. He picked it up in his right hand and saw his opportunity.

With his back now turned to Munroe, Oates never saw the arc of Munroe's swinging arm as the brass elephant was carried upward and then sharply downward. The first sensation Oates felt was intense cold. No pain. He knew instantly that his skull had been penetrated and wondered why his arms were still by his side, not even beginning to move upwards to pull the offending object from his temple. His vision was clear. Munroe's furniture looked as opulent as any he'd ever seen. *This carpet's a genuine Oriental,* he thought. *Probably worth ten grand at least.* His body turned gradually towards Munroe. *Am I turning myself, or am I being turned by someone else? Look at Munroe ...he looks like he's going to be sick. He'll probably puke all over this rug.* And for U.S. Navy Captain Henry Oates, that was his final thought.

Oates lurched once, his shoulders rising as he remained standing erect for a moment, then slowly slued right and fell. There was a soft thud as he sank to the carpet. His body twitched and jerked wildly for several seconds. After a brief period of no movement, a second more violent convulsive wave shook his lower torso. There were sounds of rapid, checked breathing, as if Oates was trying to inhale but had an obstruction that prevented him from doing so. His right leg shook unsteadily for several more seconds. Then he was still. A cold silence of ten seconds was followed by flatulence and Oates' sphincter released.

The stench was overpowering. Munroe never moved after his single, forceful thrust at Oates' skull. He watched in stunned silence the disjointed playlet unfold and now stared at a crumpled, horribly contorted mass. The trunk of the brass elephant remained embedded deep in Oates' brain. Oates' eyes were open and fixed on the leg of the armchair he'd occupied minutes earlier. As the bladder released, a dark stain blossomed on his trousers. *Was it only a minute ago that this person was a living human being leaning me up against my desk and threatening me? He looks smaller now.*

Whereupon, Oates' final thought was a prophesy.

CHAPTER FIVE

JOANNE FOUND MATT staring intently into the eyepiece of a telescope. He was fixed in place, held as if locked onto a target. She moved close to him and asked in a low voice what he was looking at. He apparently didn't hear her, and she repeated her question. He remained in place. Joanne wondered what could possibly be so intriguing that he wouldn't answer her, or even move away from the telescope to acknowledge her presence. She tried to follow the general direction in which his scope was aimed, but all she could identify was the Prudential Tower three blocks away to the west.

She scanned the Prudential, seeking out whatever might be riveting Matt's attention. From this distance, and with an unaided eye, she could see only that several offices were brightly lit, and from time to time she could spot some movement. People working late? Cleaning people? She couldn't tell if she was seeing a male, a female, a gorilla, or a water buffalo without the aid of the telescope.

Moving to his shoulder, she tried to follow the sight line of Matt's telescope again. Matt was fixed on something on the upper floors; that much she could tell. She squinted to improve her focus, but could only discern rows of office floors, most of which had their lights turned off for the night. Several were lit up, though, so she squinted even more until her eyes were nearly closed.

Was there a fire in the Prudential? Is that what is absorbing him? No sign of flame or smoke or anything else that to Joanne might be inordinately consuming of one's attention. She opened her eyes wide and turned to Matt.

"What is it, Matt?" No response. She tugged lightly at his sleeve to capture his attention. "Did you see something, Matt? Did you catch somebody undressing or what?" Still nothing. She had turned her attention to the Prudential once more when Matt slowly straightened up and moved a step back from the telescope.

He stared straight ahead, not addressing Joanne. "Incredible," he mouthed, barely above a whisper. He was not speaking to her as much as to himself.

Joanne touched his arm, looked up at his face, and noticed how ashen he suddenly appeared, even in the subdued lighting of the observatory. She could tell he was shaken and she spoke with care and comfort in her voice. "What on earth did you see, Matt? What's wrong?"

"What?" He turned abruptly to Joanne as if just realizing where he was and with whom. Moments passed in silence as he held her in a blank distant gaze. He was unfocused, Joanne a blur to which he was as yet incapable of connecting.

"Matt," she urged in a low voice, "tell me: What's the matter? You look like you've seen a ghost." Her tone was soothing as if she was speaking to a frightened child just awakened from a nightmare. She put her hands to his arms as if to steady him, and patiently waited for a response.

"I'm not sure." He shook his head, as if clearing cobwebs. "I mean, I saw two men in an office. Arguing. Then...one of them..." his voice trailed off as he mouthed the words. "I think I just saw a murder."

"Murder?" Joanne's eyes narrowed.

"I'm not sure. Maybe not. But the guy didn't get back up." He continued to stare at Joanne, through Joanne. His voice was barely audible.

Joanne kept her arms by his side. She, too, continued to fix her eyes on his. But where his were glazed and still adrift, hers were intently riveted to his.

Matt came out of his fog, gradually regaining his bearings. He shook his head again, cleared it. Directly now, he spoke to Joanne, "I just saw someone kill another man. Just now. In the Prudential Tower." His lips curled up, his brow creased, and his eyes pleaded with her; he was looking for Joanne to tell him it wasn't true, it was only a dream. But she didn't.

Instead, she held his left arm and slowly, gently, turned him towards a carpeted bench nearby. They moved slowly to the bench, where she placed her hands on his shoulders and gently urged him to sit. She sat close to him, angled in such a way that she looked him directly in the face.

"Matt, you look deadly serious about this, but I want you to sit down for a minute and talk to me." She put her hands on his as she went on. "Are you sure that you saw someone getting killed?"

"I think so, Joanne. I mean, I saw the whole thing with my own eyes."

"Matt," she asked. "Maybe we should tell the police, or call 911."

Matt didn't respond but appeared to wait for more information from Joanne.

"I mean, if you definitely saw a murder, we have to tell someone. What did you actually see?"

"There were two men, businessmen, I think. Suits They looked like they were arguing. A big argument. Something serious." He spoke slowly, looking at Joanne, seeking some confirmation that he wasn't losing his mind. "They were in each other's face. I could tell they were shouting. Then one of them hit the other one, and he went down. Like a bag of cement. Right down. And he didn't get back up, Joanne. He never got back up." He was silent for several seconds. "Then the lights in the office went out. Black." Another pause. "Nothing."

Joanne could tell Matt was shaken, but couldn't hide her skepticism. "Look, Matt. I'm sure you saw something. I mean, I know you're not making this up. But think about it. Who would commit a murder in plain view of an entire city? I mean, it's pretty stupid. Well, maybe possible, but not very likely." Matt was listening, but she could see self-doubt creep into his expression. She went on.

"You were focusing on the upper floors. Those are all executive floors, all first-class tenants. Law firms, businesses, architects, stock brokers. Not exactly people who'd be prone to physical violence on their associates."

She waited for Matt to answer, but she could see he was still partly in a funk. He finally addressed her, met her eyes squarely, and spoke. "I know what I saw, Joanne. I saw two men having an argument. That much I can tell you for sure. One guy in a suit. Another guy, a taller guy, in a uniform, like an airline pilot. You know, dark, black, maybe dark blue." He recounted the scene in stages. "An argument. The two of them getting closer to each other. A real toe-to-toe argument. Then, all of a sudden, the guy in the suit hits the other guy with something real hard. And the tall guy goes down. He stayed up for a second or two, but then he goes down. I saw it, Joanne. I think I just saw a murder."

"Look, Matt," she countered, "maybe you should call the police and let them sort this out. I mean, they're used to this stuff. Crime, fist fights, dead bodies." Matt listened, looking for confirmation. Reassurance.

It was his turn for doubt. "And if I call the police, what do I tell them? That I saw two men arguing? That I think I might have seen a fight, a push, a lucky punch?"

Joanne considered this. "Can you be sure from this distance that there was a murder. Did you see blood? Was there a gun?"

"No, no gun. I couldn't tell what it was. Not just a punch. He used something. And the guy went down hard."

"Was it a proverbial 'blunt object'? A poker from a fireplace? Did the butler do it? Or maybe it was Colonel Mustard in the conservatory with a lead pipe."

Joanne's effort at some humor didn't set well with Matt, and he frowned, hurt and puzzled by her sarcasm, her dismissal.

"I'm sorry, Matt, but let's look at this, realistically. You saw two people. Were they both men ...could you tell for sure? Were they blond, bald, wearing glasses? From three blocks away. At night. Through a carnival-quality telescope. These people are in an office, late at night, on an executive floor in the high-rent district. I'm sorry, Matt, but it sounds a little crazy. I'm not sure what you saw because

I wasn't looking at the same office. But I can tell you, I'd have a hard time convincing some police officer that he ought to check out this story. Knock on a hundred doors and check out every office in one of the biggest buildings around. You're tired. We killed two bottles of wine tonight." She strengthened her grip on his arms.

Matt shook his head. Tried to clear it. Joanne was making sense. Cool and calm. Lucid.

"And last, but not least, you were charmed by the company of a beautiful woman."

She was smiling now, and she sensed his acceptance. "That's right, Matt. A beautiful woman, whose feminine wiles wreaked havoc with your mental faculties. You couldn't think clearly because you wanted to sweep her off her feet and take her to some swamp in Peru or Bolivia."

"Brazil," he corrected.

She had reached him.

"And you wanted to ravish her on the floor of the John Hancock Tower observatory in plain sight of three bored businessmen from Des Moines and a young couple, who, by the way, probably have that very same thought in mind."

He felt lost, like a forager looking for something on which to grab hold. He reached for Joanne and held her tightly. He felt the old feelings he once had for her rise within him again. He believed that he had loved her, but was too afraid to act on his feelings then. He peppered himself with questions: *Why didn't I stay? Why did she ever hook up with that clod, Alan O'Byrne? Was she on the rebound? Did I have …could I have …?* He did not release his hug. *She's right. I'm tired, maybe a little drunk on wine, on my way to another country I've never seen, and just realizing that I probably made a major league mistake ten years ago, for which Joanne has paid the price. And now I can't even convince myself of exactly what I just saw in the Prudential; there's no way I'd convince someone else.*

"Excuse me, sir, but we'll be closing soon." A young man in a blue blazer, a security guard, was working his way from one end of the observatory floor to the other. He was approaching the businessmen now with the same message.

Matt stood, unsatisfied but resolved for now to file the improbable murder into a darker recess of his mind. He held out his hand for Joanne and pulled her gently to her feet. He felt relieved and refreshed and held her close once again. "You're right," he whispered and leaned closer, hugging her, smelling her hair. "I'm not sure what I saw. I just know that right now I love you, Joanne." She hugged him in response, then stood back and took his hand. It was time to leave. He was never sure exactly what she said, but he thought he heard her whisper, "I love you, too."

***

JOANNE'S CAR WAS parked in a lot on Stanhope Street, and they walked the two blocks huddled together. The winds that had been blowing briskly earlier had died down, so their closeness was not demanded by the weather. They walked the entire distance in silence. It wasn't until Joanne unlocked and opened the door to her tired wheels that she broke the silence. She looked up at Matt, whose face no longer bore the pale alarm she had seen twenty minutes ago, but instead reflected a rather quiet contentment. Joanne hoped, and inwardly knew, that his mellow air didn't come just from the wine.

"This is it, my Benz. Like it?" It was a Ford Escort with more than a little abuse showing. "Its fender bends here, and the bumper bends there."

Matt looked at the slightly dented and extraordinarily dirty exterior in appraisal. "It's the road salt that does it," Joanne said. "When I hose down this sucker, she looks like a million. Only a hundred and nineteen thousand loving miles on her. A real beauty. I think it's going to be a classic."

"I'll bet. It's the damned road salt, I can tell." Matt held Joanne's shoulders and gently turned her so he could look into her face straight on. "Joanne, I really enjoyed seeing you again. And I want you to know that I think I made a horrible mistake when I left. I should have said something ..."

"Matt, no," she interrupted quickly. She put a gloved finger to his lips. "It's not the time to talk about this. It's late. I'm tired.

You're tired. You did what you did for your own reasons. And for better or worse, I did what I did for my own reasons. So here we are. I had a terrific time tonight. Let's leave it at that, OK?"

"I just ...it was great to see you again. I never expected I'd run into you like I did. And I wish I wasn't going away tomorrow for such a long time."

Joanne's voice was stronger now, less gentle. "Matt, I've just gone through a real bad time in my life. Seeing you tonight was great, and maybe you still have a warm spot in your heart for me, or the person you think I am. It's been a long time, Matt."

She turned to enter her car. Matt didn't resist. When she was in, she looked up to him and continued her thought. "Matthew Keyes was...is a very special person to me. Very special. But maybe it's best that you're going to Argentina tomorrow. Let me settle my life some more; let me play with my son." She reached into her purse and found her keys. "I'd like to see you again, too, and maybe when you get back..." She let that thought sit there between them. "Maybe we can plan on that."

Matt leaned over and kissed Joanne lightly on the lips. "I understand, or at least I think I do. But I'll think of you and write to you, if you don't mind. If you'll give me your address."

Joanne nodded. "Writing is fine, Matt. In fact, I'd love to hear from you. Here," she said, tearing a piece of paper from an empty McDonald's bag left on the floor of her car. "I'll write my address and phone number on this." She ceremoniously handed him the torn-edged scrap with the information. "My card, Mr. Keyes. And why don't you give me your address in ...where are you going?"

"Don't write to me in Argentina, because it'll never get to me. Here." Matt handed her a business card with his name and Brazilian address. "I had a bunch of these printed up to give to friends, relatives, and bill collectors."

"Thanks, and yes," Joanne said as she accepted the card and put it in her pocketbook.

"Yes, what?"

"I'll write." Joanne inserted her key in the ignition, the engine turned over, and she buckled her seat belt. She reached for the door handle and pulled the door closed. Then she rolled down her window. "Stay away from the alligators, Matt."

The Ford made an ominous clunk as she shifted into gear. Joanne waved as she drove away, and Matt raised an arm to wave back.

His arm was still high in the air, and he was following the movement of her car as it rolled down the street and merged into the evening traffic.

***

ALONE NOW IN the darkness of his office, Jack Munroe fumbled with the telephone, finally using a cigarette lighter from his desk to provide sufficient illumination for him to locate the correct button on his speed dialer. He pressed the button marked "BOD" and closed the lighter. A series of low clicks and beeps told him the call was going through. The clicks were followed by a low tone; the phone was ringing. "Be there," Munroe muttered aloud.

A second ring. No answer yet.

Munroe was getting anxious. His hands, which were already trembling, began to perspire. A third ring. "Come on," he urged, "you've got to be there."

Before the fourth ring was complete, Munroe heard a click on the other end. The phone was being answered. "Yes?" was the single word address.

Munroe swallowed and began, "There's a problem."

"Yes." Again the single word, but this, time not a question.

"It's Oates. He wouldn't listen to reason."

A pause. Silence for several seconds. Then: "I'm going to ask you some questions. Just answer simply yes or no." The voice was steady, calming.

"OK, but it's a big problem." The sweat poured from Munroe's brow.

"Listen to me." Calm. Reserved. But firm and in full control. "Just yes or no. Now, is the subject still on the premises?"

"Yes, he is, but you have no idea ..."

"Yes or no is sufficient." There was no inflection. No alarm. "Can he hear or see you?"

"Uh, no."

"Good. He must be in another room, is that correct?"

"No."

"Hmmm ...Is he injured? Is he impaired in any way?"

"He's impaired alright! He's lying on my goddamned carpet, and I need some help quick."

There was sudden fury in the voice now. "Listen! Yes or no! Only yes or no!" A pause. Then the calm returned. "Are your lights off in the office?"

"Yes."

"Are the drapes drawn?"

"Yes," Munroe answered again.

"Listen to my instructions carefully. Make certain your office door is closed and locked and stay where you are. Don't move. Don't leave your office. Don't turn on any lights. Don't open the drapes. Don't answer the door if someone knocks. Earl will let himself in."

Munroe felt reassured. The only decisions he was able to make since Oates' unseemly collapse were to turn off the office lights and close the drapes. Then for several minutes he huddled in the corner of his office, frozen by fear and panic. It had taken all the reserve he could muster to keep from screaming and running wildly from the office. Eventually, enough composure returned for him to make the phone call. Now he felt better. He began to speak into the phone. "Thanks, I'll wait for Earl. You'll send Earl, right? I'll stay right here ..." But the humming of the dial tone let him know that the phone had been hung up on the other end.

***

OUTSIDE, THE NIGHT air was chilled. Keyes inhaled deeply and enjoyed the crisp coolness in his throat and lungs. He felt refreshed and began his short walk from the parking lot to the hotel. He took another deep breath and thought of the heat and humidity he would experience over the next several months of his life. His path to the hotel took him by the Hancock Tower once more, and as he passed, he was reminded of the evening's events. He slowed his pace and replayed the scene in his mind.

Maybe Joanne was right. It was several blocks away, at night. It could have been anything. But I'm sure that I saw something; I couldn't have dreamed all of this up.

Keyes was paying more attention to recollecting his vision than to where he was walking, for when he reached the end of the block, he stepped off the curb and stumbled. He regained his footing after an awkward lurch and avoided falling to the pavement. But he didn't escape the judgmental muttering of two aging and elegantly dressed women who were then passing by, witnesses to his ungraceful recovery. The only words he heard clearly were "drunk" and "shameful," and he half smiled to himself as he continued on his way to the Copley Plaza.

Keyes entered the hotel lobby that was lushly decorated in the ornate style of late nineteenth century conceit. Heavy chandeliers, deep carpeting, polished brass and mahogany. J. P. Morgan and his fellow barons surely would have felt at home here.

He remembered the first time he had seen the hotel, prior to its restoration to elegance. In an apparent fit of post World War II exuberance, the hotel's owners had imported a designer predisposed to the Early Long Beach look. To update this grande dame, its richly colored Italian tile floors had been covered with beige, wall-to-wall carpet. Its thickly textured walls had been cheaply paneled, painted in various pastel shades or covered with plastic laminate. Those efforts were, in a subsequent and very fortunate return to common sense, trashed in the mid-seventies, and the hotel's previous grandeur was restored. The Copley had been given back her grace.

Keyes approached the elevator bank and was about to press the call button when he remembered that he had left his *Boston Herald* at the coffee shop hours ago. He looked across the lobby to the newsstand that was closed. Rather than return to his room with only a television and a tiresome paperback to occupy his mind, he decided to visit the handsome hotel bar. He walked in and took an empty seat at the bar. He ordered a draft beer and drank it down quickly. He ordered another. This he would sip. His flight the next morning was scheduled for a 10:30 departure to Miami, with four more connections after that. He wanted to be awake early, packed, checked out, and ready to go by 8:30.

He sat alone with thoughts of his journey. The chance of a lifetime. With everything happening to him so fast this evening... meeting Joanne, dinner in the North End, and whatever he saw from the tower observatory...he'd given the trip barely a passing thought. Thoughts of Canutama and the project ahead of him had consumed most of his waking hours for weeks. And tonight, his thoughts were clinging to Joanne, their dinner, and finding out once more how much he cared for her.

Without question, she was as attractive to him as ever. At least part of the attraction was purely physical. He could remember many evenings when he and Joanne would return to his apartment after work. They enjoyed their nights together immensely. They were hungry for each other, and every night in bed with her was a feast. This evening, though, he sensed a different presence in Joanne, and he knew that his feelings were based more than merely on the physical. There was a special bond beneath the surface, and he felt particularly inclined to pursue it. He even found himself telling her he loved her, and it was not an idle notion. There was an unusual sense of safety in revealing himself to her that he could not remember experiencing before.

It was serendipitous to happen upon Joanne this evening, his last in the country for almost a year. His original departure plans had not included a trip to Boston at all. Keyes wondered at the irony of intersecting with Joanne like this.

Then again, the timing could not have been worse, considering Joanne's recent emotional scars. Add his imminent departure to Brazil, and the timing suddenly seemed almost tragic. He knew that the hurt that showed clearly in her eyes would not be going away either quickly or easily. He thought, perhaps if this was six months into the future, I might be calling my firm in Burlington to cancel my plans for South America. *Silly*, he thought. *Stupid. You've got too many things going on inside that head of yours,* he told himself. He decided he would write to Joanne, and he hoped she would respond. With that thought, he drained his glass. It was time to get some sleep.

***

FIFTY-FIVE MINUTES had passed, but to Munroe, all sense of time was lost. It may have well have been five minutes or five hours. Every passing moment, Munroe's heart pounded. His efforts at composure were being complicated by the redolent presence of a dead man ten feet away.

Munroe knew when he first arranged the meeting that Oates could be a problem, but he did not anticipate that outright physical violence might ensue. Munroe held that thought. Mortal force was necessary, he said to himself, to keep Oates from blowing everything. Oates failed to heed reason and common sense and striking him to end the threat was a necessary action. And in truth, this was probably as accurate as any prudent person might deduce, given Munroe's plans for the near future. Yes, Munroe convinced himself, *what I did was rein in a potentially explosive matter.*

There was no knock to signal Earl's arrival. Instead, Munroe heard a key in the outer door and the sound of confident footsteps across the floor of the anteroom. The doorknob to Munroe's office turned and squeaked almost imperceptibly. To Munroe, the sound was deafening. Earl stepped into the office, and Munroe recognized his form outlined in the shadow at once. Earl was six feet seven inches tall and over three hundred pounds. Jack Munroe had known him for a dozen years or more as a sometimes driver, sometimes bodyguard, and all time loyal aide to the Chairman of the Board. As the anointed child of the board, Munroe was tonight accorded Earl's fullest attention. And tonight, he would need it.

Earl nodded a hello. Munroe stood and approached the doorway.

In a whisper, Munroe said, "He's over there, Earl. My God, it's good to see you."

Earl said nothing. A light from a lamp in the outer office was enough to illuminate the body of the late Captain Henry Oates. Earl moved to the body, studied the scene for a moment and bent low. He moved Oates' right arm, which was bent in such a way that it rested on the floor, off the edge of the carpet. Still warm, for which Earl was grateful. Rigor had not yet locked the dead man's frame. He didn't want to have to break bones.

Earl reached inside Oates' jacket pockets and extracted a wallet, a set of car keys, and a Prudential Center parking garage ticket. In Oates' trousers, Earl found some folded bills, a few coins, and a gasoline service station receipt. He put Oates' wallet and money into his own jacket pocket, and handed the keys and parking ticket to Munroe. "Here, Mr. Munroe; you'll need these." The rest he left on Munroe's desk.

"Who puked, Mr. Munroe? You?" Earl asked the question as if he was asking about a pencil falling on the floor. There was no judgment in his voice. He shifted the corpse and turned one edge of the carpet over. "It didn't go all the way through, Mr. Munroe. Probably won't stink too bad. Just needs some Lysol or something. I'll take care of it later."

Munroe remained staring fixedly at the body. Earl had never mentioned the brass elephant whose trunk was still plunged deep into the skull of Henry Oates. Nor the fact that Oates' eyes remained opened, staring into nowhere. Nor the odor of excrement that often follows death, especially a violent death. To Earl, evidently, these were matters of less concern than the sour evidence that someone had recently suffered a bout of stomach upset.

Earl reached down and plucked the brass elephant from Oates' skull. It came out with a sucking sound, its trunk dripping blood and clumps of gray and pink brain tissue. Earl tugged the end of Oates' necktie from its gold clasp and used it to wipe the trunk of the residue. He set the elephant on Munroe's desk.

Earl then picked up the largest shards of the broken vase and disposed of them in a wastebasket adjacent to Munroe's desk.

Munroe watched as Earl, having placed Oates' body in line with the edge of the carpet, began the process of neatly rolling up the late captain within the expensive Oriental carpet. He was meticulous as he worked, periodically stopping to check and double-check his progress. When he was finished, he picked up the rolled carpet with Oates inside with all the effort a normal man might expend hoisting a forty-pound sack of flour. Oates was by no means a small man, but Earl never groaned. He faced Munroe and nodded once towards the door. Munroe stepped into the outer office as Earl followed.

"Where are you going to take him, Earl?"

"To the Farm, Mr. Munroe. I'll take him in the trunk of my car."

"Are you going to burn the body or something?"

"I don't think so, Mr. Munroe. But we'd better be going."

Munroe asked, "We? Am I going with you?"

"Mr. Munroe, you'll follow me in his car."

Munroe looked at the car keys and the parking ticket in his hand. A Ford, from what he could tell from the shape of the key. There was a tag on the key chain with several typed digits, probably the registration number. And probably government plates, considering Oates had been in Newport on official business.

"We'd better go, sir."

Munroe walked ahead of Earl, who made sure the office was locked as they left. "All the way down to the end of the hall, sir. We're taking the freight elevator."

Munroe walked like a dutiful child. The elevator door was opened and awaiting them. Normally out of operation at this late hour, the freight elevator was available to building tenants any time of day. They began their long descent to the basement's loading platform that abutted the parking garage.

When the elevator stopped, the door reopened and Earl motioned Munroe to exit. They stood on the deserted platform. Earl made another motion to indicate the direction in which Munroe should go. They exited the loading platform and entered the garage. As they walked, Munroe scanned the underground parking lot for a Ford with government plates.

Earl stopped when they reached a white Chevrolet sedan, the car nearest them. Without taking the load from his shoulder, he reached into his pocket, removed a set of keys, and opened the trunk. He placed the body, still wrapped tightly in the carpet, carefully in the trunk. Before closing the trunk lid, Earl studied the contents, apparently making sure he had not forgotten anything. "All set here, Mr. Munroe. Now, let's get you into his car and get going." Together they surveyed the remaining cars in the parking garage. There were perhaps two dozen at this late hour, a silver Cadillac Eldorado, Munroe's own, among them. At the far end of the garage was a dark blue Ford sedan. "That must be it, Mr. Munroe."

As they approached it, Munroe noted that the plates were indeed Government Issue. He looked at the numbers on the key tag from Oates' pocket to make sure they matched before he inserted the key in the door and opened it. Munroe sat, found the ignition key and started the engine. Earl leaned his frame into the car and looked at the dash. "Plenty of gas, Mr. Munroe. Now, I'll go out first, and you follow me. I won't go too fast, Mr. Munroe."

Munroe let the car idle until he saw Earl pull up in front of him in the Chevy. Earl waved for him to follow, and they proceeded to the exit and payment booth. Earl reached out and handed the attendant his parking ticket and a ten-dollar bill. When he received his change, the gate lifted and Earl pulled ahead about fifty feet and waited for Munroe.

Monroe pulled up to the booth in Oates' blue Ford and similarly handed the attendant the parking ticket, actually Oates' parking ticket, and a twenty. He was preoccupied with the weight of his cargo when the young attendant bent low and recognized him. "Oh, Senator Munroe, it's me, Lenny. Hey, I'll just put the ticket in the tenant slot. You don't have to pay, senator." Lenny raised the gate as he continued, "Go right through, Senator Munroe. But next time, try to remember to bring your parking card with you."

Munroe, nodded, tried a smile, and fumbled with the twenty-dollar bill. His parking ID was taped to the windshield of his Eldorado, and the plastic parking card was sitting still clipped to its visor. "Uh, thanks, Lenny," he said in a broken, tentative voice. The gate was lifted and Jack Munroe pulled up behind Earl, waiting to begin the journey to the Farm.

Both cars were five hundred yards away approaching the Massachusetts Turnpike entrance ramp when the attendant reminded himself to make a note about Senator Munroe. He didn't have his windshield sticker either, and technically, he was supposed to pay the parking fee. He made a note on the back of the ticket and put it in the tenant slot. He'd be sure to tell Senator Munroe's secretary tomorrow to remind him about the sticker and the parking card.

CHAPTER SIX

KEYES' INTERNAL ALARM clock went off at 5:30, a full hour before his scheduled wake-up call. He pulled open the drapes to see a dismal gray, but still dry morning. The sun hadn't risen fully at this hour, but it promised to be a day devoid of sunshine anyway. He walked towards the bathroom, stopped to turn on the television, and heard the local meteorologist concur with his prediction.

He showered, shaved, dressed, packed, and assessed his schedule. Sufficient time to eat a light breakfast, check out, and make his way to Logan Airport with time to spare. He'd use any extra time to take a leisurely route to Logan, perhaps a walk through the Public Gardens and the Common. He would have plenty of time to catch the 'T' at Park Street and ride directly to the airport.

By 7:30, Keyes was in front of the Copley Plaza, a small suitcase in one hand and travel sack over his shoulder. He had packed the bulk of his clothes, plus some books and supplies, in a trunk that was shipped from Vermont to Canutama two weeks earlier. He would have preferred that this day be filled with sunshine, warmth, and flowers, but he accepted the drear without complaint. It wasn't raining, and for that he was grateful. He walked north towards Boylston Street and the grand boulevard of the Back Bay, Commonwealth Avenue. He would approach the Public Gardens from the avenue's tree-lined concourse and enjoy the stroll.

As he walked, he completed a mental checklist. *Tickets? Jacket pocket. Passport? Right front pocket.* And so on. He was accustomed to travel and performing such exercises had become a habit, even though he had never forgotten as much as a toothbrush. Given the extent of the journey facing him today, the checklist assumed greater importance and preoccupied him for a full block's walk.

His reverie was broken by an ominous rumble. Within seconds, heavy splatters of rain began to fall. He was now surrounded by the same workers this morning that had passed him by last night. Mornings made them no more aware of his presence. He moved as quickly as he could to the southwest corner of Dartmouth and Boylston, where both subway station and bus stop were located. There, he'd seek to escape the downpour and take the less scenic journey to the airport.

Keyes and, it appeared, ten thousand others, shared similar notions about using the subway and bus. The steps at the entrance to the subway were crammed, backing up onto the sidewalk. He didn't relish the thought of a tightly packed ride, with luggage, aboard either mode of transportation and spotted a taxi dropping a fare in front of the library. With a rush of determination, fed by the dislike of being soaked to the skin, and the thrill of competing with another potential cab rider running unencumbered from the opposite direction, Keyes reached the cab and rapped the fender with his fist to capture the hack's attention. He opened the rear door, threw his baggage on the seat and leaped in. He had won, and he took particular pleasure in noting that the competition was not only much younger than he, but also immensely upset at losing. Keyes ignored the bird being flipped in his direction by the loser, sat back in the cab, and enjoyed the feeling.

"If this was my cab, I'd have to hurt you for whacking the fender like that," the driver began, "but the guy who owns this shit on wheels is a miserable SOB, so be my guest. And where are you going this fine morning, sir?"

"Logan," Keyes answered, still watching the loser frantically run after another cab.

"Terrific. Logan. We gotta take the artery this morning. The tunnel has an accident inside, Storrow Drive's a real mess and over the hill is a bitch right now." Keyes hadn't seen either Storrow Drive or the "hill" in years, but remembered them as murderous routes in the best of times. The artery, no picnic itself, was option number three, and he prepared for a stop-and-go, cut 'em-off trip.

"They keep changing the traffic directions here, don't they?" Keyes figured he'd fill in the time with some conversation, and this cabbie seemed like the talkative sort.

"Every few years the city hires some asshole consultants to tell them which streets ought to be one-way, and which direction they ought to go. Over here, we want to go up Stuart Street, see? But to get there, we have to make a right turn, cut across the Turnpike entrance, get over to the left lane and go clear around the Westin Hotel. Then, in ten minutes, we'll be at that corner right over there. Makes good fucking sense, right?"

The light was still red, but the driver gunned the engine. The light turned green halfway through the intersection, an event the driver anticipated, but which took the pedestrians crossing Huntington Avenue by complete surprise. The cab lurched, surged, and roared through the intersection, the driver ignoring the shouted obscenities. "As far as I'm concerned, they can all piss up a rope," the cabbie said to Keyes over his shoulder, smiling all the while.

The cabbie apparently enjoyed the challenge of hacking in Boston. Keyes had considered driving a cab part-time when he lived in Boston. Crane & Stewart had been paying him a livable wage, but he could always use the extra cash. He supposed he had a romanticized image of himself wheeling about town in a hired heap, sharing insights with college professors and hookers alike. *A great way to meet people,* he thought, sort of like Charles Kuralt and "On The Road." Keyes had cut short that sanitized image when a grad student at MIT, working part-time as a cabbie, met his maker on Dorchester Avenue at the hands of a mugger with a knife and a bad attitude. He wondered at the time whether the dead grad student's motivation for driving a taxi was anything like his own.

The cab jerked to a halt. Matt leaned forward and saw a clogged up intersection with little hope of relief. At Berkeley and Stuart streets traffic came to an absolute halt in every direction. Keyes looked at his watch, the cheap Timex digital that had taken several lickings and still kept on ticking. *Still plenty of time,* he considered. After all, he'd left ample time to walk part of the way. The rain, which forced the decision to take a cab in the first place, appeared to be letting up somewhat. Keyes glanced at the meter; $6.70, and he'd only traveled three blocks so far.

He sat back in the seat, not seeing any point to sitting in a cab for at least the next twenty minutes. With some luck, the rain will stop completely. "Look, why don't I hop out here? There's no point in me sitting here forever, and you can keep the change." He handed the driver $10, grabbed his luggage, and stepped out. Before he closed the door, the cab driver said, "Look, if you still need a cab in twenty minutes, come right back here. I ain't going anywhere."

Keyes stepped towards the Berkeley intersection and saw the reason for the delay. An accident. Two cars and one traffic light had met at interesting angles. He was about to make his way across the street when he was brushed back by two Boston police officers running quickly to the scene. "Out-a-the-way," one of them yelled as they ran past. Keyes stood back and saw that they had come from Boston Police Headquarters, immediately to his right.

A third officer, somewhat older and certainly beefier than the others, was exiting headquarters, walking, not running, to the scene, and dressed in a long, orange raincoat. This clearly was supervisory talent on its way. "Great day to be alive," he said to Keyes as he passed by, smiling, oblivious to the pelting rain. Keyes watched him amble between the stuck traffic. "No cause for alarm. No reason to take a heart attack. It's happened before. It'll happen again. It'll stop raining in a few minutes anyway."

Keyes stood in the shelter of a building entrance and watched the scene play out. He absently glanced at his watch and decided to satisfy the curiosity that Joanne had effectively stifled the night before. After all, the Boston Police Station, the old headquarters building, was right here. Directly behind me. Won't take a minute to ask the question. The rain began to lose its force and Matt used the opportunity to trot easily to the front steps. He admired the solid gray granite, the large, blue lanterns eternally lit and announcing its purpose.

Keyes entered and faced a dark hall and a uniformed guard

sitting at a long table. The guard was more involved in studying his clipboard than he was in actually guarding the entrance, and Matt cleared his throat to get his attention.

No words from the guard, just a look. Evidently this was Matt's signal to speak.

"I'd like to find out if there was a report of a fight or a murder last night."

Still no words, but Keyes had at least elicited a wrinkled brow. A signal to elaborate?

"I saw a fight last night, and I think someone could have been hurt or killed. I just want to find out about it."

The guard took a breath. Keyes was about to hear a voice.

"You want to find out if what you saw was a murder?" Basso profundo in B flat. Keyes nodded to this Barry White sound-alike in agreement. "And you're not sure if it was a murder, so you want to know if there was a fight? Did you report a fight or a murder last night?"

"Uh, no. I mean, I saw it from a distance. Through a telescope." Keyes knew as soon as the words came out of his mouth that it sounded stupid. And his own voice sounded like a high-pitched chirp compared to the rich depth of the guard's. If the guard's silence, cocked head, and the wrinkled brow were indications, he knew that the guard was in full agreement. He sounded stupid. Stupid and shrill. *Pisser*, he thought. He considered salvaging some shred of self-esteem by simply turning around and leaving the station at once, but decided he'd try to recover.

"I was with a friend in the observatory at the Hancock Tower last night, and I was using one of the telescopes. I saw two people fighting in one of the offices in the Prudential building, and it looked pretty serious. One guy went down and he didn't get back up."

The guard lightened when he found an opportunity to pass this case along to someone else. "You can file a report if you want. Over there, report across the hall. They can help you." Keyes followed the direction of the guard's nod to a counter twenty feet away and staffed by three officers. Two were engaged in conversation. The third saw Matt and motioned him over.

"Yes, sir. Can I help you?" Keyes was relieved. He had a feeling that he'd be able to communicate without getting a frown as his sole response. He retold the events of the previous evening. The officer with a name badge reading "Finnegan" on his uniform shirt pocket listened and even seemed to be paying attention. Periodically he jotted some notes on a pad of paper out of Keyes' line of vision. When Keyes finished, he craned his neck and saw that the pad had copious notes. "Can you come with me, Mr. ...?"

"Keyes. Matthew Keyes. Sure."

Matt followed the officer to a battered gray metal desk. The officer sat in a chair on one side and motioned Matt to be seated as well. "I'm going to check this out on the terminal, and then I'll print out your statement. I'll need you to sign it when I'm done." A computer screen on the desk glowed and Matt watched the officer type in a series of commands. "This will take a minute."

While the computer did its thing, the officer turned on a printer, positioned the keyboard on his lap and quizzed Keyes— "Your full name? Full address? What time did you witness this event?"—until he was done. Then he keyed in a command to print, waited for the report to be completed, tore it from the printer, and handed the document to Matt. "Here. Read through this and see if I got everything. If it's accurate, sign it on the bottom." Keyes took the report and began reading. The officer looked back at the screen and typed in more commands. Yes, it was accurate, so Keyes reached for a pen and signed.

The officer paged through a series of screens, scanning each one intently. He finished and turned to Keyes. "There was nothing reported by anyone else last night that comes anywhere near to what you saw. In fact, Mr. Keyes," he said as he continued scanning the screen, "it looks like it was actually a slow night around the city. A few assaults. Domestics, as usual, some breaking and entering. But nothing unusual at the Prudential Center except for a few reported shoplifters and a false alarm at a camera store on the first floor."

Keyes felt a sense of disappointment. It's not that he wanted there to have been a murder, but the fact that there wasn't even a reported assault was unsettling. He wanted the computer to burp and whistle, announcing that there was, indeed, a murder at the Prudential Center last night.

The officer sensed Keyes' anxiety. After all, he didn't seem to be some kook. But whatever he saw, it wasn't a murder, wasn't even something that warranted mention. "Mr. Keyes, I'm going to refer this report, if you don't mind." *Refer?* Keyes wondered what that meant. At least he didn't say he was going to trash the report. "That way, if anything is reported, if it relates to similar circumstances, we'll have your corroboration." *Corroboration?* Keyes saw some promise in that.

The officer rose, indicating that the session was over. Matt followed. "Thanks," he said, appreciating the official "referral" and the anticipated value that his report would have as "corroboration."

Keyes walked out of headquarters without raising a shred of interest from the guard at the front door, still busy studying his clipboard. As he approached the guard from this angle, he noticed that the clipboard was entirely blank. He paused at the top step and looked at his watch. This side trip had cost him only fifteen minutes, and during that time the rain had come to a complete halt.

Inside Boston Police Headquarters, officer Kevin Finnegan read through the report one more time. In his job at the desk, he heard all kinds of strange reports from even stranger people. After listening to people coming in with everything from complaints about litter to large-scale mayhem, Finnegan felt he was pretty good at sizing people up. He could tell when a person was being factual and when he was lying.

This man, Matthew Keyes, seemed rational. The only thing out of sorts here was the fact that there had been no reports of a fight or anything else in the Prudential by anyone near the scene. Just this telescopic view from Keyes.

Finnegan jotted a note to himself on his calendar. If nothing had been done with this report in six weeks, he'd schedule it for a quick follow-up. It just wasn't worth pulling an officer off some detail right now to run up to the Prudential and start knocking on doors.

If there was a missing person reported over the next couple of weeks and it matched up with anything in this report from Keyes, then the department would have something to draw upon. Otherwise, the report would be shipped to dead storage downstairs.

Keyes' signed statement was dropped into a metal tray marked "New Reports Filed."

***

THIRTY MILES AWAY, Senator John Munroe sat staring aimlessly out of a bedroom window of a white frame farmhouse. Still fully clothed, but wrinkled and rumpled. Sleepless. The drizzle matched his mood. Since his arrival the previous evening, he relived his argument with Oates and its terrible finale a thousand times. Each time, he heard the crunch of metal, bone, and flesh and saw the perplexed expression on Oates' face. Munroe still didn't know how he managed to follow Earl all the way from Boston to the farm. His mind had gone blank during the drive, and he recollected nothing of the journey.

Munroe clearly recalled, though, the moment of his arrival when he stepped out of Oates' blue Ford sedan. Earl, without a word, immediately moved the Ford behind the barn and left Munroe alone to face the icy stare and the seething wrath of the Chairman.

"Get inside, dammit." The command was gruff, to the point, as expected, and Munroe entered the back door of the house. He remained standing as the Chairman entered and took a seat at the pine trestle table. A respected United States Senator, he was reduced to a child awaiting his punishment.

There was a prolonged silence, followed by an offhand wave of displeasure and impatience, a motion to Munroe to be seated.

"Tell me the whole fucking story. Start at the beginning and tell me everything."

Munroe began telling the story of Oates' arrival at his Boston office, delivering a detailed account of the subsequent conversation and the rapid degeneration into a heated argument. He described the last moments of the meeting, the reach, the brass elephant, the lunge, the fall, to the point of his phone call. Not once was he interrupted. He finished with a deep sigh and searched for some reassurance and comfort in his Chairman's face. There was little from which to draw comfort.

"I suppose you did well enough under the circumstances, but you came within a hair's breadth of blowing everything wide open. Do you realize that? What if someone in an adjacent office heard you or heard the commotion?"

Frustration and fear had equal time in Munroe's thoughts. "No one else was around." It was a weak response, but all he could muster at the moment.

"Earl called me from the car and told me about the mess in your office. Of course, he couldn't recount all the details about how it happened, and he had to speak in shorthand on the cell phone. Too many ears out there where they don't belong." The Chairman reached for the cup of tea he'd been drinking before Munroe's arrival. Then he added, "At least Earl will take good care of things." Munroe sat silently and wondered at the simplicity of those words—reducing a homicide, a corpse in the trunk of a car, the car itself, to the level of a bit of dust to be swept away.

"The immediate concern is to make goddamned sure you proceed in your day-to-day activities as if nothing ever happened. Oates never met with you in Boston. There was no argument. There was no fight. I don't care what it takes, but there's so much at stake, and you can't afford to draw any undue attention." Munroe listened patiently and with some minor relief. The Chairman wasn't going to dwell on the evening's events, it seemed. Munroe felt like he had escaped a brutal beating behind the woodshed.

"Oates was married," the Chairman continued. Munroe knew that, and he had met Rosemary Oates more than once. A financial wizard in Washington, she hobnobbed with the rich and famous every day. "He's also certain to have had a busy schedule, so people are going to miss him when he doesn't start showing up where he's expected. He was in Newport before he drove to Boston, so that's the most likely spot he'll be sought out, at least to start. I doubt very much that he would have let on to his colleagues that he was going to Boston to meet with you. Oates might have been a lot of things, but he wasn't a fucking flannel mouth. He knew when discretion was called for."

Munroe asked, "What about the record of his transactions he told me about? What if he prearranged something where his association with me would be made public if something happened to him? I got the feeling he meant it when he told me about it." There was real apprehension in his voice, and the Chairman nodded at the question, expecting it.

"That's entirely possible, but we have the liberty of time to consider how to approach that problem, if it even is a problem. If he made a detailed record, then the most likely person he'd leave it with would be his wife. I don't think his wife would reveal anything without having a reason to. No reason to right away, at least. I doubt she'll react to his disappearance with a hair trigger. But Rosemary Oates is no dummy. She could be dangerous. We'll have to keep close watch over her. Also, there'll be no connection with you. No one presumably knew about the meeting except for you, me, and Oates. And his body isn't going to be found. Earl is taking care of that right as we speak." With that, the Chairman rose and moved to retire to his own bedroom at the rear of the house. "You left me a pile of lemons, and I'm going to have to figure out how to turn them into lemonade. So leave that to me and get some sleep. The front bedroom upstairs is set up." Munroe remained seated for a moment before he, too, arose and climbed the stairs to the second floor.

That was last night, and it was morning now, Munroe having remained clothed and awake at the window for hours. Throughout the night of his silence and solitude, he pondered his current position. He was wealthy beyond his needs, income from a trust accumulating at a rate at which he could never spend. He was single and available to a virtual harem of women who were attracted to him and to whom he was attracted. He had won his election to the Senate against daunting odds, and had become a favorite of the senate leadership. Munroe's star was on the rise, and the coming year would thrust him into national prominence.

And he just killed another human being. And been told to pretend nothing had happened.

Munroe wanted to take a step backwards and determine how he found himself here. He recalled making few conscious decisions to reach this point, the direction of his career having been carved out for him, fashioned in every detail, by the Chairman. He had few friends since his early years, and few periods in his life that he could describe as truly happy, at least not since his youth in rural central Massachusetts. His parents, both elderly now, had raised him with great doses of care and love. They wanted only the best for their only child and shared their time and their affection generously. The scholarship to one of the select prep schools in New England surprised John Munroe, if not his parents, and at fourteen, he was reluctant to leave home for a life among the sons and daughters of the well-to-do.

It was a turning point, and he found he liked the good life. His was an attractive face, with an easy and open smile. And now he had friends with famous parents and money to burn. And then Cornell, the Ivy League almost a given. He'd come to expect nothing less. Munroe wasn't brilliant, but in comparison to this friends and colleagues, he was equable. If anything, he might be described as unemphatic. His was a character painted in watercolors; of John Munroe, one might consider if nothing stood out, at least nothing was offensive. He accepted his good fortune with no apparent curiosity and loped through the daily routines of the young and the wealthy without breaking a sweat. He'd come to count on the good life.

Later, he found himself the beneficiary of a healthy trust fund set up on his behalf by a recently deceased relative he'd never met. Nothing appeared beyond Munroe's reach; good fortune seemed destined to come his way. And then George Washington University Law School. Not the most profound thinker in his class, he nevertheless thrived there, and fairly exhilarated with life in the shadows of the White House and the Capitol dome. A position with a respected firm in Boston greeted him after graduation, and there was no shortage of well-heeled clients referred his way, including the Chairman, who befriended him and found a willing protégé in young Mr. Munroe. The right connections, election to the Massachusetts House. Then the state senate. And then the senate of the United States. And soon, the biggest prize of all. And all along the way to this point, the Chairman orchestrating his next move. Even the business with Oates was the Chairman's idea, the recognition of Oates as an uncommonly damaged individual, whose insatiate rancor and position of power made him ripe for the boldest of propositions.

Munroe stared out the window at the new light of the dawn breaking through the pale gray. Oates' words echoed as if in a dream: greed and fear. And Munroe concluded that Oates was probably on the mark. Very likely, they were greed and fear that drove Munroe, smiling, accepting, and only slightly unaware, to this point in his life.

The uncertain penumbra of the breaking dawn developed into a drizzle and turned to heavy showers, and the rain turned the senator's view of the quaint New England farmyard into a softened work of impressionist art. Shapes were undefined and slippery. The colors, muted by the early light and the rain in that middle time of neither full night nor full day, were soothing and distracted him for the moment from his predicament. Munroe was shaken from his reverie when he heard stirring downstairs, which meant the Chairman was awake and moving about. He arose and made his way downstairs.

CHAPTER SEVEN

B Y THE TIME Keyes left police headquarters, traffic on Berkeley Street was beginning to move, directed by police officers around the accident scene. Flashing yellow lights caught his attention from the right, and he turned to see a white tow truck from the Boston traffic division slowly making its way through the clogged crowd of cars and people. No ambulance, no siren. Apparently just a case of wrinkled sheet metal. Keyes scanned the area in search of a cab.

He remembered the cabbie that had dropped him off, stopped walking, and looked around. No sign of him so he searched the damp, gray landscape for signs of another cab looking for a fare. He knew the chance of finding a cab was improving, for he understood the indirectly proportional relationship of quantity of cabs versus need for cab. Now that the rain had stopped, he knew an available cab would soon appear.

He walked past the accident scene and saw one of its victims, a sleek, silver Jaguar sedan with a menacing problem—the problem was a red Toyota coupe, twelve years old at least, dimpled with rust, and firmly affixed to the Jaguar's front end. A tall woman in a Burberry trench coat was standing next to the Jaguar, speaking loudly and pointing repeatedly and forcefully in the direction of a young female dressed in jeans and a plaid overshirt. The young female was silent in return, but shrugged her shoulders, whereupon the tall woman's voice rose to a shout, and more animated jabbing ensued.

Keyes heard bits of the conversation, mostly the higher notes hit by the Burberry lady. The younger woman said not a word. The only other conversant was the heavy sergeant Matt had seen exiting headquarters as he was entering some minutes earlier. The sergeant was positioned immediately in front of the Burberry lady, blocking her from direct access to the Toyota youth. His words were audible, not shouted, and almost soothing. "Please, ma'am, yelling is not going to get you anywhere. The tow truck is coming right along, and we can discuss ...No, ma'am, I can't give the young lady a ticket because she didn't do anything wrong ...Yes, ma'am ..., but ..." and he caught Matt with a wink as a he walked past. "Yessir, young man, a great day to be alive." Matt nodded and smiled in return.

Just ahead, Keyes spotted a cab at the corner with no rider in the backseat. He trotted towards it, nodded to the driver, who nodded back, and in seconds, he was being driven to Logan International Airport. The cabbie this time was a reticent young man and would not yield to his efforts at conversation, short of mumbling "Yes" and "No." Keyes decided to sit back and take in the scene around him.

***

IN THE OFFICES of Crane & Stewart, Joanne O'Byrne stared at her day's task list and found her mind wandering for the umpteenth time this morning. She shook her head to clear it of its meandering ways and tried to concentrate. In her methodical way, she kept a running account of her day's tasks at the corner of her desk. This helped her maintain some focus in a department where chaos could, and usually would if left unchecked, run amok. The fact that the previous evening with Matt Keyes intruded frequently left her approaching late morning with only two items scratched off her list, and eleven yet to do. She didn't like this, so she decided to get a cup of coffee, her fourth this morning, to try to get a grip.

Matt Keyes. Of all the people to run into. Where the hell was Matt when I needed him, huh? In goddamned, godforsaken Vermont! And after a few hours back in Boston, he all of a sudden gets warm and cuddly? Screw him!

"Joanne." She turned abruptly when she heard her name. "You just put your ninth packet of sugar in your coffee." It was Phyllis Rhodes, the receptionist.

Joanne acknowledged Phyllis with a nod that said, "Uh, sure. Right." She left her coffee on the counter and walked quickly back to her desk, where she fumbled for a stick of gum in her purse. Phyllis Rhodes, a venerable fixture at Crane & Stewart, followed at a discreet distance and approached Joanne confidentially.

"Are you OK, Joanne? You seem preoccupied." There was genuine concern in her voice, and Joanne had worked with Phyllis long enough to recognize it.

"A lot on my mind this morning, Phyllis. That's all." Then she added, almost as an afterthought, "By the way, Phyllis, do you have the morning paper?"

"Sure. The *Globe*. Would you like to see it? It's at my desk."

Joanne followed Phyllis to the firm's reception area and accepted the paper. Immediately she scanned page one, then riffled through the first and second sections quickly. Nothing about an assault at the Prudential. Nothing like a murder in the high-rise. "Looking for anything in particular, Joanne?"

"Nothing in particular. Thanks." She handed back the paper and headed back to her desk.

"By the way, Joanne. Mr. Jensen called a few minutes ago. He won't make his 11 o'clock meeting this morning. Would you mind passing along the bad news to the crew? I'm sure they'll be disappointed." Joanne turned back to acknowledge Phyllis and caught the wry smile at the corner of her mouth.

"Thanks, Phyllis. They'll be broken up about it."

The day is dreary enough without having Trygve Jensen around, she considered. When she returned to her desk, two engineers were there to get the good news. The sense of relief was contagious, and soon the entire unit had a brighter perspective on the day.

Phyllis Rhodes watched Joanne from a distance, concerned about her absentmindedness this morning. She hadn't seen Joanne so distracted since she went through her separation and divorce from Alan O'Byrne. Then, she was stumbling into people, spilling things, forgetting to deliver important messages. In one case, her forgetfulness nearly cost the firm an important contract. Phyllis understood that Joanne was going through a difficult period of her life, and she had kept a wary eye out on Joanne's behalf. She'd been able to deflect some of the criticisms that had flown in Joanne's direction, but if it hadn't been for Mr. Banks, Phyllis was certain Joanne would have been asked to leave. Phyllis had approached Mr. Banks after a particularly inattentive workday on Joanne's part and presented him with the predicament: losing a husband, caring for a small child, moving back in to her mother's home. These were taking their toll, but they were likely to be temporary in nature; give her a chance to make her adjustments, she asked, and Joanne would be right as rain shortly. Mr. Banks assured Phyllis that Joanne's position would be secure, and that Joanne should be encouraged to take a few days off to get her life in order, her mind focused, and her emotions a needed break.

This morning, Phyllis could see some of the same behavior in Joanne, and she paid special attention to her. Perhaps she's relapsing; perhaps something has happened to further disrupt her life. Phyllis could not have known that Joanne's distraction this day was partly the result of the emotional dissonance she experienced at having met up with Matt Keyes, her one-time lover, the previous evening. Nor could she have known that this sense was coupled with Joanne's doubt and unease regarding Matt's reaction to whatever he saw through the telescope.

**

FLYING GENERALLY DIDN'T bother Matthew Keyes. If anything, he enjoyed looking out the window, whether it was cloudy or fair. He relished traveling, whether for business or pleasure, and in spite of numerous flights of varied duration in his lifetime, he was never over the awe of being whisked in a fifty-ton machine from the ground to the tops of the clouds.

Because the rain showers were blanketing much of the eastern half of the U.S., the takeoff from Boston was delayed nearly an hour, and he felt a few good bumps and rough spots on the way from sea level to thirty-six thousand feet.

The clouds beneath him were light gray and angry, but the sky above was bright with the late morning sun. He ordered a Bloody Mary to go with his breakfast of orange juice, black coffee, a sort of prefabricated extruded cheese omelet, two lukewarm sausage links, and a clotted mass of gelatinous, beige …what, home fries? The omelet he ate, and the rest he left on his tray.

After breakfast, he slept nearly all the way to Miami, and dreamt of Canutama and the work ahead of him.

As chilled as the autumn air had been in Boston, it was a steam bath in Miami. Keyes was grateful that he only felt the heat's blast for a brief moment exiting the plane to the air-conditioned Jetway. After feeling the full cooling effects of the airport's interior, he smiled inwardly, cautioning himself to be prepared for the drenching hot weather in which he would live almost constantly for the next period of his life.

The second leg of his trip took Keyes from Miami to the city of Belem, on the northeast coast of Brazil. The sky was cloudless the entire trip. Landing in near total darkness, Keyes cleared customs and found that the hotel where a room had been reserved in his name for one night was directly adjacent to the airport. He checked in, grateful that his audiocassette course in Portuguese had prepared him sufficiently to utter and understand at least the basic phrases. In spite of grabbing several naps throughout his two flights that day, he fell to the bed, exhausted, and slept easily.

The next day's journey began with a flight from Belem to Santarem, a town along the Amazon River some five hundred miles inland. The plane was a two-engine, propeller-driven antique, but the flight was remarkably smooth. With half of the twelve seats on the plane empty, Keyes used the opportunity to scan the landscape below from both sides of the aircraft. The flight path was northwest over low marshland and forests until they reached the great Amazonas, where the plane banked left on a due west heading. They followed the course of the Amazon to Santarem, where the airport runway was an unpaved strip and the "terminal" a small aluminum hut. Three passengers deplaned and none boarded. One hour later, with the plane refueled, the plane took off for the next stop, Manaus, three hundred miles further into the heart of the continent, where the Rio Negro joined the Amazon.

As the craft headed west, Keyes saw that the ground beneath was relatively flat, the land on either side of the great river dotted with numerous small ponds and was extraordinarily lush. Boats, large and small, could be seen maneuvering along the river, and often he spotted simple dugout canoes, usually staying closer to shore. Looking north and south, he saw no towns, no signs of human habitation. This was the rain forest, and he knew that the treetops below hid a vast array of flora and fauna to an extent unseen anywhere else on earth. He guessed his altitude at about seven thousand feet and enjoyed the play of the sunlight over the umbrella of green below.

Within moments of his arrival in Manaus, where the airstrip appeared to be recently paved, Keyes found that his plane to Labrea—a Cessna with pontoons affixed for water landings—would depart at once. He rushed to the plane with the pilot at his side, threw his bags into the cavity behind the seats, and squeezed inside. The four-seater roared to life with stubborn, intermittent backfiring, and the pilot made several quick adjustments to steady the engine's rhythm. He was clad in denim cutoffs and a sweat stained, short-sleeved jersey. He had a determined look as he taxied from the grass field to the paved runway, checking his instruments frequently as the plane rumbled to takeoff. Keyes tried to comprehend the words spoken by the pilot into his microphone, but the chatter was too rapid for his untrained ear. It was when the plane ascended slowly and coughed several times that Keyes experienced the first feeling of reluctance since his journey began in Boston. The pilot twisted knobs and made more adjustments until the sound eventually smoothed. *Was accepting this assignment a good decision?*

The pilot turned to Keyes after the plane leveled off and spoke slowly, knowing that Keyes was not fluent in Portuguese. He explained that the urgency of getting started without delay was caused by weather conditions threatening to close off Manaus to air traffic for perhaps one or two days. Keyes could see darkening skies to the South, and inwardly hoped that this leg would prove as uneventful as the previous three had been.

Labrea, his next stop and the nearest point reachable by airplane to his ultimate destination, was little more than a small village. From the air, it appeared to be a collection of several adobe buildings with thatched roofs carved from the jungle, which surrounded it. He judged from the air that the thickest rain forest could be but a fifteen-minute journey by foot from the clearing that represented the central most point of "downtown" Labrea.

From there, he knew, his journey would be via a four-wheel drive land vehicle, and it would not be a brief journey, given the lack of roads in the area. The plane banked lazily over Labrea, and the pilot pointed its nose towards the center of the Rio Purus, a tributary feeding the Amazon with waters from the eastern slopes of the Andes.

When the pontoons of the Cessna met the calm surface of the Rio Purus, Keyes realized the remoteness of his position, a sense that would envelop him for some weeks hence. The pilot taxied across the water in the direction of a wooden pier at the river's edge, upon which stood a diminutive young man Keyes guessed to be about sixteen, who waited until the propellers stopped completely before expertly tossing a rope to the pilot.

The pilot held his end of the line firmly as the youth gently towed the plane towards a clearing at the river's shore, adjacent to the pier. The pilot warned Keyes to open his door slowly, but not to exit the plane until he was told to. The pilot then reached behind to the luggage, tossed it to the youth on the pier, and leaped gingerly from his seat to the pier, using the wing brace as a step. Then, using the rope, he and the smiling young man began to reverse the plane's direction in the river so that Keyes could leap from his seat, at the pilot's command, to the pier. In moments, after a quick handshake with the youth and Keyes, the pilot was back in the Cessna, turning the engine over and taxiing towards the river's midpoint for takeoff. Keyes waved at the pilot when he was airborne, unsure if he received a return wave, but sensing that this most recent leg was not yet the most rigorous he would face.

The youth smiled unceasingly, but remained silent. With straight hair the color of ink, high cheekbones, and a dark, unblemished complexion, Keyes guessed him to be a native. The young man picked up Keyes' bags and pointed towards shore and the mud-splattered Chevy Blazer that would be his means of reaching the final destination of his long trip. As they walked together from the pier, Keyes asked the youth, haltingly in unpracticed Portuguese, how long it would take to reach the village of Canutama, the soon-to-be home of Matthew Keyes for the next ten months.

"Two days, more or less," was the answer in unaccented English, the smile still frozen. "I will drive you there."

"My name is Matthew Keyes, but I'm sure you knew that. What is your name?"

The young man turned to Matt as he walked. "Mine is a very difficult name to pronounce. It is a native name that is very long. It will be easier if you just call me Jimmy." No change in the smile.

They reached the Blazer and Keyes climbed in. The vehicle was thick with crusted mud on the outside, but clean and uncluttered inside. Jimmy started the engine, shifted into first gear with a crunch, and drove north along a gravel path that passed directly through the center of the village of Labrea. Within minutes, the road deteriorated from gravel to well-rutted packed soil with thick vegetation brushing the sides of the vehicle. "We will drive for three hours until it is too dark to see the trail," Jimmy said. "I have food in a cooler in the back. It is a long drive, and we will be hungry. Do you like fried chicken?"

Keyes nodded and smiled back at Jimmy.

"I will be working with you at the project site," Jimmy remarked.

"Have you been at Canutama very long?" Keyes was eager to learn about the community in which he'd live.

"Actually, the project site is northwest of Canutama by about twenty-five miles. But since where we are going has no real name and Canutama is the closest ...you see?"

Keyes didn't really see, not yet. "I have been to school at Sao Paolo University," Jimmy went on. "I took my degree in mathematics. There are seventeen people working on this project now. You are the fourth engineer, but the only expert in flood control and erosion."

Keyes was surprised that the youth had graduated from college. That would place him in his early twenties. "I was trained in geology and soils," Keyes said, "but I also have some experience in underground water movement. Based on what I have seen in the proposal and the plans, this project will test how much of an expert I am."

Their conversation went this way for some time. Jimmy turned out to be a talkative sort, and he gave Keyes such descriptions of all the other project participants, their looks, and their habits, that Keyes was certain he'd know them all as soon as he arrived.

Keyes reached for the cooler and they both ate while they traveled. He found the chicken to be delicious and hoped that his meals in the coming months would be as good. Twice he offered to share the driving. But the roads were so primitive and the going sometimes so treacherous that he was pleased when Jimmy politely acknowledged the offers but declined.

When darkness fully settled in, Jimmy stopped the Blazer in the middle of the path and turned off the lights. They slept in the Blazer, Keyes taking the backseat and Jimmy taking the front. With an arrangement of fiberglass screening and clips, Jimmy sealed the Blazer sufficiently to allow some movement of air without permitting the insects of the jungle to feast on their passengers.

They started early in the morning, nourished with the juice and pulp of several fruits Keyes did not recognize. As Jimmy drove, Keyes glanced at the lands passing by and considered the challenge before him and the entire Canutama project team. It had been the world's insatiable appetite for wood products, this time for mahogany and teak, which had robbed this rain forest of its strength.

The rain forests of Brazil have only in the last decade been found to be one of the planet's major sources of oxygen. The vast expanse of vegetation generates enormous benefits for every living thing on the face of the earth, and indeed shapes the world's weather to a great extent, yet it suffers from ignorance, greed, and distance from most of the world's power centers.

Stripped systematically and relentlessly in the last quarter century for its lumber and other resources, the Brazilian rain forest shrank considerably. By century's end, fully one third had been destroyed, and climatological effects were being felt around the world. At least a portion of the effect called "global warming" was attributed to the shrinkage of the rain forest. Overstressed in its efforts to consume heat-inducing carbon dioxide from the atmosphere, the forest was incapable of performing to its maximum effectiveness, and gradual warming of the environment resulted.

Long a focus of conservation groups calling for a halt to the slashing and burning that threatened to destroy it, the rain forests of Brazil gradually and fortunately gained some standing among some of the world's great nations, meaning those countries sufficiently wealthy to contribute to a poor and beleaguered Brazil and its efforts to rein in development and destruction that threatens to cause cataclysms as yet unheard of.

Matt Keyes' part in the Canutama Project would be to direct the design and field testing of methods to help reverse some of the destruction wreaked upon the region over the past three decades. Using reforestation and soil retention techniques, project planners hoped to turn a corner that would eventually allow them to depart the area and allow it to thrive and regenerate on its own.

The particular area of his involvement was to assess the extent of the damage already done to the soil and to prepare schemes to preserve what was left from further destruction. Unprotected by the moisture-preserving umbrella of trees and exposed to the relentless drying heat of the sun, millions of acres of land saw its soil being turned to powder and washed away by the rains. Hundreds of rivers and streams swept the soil eventually to the Amazon River. The entire complexion of the river had been affected, with many species of fish and amphibians disappearing entirely. Time was inexorably passing and with it the chance for the rainforest to recover.

This was so unlike the New Hampshire woodland Matt had known as a youth. There, the land positively insisted on being forestland and relentlessly rebelled at man's efforts to make it into anything else. Before the Mayflower had landed, fully ninety percent of the area they chose to call New England was covered with trees. Oaks, elms, maples, and softwoods like pine and balsam. But the craving of the new settlers and their descendants for wood products was so vast that, towards the end of the nineteenth century, just a century and a half following the first Thanksgiving meal, less than twenty percent of the land was left to the trees. Wood for houses, for ships, and most of all, for fuel, had stripped the land and left it bare and exposed.

Keyes' curiosity in the ways of the land had its roots in his early walks through the thick woods of southwestern New Hampshire. There he saw stonewalls, obviously placed in rows by human beings, winding through the woods and serving to separate no pastures, no meadows. Only more woods. What happened to the pastures where cows and goats and sheep must have grazed, and where farmers penned their stock? Where were the small gardens and the farms where rows of corn and squash once thrived, and for which these stones were pulled and laid end-to-end?

It was later that Keyes learned precisely what happened, and why hundreds of miles of rugged stone walls could be found lying fallow in almost every grove of trees throughout his corner of the country. If left to its own devices, he found, almost any thoroughly cleared and empty plot of land in New England, whether it was a single lonely acre or one hundred acres, will sprout healthy saplings in three years. In ten years, trees the height of a grown man will surge upward to the sun. In twenty-five years, these trees will be forty feet tall, and the earth will be matted with a thick layer of rotted, mildewed leaves, restoring and energizing the earth and making it strong against the winds and rains. To Keyes, this was nothing short of a miracle.

As he absorbed the scenery around him now, he considered the irony of this odd pilgrimage. He was from New England, coming to a landscape where elms and balsams would never sprout. Keyes silently hoped, however, that this land would, like his own, have the resilience and the will to become again what it wanted to be.

***

THEY REACHED THE project site in the early afternoon of the second day. Keyes was dozing when Jimmy stopped the Blazer directly in front of a small bungalow-type structure. Jimmy gently nudged him awake and said, "This will be your home. Your trunk arrived here last week, and I put it inside." Matt turned his head and rubbed his eyes, the dreams and cobwebs still holding him in half-light. When he opened his eyes in full wakefulness, the hut to him seemed somehow familiar. He'd seen photographs and read descriptions of it, knew its approximate dimensions and its basic construction. It stood in a light-dappled opening, perhaps twenty feet separating it from its similar neighboring huts, and set, he presumed from this vantage, some fifty or fewer yards from larger huts for the common project workspace. This was still the forest, the treetops seemingly hundreds of feet above, nearly silent but for the steady hum of a generator some distance away, and the occasional squawk and chirp of fauna roaming the limbs and vines of the forest ceiling. Hanging on the frame of the front entry of the hut was a sign, handprinted on cardboard that read, "Welcome, Matt, from all of us on the Canutama Team." A collection of signatures surrounded the words.

He alit from the Blazer and stepped inside. Home was now no wider than nine feet and perhaps twelve feet deep. There was a cot with a thin foam mattress, bedding neatly folded, a small table with a chair, a bookcase, a small table with a basin and pitcher, and to his surprise, but not amazement, an old-fashioned oil lamp. His trunk, packed with extra clothes, reference books, and some basic drafting tools, was placed squarely at the foot of his cot. Keyes felt as if he had stepped back in time at least half a century.

"I'll show you around," called Jimmy from the open doorway. He saw that Jimmy had placed his two pieces of luggage inside.

"Sure, Jimmy." Matt felt curiously resolved, a sense that he had finally arrived at the gates of a dream. And he felt fully refreshed, in spite of the dampness and heaviness of the air for which a lifetime in New England had not prepared him. "Show me around."

CHAPTER EIGHT

T HE FRIGID DRAFT coming through the leaks around the windows on the second floor of the former Boston Police Headquarters was ruffling the sheets of paper stacked up in Jerry Wetman's in-tray. This was Homicide. Temporary quarters for the past six months while the division's regular offices in Area D in South Boston underwent renovation. Renovation by wrecking ball would be the most appropriate method as far as Sergeant Wetman was concerned. These were poor, crowded quarters to be sure, but they still provided far better conditions than those to which he'd become accustomed in Area D. When Fatima Cabral dropped a heavy manila envelope on the top of the stack as she swooped by, the ruffling came to halt. The thud of the envelope was followed by a shrill, "Goo-ood morrrning, Sergeant."

At 8:30 on a frigid winter morning, Jerry Wetman felt no one had a right to be cheery. He had been awake since 5, after only three hours of fitful sleep, and his third cup of strong, black coffee wasn't yet sufficient to kick-start his engine this morning. Not that Wetman felt that anyone had the right to be cheery at 8:30 *any* morning. But especially in the dead of winter, Fatima's smile and earthy bounce made him sick.

"Oh, come on, sergeant, snap out of it," Fatima said as she passed by his desk once more, delivering more paperwork. "It's five degrees outside, and the streets are iced up. Be thankful you're not out there directing traffic!"

"Look, Fatima, it was a long, rough night, and I'd just as soon you kept your perky thoughts to your perky little self." "Little" was not frequently used to describe Fatima Cabral, a woman of ample breadth, as sturdy as a fire hydrant, and Wetman's remark earned him a forty percent sneer. "Where's Collins?" he asked her.

"I don't kno-o-o-w, sergeant," Fatima said with a dismissive wave of the hands, exaggerating her coo to make utterly certain she'd get under Wetman's thin skin.

"Well, when he comes in, tell him that the miserable little pissant he interviewed on the Hoffman case took a header off the Mystic Bridge last night. He'll love to hear it."

Fatima looked up, serious now. "Really? The one you said was lyin' through his teeth?" The Hoffman case was a particularly brutal stabbing murder of a young male in Boston's South End two days earlier. Ronald Hoffman, forty-one and the father of two girls, worked nights as a clerk at a corner convenience store to supplement his earnings as a meat cutter for a supermarket in Roslindale. Ronald Hoffman had apparently refused to relinquish the convenience store's receipts without first challenging the two perpetrators with a loaded, but unfortunately jammed, thirty-eight caliber pistol he kept under the counter. The two perpetrators, initially stunned by the unanticipated appearance of a loaded weapon, laughed at Hoffman's definite and immediate predicament. The pistol turned out to be as helpful as a paperweight. When Wetman and Collins arrived at the scene, Hoffman had been removed by ambulance and was already slipping into oblivion in the emergency room of Boston City Hospital. The first responding officers had been so certain that Hoffman was already dead that they reported it as a homicide; hence the call came to Wetman and Collins.

Among their colleagues, Wetman and Collins were often referred to as Mutt and Jeff, a curious pair. Wetman was small, wiry, and mouthy, raised in Mattapan, and nicknamed "Weasel Wetman" with good cause in his childhood. Collins was the so-called Black Irishman from Mission Hill…"skin so black, it's blue," Wetman would say…tall, given to a slight paunch, younger than Wetman by a dozen years, the more reserved and definitely the more refined of the two.

"Man, the blood's still runnin' across the floor," Wetman muttered as he stepped over the yellow crime scene tape. "Guy can't be dead five minutes."

Collins wasn't paying attention to Wetman, who always muttered to himself. Instead, he was already engaging the senior uniformed officer in a question-and-answer session.

"How long ago?"

"Call came in at 9:38."

"Any witnesses? Anyone around?"

"Nobody. The call was from a cell phone to 911. By the time the first officer arrived at 9:46, the whole area was empty. When he came in and saw the blood, he figured the guy was already dead and called it in. Then he saw some movement and radioed for backup and an ambulance. They took him away around 10 o'clock, but from what I hear, even the EMT thought he was dead. Then the guy starts to scream. Something about "Bobby" or "Buddy." That was it. Man, the blood was everywhere, and this guy starts yelling. Real loud. Freaked me out."

"Then what?"

"They rushed him out. You showed up. Now you know as much as I know. And I know as much as anybody here."

"Thanks," Collins said, then he slowly scanned the scene for the first time. Wetman was still muttering, something about the quantity of blood on the floor.

"Look, Collins. Look at this skid mark in the blood. Must have been one of the EMT's almost fell on his ass in this shit. Christ, this guy was stuck good."

Collins nodded, then continued slowly panning the store. Wetman tiptoed behind the counter, carefully avoiding the blood, and carefully eased open a door to a small back office. The crime scene photographer had not arrived yet, and Wetman was cautious about not disturbing anything. He craned his neck around the doorjamb and let out a slow whistle.

"What's up, Jerry?" Collins called to him.

"Oh, nothin' …just a little security camera back here aimed at the counter through this little peephole here."

"No shit." Collins didn't smile, but even though he couldn't see Wetman's face, he knew he'd be wearing a grin a mile wide.

Wetman stepped back out of the area. "Nice little model, the kind you see at banks. I'll bet we can get nice eight by ten glossies in a couple hours. Whaddya think, Collins?"

By midnight, Collins and Wetman were in the photo lab staring with dismay at the gradual appearance of light gray patches of mud against darker gray patches of mud. At best, one might be able to make out three blurs, probably Hoffman and two other men. If one squinted and used some imagination, one might be able to make out a pair of glasses and a white hat on one of them. "Shit," Wetman said. "Shit, shit, shit. Goddamned camera must have been focused on the moon."

Collins nodded in concurrence, but said nothing. If he spoke one word, Wetman spoke thirty.

Wetman picked up the photographs, still damp, and turned to leave the lab. "Come on, Collins. Let's head back over to the store."

On the way out of headquarters, a caricature of a crime reporter was waiting, nervously poised with spiral note pad and ballpoint pen to take notes. "Sergeant Wetman, can you tell us if you have any suspects?" Wetman stopped abruptly, Collins nearly bumping into him. Wetman was all seriousness, even holding up the envelope with the worthless photographs close to the reporter's nose. Collins watched Wetman go to work. In thirty seconds, the reporter was on his way, anxious to get his report into the morning edition.

An hour later, Wetman and Collins had collected seven assorted names from the area's denizens, based on vague descriptions and the name "Bobby" or "Buddy." Within an hour after that, they had conducted four follow-up interviews with weakly described suspects. None were solid, but one appeared to be especially edgy. A real squirrel, wiry, probably doped up, trying to wise off with Collins, but doing a miserable job of it. A real pissant, in Wetman's view. Collins pressed him, came up empty, and made sure the little squirrel overheard his aside to Wetman as he walked away: "Let's go back to the lab and check out the surveillance photos from the store. They should be done with the enhancements by now."

Wetman knew that he would be wise to keep one eye assigned

to this pissant. And before a day had passed, who goes tumbling off the Mystic River Bridge but Mr. Squirrel himself. A jumper? Pushed? Wetman guessed a jumper. That leaves one bad guy. He'd make sure they'd do another check around, visit the pissant's friends, if he had any. Who knows? With a little luck, once in a while these things get closed quickly. At least there's one stiff that the Commonwealth doesn't have to defend, feed, house, parole, and so on, and so on.

At twenty minutes to nine, Collins entered the cluttered office, removed his parka and slipped it over the back of his chair. A nod to Fatima and a soft half-smile; "Good morning, Fatima." He had set a paper cup of coffee on the corner of his desk and now focused his attention on removing the lid. At this hour, after the nights he'd been putting in, one must take things one step at a time.

He took a sip, set the cup back down on the desk, and leaned back in his chair. "I guess it's time to say good morning, Sergeant Wetman."

Ignoring the feeble greeting, Wetman never looked up from the paper in which he had just started the crossword puzzle. "Did you see the *Herald* this morning, Collins? Chelsea dragged an unidentified out of the Mystic River."

"So? Another jumper. Do we know him?" The Mystic River separated the cities of Chelsea and Boston. The Mystic River Bridge …or the Maurice Tobin Bridge as it formally known …is a heavy steel girder contraption with an upper deck taking drivers from the north into Boston and a lower deck to take them out. The upper deck has served as the final launching pad for countless individuals over the fifty years of the bridge's existence. Most jumped. Depressed, suicidal types. Drunks. Dopers. And a few were encouraged, so to speak, from the precipice. Usually these were connected somehow to organized crime. It is safe to say that the dive to the river below is generally of a fatal nature. Fortunately, at least for Boston, the tides tend to take the remains towards the less fortunate city of Chelsea, which, therefore, earns the privilege of fishing the corpse from the river and notifying the area police departments. And the frequency of the deaths was usually sufficient to merit only two sentences in the daily papers.

"Well, it seems that the recently departed bears a remarkable resemblance to one of your favorite buddies. One Benjamin Fredericks, AKA 'Pissant,' from the South End. Your wiseass squirrel from the Hoffman case. Man, Collins," Wetman went on in mock seriousness, "what on earth did you say to drive the youth to this sudden and tragic end?"

Collins took another sip of his coffee. "Fine. One down. Any witnesses?"

"Course not! But what the hell, it's still a point for the good guys."

Collins didn't share Wetman's cynicism, but unlike his partner, he had not been assigned to Homicide for eleven years. By comparison, Collins' twenty-nine months in Homicide made him a relative rookie. He liked the job and its challenges, especially after an uninspiring five years as a uniformed officer, but he was conscious that the disappointments associated with it, and the high rate of failure that accompanied murder investigations, could very well jade his view over time. He didn't want that to happen. At least not so soon. So he tried to fight it.

Nevertheless, Collins reasoned that with Benjamin (Hoffman was trying to say "Benny"?) Fredericks out of the picture, at least he wouldn't be holding up any more innocent store clerks. Wetman had a point.

Wetman stepped over to Collins' desk and picked up the manila envelope that Fatima had dropped there earlier. He moved it and tossed it a bit as if trying to guess its weight. Then he closed his eyes and put one hand to his forehead. "Enclosed in this envelope, I will estimate with my usual clairvoyance, is a great bag of manure from the man upstairs, designed to keep you busy and out of trouble for at least half a day." Collins had to smile because Wetman was right. Cold cases. Old unsolveds. Usually a few rarely useful bits of new evidence on stale cases. Collins took the envelope from Wetman's hand and opened it. He looked through the sheets of paper, some with only a sentence or two of information. Some multiple page reports. He made mental notes and a few written ones as he perused the pages. One report involved a claim by a witness to a robbery and shooting in South Boston, the case of which would begin trial next week, that her original statement was flawed, that she couldn't, upon serious reflection, be absolutely certain of the identity of one of the suspected perpetrators. Of course, the original report, Collins recalled, had no such ambiguity. The witness was sober, clear-eyed, and definitive. It didn't take much to imagine what happened here.

Another was a brief report noting the discovery of four spent bullet jackets, all .44 caliber, in an alley adjacent to the scene of a homicide that occurred seven months ago. There might be something here worth looking into. Collins recalled that the victim in this case was a fourteen-year-old boy with a hole the size of a baseball where his navel had been. There was a short list of suspects, but not enough evidence to arrest. The casings might be worth nothing at all, but there just might be a print or two. He set that report to the side and continued his perusals.

One report involved a homicide from three years ago. Still unsolved. The victim's family had taken over the investigation when the police gave up. The victim, a twenty-four-year-old female flight attendant, was found gagged and knifed in the trunk of her car in an East Boston parking lot. There were no solid leads and no witnesses were ever found. The vehicle had been dusted and gone over meticulously, and not a single print was found except for the victim's. The police hit a dead end.

With relentless energy and determination, the woman's parents continued their questioning and canvassing of the area where the body had been found, certain that an as yet unturned stone hid an important clue. Posters featuring a photograph of the stunningly attractive woman were nailed to telephone poles for several miles in every direction, with requests for information and a telephone number for people to call. No new information had been reported, but Collins noted a handwritten message from a deputy commissioner: "This deserves personal follow-up visit by Homicide.

No activity six months. Report requested w/i 14 days." A visit was unlikely to yield anything of value, save for some reassurance to the parents that their daughter was not being forgotten. Collins set this report aside as well, and wondered at the depth of anguish that the parents must feel.

The final report in the stack was a real poser. A reported homicide-slash-assault-slash-question mark. No body found. No missing person reported which might fit the description or the time involved. The report was filed in November by a person named Matthew Keyes, and it was accompanied by a single paragraph signed by Jim Finnegan, a fellow officer and friend of Collins from the academy. Jim had taken the report from Mr. Keyes: "Reporter appeared rational, in control, sincere. Appeared certain a serious assault took place. Not a flake." So why did he make a report if there was no body, no missing person reported? Only identification was "likely white male victim in dark suit, possible pilot uniform?? Perp also likely white male, business suit." The report noted that the alleged assault occurred somewhere between the fortieth and fiftieth floors of the Prudential Tower. Collins read through the entire report once more, but more slowly this time around. Mr. Matthew Keyes listed an address in Burlington, Vermont. Great. No local contact number, just the telephone number of his employer. Will be out of country temporarily on assignment until October. That's even better. Collins set the report down on his desk and closed his eyes as he considered a next step. After a few seconds, he turned to the computer on his desk and entered a command that brought up the city's street directory. He searched through the directory until he found the names and addresses of every office located in the Prudential building. It was an extensive list. Insurance offices, banks, lawyers, architectural firms, consultants, advertising agencies. But there was no indication on the directory as to which particular floor in the fifty-two-story landmark any given firm might be located. Collins could feel his wheels spinning, and he hadn't even got started.

He turned back to the report. Keyes had listed another witness as Joanne O'Byrne with an address of Melrose. No street given. No telephone number either. Collins decided to give it another shot and dialed information for the city of Melrose. No O'Byrne listed or unlisted. A further check of that city's street directory also showed no one with that name. Collins set the report aside. He admitted defeat, at least for now, and decided instead to follow up on the report involving the four bullet casings. At least that held some shred of hope. And after that, he'd call the woman who changed her story about being able to identify the shooter. The Prudential Tower homicide without a corpse would wait for another time.

***

AT THE POINT at which Collins set the report from Matt Keyes aside, the star of this evening's national news was stepping out of his silver Eldorado in front of Symphony Hall on Huntington Avenue. Earl drove off to find a place to park and Senator Jack Munroe walked briskly to the hall's side entrance. Press releases referred to him always as "Jack" now; more connection with the voters, consultants advised. He was early, well ahead of the supportive crowds that were being bussed in for the event from communities throughout the region, but Munroe wanted plenty of time to feel comfortable with the microphones and the lights. This would be the first crucial appearance in what would be a long line of crucial appearances. Munroe understood the importance of appearances and wished to come across properly to the American people.

At 10 o'clock this morning, Jack Munroe would announce to the people within this magnificent building, to all of the nation, and to the world by satellite link, his intention to run for the office of President of the United States.

Everyone present in the hall, except for news media representatives, was carefully selected to be in attendance for Munroe's announcement. They would be certain to cheer and applaud at all the right places, such as the line near the beginning where he says, "Why is it that so many Americans feel powerless? Because so many Americans know that whatever power they might have is being stripped systematically by complex and unfair tax laws and the frustration of political maneuvering."

Or near the end when he calls for "an end to satisfying the voracious appetites of politicians and bureaucrats for your hard-earned money." And when he cites the incumbent President as "a fine gentleman, but a man who never saw a dollar he was unwilling to tax."

Jack Munroe was handsome, distinguished, and sufficiently popular in his home state to win his seat in the U.S. Senate by the widest margin in the past twenty elections. He would be a late starter in the Presidential race, he knew, yet the timing was perfect. From a closely guarded source, Munroe learned that the sitting President would soon announce his intentions not to run for a second term. He would blame it on his health, he being a man given to some physical frailty, but the timing would be such that he could just as easily be viewed as backing away from a battle with Jack Munroe. And the President's heir-apparent to run in his place, his Vice President, was deemed eminently beatable by Munroe and his backers.

Munroe had leaped into the national spotlight last year when he championed the reduction of military aid to Japan. He was articulate, telegenic, and seen as having the boldness and strength to face up to the fallout of criticism. The President argued futilely to maintain the level of military support to Japan. When the votes were counted in the Senate, the President lost and Munroe came out a big winner.

Over the late months of the year, Munroe's own party had seen nine separate contenders announce their intentions to run for President. Of them, three had an honestly strong chance of succeeding. They had the money behind them and the stamina to slug it out over the coming election year. But the infighting served only to fracture the party into weak segments, and there was, so far, no apparent willingness to form coalitions and to settle on a clear candidate. With the New Hampshire primary only weeks away, polls showed that the likely winner would take no more than twenty-four percent of the vote. So if mid-January was late, it was also the perfect time to make the announcement.

Jack Munroe stood at the podium and faced empty seats,

preparing himself for 10 o'clock. A wrinkled gaggle of political newspaper columnists sat together in the balcony, telling each other raw jokes and tall tales about the stories they almost wrote. They made no attempt to control their chatter. On the orchestra level below them, a number of television correspondents were clustered, polished, and prepped for their videotaped reports. One of them, a young and lithe blonde from CNN, looked hard at Jack Munroe as he practiced on stage. Munroe pointed his finger in the air and gestured as he ran through his speech in a low voice. She kept her gaze on the senator, watching his rehearsal. "That smile ..." she said to no one in particular. "He'll get ten points on just the smile."

***

BY THE MIDDLE of January, after only six weeks there, Keyes felt like a veteran of the Canutama Team. He had settled into a daily routine and was learning to speak Portuguese with some facility. Most important to him, he felt he had already made some progress in developing methods of preserving the endangered soil.

Keyes' teammates in this effort of preservation and restoration were an eclectic group of engineers, scientists, and native labor. The leading figure in the project was Danish geographer, Bjorn Palenius. True to his name, he was a bear of a man. With a mop of roguish red hair, a full beard, and a tangled forest of eyebrows, he looked and played the part of the noble warrior Viking. It was Palenius who was the driving force behind the project from the beginning. He was the first to approach the Brazilian government with the concept of a project team to research the potential reforestation of the denuded swaths of the once lush rain forests in the Amazonas.

Understanding the financial limitations of the Brazilian government, Palenius convinced the Brazilian leaders to approach the United Nations with a multinational proposal. In an impassioned speech before his UN colleagues, the Brazilian representative gained broad support for the proposal, and the Canutama Project was born.

The United States participated in the UN plan, and it was

Keyes' firm in Vermont, at Keyes' urging, which submitted the winning bid to conduct research and prepare a proposal for restoring the soil to suitable growing conditions. For Keyes, winning the bid was the chance to fulfill dreams he'd had when he first chose his career. It also provided a modest revenue stream for the firm's overhead and profit, but winning the bid in competition with dozens of better known, more substantial firms was a public relations coup. A consortium of European nations contributed machinery, equipment, and supplies to the project. Other nations supplied botanists, chemists, engineers, and other specialists.

The Canutama Project was expected to span sixty months, and most of the scientists were there for periods of three to thirteen months. Palenius, as leader, expected to be in Canutama for the full five years of the project, although he was able to take stretches of one month off each year. Keyes admired the Dane, who considered every development or discovery by a member of the team, however small the achievement, as justification for public recognition and celebration. He always did so publicly, usually at or after a communal dinner, and his honest enthusiasm forged the central link that held the group together and made them reach deep within themselves to achieve more.

Upon seeing what he termed "significant developments," Palenius would reach into his battered brass trunk and extract a bottle of Danish aquavit. Project participants would each throw back at least two or three toasts in honor of whoever the exalted party might be. Having been a member of the team for six weeks, Keyes estimated that there were usually two "significant developments" a week by the Palenius definition, usually spaced a few days apart.

Keyes easily fit in with his colleagues, and he found their dedication to the project refreshing. Their shared sense of purpose and the urgency of the reforestation mission combined to focus every participant's attention on the common goal.

What a world away were the drainage projects, the sewer lines, and the flood control gates Keyes had left behind. Once, in conversation with a Canutama colleague who had been a structural engineer in Spain, Keyes learned that he had spent the prior three years designing roof trusses and other supports for an industrial fabricator near Madrid. Canutama, he said, represented "a chance to live the dreams" that propelled him into an engineering career in the first place. Keyes understood exactly what his friend was describing, for he too had never before expended such energy towards so lofty a goal.

Keyes developed his closest friendship with Jimmy, his young driver, and was impressed with his knowledge of the region's ecology. Jimmy was a keen observer, and often drew Keyes' attention to the simplest solutions as they worked. At Keyes' request, and to his pleasant surprise, Jimmy was assigned full-time to work with him as his assistant.

Keyes was daily amazed and overwhelmed by the immense scope of the project, and had more than once considered it a task exceeding his skills, and perhaps that of the entire team's. But as often, Keyes was convinced that the collective efforts of the project team would yield positive, and hopefully, astonishing gains in the preservation of the region's precious and fragile ecosystem.

Frequently, during their working hours together, Jimmy would point out to Keyes the unusual animals who co-inhabited the region. Once, taking Keyes with him in a dugout canoe, he spotted an extended family of crocodiles lazing on the banks of the Rio Purus. Keyes saw more varieties of brightly colored hummingbirds than he knew existed and watched an earnest coati pursue, nab, and devour a tarantula as big as a man's open palm.

For the participants in the Canutama Project, the days were usually long, and at the end of each one, Keyes felt an exhaustion he never before experienced. The extreme heat and humidity, especially during the hours of midday, took its toll, and Keyes learned the value of taking frequent breaks from his work to drink quantities of water, and of relaxing, even napping, when the equatorial sun was at its peak. Nevertheless, whether he was deep in muck taking test borings and measurements, or poised over his drafting table under the protection of the large, screened working area that comprised the

Canutama Project's operations center, Keyes felt an exhilaration he had hoped for when he first considered signing on to the project.

As remote as the team was from civilization, there were some distinct signs that this was indeed the start of the twenty-first century. The project's operations center was composed of a rustic, wooden-beamed rectangular structure, a roof of reeds and fronds, and screens on every side. Electricity was supplied by a pair of Ingersoll-Rand gasoline-powered generators housed in their own open hut some forty yards away. Enough power was supplied by these workhorses to provide for six desktop PCs, sufficient fluorescent lights for the main hut, several electric fans, and a pair of small refrigeration units.

Food, fresh water, provisions, and gasoline for the generators were supplied every two weeks via barge from Manaus. If the need arose, the Blazer could be used to travel to Canutama, but the time required and the travel conditions down and back meant that this was a rarely used option.

The operations center had two telephone lines, one reserved for data transmissions. This way, in spite of the distance, both physically and culturally, and the limitations on electricity to power the computers, the team members could communicate with the outside world rather frequently, and even surf the Internet when they had the time and the fuel.

For emergencies, a circular clearing eighty feet across and one hundred yards from the operations center could be used to land a helicopter. So far, during Keyes' brief tenure, that need hadn't arisen, and the clearing, instead, served as a baseball and soccer field. Keyes and his colleagues felt reasonably secure in knowing that the link to the rest of the world, while not always easy to access, was there, if they needed to use it.

Keyes immersed himself in the work at hand, often oblivious to the outside world, and frequently unaware of the date or the day of the week. Workdays began early with the sunrise, paused at midday until the sun's intensity abated, which could be as late as 4 o'clock, and recommenced until 8 in the evening. Periodic sudden rainstorms would force most of the team members under cover, but

Keyes and Jimmy often used these times to study the rate at which the soil would absorb the water, and, less fortunately, how much soil was washed away into the river.

Each evening's dinner was the social and cultural high point of the day, and indeed, the team had its own cook on staff that doubled as the launderer, baseball umpire, and source of local lore. Nicknamed "Joe," for his real name was as long and as unpronounceable as Jimmy's, he was Jimmy's distant cousin. Often, to supplement the foods shipped in from Manaus, Joe would set off in the dugout canoe in search of fish and other game. In spite of the varied cultural backgrounds of the Canutama project team members, the meals Joe prepared from the native animals he captured were the most popular. A stew of tree frogs or fried baby crocodile tail would attract cheers from Joe's diners.

It was in January, after one of Joe's superb dinners of eel and steamed vegetables, that Keyes first caught himself missing home. The Christmas holiday passed almost unnoticed at Canutama, save for a more elaborate meal prepared by Joe for the occasion. New Year's Eve was celebrated with gallons of warm wine, party hats creatively crafted from enormous leaves and palm fronds, a series of sloppy toasts at midnight, and a painfully off-key rendition by a Texas botanist of "Auld Lang Syne." Other than these occasions, however, life at the Canutama Project was very much a steady diet of research, testing, surveying, observing, and studying the damaged rain forest and its prospects for survival. To Matthew Keyes, who saw Canutama as the chance to fulfill a dream, the project was proving to be everything he'd hoped for, and more. Still, he sensed a growing ache. Whether his yearning was borne of mere absence or a real need to connect, he wasn't prepared to claim. He just felt the ache.

When the barge arrived on the fourteenth of January, all seventeen members of the team waited eagerly for seventeen different reasons. For one, it was the anticipation of receiving a copy of a first edition of a college geography text he had co-authored. For another, a carton of jarred pickled fish from his mother. A collection of at least a dozen professional journals was tied together with baling string for still another. The barge carried three Christmas cards for Keyes. One was from the associates of the firm in Vermont, with each of their signatures accompanied by phrases like "Greetings from the northern hemisphere," and "Try to stay warm!" A second, from his sister and her family in Maine enclosed a lengthy letter describing, among other events, the fierce winter they were experiencing. The third card was from Joanne and enclosed a short note saying how wonderful it had been to meet up with him, hoping he was doing well and enjoying his work, and that she hoped he would write to her. She said she would write again. It was dated the eighteenth of December.

Amid the noise of everyone else chattering over their packets and moving off to their bungalows to enjoy their treasures, Keyes felt a need to be alone with his thoughts. He walked over to the battered John Deere six-by-four utility truck used for a variety of odd jobs, started it up with the key that was permanently left in the ignition, and drove off slowly to the perimeter road of the project compound. Once there, he pulled off at a narrow clearing overlooking the river, a favorite spot for him. Keyes never considered himself a sentimental sort. In fact, he mused, his lack of sentimentality was probably a most effective defense mechanism. He had developed some friends over his adult years, but none he would call close. Joanne was perhaps the person to whom he felt closest, and even then, he had never called or had written to her since his departure from Boston to Burlington some ten years before. Their chance meeting in Boston had been just that. As in most other aspects of his life, he avoided establishing closeness and tried to live life as it came. In rare moments of reflection, he had agreed that life was to him serendipitous. Its pleasures and rewards, if they came his way, simply did so; if they did not, then few questions arose within. No purposeful plans, at least of the personal sort. Limited investment of the soul. No getting close to the light, so no chance of getting burned.

He reread Joanne's card again and felt a sea change. It would have made the prospects of his future much easier to calculate if he could forget about her. It would be more convenient if he could dismiss her now from his thoughts and think instead of the other women he had known, and to whom he felt little attachment. There were plenty of them around for short-lived romances. But he found himself truly longing for Joanne. It wasn't just for the prospect of reliving the moments they had shared years earlier when he had lived in Boston and worked with her at Crane & Stewart. Certainly he desired the touch once again of her hair and her skin against his. There had been heat and passion in their relationship while it lasted.

But his appetite was for a stronger union with Joanne than one built strictly upon physical intimacy and momentary possession of each other in bed. The ache he felt now was an unfamiliar and uncomfortable sensation. He wanted, at that moment, to be with Joanne, to share with her the excitement he was feeling as he literally dug deeply into the Canutama Project. He wanted to hear her voice, her laugh, and to listen to her tell about the events of her day.

It was not melancholy. Indeed, he felt good when he thought of Joanne. The sadness he felt was born of his own making. He saw himself as the one who rejected her several years ago when she wanted him, and he felt a degree of shame and guilt that her subsequent turn towards Alan O'Byrne eventually bore her grief such that she might never make herself vulnerable to Keyes' embrace again. His memories of Joanne gauged the depth of his loss.

He turned once more to her card. He hoped that the polite wishes she expressed contained an underlying sentiment of affection. His mental picture of Joanne presented a cheering image, and he felt a smile cross his face. As he was learning every day in his work, he had a facility for facing uphill battles. Without making the attempt, he would never know whether his future and Joanne's might be a shared one. He would send Joanne a letter. This he resolved as he climbed back into the utility truck and returned to the compound. But then, the only way to send mail was to wait for the barge, and he quickly calculated, that was still thirteen days away.

When he shared his frustration with Jimmy later that evening, it was Jimmy who convinced Keyes to take fuller advantage of their access to the Internet and E-mail. In the late evening quiet, when most of the team members were reading in their bungalows or asleep, with Jimmy at his side, Keyes sat at the keyboard and made repeated attempts to find the electronic address of Crane & Stewart in Boston. It took them nearly an hour to accomplish, but the next morning, when Joanne appeared at work, Phyllis Rhodes printed off a copy of Keyes' letter and handed it to her wordlessly, but with a knowing smile.

Later in the day, Jimmy showed Matt how to retrieve his own messages on the system. One would be there, Jimmy felt confident, and he was correct. From then on, Joanne and Keyes communicated daily.

***

WHILE THESE THOUGHTS and events ricocheted through Keyes' mind in a remote outpost in central South America, the body of the late Captain Henry Oates began to rise from the silt in the deepest section of a small lake in eastern Connecticut. The combination of the deteriorating ropes wrapped around his corpse and secured to eight large cement blocks and his slowly rotting flesh had allowed for some slack. The body, bloated with the methane of decomposition, but still remarkably well preserved in the cold waters of the lake, drifted upward six feet until the ropes went taut once more. Had anyone seen the specter, the report would have been of a foolishly smiling ghoul, one arm raised in a slowly drifting salute.

CHAPTER NINE

THERE'S THAT SMILE. A little uneven, deep dimple on the right cheek. Great teeth. Jack Munroe was knotting his maroon and gray Italian silk tie, but focused on the smile. He turned a little to his left and picked a thread from his shoulder. Then a little to his right. He slipped on the jacket, shrugged once quickly to drape the shoulders just right and looked once more. The mirror didn't lie. Perfect. He reached for his hairbrush and gave a few flicks to his sideburns. Not too long, just enough to show the silver flecks. Maturity. Wisdom. And that damned smile. With his looks and a great stump speech, he'd get these folks in Altoona wishing the election was tomorrow, just so they'd have a chance to pull the lever for Gentleman Jack.

The smile had indeed been worth ten points and more as the primaries wore on and the time arrived for the convention in Dallas. Seven of his party rivals for the nomination had dropped out at various stages of the campaign. Two after New Hampshire. Another two after the Southern primaries. California, New York, and Virginia each claimed one victim as their own.

There were three left. Patrick Cummings from Oklahoma, a two-term governor and a member of Congress for two terms before that. Warren Day, a four-term member of the House and representing the enormous electoral block called California. And Jack Munroe made three.

Flying into Dallas and the convention, Munroe sat with Leland Hayes, his campaign coordinator, former assistant deputy secretary of the Treasury for the current administration, and the source of the advance information that the sitting President would choose not to run. Hayes was confident of a victory in Dallas, a view that Munroe did not entirely share. Munroe saw the key as picking the right candidate for Vice President, and that only a bargained coalition would provide him with a clear mandate from his party on the first ballot.

"You're already thinking out your fallback position, Jack, and the bell hasn't rung yet. I think you're being premature." *Hayes is an optimist*, Munroe thought. The people watching the convention at home on television and on the news don't want to see a drawn out battle that goes to three or four ballots. They want to back a winner.

In the end, Munroe was right. He bargained hard with Cummings and Day. Pat Cummings brought leadership and vision. He was extraordinarily successful in his home state in challenging the status quo and winning. Oklahoma had emerged from the cowboy and oil days and was stepping eagerly and was preparing for the twenty-first century under the serious, but inspired leadership of Patrick Cummings. And he scared the daylights out of Jack Munroe.

"Bo" Day was a less inspiring leader, but brought his own set of important assets. One was his position on reducing military aid to Japan, which mirrored that of Munroe. Another was his quick wit and easy manner. This would help on television, where he had demonstrated on several live interview programs his ability to deftly dodge potentially fatal bullets. He was quick on his feet and funny. Nobody ever accused him of being terribly deep, but he also came from California, the state with the highest number of electoral votes, and that might be the greatest asset of them all.

That and his mixed racial background. Son of a black mother and a white father, he had used his medium skin color and ambiguous features effectively when appealing to primary voters. He once told Munroe that his mother was the daughter of an Australian aboriginal couple, and she had emigrated from Australia to the U.S., when she was orphaned as a child. His maternal grandparents had been killed in a bomb attack by a renegade Japanese pilot fifty-seven days after Tokyo's surrender of World War II, which explained, at least in part,

Day's position on Japan. Day's mother was discovered by a group of American Episcopalian nuns, and they arranged for her adoption by a minister and his wife in Sacramento.

Ever a pragmatist, if African Americans wished to see him as one of their own, Day would not deny them that view. This worked in his favor, even if he did not personally identify with the African-American experience.

Munroe confided to Hayes that "Bo Day is half Aborigine, one quarter Harp, and one quarter Wop. He's about as African as I am, but if it works, who cares?" Hayes did not dispute that there was some merit to this thinking. "Besides," Munroe went on, "Bo is happily married and the father of four kids. I'm single, and Pat Cummings is twice divorced."

"If you take Day on the team," Hayes said, coming around to Munroe's position, "Cummings will have to feel the heat. If he wilts, we'll still have to offer him something big, like Treasury or Commerce, to get him to back off and throw his support to us."

Throughout the night before the convention officially opened, negotiations between the rival camps were frequent and grueling. Cummings, Munroe conceded, would make a fine President. Whether or not Day saw Munroe in a similar light was not nearly as important as Day's having the chance to at least run the race. And Day, Munroe knew, was running out of money. Cummings had a greater degree of financial wherewithal, but Munroe had his Chairman of the board. And Munroe's Chairman let Munroe and Hayes know that they ought to pay attention to the race, not the money. The well was not without depth, the Chairman once told Hayes, "but I'll let you know when I can smell water."

It was Day who was asked and Day who accepted. Munroe/Day posters were ordered printed that evening for delivery the next morning.

Two sharp raps at the door followed by a pause then a third rap, and Munroe knew that Earl was signaling his arrival. He checked his file card for this day: Breakfast at 7:30 with the mayor and his wife; meet with the mayor's staff and hangers-on at city hall at 9:00

to shake hands; taped interview with the local news anchor at the station at 9:40; visit the elementary school at 10:30, coffee with superintendent and school administrators, where they'll present him with a list of their grievances about the sad state of education in America today; deliver the speech to a crowd of supporters on the steps of the school at 11:10; reception and lunch at the Olive Garden at 12:15 with a dozen business leaders. The schedule went on like this all day until 5:30, when he'd catch his charter to Chicago. The Chairman would phone him during the flight. Then a crowd of supporters would be organized to greet him and cheer when he arrived at Midway, where he'd give the short speech, three minutes of "The Spirit Of Change Sweeping This Great Nation," just in time to make the late news.

Munroe opened the door and Earl stood tall and ready. He was still Munroe's chief bodyguard and babysitter, although the gentleman in the navy-blue suit and dark glasses standing at Earl's side was there for Munroe's protection as well. Jack smiled broadly at the pair and asked them to enter. Earl's companion was Todd Bernard, twenty-seven and on his first full-time assignment since his employment by the United States Secret Service. Every official candidate had Secret Service protection, as did candidates' spouses and family members during the campaign. Jack liked the fact that Todd was strong, quick, and armed with a nine-millimeter pistol. Earl's expression was one of tolerance when it came to the Secret Service. There were two assigned to Munroe, but the other was asleep, having spent the evening in a chair outside Munroe's hotel room the previous evening. Of the two, Earl favored the other over Bernard. Waylon Jump's personality and demeanor were more Earl's style. Understated. But they're all the same. And he was older, past forty, and an old hand at keeping an eye on the crowds. Todd, on the other hand, was still in awe of his position. Now that the elections were getting closer, Earl knew that there would be more agents assigned to Munroe, but he had not yet made their acquaintance. Without being asked, Earl picked up Munroe's briefcase and followed Munroe and Bernard from the room.

The day began well for Munroe. Earl had slid the morning paper under Munroe's door at six, but not before reading the front-page article on the candidate and seeing the color photograph above the fold. The news was good and getting better each day. Here was Munroe, in the sitting Vice President's own backyard, and he was four points ahead in the polls already. Earl had heard the stump speech often enough to know that it hit the right buttons. And he'd seen Munroe work the crowds. Munroe was just hitting his stride, and by the end of this trip, he'd likely be another four points further in the lead.

Munroe was greeted at the far end of the lobby at the elevator bank by his press secretary, Lisa Sobolewski, whose arms were loaded with stacks of papers and whose mouth was running at eighty miles an hour, as usual. Munroe presented an air of energy and enthusiasm, whereas Sobolewski presented an air of a whirling dervish on amphetamines. "I've got press releases on your school appearance ready to go. Remember to stress your stand on educating America's youth. Don't forget to call it 'Priority One.' It's important. That's the name of the committee you're promising to form as soon as you're elected. You've had three calls from the *Times*; they want an interview by Wednesday for a Thursday run. I put them off until the Friday morning edition. And I think I can get them to spill some over into Sunday. The campaign chairman from Hawaii called last night; he knows how much time it takes out of your schedule to go there, but he said he'll tie in your trip with a business round table symposium and help you establish credibility on Pacific Rim issues. It would also help to be seen stepping into the fire on the whole Japan thing. If you lose Hawaii, it's not a big deal. But it will definitely play well back here. I told him I'd let him know. Leland thinks it's not a bad idea."

Todd leaned in Earl's direction and whispered to him while Sobolewski continued without interruption. "Great lungs." This was the not the first time he'd made this observation to Earl. It was a testament to Lisa's ability to speak for great lengths of time without seeming to pause for a breath. It was also a comment on her breasts.

Today, as every other day, she wore a simple, open-collared blouse that exposed just enough to be alluring without being plainly guilty of immodesty. Many men, including Munroe, tended to catch themselves staring at the curves of her breasts while she spoke. She kept up her commentary, questions, and updates unceasingly as they all boarded the elevator together. Todd always looked inside before letting the entourage on, and the first off at the lobby before allowing them to exit.

The mayor of Altoona was stationed a few yards from the elevator in the lobby, standing with his wife, Celeste. Next to her was Munroe's Pennsylvania campaign coordinator and yet another Secret Service agent. The mayor smiled and extended a hand to the candidate while camera flashes popped and floodlights lit the scene for the video cameras. Munroe nodded quickly to Lisa as a signal to stop talking, which she did mid sentence, and Munroe simultaneously reached for the mayor's hand and clasped his shoulders in an embrace.

Observers would think this was a meeting of longtime friends who were thrilled to see each other after a long absence. In fact, Earl knew this was the first time Munroe had ever met the mayor. Just saw his picture last night so he'd be ready to shake the hand of the right person. Knew his wife's name and the name of their son, a nose guard on the local football team. Munroe never went anywhere unprepared.

Agent Todd Bernard stood never more than six feet away and scanned the surroundings. Earl surveyed the scene and saw that Munroe's smile was turned on for the cameras, and that he was calling the mayor by his nickname, "Tuffy," of all things. The group walked together into the hotel dining room for breakfast.

***

AT THE FARM, which served as the principal home of the Chairman of Munroe's "board," a meeting was convening in the barn, some fifty yards from the main house. The scene was prototypically New England, with a wide porch surrounding the white clapboard house, several outbuildings of weathered fir, and a well maintained Ford tractor parked next to a post and rail fence. The morning sky was clear and blue, a rare puffy cloud hanging about for appearances only. It was a delightful start to the day.

In the gravel driveway near the barn were parked a green Jeep Grand Cherokee, a Buick Riviera, and a BMW 535i. The barn looked rather like any other barn on the outside, with its faded red paint peeling and flaking from the wood siding and a rusted weather vane with a rooster on top, sitting at the peak of the shingled roof. But the interior was unlike any barn on earth.

Two board members were seated at a rectangular table of deep cherry wood. The chairs in which they sat were stuffed wing backs upholstered in damask of deep maroon and shades of green. The floor was polished red oak covered in an exquisite Indian *Bijar* and measuring at least twenty-by twenty-six-feet. The walls were painted a muted blue-gray, with brass sconces providing subdued lighting of the interior's perimeter. Along one wall were handsome bookcases of oak holding various signed first editions from the early twentieth century, plus an assortment of mementos and objets d'art. Directly behind the Chairman's seat was a large desk of a type and color similar to the table, plus a credenza and a side table on which was mounted a desktop computer. Two phones and a lamp sat on the desk. Otherwise it was bare. Overhead, beams from indirect lights ricocheted from behind cross braces and collar ties to provide even lighting and few shadows. There were no windows to the outside.

A formal meeting of the full twelve-member board would begin in forty-five minutes. In a quiet corner of the room, the Chairman chatted with a friend and fellow board member as they waited together for the arrival of the rest of their colleagues. "I'm going to begin the meeting this morning by reporting that the next President is in Altoona, Pennsylvania, as we sit here, winning over the locals and making the current Vice President look weak in his wife's hometown. The polls in *USA Today* have Jack at 43, the Vice President at 39, with that whacko from Texas taking seven. Eleven percent are undecided. I'd say we have some cause for feeling pretty good about the way matters stand this morning.

"Tonight," the Chairman went on effusively, "Jack's in Chicago and tomorrow's rally will probably be the major campaign story on the national news. Ten thousand people will be there, and there'll be a concert in Grant Park. We're still coming up short in Illinois, and we really need this rally to get us jump-started in the Midwest."

The Chairman adjusted his glasses and looked at a pad of notes in front of him. "We'll also need to talk about Hawaii. Leland is getting calls to schedule Jack for a trip there, and there may be good reason to work this in." He looked up at his friend and expected him to be smiling at the news he was delivering. But his friend and ally wore a stern visage. "Well, what is it? You don't like hearing about Jack's successes?"

"Of course I like hearing about them, but I have some news of my own, and I'm afraid you're not going to like it."

"Speak up. We have to deal with all the news, good or bad."

"This is not necessarily the kind of news you'll want to share at the meeting." He whispered to the Chairman in an aside, "Someone saw Oates' skull getting cracked in Jack's office."

There was an audible gasp from the Chairman.

His friend went on. "Someone saw the whole thing and reported it to the police."

"This is awful!" The Chairman was stunned, found his seat, and slumped back limp.

"Hold on. There's a police report on file, but the witness who filed it claims he saw it from the Hancock observatory, looking through a telescope. Apparently, he can't identify anyone. And the police don't have anything else to go on. There's no tie-in to Jack or Oates. Just this report. It's going nowhere as far as a police investigation is concerned. But you need to know."

"So why is this coming up now? That happened months ago!"

"The report turned up in a routine follow-up. All of these do at least once. But there's still no report of a body. And the missing persons report on Oates that his wife filed placed him in Newport that day. You told me that Earl arranged to drop his car off at a casino parking lot in Connecticut, and that's where the authorities found it. There's nothing so far that links Oates to Boston or to Jack. As far as Oates is concerned, his body still hasn't turned up. Hell, as far as I know, Earl is the only person who knows where the body is, and he's never told me. I don't want to know."

"So, we'll leave sleeping dogs right where they are. That's what you suggest?" The Chairman was anxious to have this suggestion confirmed.

"The police are treating the report as far-fetched, and we ought to do the same."

***

WALKER WHITE WAS lean and wiry. For a man of seventy years, he was healthy and strong. The lung cancer that would eventually kill him eight years later was as yet only the size of a small pea, fastening itself to the left lobe, and he lit another Marlboro without breaking stride as he crossed the dirt path on the way to the pond at the edge of his property in Lebanon, Connecticut. He loved to fish, and today was a fine day to sit on the pier he and his son had built last year and catch some trout. The sun was barely crossing the horizon and the morning dew hung on the tall grass and dampened his trousers as he walked. Next month, his grandson would come to visit and they would spend much of that entire week fishing, catching turtles, and wasting whole days enjoying the fresh air and each other's company. At six years old, his grandson would soon find more interesting things to do than sit around all day with Buppa. He'd have friends and then girlfriends, then a car, and what the hell. Walker White would take life one day at a time.

Walker White loved to fish, and as he neared the pier he recalled meeting the famous fisherman Gadabout Gaddis on a pier like this on a lake in Maine twenty-five years earlier. Walker was in Maine visiting his brother at the time, and one morning before everyone else woke up, he stole across a meadow behind his brother's house to fish in the nearby lake. He had hoped to catch something he could cook up for breakfast, and he did nab a fourteen-inch trout that would cook up nicely. But the best catch of all was the chance to spend two hours swapping stories with one of the most famous fishermen of them all.

He made his first cast of the morning and stood breathing in the morning air. He was facing southeast, and the sun on the water glared strongly. He squinted to compensate and to try to watch his fly on the surface. He heard some activity in the water along the shore, which was not unusual.

Turtles, bullfrogs, and other animals routinely splashed along the water's edge. Once in a while he'd catch sight of a fish leaping to snag an insect hovering near the surface. Years ago, he saw loons swoop over this same pond and dive for fish. The loons weren't here anymore, but there were some mallards making their home here now, and perhaps they were the source of the noise of water being slapped and splashed about this beautiful morning. He reeled in his fly and prepared to cast again when some movement caught the corner of his eye. They weren't mallards at all; sonnavabitch, they're muskrats. *Damn*, he thought; he'd just as soon have those ugly rodents move somewhere else on the pond, especially with his grandson coming. Walker White stepped back off the pier and picked up a handful of stones. He could see the muskrats about fifteen away, three of them, and they were making a racket. He chucked one stone and another in their direction, and he was sure he'd hit them square on at least a few times. He counted two of them swimming away, but a third was holding his ground. He squinted some more to see what was keeping the muskrat's attention. What he saw caused bile to rise in his throat.

Walker White had never met Captain Henry Oates, but there was Oates' shoulder serving as a perch for a stubborn muskrat intent on tearing at the remains of Oates' bloated face and neck.

It usually took Walker White a full five minutes to walk from his house to the pond, all downhill. This morning, it took barely two hundred seconds for him to race back uphill to reach his home and grab the phone off its cradle. It took him another one hundred seconds to catch his breath and composure sufficiently to place a call to the Lebanon police station.

CHAPTER TEN

THE GRANDFATHER CLOCK had just sounded eight chimes when the telephone rang at Anne Stowe's home. Her daughter Joanne was just putting Anne's grandson to bed, and she could hear her saying "I love you" to Joshua. Anne Stowe picked up the phone and answered.

"Mrs. Stowe?"

It was a clear connection, but for some reason she knew this was a long-distance call, a very long-distance call. "Yes. Who's this?"

"Mrs. Stowe, this is Matt Keyes. I'm calling from South America. How are you?"

"God in heaven, it's Matthew Keyes. It's so nice to hear your voice. Joanne told me you were down there in South America. Why that's the other side of the Equator, for goodness sake. It's the end of summer here, so you must be having winter where you are."

"Actually, Mrs. Stowe, it's summer where I am all year round. Uh, is Joanne at home?"

"Why, yes. I'm sorry, I should have called her to the phone as soon as I heard it was you. I'll get her right now."

Joanne was just reaching the bottom step when her mother called her to the phone. "It's Matt Keyes, Joanne. He's calling from South America."

Joanne's face brightened when she heard that Matt was on the line. Thanks to Jimmy, they had been able to communicate by E-mail with each other, but she preferred to send, and receive more personal handwritten letters. Matt's last letter, she knew, was still sitting on her bureau upstairs. Now he was live and almost in person by telephone. She had been pleased to see him when he appeared on the sidewalk in Boston last November, but she felt a need to stand back for a bit. Especially now. And especially from Matt. Whether she recognized it at the time or not, her decision to accept Alan O'Byrne's proposal of marriage was at least partly due to the hurt she had felt when her relationship with Matt had come to a halt. When she was seeing Matt several years ago, she let down her defenses, and she even hoped that they might spend their lives together. Her hopes were dashed when Matt announced, with a smile, damn him, that he was being offered a great job in Vermont, and was moving there in two weeks time. No invitation to join him. Nothing.

Joanne confronted Matt then, and demanded to know if he was moving far away to get away from her. Did he just not have the guts to break it off? Did he have to fall into such an excuse as another job offer to make a separation? She hated him then. And she hated herself for having shared so much of herself with him.

The physical part was one thing. Matt wasn't exactly Mr. America, but she was attracted to him. Their bodies had meshed well, and Matt was a patient and gentle lover. From time to time, he had been close to the edge of letting her into his emotional world. But he was never fully prepared to let her in all the way. So she was the only real giver in the relationship. And the realization that he would run away with such haste and vigor instead of facing her with the truth made her so full of rage that she ignored every call from Matt that time on. He wanted to take her to dinner on his last night in Boston before moving to Burlington. Fuck him! Matt tried to talk to her at work during his last days at Crane & Stewart, and she made a point of calling him a gutless wonder in front of several of their coworkers. When Alan O'Byrne called her two weeks after Matt departed, she quickly agreed to dinner and a movie.

Alan O'Byrne wasn't a bad person. He was a dull person. A nonperson. Where Matt had been attentive to her, Alan was tolerant. When Joanne had a crazy idea, Matt was one to encourage her; Alan was merely agreeable. Matt wasn't reckless, but he wanted to reach out beyond himself and try to accomplish good. Alan, on the other hand, was content to go along.

Alan came from a far more privileged background than Matt

and was the son of a philosophy professor at Harvard. The O'Byrnes lived in Lexington, and it was clear that Alan, an only child, would be taken care of financially for life. Matt, on the other hand, was from a blue-collar mill city in New Hampshire, where his father taught high school math and his mother waitressed. Matt's younger sister, Kristen, was bright, beautiful, and, Joanne recalled, in love with a cabinetmaker. Matt's older brother, Jeff, had died of leukemia when he was seventeen. At the time, Matt was fifteen and anything Joanne knew about him came from Matt's stories of their youth. Joanne sensed that Jeff had been Matt's hero, even if Matt didn't talk about him often. Joanne just had the sense that if she could look into Matt's mind, she would see a shrine to Jeff there.

Joanne never met Matt's father, for he died before she and Matt ever met. His mother, though, was one of Joanne's favorite people. Linda Keyes was smart, quick-witted, and so full of life. Like Joanne, she was a great reader, and loved to read books set in foreign countries. She remembered talking with Mrs. Keyes one time about Cervantes, one of their favorite authors. Mrs. Keyes told her that she had been was so wrapped up in *El Cid*, that her children were nearly named Fernando, Sylvio, and Carmelita. It was her husband who gently persuaded her to gain a firmer grip on reality and settle on names for which their children's psyches would not be scarred forever. Mrs. Keyes laughed with a roar as she told stories like this. Whenever Joanne left Matt's mother's home, there were hugs and kisses, and genuine wishes that they'd all see one another soon.

Alan's parents, Edward and Evelyn, were hardly as demonstrative. The O'Byrnes were good-hearted and affable people, but bland by kind comparison. Mrs. O'Byrne called her son "Ally," she recalled, which rubbed Alan like sandpaper on an open wound.

Alan and Joanne announced their engagement within months of the start of their relationship, and the wedding was held at the Paulist Center in Boston six months later. The Paulists were Joanne's idea. She had been raised Catholic, and the O'Byrnes described themselves as lapsed Catholics who were now active Unitarians. "Then you'll love the Paulists, Mrs. O'Byrne," she had said at the time to a benumbed Evelyn O'Byrne. "They're a lot like Unitarians, but they still use incense."

The lovemaking shared by Alan and Joanne O'Byrne was as bland as their overall relationship. It didn't have to be that way, but Joanne found early on in their marriage that Alan had a peculiar need to be dominated, and he once brought home a leather mask and handcuffs. When Joanne asked him about the paraphernalia, he haltingly explained that he needed to be punished, that he had been a bad boy. Joanne didn't consider herself a prude when it came to sex and was not averse to the occasional erotic experiment. Spanking her masked and handcuffed husband while he lay across her lap did give her pause, though.

When Joanne later announced to her mother that she and Alan decided to separate, Anne Stowe was horrified and urged her to reconsider the decision. "Jesus, Mary, and Joseph, how can you be thinking about divorce when there's a small child involved?" Alan, in Anne's opinion, may not be especially personable or warm, but he was the father of her grandson, offered financial stability, and was a generally gentle soul. "Every marriage has its difficult moments, Joanne," she explained, "and now that you've made your bed, you have to sleep in it!" Famous words to Joanne who heard them countless times from her mother in response to complaints of life's various adversities. Joanne pressed her case, but Anne was unyielding, citing the sanctity of the marriage vow. Joanne finally decided that the truth might make an ally of Anne Stowe.

"But, honest, Mother, he wants to be spanked!" That stopped her mother's argument in its tracks, and Joanne's reluctant description clinched the debate. The disclosure was sufficient to satisfy Anne Stowe that a separation from Alan O'Byrne ..."that sick so-and-so" is how Anne referred to him ...was perfectly understandable.

Whatever needs Joanne might have had in the bedroom were simply never a subject of discussion between her and Alan. So when she became pregnant, rather miraculously, she thought at the time, she was eager to grab the excuse that she was too tired or too ill or too anything for lovemaking that night or any night. When she thought of this, she wondered if it contributed at all to Alan's more unusual proclivities. Then she dismissed the thought.

Joshua O'Byrne arrived on time, but with great fanfare. Joanne wanted to remain working as long as she could at Crane & Stewart, this over the strenuous objections of Alan's parents. As matters turned out, she worked until precisely forty-eight minutes before Joshua appeared. Joanne, in fact, never got to see the inside of a delivery room, Joshua having insisted on arriving in a hallway at Brigham and Women's Hospital. Anne Stowe had noted that same evening that she always thought that Joanne was "built for babies." She went on to describe that she, and her mother before her, experienced very short labors. Joanne took comfort in this. As she snuggled her newborn son, she whispered, "You'd better understand this from the start, Joshua. The only part of you that's O'Byrne is your name, get it?"

Joshua was, indeed, much more a Stowe than an O'Byrne, in habits and character. He was lively, expressive, mischievous (she could never imagine Alan in any sort of mischief as a kid, no matter how she tried), and irreverent without being a bratty kid. Joanne was proud of her son and joyful in his presence.

Family outings to Lexington were stultified occasions, and when Alan agreed to separate and later divorce, one of Joanne's quiet gratifications was the knowledge that these outings would occur less frequently.

Joanne's life since then was a combination of three elements: her son, her mother, and her job, in that order.

She took great pleasure in returning to work when Joshua reached his fourth birthday and Alan left Crane & Stewart for California. Many of her closest friends were those she made at work, and she truly enjoyed their company. Mr. Banks was particularly pleased when Joanne returned to work, and made sure that a vase of fresh flowers and a card from him were on her desk the day she came back. Marshall Banks was the kindliest and gentlest man she knew, and his stature, socially and professionally, was such that he did not have to do things like this without others thinking any less of him.

She was reminded of something her mother told her when she came home from her first day back to work. "The real test of a person is how he treats people when nobody's looking." Mr. Banks was a jewel of a human being.

So now, here, in her mother's kitchen, was a telephone in her hand, connected by electromagnets, fiber optics, and a satellite to a man she had once alternately loved dearly and hated deeply. Over the past several months, she had many opportunities to consider her feelings for this man. First, she felt important to him, and she thought that was a genuine sense based in reality. That she made a difference to Matt.

But, she reconsidered, I felt that way before about him, and we know what happened there. She also felt connected to him. And this was a little different now than it was before. There was a give-and-take that wasn't nearly as evident earlier. His letters were more self-revealing, and he wrote about feeling lonely sometimes and happy other times. Before, when we were together, he talked about things, events, other people, and objects. Not his dreams, not his fears like he does now in his letters. Although he does write about other people, it's those who make a difference to him, people he cares about, like this person named Jimmy. *I feel like I know Jimmy from Matt's letters,* she thought, *and I hope I'll have the good fortune to meet him in person someday.*

This Matt is a different Matt than the one who left for Vermont seven years ago. Hell, she paused, *I'm probably a different Joanne than I was, too.* She brought the telephone to her ear and said, "Hello."

When Matt returned to his bungalow, Jimmy was waiting for him. "You are going soon, aren't you, Matt?" Jimmy had become Matt's closest friend in the world during their past months in Canutama. From their meeting at the dock on the river near Labrea, Matt had found Jimmy to be open and friendly and kind. They enjoyed each other's company from the start.

They worked closely every day. At the beginning, Jimmy's role was simply interpreter and guide, helping Matt get accustomed to the ritual of living in a jungle compound with sixteen other strangers.

Their number had alternately grown to twenty and shrunk to twelve over the period of Matt's work at the Canutama Project. It was back to seventeen now, exactly as it was when he arrived.

Fortunately, Matt and Jimmy found that they genuinely enjoyed each other's company, and Jimmy moved easily from interpreter/guide to valued personal and professional assistant after the first few weeks. By then, Matt felt sufficiently comfortable in Portuguese to communicate with the native Amazon Brazilians attached to the project, and had learned that their facility with the Portuguese language was as uneasy as his own to a large extent. Their native language was a curious blend of tongues, including a dash of Spanish and Portuguese, but more prominently a largely unwritten language they inherited over the centuries from their ancestors, who had inhabited the land for millennia.

Jimmy felt an attachment to the project much deeper than any of the other engineers who were nonnatives ever could. He once told Matt that he wanted to study engineering so that he could bring the land back to a condition of which his ancestors could be proud. He was born here, knew well what the rain forests could be without the devastation, and wanted to work and learn so he could be a part of the restoration process.

In spite of the multiple nationalities represented at the project site, Jimmy remained keenly aware that his was a less privileged lot. In a reflective moment, he once confided to Matt that he felt a kinship with, in his words, "the darker people of the planet." He remained, however, reluctant to feel the fear of being brutalized by those lighter than him. Just as firmly, he was reluctant to feel that fear that he, and others, might deserve it. "We are not heroes," he remarked, "and we are not villains, either. Some of my brothers here would say something different, but this is the truth. At least, this is what I think."

It was Jimmy who was key to a particular finding which would play a major role in the Canutama project's strategy for reestablishing the rain forests on the Amazon region. It began with Jimmy spending at least an hour alone each evening working on what he called "my silly idea." As a child, Jimmy told Matt, he remembered that there were gnats and biting flies, but not to the same extent to which these insects proliferated today. Growing up, he didn't notice any sudden change in the insect population, but rather a gradual increase in it. Indeed, in the project compound, he noted, mosquito netting surrounded every bunk. Such would not have been as much of a requirement years before.

When Matt once visited Jimmy in the bungalow he shared with several others on the project team, he found Jimmy nailing narrow wooden boxes together. He had a stack of finished boxes on the floor next to his bunk, and when Matt picked one up to examine it, he noted that one end was left open. He guessed the scheme behind Jimmy's diligence: "Bats," he said to Jimmy, with certainty. "You're building bat houses."

Jimmy was building bat houses, as many as he could build out of the scraps of wood from pallets he collected when the supply barges arrived. He nodded to Matt and said, "I have an idea that will help you, maybe. Do you know how?"

Matt picked up one of the finished houses and studied it carefully. He guessed that each house could hold a dozen or more bats and asked Jimmy, "If these houses attract bats, do you think it will cut down on the insect population, Jimmy?"

"The bats will help, yes." Jimmy's smile, ever present, was coupled with a glint in his eye, and Matt knew that Jimmy's idea went beyond his brief reply. Matt counted the boxes already completed and stacked. There were twenty finished, and he estimated that Jimmy had a sufficient supply of wood scraps to build perhaps six more. "So how many bats do you figure you can attract with these bat houses?"

Jimmy answered, "One hundred to one hundred fifty."

Matt figured that Jimmy was estimating only five bats per house. Matt had seen some bats in the area, especially at dusk, flitting and darting across the sky eating their evening meal. But to have any serious effect as mosquito controllers, Matt considered that Jimmy would need perhaps ten times as many bat houses for the area surrounding the compound.

"You are calculating, Matt," Jimmy observed, smiling and banging nails without pause.

"Yes, Jimmy, and won't you need many more bats to have any impact? Even two hundred bats won't be enough, will it?"

"Ah, yes, two hundred would not do. But, my friend, the bats crowd together when they sleep, and they are small. Each house will hold one hundred to one hundred fifty. Now, calculate again."

Matt was amazed that as many as one hundred fifty bats could squeeze into each of Jimmy's houses. At that rate, his creations would house over four thousand bats. "Now you're talking insect control, Jimmy. Four thousand bats should keep some of the mosquitoes under control." Matt reclined on Jimmy's bunk, self-satisfied for the moment, having cut straight to the heart of Jimmy's plan. More bats mean fewer insects. Fewer insects will make this place more habitable.

Jimmy's work and Matt's attention were abruptly halted by the shouting just outside the walls of the bungalow. Two of the project workers were engaged in a harsh battle of words. Matt couldn't make out their words, partly because of the rapidity of their delivery, but more so because their language was not one Matt understood. These were evidently natives speaking their own dialect. Matt looked to Jimmy for help in learning the content of the heated argument. Jimmy motioned Matt to be silent and listened. In seconds, the exchange ended, and Jimmy explained.

"The man you know as Masso is complaining to Joey that he passes wind in his sleep, and the smell disturbs Masso and wakes him up. Joey told Masso that it is only a sign that he is healthy, and that Masso's mother was known in the village as the person with the biggest wind of all, and that Masso should be used to the smell by now because he grew up with it. Masso is insulted. That is really all there is. I think they are both probably a little drunk."

Jimmy bent back to his task, and Matt saw that the glint in his eye hadn't disappeared. He knew there must be more Jimmy wasn't telling him.

"Why are you smiling, Jimmy? Did they say something else that you aren't telling me?"

"No, I am just thinking that they are arguing about making bad smells. And I am working here to bring bad smells." Jimmy looked up at Matt, but his hands kept working. His broad grin was even wider than usual.

"I'm not following you, Jimmy. You said that the bats would help, but there's something more than just eating mosquitoes, am I right?"

"I will tell you something, Matt. Bats will eat the mosquitoes, and they'll also eat fruit from the trees. Four thousand bats will probably eat very many bugs, but they'll also eat quantities of fruit. You know the word 'guano'?"

Matt nodded. Bat manure is known as a rich source of nutrients and serves as an excellent fertilizer.

Jimmy continued. "You have not smelled wind as bad as guano, Matt. If the bats like my houses, and I believe they will, they will stay around this area, and eat bugs and fruit. And then they will drop guano, guano with many seeds, across this whole area. If that is true, we will see small plants taking root wherever they can. Every drop of guano will carry its own seeds and fertilizer. Some of the seeds will never sprout, and some will sprout and die. But some of those seeds will take hold. And those plants will grow, and maybe your work in helping the soil come back to life will be helped by my bats bringing plants and holding the soil together."

Matt was intrigued and described Jimmy's idea, with his permission, to the other engineers working at Canutama. One, a meteorologist from Chile, dismissed Jimmy's plan as foolish, but another, a biologist from London, called it "utterly elegant in its simplicity." While the plan never received official sanction, it was deemed harmless enough, and at worst, a curiosity.

Jimmy was keenly aware of the value a replenished rain forest would have on the entire planet. He expressed from time to time that he would like to see more of the planet for which this rain forest was so responsible. He had traveled from Caracas in the north to Buenos Aires and Montevideo in the south, and all the way to Rio de Janeiro. The rest of the continent, the west coast to the tip of Cape

Horn, was foreign to Jimmy, and he was anxious to see it all. "If I can, I will travel in my lifetime," he told Matt. "I once met a man from Santa Maria in the Azores," he went on. "A fisherman. And he told me about life on the sea, about Portugal, and about the United States, where he lived for eight years. He was on a ship that went to Japan once, and he told me about that trip, and the Philippines, and Borneo, and so much, Matt. I want to see the world, too. There are so many people here on this project from all around the world, and we are so different and so much the same. I feel hungry to see snow on the mountains. And I'll go to Boston where you lived and see MIT and go to Fall River, where my friend from the Azores lived. I want to see so much."

Matt had described Boston at length to Jimmy. He told him about his early years at Crane & Stewart, and later, about Joanne. It struck Matt that when he talked about Joanne, he was talking about her for the first time. As close as he'd been to Joanne, he'd never before told anyone else how deeply he felt about her, how he regretted moving away when and as he did, how much he had hurt her in his own adolescent efforts to protect himself. And how he hoped that when he returned, he might be able to regain her trust. He told Jimmy about his fear of becoming committed. How he felt so close to his brother, Jeff, and felt so abandoned when he died. To Jeff, Matt told Jimmy, he had bared his soul. He didn't know any other way when he was growing up. "Jeff would listen to me," he said, "and he helped me grow up. When he got sick and it turned out to be leukemia, I cried with him in bed all night. I was so angry with God and the world. When he died, it wasn't peaceful or gentle. He was screaming all night. We were all at the hospital, and he was so damned afraid, and he didn't fake it. A priest came in that night to say some prayers, and my mother told him that he was welcome to pray only if Jeff said it was OK. When the priest bent over my brother's bed and asked, Jeff told him to take his rosary and stuff it up his ass, bead by bead. When the priest left, Jeff laughed for the last time, and he asked me to hug him and he told me, 'Go tell the priest it's OK. I'm not pissed at him, just at his boss.'"

Jimmy laughed at the story, and so did Matt, through damp eyes. Over time, Jimmy told Matt stories of his own. They laughed together and wept occasionally at each other's stories. And Jimmy had passed from assistant to, alternately, professional colleague, confessor, teacher, and always and best of all, friend.

"So WHEN'S THE BIG DAY, my friend?" Jimmy was trying to maintain his composure, but he could feel, and Matt could see, tears welling in his eyes. "Are you the one on the plane next Thursday?"

Matt nodded. Yes, he would be leaving Thursday, and he invited Jimmy to stay for a while. "I wasn't scheduled to leave for another few weeks, but the plane is being ordered early to replenish some medicines and bring in some equipment. There didn't seem to be much sense in having him make another long run just for me later."

"You called Joanne? Is she OK?" Jimmy had come to know Joanne well from Matt's conversations, and he added, "Tell her I think she is a wonderful woman, and if she has any sense, she should wait for me. I'll show up someday, and she'll toss you out like an old rag, and she'll run away with me to my jungle. Don't forget to tell her that. I don't want her to make a mistake and think you're a nice man or anything."

"I'll be sure to tell her that. But I really think she's happy I'm coming home." Jimmy smiled at that, happy for his friend, for he knew that Matt was afraid she might not feel as strongly for him as he did for her. "I left her before. I knew she loved me, and I knew she hated me for leaving. I was afraid it might be the same this time, even though her letters were, you know, friendly and encouraging. I'm happy for the way she sounded to me over the phone."

"My mother told me once," Jimmy said, "that love and hate are very close friends. But their enemy is not caring either way. She's right. And I think Joanne will love you when you return. And me, my friend, I will hate you for leaving."

CHAPTER ELEVEN

DOC DESROSIERS WAS as ready as he'd ever be. The corpse, what remained of it, was being wheeled in on a stainless steel gurney. Desrosiers shook his head slowly back and forth, his lips pursed.

The doc's assistant, Delbert Nelman, saw the look on doc's face. This case, Delbert knew, would be a trying one for him and doc. *The poor stiff,* Delbert thought, *has been wet for months, and as soon as he's fully thawed out, this place is going to smell like nothing else on this earth. But this is not a time for the faint of heart,* he gamely recognized, *because the doc and I have got to find the truth.* Delbert knew that theirs was, indeed, a noble profession.

It wasn't Doc Desrosiers' concern about determining the truth that caused him to purse his lips and nod his head in dismay. It was the recurring recollection that he would be marking his thirty-fifth year as a physician soon, and this is not what he had in mind when he first enrolled at Johns Hopkins Medical School. He thought he'd spend most of his time healing the sick, comforting the infirm, and enhancing the health and well-being of his small-town practice in rural Connecticut.

This wasn't what he had in mind when his good friend and mentor, Doctor William Vick, asked him to give him a hand and cover for him as Windham County's Medical Examiner. "It's just for a week, Louis," Bill Vick pleaded. "Doris and I haven't been away on vacation for fifteen years. Beside, Louis, you'll get paid just for being on call. Chances are, you'll get a nice check for doing almost nothing at all."

Bill Vick was right. He only got three calls, none urgent, to certify the causes of death of an elderly man (four heart attacks in the last four years), an elderly woman (a stroke three weeks earlier), and a twenty-six-year-old suicide by hanging (treated for chronic depression for the prior six years). The check came in handy, too.

When Bill Vick asked him for a second favor six months later, Louis Desrosiers gladly agreed to help out. *This was easy work*, he thought.

Then Bill and Doris Vick had the nerve to die in a plane crash coming back from Fort Lauderdale, and Louis Desrosiers found himself permanent Medical Examiner of Windham County.

That was nineteen years ago, and Louis Desrosiers had had enough. *Truth? Sure*, he thought on occasion. But one of these days, I'm going to chat up that new internist over in Putnam, Chad Whatever-It-Is, and see if he won't mind covering for me just once.

Delbert Nelman was Louis Desrosiers' dedicated part-time assistant. Taller and younger than the doctor, his sloped shoulders and thinning white hair added years and reduced his height. He was a Licensed Practical Nurse with a few personality flaws. Well schooled and a willing and eager worker, Delbert's unfortunate tendency to see darkness where there was hope made dealing with living people difficult. Day Kimball Hospital made several unsuccessful attempts to find a place for him. Emergency Medicine, Pediatrics, Coronary Care, Day Surgery. Everywhere he went, Delbert sowed seeds of cheerlessness and despair. Patients who rallied after difficult bouts with accidents and disease would suddenly take turns for the worse when Delbert was around. Children recovering from minor surgery would be discharged in tears.

Then someone in Human Resources suggested at a meeting that Delbert be placed in charge of the morgue. The idea gained merit as it passed around the room, but there weren't a sufficient number of dead bodies in the small hospital to warrant making that a full-time job. So Delbert had a split assignment. Tend the morgue and assist in Geriatrics, where every effort would be made to permit him contact with only the hearing impaired or those with severe Alzheimer's. Those who could neither hear nor recollect what Delbert Nelman was saying were thus provided quite excellent care.

Delbert wheeled the gurney to its proper place beneath the lights. He made sure Doc's cassette recorder was functioning and in a grand gesture, pulled the sheet from the cadaver.

He and doc stood there silently and stared at the remains. Doc's best guess was that it was male. The necktie was one clue. The lack of darts on what remained of the blue jacket was another.

Doc Desrosiers placed a menthol cough drop under his tongue and went to work. Delbert preferred to fight the odor with well-placed dabs of Vapo-Rub in his nostrils. Over the next three hours, the corpse would be cut open, its organs removed, weighed, and bagged, and slices taken for slides. Desrosiers systematically went about his work and looked for evidence as he did so. He confirmed the body to be that of a white male, estimated its age as between thirty-five and forty-five years, and gauged its height at approximately seventy-four inches. The muskrats had done a job on the head, so eye color was undetermined. There was no evidence of disease in the organs, but the lab work that followed would provide better data. The consistency of the lungs did not indicate death by drowning. In spite of the corpse's extended immersion in the pond, the intact alveolar sacs were empty and flat. A wound in the temple was roughly round and twenty-four millimeters in diameter. He would later draw a replica on graph paper and make it part of the file. "A betting man," he told Nelman, "would probably lay odds that whatever caused this man to expire would be directly connected to this hole."

With the Canon F-1 his wife had given him for Christmas many years ago to capture family memories, Desrosiers snapped dozens of photographs of the corpse as he worked. He particularly wanted to get close-ups of the dental work. If anything can help put a name on the corpse, these could.

***

WHEN THE CESSNA finally broke the sticky grip of the water's surface and lifted into a gentle, sweeping arc over the Rio Purus, Keyes looked down to see a solitary figure waving to him, getting smaller as the plane rose into the sky. Jimmy, the wiry young man with the relentless smile, had made a difference in Keyes' life in ways he would not have imagined when he first saw this same scene upon his arrival last year.

The pilot, the same who had dropped him off at this spot, had welcomed Keyes with a nod, recalling their language barrier. It was only after they had leveled off at five thousand feet and Keyes opened up in rapid-fire Portuguese that the pilot responded. Unlike their first trip together, which was filled with only the sound of the droning engine, the return haul was filled with conversation, joke making, and laughter. At Manaus, Keyes deplaned and waited for three hours for the next plane to appear. He again retraced his journey, stopping briefly at Santarem's grassy field for fuel and arrived in Belem late into the night. His next flight, from Belem to Miami, was scheduled to leave at 9 AM, so Keyes retired to his hotel room.

The flight from Belem took him over the enormous mouth of the Amazon delta, its mud and silt mingling with the deep blue, briny waters of the southern Atlantic Ocean. Keyes knew that the work he had accomplished as part of the Canutama project team would perhaps reduce the volume of rich earth sloughing off from the rain forests of the continent in the years to come. Among other discoveries, he found certain vegetation which extended roots quickly and deeply into the threatened soils. If the soil could be stabilized sufficiently by these smaller plants, it would foster the growth of larger plants and trees, so that a sheltering umbrella would be better able to maintain the steamy conditions of a replenished tropical habitat. Coupled with a simple gravity irrigation system using the flow of the river to propel quantities of water two inches beneath the powdery soil, the young growth would have excellent chances of survival. Keyes hoped that the denuded plains of the once lush rain forests would begin to diminish, and reforestation would flourish.

He smiled to himself as he considered Jimmy's bat houses, how they, indeed, became the homes to thousands of small bats. While any beneficial effect of the bats upon the local mosquito population was a subject of debate from time to time among all of the members of the project, Keyes saw little difference. But there were two noticeable changes, both predicted with a considerable degree of scientific certainty by Jimmy. First, the odor caused by the guano was horrid and took some getting used to. Jimmy once joked that the Canutama camp made him long for the village where he grew up, for the stench of the guano was even worse than that of Masso's maligned mother. But the other, and more felicitous discovery, was the fact that the bats did present a wonderful source of seeds embedded in their own private cocoons of fertilizer. Tiny roots stubbornly fought to establish themselves in the damaged soil. Keyes was certain that the eventual vegetation only improved the likelihood and speed of the reforestation effort.

Keyes felt deeply invested in the process and progress of the reforestation, and before he departed the project, he arranged to maintain continuing contact with the team. He wanted to keep tabs on the small steps and greater strides that might be made over time in the collective efforts of the Canutama Project.

The flight path from Belem was generally northwest, crossing the wide delta and entering the northern hemisphere over the northern most coast of Brazil. He scanned the low mountains and deep forests of French Guyana and Suriname, reaching the Atlantic once more at a point directly over the city of Georgetown, capital of Guyana and the site of the Reverend Jim Jones massacre twenty years earlier. Keyes did not remember all the details, but he recalled seeing the photographs of corpses, hundreds of them, including those of small children who were somehow convinced to drink poisoned Kool-Aid in a twisted sense of religious righteousness. His plane continued to follow the coast, passing over the Orinoco delta with the island of Trinidad on his right. Then Margarita Island appeared, followed by Tortuga, and later the Netherlands Antilles. He had once visited the island of Aruba, and it struck him then as a dusty, hard-packed barren place, with the redeeming features of magnificent white beaches and changeless, perfect weather. But Aruba stood out from most of the other islands below him that were lush and green. Aruba's only significant vegetation, he recalled, were the rather lonely looking divi-divi trees growing low with their trunks bent at right angles to follow the constant breeze. As he watched the island pass beneath the wing, Keyes dozed off.

***

IN THE BARN at the Farm, an unusual Saturday morning meeting was being held. There in their usual seats were the powerful individuals who comprised the board. Standing at the side of the room apart from the others was the head of Jack Munroe's campaign for the Presidency, Leland Hayes. The board members were dressed in weekend casual attire, but Hayes, in preparation for meeting his charge before the senator's scheduled lunchtime speech at Boston's Long Wharf Marriott, was in a medium gray suit, blue shirt, and maroon tie. He was making notes on a pad before him when the Chairman entered and motioned to him. The Chairman wished to speak with him privately.

In a dark corner and out of earshot of the others, the Chairman began in a low, determined voice. "Leland, it's fair to say that we're generally pleased with the trends so far, but the purpose of this meeting is twofold. First, I want to keep my colleagues fully informed as to what is going on in and around this campaign, and second, we need to make sure that the strategies for the weeks ahead meet our collective objectives." He lowered his voice to a nearly conspiratorial level as he went on. "How is Senator Munroe faring these days?"

"I would say, sir, quite well. He is in excellent physical shape, sir, and I know that his spirits are quite high. At the moment, he should be in his hotel room in Boston rehearsing his speech."

"Fine. We're going to begin our meeting in a few moments, and you'll be on your way. However, I believe that you should be aware of some news that will appear in tomorrow's newspapers. It seems that a body surfaced last week in a pond in Connecticut, and that it has been positively identified as that of a Navy Captain Henry Oates." The name meant nothing to Hayes. "The police suspect foul play because of a hole the size of a quarter in his skull. Tomorrow's papers will run the story, but we do not believe that anything will develop any further. The pond is within nine miles of where his car was found, and the police have nothing else to go on beyond those two discoveries. I want you to relay to the candidate, Mr. Hayes, that he should be prepared to see the news, but there's no cause for him or for us to be distressed. Is that understood?"

Hayes nodded, perplexed, a question mark written in his furrowed brow. What Leland Hayes did not hear was that it would also become news very shortly that Mrs. Henry Oates is no longer to be found residing at her handsome brick colonial in Fairfax County. Rosemary Oates had departed her home and the area several weeks ago and now lived on the lovely island of Antigua in a luxurious three-bedroom condominium. She and the captain had also acquired a home in Switzerland outside Geneva, and that is where one would expect the grieving widow to spend her summers. Those few who knew of Captain Oates' unusual business ventures might guess that his spouse had developed access to a significant source of funds, and whether or not Oates' involvement in arms trading ever became public knowledge, it appeared that she intended to maintain a good deal of distance between herself and the United States.

The Chairman's voice rose as he took the uncertain Hayes by the elbow and steered him towards the door. In a voice clearly louder than it had been moments earlier, he said to Hayes, "I don't believe that there's any reason for you or for Jack to give the episode another thought. It is important that neither you nor the senator be distracted from the task at hand, which, although the pointers are all aiming up, needs the fullest attention of us all." The way he said this, everyone present knew that the meeting would begin and that they would move directly to their agenda. The Chairman shuffled some papers, found the page he sought, and looked at the others.

"Finance, gentlemen. That's the next item on our agenda." He turned to Hayes and said, almost as an aside, "Excuse us now, would you, Mr. Hayes? Perhaps you could join Earl in the house for a cup of coffee before you head to Boston."

Hayes didn't like the fact that he was excluded from the discussions; it made him feel a bit childish every time this happened.

Nevertheless, he understood well on which side of his bread he would find the butter, and he said his farewells quickly to the group.

***

WITH EVENING SETTLED in, Keyes' flight made its gradual descent towards Logan International Airport in Boston. Landing to the north, Keyes could see the lights of Nahant and the dark shapes of the Boston harbor islands. It was a crystal clear night with the moon nearing full, and he watched its reflection race across the water as the plane settled down on the runway. He checked his watch. The flight had arrived twenty minutes early.

Keyes walked the length of the terminal, bought a copy of the *Globe* from a newsstand, and headed for the taxis. From a PC terminal at the Canutama compound, he had made his flight arrangements and reserved a room at the Lenox Hotel. It didn't provide the same level of elegance and amenities as the Copley Plaza, but because he was planning to pay for the next four nights out of his own pocket, he failed to see the need to spend the extra hundred dollars a night.

The line for taxis was thankfully not a long one, and he was about to step into the line when he saw Joanne walking in his direction.

She was smiling broadly as she approached, threw her arms around his shoulders, and welcomed him home with a long kiss. "It's good to see you, Matt."

"Joanne, I missed you." He kissed her again. "It's wonderful to see you."

"Let me take one of your bags. I'm parked in the central garage. Have you eaten yet? Your plane got in early, and I almost missed you." Keyes reached for her free hand and they walked together slowly, talking and smiling. She invited him to stay at her mother's house in Melrose, and he immediately called the hotel to cancel his reservations. His schedule called for four nights in Boston before his return to Burlington, and they spent the next hours sitting at her mother's dining room table eating, talking, and sipping ice-cold Diet Coke. Joanne's mother was pleased to have him as a guest, and there was certainly enough room in her large home to accommodate several visitors. "You missed Joshua tonight," Joanne said. "But you might find the face of a four-year-old boy staring at you when you wake up in the morning. I've told him a good deal about you and where you've been, and he thinks it's great that you've lived in a jungle. I'm warning you ahead of time: There'll be lots of questions."

"You've got towels at the foot of the bed, and you can use the bathroom at the end of the hall," said Anne Stowe as she climbed the stairs. "I don't have air-conditioning, Matthew, but there's a fan in the closet, if you need it."

Joanne gave Matt a hug and kiss before saying good night. Tomorrow was Saturday, and she was hoping that he could meet Joshua and perhaps the three of them might spend the day together. Keyes agreed, and he was looking forward to it. Before he retired to the guest bedroom, he picked up the *Globe* he had bought and carried it with him. As he settled into bed, the first real bed he'd slept in for nearly ten months, he reached for the newspaper and was only three paragraphs into the lead story on the Presidential election campaign when he fell asleep.

"Hi."

KEYES OPENED one eye and saw a brown-haired young boy dressed in shorts and a T-shirt and holding a teddy bear. "I'm Joshua," he said, extending his hand straight out.

Keyes wasn't fully awake, but enough to know that he should accept the hand in response. They shook. "Hi, Joshua. I'm Matt."

"I know."

"Uh, Joshua," Keyes was glancing at his watch, "it's 6 o'clock in the morning. Is your mother awake?"

"No. She's still sleeping. But Gram is up. She made me some toast. You want some toast?"

Keyes was intrigued by this little man and knew that he was being studied very seriously. Joshua had yet to smile.

"Look, I'll just get up and get dressed. Tell your Gram I'd love some toast, and I'll be down in five minutes."

Joshua was off and running before Keyes was standing. He put on his jeans and the shirt from the night before. He'd shower later, knowing that Joshua was waiting for him downstairs.

Joshua bent Keyes' ear with stories about his neighborhood, his friends, his new sandbox, and his toys, especially his toy trucks. "I like the street because there aren't many cars on it. And my friend Philip is only four houses away. He's a little stupid sometimes, but my next best friend is way down the end of the street, so Philip's not so bad."

"Joshua," his grandmother admonished. "You shouldn't speak of Philip that way."

"I know, Gram."

In a conspiratorial low voice, he leaned over to Keyes and said, "Philip is really stupid sometimes, and Gram knows it, too."

The child was animated in his speech and actions, and reminded Keyes of his sister, Kristen's, children. Joshua, it appeared, inherited his dark hair and brown eyes from his father, but he was pleased to see that he had his mother's spirit.

As the morning progressed, Joanne awoke, rising lazily at 9. After showering and getting a basket of sandwiches ready, Matt, Joanne, and Joshua drove to Drumlin Farm in Lincoln. There, Joshua had free range to roam, and by 1 o'clock, they were ready to eat lunch. As they picnicked, Joshua peppered Keyes with questions about living in a jungle. What little Joshua knew about jungles he learned from his mother. Joanne read to Joshua every night and had borrowed several books from the library with a jungle theme. Were there pythons? Tigers? Did he ever swing from vines? Did he see any monkeys? Gorillas? By 2 o'clock, Joshua was sound asleep on the blanket.

Keyes asked Joanne about work, whether anything new had been happening at his old employer, and her current one, Crane & Stewart. "Mr. Banks," she said, "seemed to be aging rapidly, and was coming into the office less often. Trygve Jensen, he of the foul mouth and fouler mood, had retired rather abruptly a month earlier. No notice. No good-by party. The polite but uninspiring Mel Kennedy was assuming the role of major honcho in charge. Crane & Stewart,"

Joanne said, "doesn't have much spark in it right now. It sort of goes from one day to the next, drifting along. Two young engineers with a good deal of promise had just resigned that week. The place needs a good kick in the pants. Mel needs to snag a good project and get the group back into some focus." Keyes trusted Joanne's instincts, and didn't doubt that her assessment was accurate. When he had worked at the firm, he found Joanne to be unfailingly perceptive.

Joanne brushed breadcrumbs from Joshua's knees as he curled up on the blanket. Keyes watched her, and Joanne was in another world for a moment. He remained quiet as a smile crossed her face. She was a picture of serenity.

She turned back to Keyes and left that world in an instant. She was holding her hands on her lap, looking Keyes in the eye, but with her head barely tilted down. "Matt, there's something you ought to know, and I probably should have told you last night." Keyes looked up, not imagining what she might have withheld. "When you called from Brazil to tell me you were coming home early, one of the things you asked me was whether anything ever came of that night we were in the Hancock Tower. The night before you left."

"And you told me that nothing had come of it. That I must have dreamt it. I remember those words."

"Well, I lied. And I'm sorry. Now I don't want you to think that it was just as you thought, or anything, because it wasn't. But I had a call at work a few weeks ago from the Boston police. A detective was following up on a report that you filed before you left."

***

THE REPORT WAS ten weeks old when Detective Collins saw it for the first time. As Wetman described it, "It's so old, it's got hair on it." Nevertheless, Collins had done some cursory checking by looking through reports of missing persons and searching through the Prudential's tenant list. Getting nowhere, he set it aside for more urgent cases.

Months passed before the report, destined for the basement file room, caught Collins' attention once more, and he decided to make some calls. First to Burlington to find that Matthew Keyes was working on a project in the Brazilian interior until the fall, but they could arrange to get him a message if it was important. Because he was calling from Boston, Keyes' Vermont colleague did volunteer that Matthew Keyes had worked in Boston at Crane & Stewart before moving to Vermont some years before. That prompted Collins to call Keyes' former employer.

He did and reached a receptionist. Collins could tell from the voice that he was speaking to someone at least as old as his Aunt Alice, which would put her near seventy. He was told that Keyes had worked there, that was some years ago, and that she didn't know how to reach him. She was making every effort to cooperate.

Collins then asked about a possible companion or friend, Joanne O'Byrne, to which she responded that there was such a person in the office, that she was off for the day, and could she take a message. Collins left his name and number.

***

"I DIDN'T WANT to call him back, Matt, and for a while I was really angry with you. You never told me that you were going to the police."

"Why didn't you tell me, Joanne? Have they found the body?" Keyes was excited with the thought that the event he had witnessed had finally developed some credibility.

"Hold on. They don't have a body," said Joanne, careful of his feelings, but not wanting to let his imagination run wild. "They're just following up on your report. They couldn't locate you, and they called your office in Vermont. They gave the detective the name of Crane & Stewart, and that's where they found me. It was a routine follow-up, that's all. Matt, why didn't you ever tell me you spoke to the police?"

"I knew you were trying to convince me that I hadn't seen anything worth telling the police. But the morning I left, I just stopped in to the old police headquarters and asked if anything suspicious had been reported that night. I told them what I saw, and they took it down. It only took a few minutes. I didn't think it would go anywhere."

Joanne related how the call from Collins had been relayed to her at Crane & Stewart, and that his call had caused quite a stir among her coworkers, especially Phyllis, the receptionist. Collins arranged to meet Joanne and asked her some questions about that evening. He was curious about the report, but more curious about Keyes. He seemed genuinely concerned and mentioned that the report sounded like one from a very credible witness. When Joanne couldn't provide him with any details that weren't already recorded, he asked her to give Keyes his card and to ask him to call when he returned. "He said he was trying to tie up some loose ends, that's all." She reached into her pocket and handed him Collins' card.

***

TWENTY MILES AWAY, a telephone rang. After the second ring, the caller heard the phone being raised from its cradle and a voice came on the line. "Hello." There was a pause.

"This is old news, sir, but you should probably be aware of this."

"Tell me," was the response.

The caller reported that a detective was asking some questions about the events at the Prudential. That he had interviewed one person and was scheduled to interview a second.

"Do these people have names?"

The caller relayed the names of Joanne O'Byrne and Matthew Keyes. He had no addresses at this time.

There was a sudden intake of breath, then an extended pause. Then, "Is there any more?"

The caller responded in the negative. He added that he could not develop any further information without Collins becoming suspicious. With that, the call ended.

CHAPTER TWELVE

"HELLO, MY NAME is Matthew Keyes, and I was told that you wanted to talk to me."

Collins was at his desk on what should have been a day off. The fact that the front desk put a call through to him anyway only angered him. Impatience and hostility attached to every word: "What case does this involve? Give me name."

Keyes wasn't sure how to respond. He was not prepared for Collins' animosity, nor had Joanne said anything about the case having an official name. "It involves a report I filed last November about an assault or a possible homicide that I saw take place at the Prudential Center. I just returned from South America, and I'm going to be in the Boston area for a few days."

Collins had planned the morning to be a cleanup morning. That meant he would sit at his desk, uninterrupted, and go through the piles of paper stacked there. It was a routine he put himself through once every few weeks. At the end of two or three hours, he would have neat, organized stacks of files and folders, and he would be able to locate the correct ones quickly. At least for a few weeks, then he'd have to do it all over again.

This morning he found the going slower than usual. In the heat of late summer, he saw too many dead young men.

Boys really. Twelve, thirteen years old. Usually because someone said the wrong thing to the wrong person. "Dissed somebody." That's what he despised most about the summer. And over the past six days, he had too many of them with which his time was occupied.

"I remember the case now, Mr. Keyes, but I've got a bunch of real dead bodies staring back at me right now, and they are all staring at me with real dead eyes." Collins didn't stop sorting through papers while he bent his neck to hold the phone to his head. "All I have with you is a report that you might have seen something. Might not. You can't see me right now, but I'm shrugging my shoulders."

Keyes bristled at Collins' dismissal, and his voice didn't conceal his exasperation. Collins sounded to Matt like a whining, harassed bureaucrat. "Look, the message I got was that you wanted to speak to me. If that's not the case, then maybe..."

"Look, I'm sorry," Collins interrupted. His tone changed in an effort to ease the tension. "You're right, Mr. Keyes. I said I wanted to speak to you, and I will. Can you come down to the old headquarters building on Berkeley Street today, like this morning, say before eleven?"

"I'll be there. Where should I meet you?" Matt's voice had lost none of its irritation.

"Just tell the sergeant at the front desk that you have an appointment with me. He'll tell you where I am."

***

JOANNE DROVE MATT into Boston. Since it was a Sunday, traffic was light, and the trip from her mother's home in Melrose to Berkeley Street in Boston's Back Bay took less than a half hour. That time gave Matt's annoyance with Collins a chance to abate.

Joanne found a parking space on Columbus Avenue and they walked the half block to the old Boston Police Headquarters building. After telling the officer at the front door the purpose of their visit, they were directed to Detective Collins in Homicide on the second floor.

Collins was still sorting through piles of papers when Keyes stopped at the open door of the office and rapped his knuckles on the doorframe. Joanne was standing at his side, and Collins smiled when he looked up and recognized her.

"Come on in. Hello, Miss O'Byrne. It's good to see you again." Collins stood and dragged two chairs closer to his desk. "Welcome to my world." Collins swept his arm over his desk, still smiling but letting any observer know the level of frustration he felt at the condition of his desk. Had they seen it an hour earlier, they would have been impressed with his progress. "You must be Mr. Keyes."

When they were both seated, Keyes glanced at several tall stacks of notes, reports, and photographs. He didn't fail to see a particularly frightening color photo on the top of the stack nearest his chair of what appeared to be a human upper torso, but with a massive gaping hole at the place where a throat should be. Collins followed Keyes' eyes and saw what had his attention. "That boy had a thirteenth birthday party about six hours before he took a bullet in the back of his head." Speaking in a low voice, Collins' voice carried intense sorrow and respect. "What you're looking at is where the bullet came out." He put an empty file folder on top of the photograph, then turned to Matt and Joanne. "There are three new stacks of paper on my desk this week. All of them like that one. After a while, you have to wonder what it's all about.

"That's why I probably sounded a little on edge this morning. That boy you just saw? I have the weapon. It was identified by ballistics as one that was used in another homicide last year. I've got fingerprints on the pistol. And I've got a reliable witness who saw the whole thing happen from her front window, and she gave us the name of the guy who pulled the trigger. If I have trouble with a single sheet report where I can't find a body, never mind a weapon, or even an exact location, for that matter, not even a report that someone might be missing that fits the whole thing, well, you've got me, Mr. Keyes."

Matt and Joanne were silent, still absorbed in the image of the photograph they had seen.

"I've got ten minutes," Collins remarked as he picked up another file folder, slid a pen between his teeth and opened it up on his lap. "Tell me what you saw and let's see if this goes anywhere. Is that OK with you?"

"Uh, sure. I'll tell you the whole thing." And he did. He described the night, how Joanne had been using one of the telescopes and how he happened across another, how he panned the landscape and how the activity in one particular office had caught his attention.

"What I saw was an argument between two men, and one was really crowding the other, not pushing him, but threatening him. I could see that much."

"Who was doing the threatening?

"The pilot. I mean, that's what I call him, but he was the one doing the threatening."

"But he's the one you say got hit, right?"

"Right. The other guy in the gray suit, he did it."

"Gray suit? That wasn't in your report."

"I'd say it was gray. At least, it wasn't as dark as the other guy's. That much I can recall. He reached for something. Something shiny and slammed the other guy, the pilot, right in the side of the head. In a second, the pilot stepped back, did sort of a spin, and fell."

Collins held up his hand to stop him. "You said something shiny. Could you tell what was?"

"No, not from that distance. But it was shiny, because I remember the reflection. Whatever it was, it was sitting on a bookcase or something. And after he hit the guy in the head, whatever it was stuck right there."

"What do you mean? Was it a knife?" Collins had been jotting some notes in the file while Keyes replayed the scene.

"It just was stuck in his head. But I'm not sure what it was."

"Then what happened?"

"The guy in the gray suit ...He just stood there for a while, looking down. The other guy didn't get back up. Then, all of a sudden the one in the suit walked over to a wall and turned off the lights. I couldn't see anything after that. Then the telescope I was using ran out of time. That was it. It probably took a minute from start to finish."

"You didn't report it that night. Why not? If you thought you saw someone get injured, probably seriously, why didn't you do anything then?"

Joanne jumped into the conversation. "That was my fault. I told him it must have been his imagination. We were having a good time, had a few drinks, and ..."

IN THE COMPANY OF STRANGERS

"Hold on." Collins interrupted and leaned forward. "Tell me about the few drinks. Were you drunk?" Collins looked at Matt sternly. If he had wasted this time on a report by somebody who'd been drinking ..."How much did you have to drink?"

"We split a couple bottles of wine earlier that evening at dinner." Keyes was answering Collins, but he was looking straight at Joanne while he did so, and it was not a look of bliss. "We weren't drunk. We ate dinner in the North End, and this was quite a while later."

Joanne was about to jump in again when Collins held up his hand and stopped her, just like a traffic cop. To Keyes, he asked, "Do you have anything else to add?" Keyes shook his head. Collins stood up. The interview was over. "Thank you, Mr. Keyes. I'll go over this with my supervisor and be in touch with you if I need anything else." Collins knew that he wouldn't run this case by Wetman on a dare, but their time was up; it was 11 o'clock, and Collins wanted out. Matt and Joanne also knew the direction this whole investigation had just taken, and it was all downhill. They shook hands with Collins and left the office.

Matt and Joanne stood silently at the foot of the steps of the building. Joanne could see that he was deep in thought, and she was prepared to wait as he sorted out the conversation they'd just completed with Collins. He finally turned to her and asked, "Well, what do you think?"

"About Collins?"

"Personally, I think he's wondering why he even wasted his time on me."

"What I said about the wine didn't help, did it?" Joanne's tone acknowledged her blame.

"Well, no, it didn't help, but it was true. He just used that as an excuse for himself so he could end the discussion. And that's exactly what he did. That, Joanne, is what's called a bum's rush."

They hadn't moved from the front of the building as they talked, and they saw that Collins was exiting the front door and angling his way quickly in the opposite direction down the wide steps. He glanced up briefly as he made his way out and was about to pretend he hadn't seen them when he abruptly changed his mind and direction. He walked over to the pair and said to Keyes, "I didn't ignore you, you know. I checked with the building manager at the Prudential, checked all the police reports and 911 summaries for the whole city for that night and the next few days, looking for anything I could find. But, let's face it, there's no body, not even a missing persons report for that time period with anybody coming close to the description you gave me. I even checked with adjacent police departments…Newton, Brookline, Milton, Cambridge, Chelsea…to see if they had anything. Nothing came back. If you had something concrete to go on, maybe I could help." He shrugged his shoulders and started to move on. He had his car keys out of his pocket when Keyes called to him.

"Maybe they moved the body. Maybe the guy wasn't reported missing for a long time. Maybe he wasn't even from around here."

Collins turned halfway around to answer, but didn't stop moving towards his car. "Look, you want to help? Check the newspaper morgue at the library. See if you can find a report of a missing person from further outside Boston. But you're on a real wild goose chase, my friend. Look, I gotta go."

***

THE BOSTON PUBLIC Library is an imposing structure consuming the city block bound by Boylston, Dartmouth, Huntington, and Essex streets in the Back Bay section of the city. It has the solid, classic aspect that all libraries should have. The main facade features two statues of muses, one sitting, one reclining, at the entrance, and tall windows crosshatched with iron bars. It's a preserve. A vault. And entering it reinforces that sense. Every trifling noise ricochets off the marble floors and high frescoed ceilings, so people speak in hushed voices and tend to walk lightly.

Keyes asked the guard seated at the front desk where he'd find the newspaper morgue and was directed to a side gallery. "You want Microtext. But before you go there, you need to get a card upstairs. Straight up, to the left. It only takes two minutes." After filling out the appropriate forms and receiving their cards from a friendly woman at the main desk, they went back downstairs to a large, dimly lit room at the end of the hall with a cardboard sign taped over the door frame reading "Microtext." The librarian in this room was a small, bird-like woman, who was busily moving stacks of papers and folders from a desk to a long table. She appeared to be extraordinarily occupied in her work. When Keyes took in the entire room, he saw that he and Joanne were the only patrons present. The room contained about a dozen cubicles, each with a microfiche reader positioned on a tabletop. The walls held bookcases filled with reference books and indices of several newspapers and periodicals. Behind the librarian were positioned tall file cabinets of varying age, condition, and institutional colors. She glanced in Keyes' direction, and he asked her for information and directions on how to access editions of newspapers dating from the previous November. The *Boston Globe, Boston Herald, New York Times* and *Washington Post* were microfilmed regularly and readily available, they learned, as were several other major newspapers. He and Joanne split the task: Matt would take the *Globe*, Joanne the *Herald*, setting aside the *Times* and *Post* for now. They selected the start date as the day after the event in the Prudential Tower last November. After being handed the appropriate microfiche tapes in small boxes, the librarian explained how to insert the end of the film into the reader and how to use the positioning lever to scan up, down, and across. Matt and Joanne each selected a cubicle and adjusted to the darkness; low lighting was essential to get a clear view of the pages.

It took Keyes a little while to learn the feel of the fiche reader, but Joanne flew through the tapes quickly. They paused after an hour when Joanne walked over to Matt and said, "I need a break. I've gone through every *Herald* from last November until May first, and I'm coming up blank."

Matt continued paging through as he responded. "You're lucky. The *Herald*'s a skinny paper with lots of pictures. I only just started going through February. But look at this." Matt slid a piece of paper in Joanne's direction. She had to squint to read his notes in the dim light. Matt had three names listed, with two crossed out. He said as he focused on the *Globe* for February third, "The last one's a real long shot, I admit."

"What about the first two? Why did you cross them off?"

"The first one was an older guy from Belmont. A retired policeman. But they found him in a snow bank a few days later. Apparent heart attack. The second guy is from Wellesley, a lawyer reported missing by his wife in early December. I really thought he could have been my man. The paper had a picture of him, and he's white and forty-four. But I just found an article on him and he was located in Jamaica in January, living on a boat with his gay lover. Sort of messy, because he cleaned out his clients' trust accounts before he took off. All elderly ladies in nursing homes."

"The asshole was a real pillar of the community, wasn't he? But what about this third name? What is it, Julius Membek? I can't read your writing."

"Julian Webber. A truck driver for Federal Express. Lives in Natick. Never came back from his deliveries the day after Thanksgiving. Nothing turned up yet."

"You think he's your missing body?"

"The time is about right. He's thirty-nine. He wore a uniform."

"Any picture?"

"No. But he's the best I've got so far."

"Why didn't I see these stories in the *Herald*? I mean, the lawyer from Wellesley should have been covered, wouldn't you think?"

"Like I said, skinny paper."

"Are you going to take a break, Matt?"

"In a minute. I'm sort of getting into this."

Joanne stepped out into the hallway and the relative brightness hurt her eyes until she adjusted. She decided to take a walk and wandered to the central gallery that opens onto a quiet outdoor garden fully enclosed by the walls of the library. She was alone and sat on one of the black Windsor chairs positioned on the perimeter, watching a blue jay pester two sparrows at a feeder. She thought about Matt, their meeting with Collins, and Collins' comment about chasing geese. She thought about the last name on Matt's list, Julian Webber. Federal Express. Matt was really reaching. Just because the guy wore a uniform …She took a deep breath, rose, and went back in to face the *New York Times*.

Matt was still sliding through the fiches of the *Boston Globe*. When she looked at his piece of paper, she could see that Webber's name was still there, not crossed out.

She had few expectations of finding anything worthwhile in the *Times*. She scrolled through the first fiche until she reached November, then slowed and scanned each page for headlines. A tedious task. There was one story that she found early in her search that she would otherwise have liked to pause and read about, a philanthropic socialite reported as missing and the curious circumstances surrounding her disappearance. She was leaving the opera with friends one moment, and she never reappeared at her apartment. The daughter of a former ambassador to the United Kingdom, she was known to be rather eccentric, especially about Dalmatians, of which she owned eleven. But it was a lengthy article, and she decided to skip over it.

She spotted another missing person report, but it was datelined Washington, and she would have skipped past it had it not been for the subject's photograph. He was Caucasian, 48 years old, and clad in full dress Navy blues. "Captain Henry H. Oates, United States Navy, failed to appear at a session of senior allied military officers at the U.S. Naval War College in Newport, Rhode Island, on Friday. Oates was participating in the planning of a joint field exercise with military counterparts representing four allied European nations. He had attended the first day of meetings on Thursday, but after failing to appear at Friday's session, he was reported missing by U.S. naval authorities. Oates had requisitioned a vehicle after Thursday's session, but it had not been returned and its whereabouts is unknown. Oates, 48, is a recognized authority on high-tech ordinance and has been a frequent lecturer at the War College. Stationed at the Pentagon since 1993, Oates resides in Alexandria, Virginia."

Maybe the man Matt saw was in a military uniform, she considered. This case wasn't exactly from a Boston suburb, but Newport was only about ninety minutes away.

Joanne marked down the date and page, and continued her search. She picked up a pattern, but not one that fit Matt's purpose. About every ten days or so, she would spot a repeated headline, "Bus Plunge in India Kills 19," or "27" or "22." Every time, the headline was followed by a two-sentence, one-paragraph story about a bus running off the edge of a cliff in India. The numbers of dead changed, as did the names of the cities. Beyond that, each story was identical. She wondered if there really could be that many plunging buses in India, or if they just kept the blank story on file for starchy filler when they needed an inch and a half.

She chided herself for being amused at the thought. After all, if the stories were true, which they probably were, these were real people, real pain, and real deaths.

Nothing in December's papers held any promise. Or January's, or February's. She finished March, looked up and saw that Matt had left his seat. *Fine*, she thought, *maybe he needs a break*. Then she saw him walking back to his seat with another stack of small white boxes. He saw Joanne and said, "*Washington Post*. The lady told me you had the *Times*."

"What about Webber?"

"Nothing in the *Globe* about finding him. I figured I'd check it out with Collins tomorrow. That shouldn't take him long. How about you?"

"Something interesting, but I'm almost finished. I'll come over when I'm done." She slid the first April microfiche into place. She was not hopeful and about to finish the month when she spotted a one-column article, about three inches, which told the grim story of finding the late Captain Henry Oates. The headline read, "U.S. Naval Official Found Dead in CT Pond." The article began, "A badly decomposed body which surfaced six days earlier in a Connecticut pond had been positively identified as that of U.S. Naval Captain Henry H. Oates, 48. Oates, a resident of Virginia and a senior Pentagon specialist in high-tech weaponry, had been reported missing in November. Oates apparently drove from the Naval War College in Newport, Rhode Island, after the second day of a week-long meeting with several European military counterparts. After failing to appear at the session the next morning, he was reported missing. The body was found in a small pond in Lebanon, Connecticut, by a local resident who was fishing from a nearby pier. The body was taken to the county morgue in Putnam, where dental records were used to identify the body. The probable date and cause of death have not been determined, but foul play has not been ruled out, according to Dr. Louis Desrosiers, Chief Medical Examiner of Windham County. Oates leaves a wife, Rosemary."

Joanne finished reading and was gaining enthusiasm. At least she had found something. She marked down the date and page and asked for help in getting prints of the two articles on Henry Oates. The library aide was quick to help, and for twenty-five cents per page, Joanne had the copies in her hands in moments.

She was approaching Matt's cubicle when sudden movement from the doorway of the Microtext room caught the corner of her eye. She turned to look and saw an older gentleman quickly back away. It was evident that he didn't want to be seen, but Joanne recognized him nonetheless. She had worked too long at Crane & Stewart not to recognize Trygve Jensen. Without getting Matt's attention, Joanne sped to the entry and looked down the hallway. No sign of Jensen, except for the door to the interior garden that had not quite stopped swinging. Someone had just passed through. She raced through the doorway and reached the center of the garden walkway. There was no movement evident. She looked in every direction. Pachysandra hugged the grounds, and mounds of hosta framed a corner. Various shades of impatiens splashed the garden with color. But not a sign of Jensen or anyone else.

Joanne turned to go back in and tried to reason why Trygve Jensen, Miserable Bastard and Chief Engineer, Retired, would be spying on them.

CHAPTER THIRTEEN

WHEN KEYES AWOKE the next morning, he reached for his watch on the nightstand and saw that it was past 9 o'clock. The night had been hot and humid, and the hum of the window fan had lulled him to sleep. When he turned off the fan and opened the shades, he saw that the day was overcast and the air heavy. It was near tropical and promised more of the same.

He showered, dressed, and called a cab to take him to the T-Station. He left the house by 10, Joanne's mother protesting that a single cup of coffee and a slice of toast was an insufficient breakfast. Joshua waved to Keyes from a sandbox in the side yard.

Keyes reached the offices of Crane & Stewart before noon and paused at the front door to appraise the building before entering. The structure itself was not visually remarkable. It could, in fact, be described accurately as awkward and even ugly. Built with little style and less imagination in the years immediately following World War II, it reflected utility and economy. A convenience store shared the first floor with a bank branch and a greeting card shop. The building's flat exterior was flush with the sidewalk, out of character with most of its neighbors, whose bay windows and heavy cornices defined their spaces with depth and shadows and richer textures. Instead, panels of olive-green plastic laminate separated the window mullions of each of the building's seven floors. Some architect in a cubist frame of mind. A former colleague of Matt's once described the building as "Cleveland Revival." Crane & Stewart occupied the top three floors.

When he stepped off the elevator on the fifth floor, he saw that little had changed in the ten years since he'd last been there.

The furnishings were unaffected, comfortable, and of high quality. Cherry, mahogany, upholstered wing backed chairs. Brass table lamps anchored the corners of the room. Customers would sense from the start that C & S was not a shabby outfit. The receptionist's desk on the left was vacant, but Keyes saw a familiar name on the nameplate. Phyllis Rhodes. At that precise moment, Phyllis herself rounded the corner holding a cup of coffee. She glanced up, saw that a customer had arrived, and began to apologize. "I'm sorry, sir. I hope I haven't kept you wait ...Matthew Keyes, as I live and breathe! Is that you?" Phyllis was smiling as she came around her desk and hugged Keyes warmly. *She didn't appear any older*, Keyes thought, as he returned the hug. If Mr. Banks was the eldest of the C & S clan, Keyes considered, Phyllis Rhodes must be the runner up.

"Joanne told me that you were back in Boston. You look wonderful, Matt. Let me call Joanne and tell her you're here."

"Thanks, Mrs. Rhodes." From habit, Keyes called her by her proper name, and she didn't object to the formality.

"Joanne told me all about your work in Brazil. What an adventure! Did you enjoy it?" Keyes spent the following minutes describing the Canutama Project. Soon, Joanne appeared and motioned him to follow her.

As he walked past the offices, Keyes saw a few familiar names on office doors. Joanne held an armload of files as she led the way to her office in the rear of the building. "So what time did you finally get out of bed, Matt? When I called home at 9, my mother told me that you were still asleep."

"It might have been the phone that finally woke me up. I probably would have slept until noon." Keyes looked left and right as he walked behind Joanne. Mel Kennedy's office was on his left, and he paused to look in. Mel was seated at his desk, poring over the contents of a file folder. Keyes stopped and rapped at the door.

Mel looked up, squinted, and said, "I'll be there in a minute. Tell Audrey to bring in the expense reports, would you?" He returned his attention immediately to the folder, and Keyes shrugged his shoulders and continued down the hall.

The walls of the hallway held numerous photographs and artists' renditions of projects past. Memorials and testaments to the success of the organization. One was an aerial photograph of a senior citizen housing project in Wayland, handsome Georgian brick buildings with porticoes and white-fluted columns gracing each facade. Another captured the scene of a groundbreaking, a young Marshall Banks standing at the edge of the gathering. Dated 1969, it depicted the start of a new regional transportation center in Lynn.

Several photographs bore the MBTA logo on brass plates. Crane & Stewart had a long history with the Boston subway system. Several station rehabs. The rerouting of underground rail lines, closing off abandoned stations, and building new ones.

A group photograph of Marshall Banks, Trygve Jensen, and Mel Kennedy with former Governor Dukakis and several others held Keyes' attention. The governor looked silly in a hard hat, and Keyes remembered meeting him at that same groundbreaking ceremony. A new water treatment plant in Worcester. He was still scanning each face in the crowd when Joanne tapped him on the shoulder. "Hey, I thought I lost you on the way."

"Sorry. Just looking at old pictures."

"That's a good one of just about everybody. Mr. Banks, Mr. Jensen, Mel Kennedy. By the way, Mr. Banks won't be in today. I checked with Phyllis, and she said he wasn't feeling well. I was hoping you'd have a chance to see him."

Keyes looked back at the group photo. "There's Trig Jensen on the end. He's still a real puzzle. Why on earth would he be sneaking around the library, Joanne?"

"I don't know, and it gives me the creeps when I think about it. His office is down the end here, and wait until you see it." Joanne led the way, stopped at the doorway of the darkened office, and reached in to flip on the lights. Keyes stepped in. It had the appearance of an office of a very busy individual who had just left for a moment. Work papers were stacked high on a sideboard. Blueprints opened and spread out across the desk. Phone messages in a stack next to the telephone. "I told you he left in a rush. Look at this. It looks like he just decided one minute to leave. Even his valise is still beside his desk."

"Does anybody ever say anything? Does anybody miss him?"

"Nobody misses his tongue, that's for certain. But there's definitely something missing around here. As much of a royal pain in the ass he was, he breathed some fire into this place. There always seemed to be something new coming along. Another big project to work on, or bidding on a major job. Mel Kennedy's taken his place, and he's a nice enough man, but he's not a driver. He makes a good passenger. Do you know what I mean?"

Keyes knew precisely. Trig Jensen ran the Structural Unit like a bull. He recalled how he would bark orders, bang the telephone down, toss plans and reports around the office, and generally drive the younger engineers on staff. Keyes had considered himself fortunate to be in another unit and not under the whip of Trygve Jensen. But, after all the abusive language and demands, the projects he oversaw were the ones that were delivered on time, on budget, and well done. And several of his staff engineers, even the ones who most loudly resented Jensen's style, went on to hold top positions with other fine firms after their days with Crane & Stewart.

Keyes visited with Joanne for several minutes when her phone rang and she excused herself to attend a budget meeting. He said that he wanted to stop to see Detective Collins and give him the copies they made of the newspaper articles on the discovery of the body of Captain Henry Oates. Then he'd do some strolling around downtown Boston for the day and return at 4 o'clock, then they would go to dinner that evening.

***

"I'M SORRY, BUT Detective Collins is not in right now and I'm not sure when he'll be back. Can I help you?"

Fatima Cabral was seated behind a gray metal desk in the same room where Keyes and Joanne had visited with Collins the morning before. She was alone in the room.

"Yes. My name is Matthew Keyes. I'd like to leave these for him," he replied, holding the photocopies in his hand.

"Certainly. Here's an envelope you can put them in. I'll be sure he gets it." She handed him a manila envelope with a clasp. He thanked her and folded the pages to fit them inside. "Why don't you write your name on the outside so he'll see it." She handed him a pen and smiled.

Keyes wrote his name on the front of the envelope, closed the flap and handed the packet back to her. She placed the envelope in a tray with Collins' name taped to the front, and said, "He usually stops in at least once a day, even on his days off, so I'm sure he'll see this and get back to you."

Keyes thanked her and left. When he stepped outside the front door of the station, he felt a sense of accomplishment. He and Joanne had come up with a plausible body in Henry Oates. If Collins could do some checking on his end, maybe he could make some sense out of this.

The day's overcast skies threatened rain, and some did arrive with little effect in the afternoon. Keyes used his time to visit Cambridge. The subway's Red Line delivered him to Harvard Square. There, he decided to eat a corned beef sandwich and drink a draft beer at the Wurst House before dividing his afternoon between the Coop and two bookstores. He had just paid for three books when he glanced at his watch and saw that it was 3:30. He opted to head back to Boston and make his way to meet Joanne. Somewhat wistful at leaving Cambridge, Keyes stepped quickly across Harvard Square to peer into the yard for a last look. He remembered the first time he took in this same scene. He was a high school junior and drove to Cambridge with a friend on an autumn weekend. His friend was intent on attending Harvard and wanted to see the school close up. As he stood today at the yard entrance, Keyes remembered the long hair, the tie-dyed T-shirts, the fatigue jackets, and the smell of marijuana that were present that day many years ago. He remembered the sensations he felt then, that for whatever it was worth, this place had a life, a personality, and an energy he had never witnessed in a single narrow piece of geography before. That the young people who were students there, in spite of the defiance and apparent scorn for authority they exhibited, were nevertheless aware that they were somehow destined to lead, to take their place at the head of the world's table. He wondered as he walked what a present-day census of the yard's population would reveal, and supposed his assessment then would prove correct.

***

AT 4 O'CLOCK sharp, at the same time that Matt Keyes stepped off the elevator at the Crane & Stewart offices, Fatima Cabral slipped a cigarette out of a package she kept in her purse. This was a habit she went through every afternoon since the police department banned cigarette smoking four years earlier. When she took the first step out the side door, she wanted that cigarette in her mouth, lighter at the ready.

It had been a quiet day for Fatima, and she liked quiet days like these. Neither Collins nor Wetman had returned to their desks during the day, instead, spending three hours in a courtroom in Dorchester in the morning, and the entire afternoon at the office of the district attorney reviewing the facts and evidence surrounding three cases then in trial status. Wetman had called at lunchtime to retrieve his messages, and there were several files that needed follow-up and on which Fatima concentrated her attention. Both Collins and Wetman, she knew, would return to their offices sometime later on, but she wouldn't see them.

Fatima left the office and closed the door behind her. Before she had reached the station's side entrance and taken her first drag, that same door was reopened. Noiselessly, the intruder unobtrusively slid into the office, closed the door, and skirted Fatima's desk. The contents of Collins' tray were removed and searched quickly, silently, and thoroughly. The manila envelope bearing the name of Matthew Keyes printed in block letters was carefully transferred and slid into a pocket. The balance of the contents of the tray was returned. The intruder scrutinized the tray, noted no sign of disturbance, and edged back out. It was imperative that a telephone call be made at once.

***

JOANNE LOOKED TIRED and frustrated when she stormed back to her office from her meeting, and Keyes listened to her tirade patiently. "Bean counters! Three hours with goddamned bean counters! If Joshua ever tells me that he wants to be an accountant, I swear I'm gonna throw up."

"How does a cocktail and some shrimp at the Parker House sound?" Keyes was seated at a chair next to Joanne's desk.

"I'm with you," she responded sharply. She emphatically dropped a thick file on her desk, ignored the mess of accumulate papers and messages, and grabbed Keyes by the arm. "This place can wait until tomorrow. Just let me stop in the ladies' room for a minute and we're out of here. Why don't you wait for me up front? I'll see you there."

Keyes passed the few moments by speaking with Phyllis Rhodes. A delightful lady, she engaged him in pleasant conversation. Yes, Mr. Banks would be so regretful at having missed him. And Mr. Jensen, his departure so sudden, a man so vigorous and purposeful, his presence would be missed. Keyes was charmed by her grace and gentleness. Dressed ever elegantly, Phyllis was mindful that, as the firm's receptionist, she would likely be a client's first contact with Crane & Stewart. She recognized the importance of the first impression upon potential clients, and she strove, quite successfully, to present an immediate image of dignity and strength. Joanne reappeared at the desk and took Keyes' arm in hers, and he bid farewell to Phyllis. It had been a charmed few minutes.

Audrey Coyne, secretary to Mel Kennedy and a longtime friend and colleague of Phyllis Rhodes, watched Joanne and Matt leave together before approaching Phyllis' desk with pursed lips; Audrey thrived on negativity. "Phyllis, I just saw Joanne in the ladies' room, and I suggested to her that reestablishing a close relationship with Matthew Keyes may not be in her best interests, especially at this time. Becoming involved with any man, but especially Matthew, could complicate her life and compromise her self-worth at a time when she is still struggling emotionally."

Phyllis listened, recognizing from years of experience that Audrey tended to see the dark lining in every cloud. "Audrey, I think Joanne knows what's right for her. She's not a child. She's been alone for some time now, and it's been a year or more since her divorce. She was in love with Matthew Keyes at one time, but that was many years ago, and I think she's recovered nicely. Besides, I can see it in her face."

"Phyllis, Joanne is merely smitten." Audrey's cloud reappeared. "She's jeopardizing her recovery. What she needs most is time. Time for the scars to heal."

Phyllis Rhodes removed her glasses and glared at her longtime colleague and friend. "Audrey, what Joanne needs most right now is a good long ride in the saddle. Did you see those two when they left? If I'm any good at reading people, if she doesn't get the big salami from Keyes tonight, she's never going to get it from anybody."

The telephone rang. Phyllis replaced her glasses and answered in her polished receptionist voice: "Crane & Stewart Engineering, may I help you?"

***

AFTER COCKTAILS AT the Parker House and dinner at the Cafe Marliave, Joanne and Matt walked to Boston Common and sat on a bench. The sun was still out and they were enjoying their evening in each other's company. Keyes raised the issue of his approaching departure and return to Vermont.

"I'll be leaving the day after tomorrow, Joanne."

Joanne didn't reply but sat looking at her hands.

"I don't want to leave you, and I feel like we're just getting started, like we're just getting to know each other all over again." She looked up and looked into Keyes' eyes as he spoke.

"I want to see you again, Joanne." He paused and struggled with his words. "More than that; I don't want us to just split and go our separate ways. I did that once before, and I know what a stupid move that was. Joanne, I want to be with you."

"And I want to see you again, too, Matt. What's past is past, though. And whatever you or I did then, we can't change. If it was a mistake for you to leave then, maybe we wouldn't be here together right now. And right now is what I'm concerned about."

He leaned over to Joanne and put his arms around her. He kissed her hair, her neck, and then her lips. "I love you, Joanne." He held her tightly and she responded.

"Matt, I love you, too." Her eyes were filling with tears, and when they separated, Matt saw the dampness and said, "I'm sorry, I didn't mean to make you sad."

"Oh, Matt, I'm not sad. These are happy tears. I'm just happy to be with you."

Matt hugged her once again and stood. He gave Joanne his hand and she pulled herself up. They started walking through the Common, hand in hand. The sky was turning dark pink as they walked. Neither spoke until they reached the sidewalk on Charles Street. Matt was the first to break the silence.

"Joanne, would you like to stay in Boston tonight with me?"

"You mean get a hotel room?" The tone was one of mild shock.

"Sure. We could get a room at the Copley, or the Lenox. Wherever. What's important is we'd be together."

Joanne looked at Keyes with a twisted grin. "I suppose we could. I mean, as long as your intentions are honorable."

"There's not a damned thing honorable about my intentions, Joanne. Will you stay with me anyway?"

"You are such a smooth talker, Keyes." Joanne chuckled, turned to him, and kissed him lightly on the lips. "You bet."

Together they walked across the Public Garden, then the tree-covered center path of Commonwealth Avenue. At one corner, Keyes spied a pay telephone and suggested that they stop so Joanne could call her mother so she and Joshua wouldn't be worried. Joanne tugged his arm and feigned meekness. "I sort of told her this morning."

Keyes was caught unaware. "Am I that transparent? I mean, if you had me figured out so far in advance, why not let me know so I don't have to work so hard?"

Joanne continued, "And I already let them know at work that I'd be taking tomorrow off."

"You did what? Joanne, I'm offended," he went on in feigned outrage. "What do you take me for? I'm scandalized!" Together, they walked to the Lenox Hotel where Matt rented a room on the ninth floor.

***

THEIR LOVEMAKING BEGAN slowly, easily. Matt held Joanne in his arms after he closed the door and kissed her, all the while gently stroking her back, her shoulders, and her hair. Joanne's tongue teased his lips. He responded by meetings hers with his own. He slid his mouth to her neck and gently nipped and licked the soft sensitive spot behind her ear. A smile crossed her lips as she remembered instantly how he had done the same to her years before and how arousing the sensation was. She could feel his breath hot on her neck, and she held him close, gently scratching with her fingers up and down his back.

Matt worked his way to the hollow of her throat. Her eyes were closed as she leaned her head back and invited the sensations. He slid his hands to her breasts and squeezed them gently through the fabric of her cotton blouse. She cooed with pleasure, encouraging him, making clear that she enjoyed the relaxed tempo. She wanted to make these moments last.

She could feel his erection pressing against her, and she slid a leg between his and purposely, slowly returned the pressure with her own. She began to grind her pelvis against his, and she hungrily searched for his lips with a deep, lingering kiss. She slid her fingers into the waistband of his jeans and slowly began to pull his shirt up.

Matt was straining to be released, tantalized by the slow, regular pushing from Joanne. He moved back slightly from their embrace, locking eyes with her. He slid his hands across her chest, reached for the top button of her blouse, and undid it. Even though the air-conditioning was on and the room was cool, each could sense the steam building up in the other. She slid a finger between his lips and he tongued it. He whispered, "I love you, Joanne. I want to hold you, to touch you, to make love to you." She whispered in response, "I want that. I want you." She took his hand and lay back on the bed.

Time meant nothing. The pair alternated between slow, slippery pressure and release, and greedy, delicious pushing. "Make love to me," she breathed to him, and he would slow his pace, luxuriating in every flowing movement. "Now," she growled, with heat and passion, and he would push himself rapidly and intensely into her.

They finished in a wet flourish of groans and squeals. And they slept where they lay.

***

HAD JOANNE BEEN more aware of her surroundings when she and Matt first entered the lobby of the Lenox, she might have noticed the thin man with the pockmarked face who had followed them in. She might have seen him staring at Keyes as they checked in. He was tall and dressed in a dark green blazer. She might have remembered him from the Parker House lounge, where he occupied a corner seat at the bar. Or across the street at the Cafe Marliave, where he paced the street, alternately reading a newspaper and smoking cigarettes. She might have even recalled him that morning as he followed her to work, keeping a sensible distance from her in traffic, but watching her nonetheless. Over the past few days, he was getting to know Matthew Keyes and Joanne O'Byrne quite well.

But neither her nor his attention was on anyone else this evening, and the tall thin man was well aware of that. After seeing the two of them enter the elevator, he walked outside and made some notes in a small notebook that he took from his jacket pocket.

***

THE CHAIRMAN HAD been in a glorious mood to begin his day. The sky was cloudless and blue, and he expected that the good news he'd been seeing over the past few days could conceivably continue uninterrupted through election day. The evening before, he had sat in front of his television, watching the candidate masterfully manage his way through a potentially difficult interview with Larry King. Jack Munroe, ever the charmer, smoothly weaved his way through the minefields and established himself as tough on defense, a man of high principles, and one who would lead America proudly. It was mostly hogwash, the Chairman grinned. Jack Munroe, he determined, was basically a modern political hack. A good hack, and a good-looking hack, but a hack nonetheless. And, most important—my hack.

The late local news led with the interview, which was a very positive sign. The national network news described Munroe as "formidable." The Chairman liked that. *Formidable*, he thought. *Jack's been a decent senator, in fact he'd done a solid job for the state, and he always does his homework. The people like him, and he likes them. He'd probably be reelected senator as long as he wanted the job.*

But "formidable"? That's a laugh. They wouldn't describe him that way if they knew how he buckled with Oates. Caved-in. Fell apart. Not that Oates could have been kept around for much longer. He was too much of a threat. He knew the game too well. Would have spoiled the campaign, or at least have held it hostage. His untimely passing was just as well. And just as well that Jack had done it, even if by accident. It was at a time like this that the Chairman questioned his own judgment: Was he betting too much on Munroe? Could Munroe hold up under the relentless microscopic scrutiny of newspaper and television reporters' demands? Did Munroe have the inner strength to shrug off the adversities and criticisms that would certainly come his way? And it was at a time like this that the Chairman reached the same conclusion: Munroe was his. Period. Whether or not the senator had caved-in during the Oates fiasco in his Prudential Tower office was immaterial; there was no way to go back and make changes. The senator and the campaign had survived and thrived. Spilled milk, the Chairman acknowledged; as he done so many times before, he dismissed the doubts and looked forward. There was excellent reason to celebrate the fact that Munroe was on his way to the Presidency. He accepted that fact as overriding. Everything was going well, and there was no reason to think otherwise.

The Chairman had good reason for being in a good mood this morning. Until the call came in from his associate that rocked his sensibilities and brutally turned his gladness upside down. The call turned the Chairman suddenly into a raging animal, snarling and rabid with fury. Matthew Keyes, his caller told him, had recently delivered a packet of information to Collins' attention in the Homicide division. The packet assembled many of the details about the untimely death of Captain Henry Oates. It would have been only a matter of time before the police filled in the pieces. Had not that parcel been taken from Collins' office, the detective would have been tempted to start taking Matthew Keyes and Joanne O'Byrne much more seriously. They're far too curious for their own good, the Chairman knew.

He slammed the phone down without thanking the caller for his diligence and good judgment. He needed to calm down. And to think.

The Chairman sat at his chair and attempted to consider the facts as he knew them. His rage, he acknowledged, however entitled he was to own it, could only serve as a distraction. He needed to focus. Detective Collins, he concluded, even if he had received some basic information about the late Captain Oates, might not make the connection. It was Keyes who mattered here. Keyes was the eyewitness, and Keyes would have to be followed. The fact that he'd learned of Oates' death and saw fit to notify Collins meant that he was still trying hard. Even without any way of connecting Oates to Munroe, if he started to draw conclusions too close to the truth, he would need to be disposed of. That meant O'Byrne as well.

The Chairman's eyes narrowed as he considered his next move. He would have to act quickly and decisively.

***

ONE WEEK LATER, at dusk in the Canutama camp, a special dinner was prepared by Joey and was followed by a celebration, the extent of which was rare to the project. The object of the celebration sat in a chair placed in the middle of the room. Jimmy was enjoying this, and his grin, even broader than usual, reflected that sentiment. The entire project team had surprised Jimmy with a series of aquavit toasts and hip-hip-hoorahs, courtesy of the Dane and the Englishman who organized the affair.

The purpose was to semi-officially recognize Jimmy for his scheme of building the bat houses. What had been dismissed by some early on as a wasted effort had proven itself to be a notable success. Vegetation had indeed sprung from the guano, as Jimmy predicted. Already a coat of green was creeping across portions of the damaged rain forest closest to the wooden houses Jimmy had erected.

Further, Jimmy's bat house project did have gradual, but measurable effects on the insect population. Anecdotally, there had been some growing suspicion that the mosquitoes were somewhat less ferocious of late. But one project member, a retired biology professor from Georgia, decided to construct an experiment to put these reports to a series of simple tests. The first was the placement of spirals of flypaper which he surveyed daily, recording the counts of mosquitoes. The second required two volunteers to stand immobile with arms bared in particularly mosquito-infested areas around the camp for four minutes at the same time each day and to count the number of bites. The results indicated that the number of mosquitoes had declined by nearly fifteen percent over a two-week period since the bats were seen in force.

Even the most skeptical of his colleagues stood in turn to offer appropriate praise to Jimmy. One by one, his colleagues rose, aquavit freshly refilled, to cite one or more of Jimmy's contributions. With nineteen separate orations, that meant nineteen separate splashes of aquavit, and most of those present were sufficiently inebriated after the first eight or nine to render the balance of the toasts somewhat sloppy and blubbery. As the honoree, Jimmy was required to participate in the toasts, and he was the sloppiest and the most blubbery of them all. To further muddle the scene, because Portuguese was not the principle language of many present, their words got lost occasionally and the slurring praises degraded rapidly.

At last, when the final speech was made, Jimmy was presented with a series of gifts. Among them were a hat made of straw from Masso, an autographed first edition of *Focus On Plate Tectonics*, a college textbook, from its co-author, a bottle of aquavit and a jar of herring from his Danish friend, a Christ College necktie from Liberty's of London from the Englishman, a Shrade folding knife with deer antlers etched on the blade, and, most treasured by Jimmy of all the gifts, twelve frequent flier coupons from the Georgia biologist.

These were later brought to the table nearest the sleeping Jimmy, who would not awaken until late the following day.

***

BY THE TIME Jimmy did wake up in his bungalow at Canutama, Matt Keyes was easing his Jeep into the early evening traffic on Vermont's Interstate 91 outside Burlington. He had left work earlier than usual this day to retrieve his trunk at the airport cargo area. American Airlines had called him at his office to advise him of its arrival. His ninety-minute wait in the customs office at the terminal was interrupted by requests to sign a raft of government forms. When he finally received his trunk, he was not inclined to argue about its dilapidated condition. He accepted it, took his copies of the forms, and left. Now stowed in the rear of his Jeep, the trunk was returned to its point of origination.

His own homecoming days earlier had been relatively uneventful. A sign was hung on his office door welcoming him back. And his boss took him to dinner one evening at a fine restaurant outside Burlington. It's not that Matt didn't have friends in Vermont, but he had no close friends. Within a few days, for Keyes, it was business as usual. A drainage project for a community habitually flooded by the LaPlatte River was the biggest project on his desk when he left for

Canutama. That had been replaced by a project to design a physics laboratory to be built into a hillside for St. Michael's College, some twelve miles to the north. The names had changed, but the routine had not. His workdays were longer since he returned because he had to catch up with the projects his firm had in progress.

The single biggest change in his life became the thirty minutes of telephone conversation each night with Joanne. Precisely at 8:30, he would press "Memory One" on his telephone that he had programmed with Joanne's Melrose number. Thirty minutes had been agreed upon in an effort to avoid becoming a major debtor to MCI. Eight thirty had been established so that Joshua would be asleep and the dinner dishes put away.

"My trunk showed up today."

"I thought you didn't expect it for another week or so."

"The barge must have showed up early. You should see it. It was opened by U.S. Customs and sealed back up with red tape, but the lock is missing and the insides look like they were dumped out on a table and just mashed back in. I had a wooden bowl made by one of the cooks that was broken, and a carving of a tree monkey that's in four pieces now." Matt's voice was low and he sounded tired to Joanne.

"Are you feeling OK, Matt? You don't sound very happy tonight."

"I miss you, Joanne. That's all. I wish I could be with you tonight."

"Matt, I thought we agreed when you left that we ought to give ourselves at least a month apart. It's only been eight days." Joanne was sounding like a mother reminding her child that the candy would have to wait until after dinner.

"I guess that patience is not my strong suit right now. I'd much rather be with you tonight than here in my apartment all alone."

"Do you have any plans for tonight? Maybe you should go to a movie or get into a good book. I was going to rent a movie for my mother and me tonight, but I didn't get out of work until 6. I barely had time to have supper and read to Joshua."

"How are your mother and Joshua?"

"They're doing fine. Joshua misses you. I told him that you had to go back to your home, and I showed him where Burlington is on a map. I think he likes you, Matt."

"Tell him I said hello, would you?"

"Sure. And my mom says hi."

"Any call from Collins yet?" Keyes was dismayed that Collins never responded to the envelope of newspaper articles on the discovery of Captain Henry Oates.

"Not yet, Matt. I really don't think he'll ever call. Maybe you were right. Maybe he was just blowing us off when he told us to go to the library and look for reports on missing persons. And besides, there was another gang murder yesterday, so I'm sure he's up to his neck in work right now. Like he said. Real bodies. Real weapons."

Their conversation went on like this for a few minutes when Joanne reminded him of the time. They had been talking for thirty-five minutes, and it was time to say good night.

After hanging up, Keyes opened his kitchen cabinets and opened a can of salmon to begin a late supper. He set a pot of water on the range and was waiting for it to boil when he went to the television and turned it on. It was tuned to the Discovery Channel and another program on wartime aircraft. He left it there and turned his attention to dinner. Tonight he'd make creamed salmon on toast, a dish to which he had become accustomed as a child, and which he still enjoyed today. The smell of the kitchen brought him back to his growing up years in New Hampshire, and it was his mother standing at the range, cooking supper. His brother and sister and father were seated, waiting at the table and talking about their days. There were other meals Matt would make from time to time which put him in similar strains of remembrance. Baked beans on cold Saturdays filled his apartment with the sweet aroma of molasses, brown sugar, and mustard. Or corned beef and cabbage, or a pot roast of beef and winter vegetables. They formed the framework of a reverie Keyes would occasionally welcome, and tonight he welcomed the memories.

He thought of the late summer nights when he and his brother would negotiate with their mother to sleep outdoors in their father's army surplus pup tent, pretending they were far from the comforts of home. There, they would plot the next day's events, when they would rise, where they would go. The railroad tracks behind the dairy farm were a favorite. And the bog near the river where Mr. Nichols built a tree house for the neighborhood kids and where their friend, Gerard "Pig Ears" Thibodeau, used his buck knife to deftly skin a beaver he'd found dead on the side of the road one. That was a red-letter day. Fat and generally surly, Pig Ears earned his nickname from the way his unusually small ears came to a point and angled from his skull; his bulk and ill-mannered demeanor did nothing to discourage the porcine comparison. He gained a reputation, one that he relished for the balance of that summer and into the early weeks of the school year, for his boldness and skill as he artfully cut and peeled the beaver pelt from its owner in front of a dazzled group of nearly a dozen pre-pubescent neighbors. One girl threw up on the spot. At least two other kids ran home crying before the deed was done. But the rest stood awestruck at Pig Ears' imperious performance.

The sound of the water reaching a boil brought Keyes back to the here and now, and he wondered if kids played the same way today. His thoughts went to Joshua and he wondered what memories might some day be evoked by the smells of his grandmother's kitchen.

Matt tossed two handfuls of dry noodles into the water and stirred the creamed salmon in a fry pan. Minutes later, seated at the corner of his kitchen table so he could view the TV screen, Matt used the remote to turn to CNN. The Presidential Campaign was in full battle mode, and tonight's program would feature the biographies of the contenders. Matthew Keyes was a voter, but not a political junkie, so he was only half listening, half scanning the day's mail, as he ate.

"...a degree in history at Cornell, followed by law school at George Washington University. The senator worked briefly as an administrative aide for the State Bureau of Housing in Maryland, before returning to his home state as a junior clerk for the Massachusetts Supreme Judicial Court. He wasn't there six months before he joined the most prestigious law firm in Boston, where he forged friendships and alliances that would serve him well in the years ahead. John Bennett Munroe first ran for political office when he was only twenty-seven and challenged the incumbent in a race for state representative from his district."

The announcer's voice droned on as Matt continued sorting through the day's mail. The electric company was charging Keyes' for turning his service back on when he returned home, even though he had been told that a temporary suspension would not result in any such charge. Keyes set the bill aside to be dealt with tomorrow. A bank in Delaware was promising low interest rates on his MasterCard if he'd transfer balances from another credit card company. That hit the wastebasket.

"...in his Boston office high over the city in the beautiful Back Bay area. Senator Munroe, thank you for taking time out of your schedule to speak with us."

Keyes heard the name of his favorite American city and glanced up at the screen. The scene was a wide shot of the interviewer and the senator, both seated in the senator's office.

The camera cut to a close-up of Senator Munroe. A broad, confident smile alternated with a wrinkled brow of seriousness and a set jaw of determination. To Matt Keyes, John Munroe looked like a thousand other politicians. Keyes searched the face of the candidate as he answered a few softball questions.

"...time for the country to get back on course ...target the problems of the inner cities ...the spiraling costs of government ..."

So far there was nothing to distinguish this guy from any of the rest.

Keyes went back to his mail. The Friends of Animals asked for "anything you can give," and a furniture advertisement promised "the best leather sofa at the lowest possible price." The Animals stayed on the table; the leather sofa hit the trash. A thick envelope of coupons never got opened. It was followed by a car dealer's "absolutely last chance for the minivan of your dreams." He looked up to the screen once again when the interviewer thanked the senator for "the opportunity to visit with you off the campaign trail." The camera shot widened as the senator stood, slipped on his jacket, and walked to his desk. Something struck Keyes as familiar in this scene. The senator standing tall with the U.S. flag on the wall behind him. Matt stared at the screen trying to register the scene with one he was sure was stored somewhere in his memory bank. It was too familiar. Then the scene changed to the home of Munroe's opponent, the sitting Vice President, where he sat on a porch, dressed in khakis and polo shirt. Evidently it was the "a man of the people" approach for this guy.

Keyes didn't pay attention to the words or the picture.

***

AT THE FARM, the Chairman was flipping through a series of phone messages and mail. The taping of Munroe's interview for CNN that morning had been well done, and the Chairman was pleased. The polls were indicating a close campaign so far, but there was reason for confidence. Munroe's money supply was still strong; his opponent was starting to show up at fund-raising dinners in far-flung cities without seeming to be coordinated. That could mean that money was tight for the bad guys, and their ads would start dropping off, especially television commercial time. Munroe had no such worries, and a new thirty-second spot was scheduled to be out tomorrow night.

In addition, Keyes had been back in Vermont for over a week, and Collins did not appear to be making any more out of the case. Maybe he would just let the matter die of natural causes. To be safe, the Chairman would continue to have Joanne O'Byrne watched for a while, just in case. Earl would assign someone to that. And the telephone monitoring would go on. Based on the tapes of the conversations between Keyes and O'Byrne that he had heard so far, Keyes was frustrated about Collins' apparent lack of interest.

And based on the reports from the Chairman's contact at police headquarters, as far as Collins knew, Keyes had simply quit the chase and gone back home to Vermont. Keyes' photocopied news articles on Oates disappearance and discovery never saw the light of Collins' day. There was reason to feel good again about the way things were working out.

***

IN ANOTHER CORNER of the country, in the Oregon capital of Salem, Jack Munroe's running mate Bo Day reached for the TV remote and turned off the set in his hotel room. *Damn*, he thought, *but that man looks good.* Day was thinking about Jack Munroe and the just completed interview of the Presidential candidates on CNN.

Day sat alone. He had started his day in San Francisco, where a brief appearance at a Union Square rally was greeted warmly. This was Day's backyard, and he was popular in his home state. He took the podium just after a rousing speech by the state party leader. By the time his turn came around, thousands of supporters were cheering loudly for him.

What a change, Day thought. *I like this idea of running for Vice President. A few months ago, I was speaking in this same place, at this identical podium, and I felt on edge, stiff, and ill at ease. My campaign was running on empty, and none of my workers had been paid for three weeks. I know I didn't come across well. I think they could sense my disheartenment. And this was in front of a friendly audience.*

Now, he mused, *here I am again, and those money problems are in the past. Munroe's campaign took care of my workers, and I don't have to worry about kissing anyone's ass for donations.*

Day surveyed the applauding crowd before him and soaked in the encouragement, the noise, and the acclaim. He felt strengthened by the people before him. He raised both arms and motioned the crowd to be silent and let him speak. He smiled as the crowd clapped and cheered even more wildly. He leaned to the microphone and said, "Thank you" repeatedly. Finally, the crowd slowed its rooting, and he started to speak.

"Thank you, my friends, thank you. Thank you. I stand before you today, proud of my role on the Munroe-Day ticket, proud of my family and my friends. I stand here proud to be a Californian!" The crowd went wild again. "And proud to be an American.

"Later today, I will have the pleasure of visiting with the governor of Oregon. We have much in common with our neighbors to the north. Our shared pursuit of a safer and cleaner environment is at the forefront. Jack Munroe and I have made it clear that we will do everything in our power to preserve and maintain this beautiful earth, with all its richness and bounty, so that your children and mine, so that your grandchildren and mine, will receive this planet in better shape than when we arrived."

More cheering followed.

"And that is a key statement of our campaign. It imbues every part of our platform. Jack Munroe and I both believe that we can, and we must, leave the world a little better place. There are, my friends, those who will couch their words in grand phrases when they speak of this planet and how they wish to do the same as Jack Munroe and me. They are draped in a flag of forest green, while at the same time, they seek to harm, abuse, and exhaust the great natural resources of our collective home." Munroe's opponent supported the mining industry's plans to pull valuable ore from the mountains of Wyoming and Colorado, and Day knew how hotly this crowd was opposed to those efforts. "And, ladies and gentlemen, my friends, with your help and support, with your continued assistance, we will stop nourishing the greed of those who would scar this beautiful land and leave our descendants a barren wasteland.

"We have a long fight ahead of us, and I need to count on you, my friends and neighbors, to stand with us in the battle. Thank you all, and may God bless you."

Day waved to the audience as he stepped from the dais and walked briskly to his waiting limousine. The crowd's enthusiasm invigorated him, and he looked forward to the balance of the campaign. His debate with his counterpart on the opposition ticket was still a week away, but he felt stronger each passing hour.

CHAPTER FOURTEEN

A S THE DAYS passed by, Keyes spent increasingly more hours at work, timing his return home to arrive just moments before his scheduled 8:30 call. Free time, he found, only made him more acutely aware of the time and distance between him and Joanne. He wanted to make plans to drive to Boston to visit Joanne soon. Maybe as soon as next weekend. He'd been loaded with work since his return and wanted to make sure he got his assignments caught up before he planned on a weekend away. He was pushing himself, he knew. Whether or not this was a way of deferring serious thoughts about commitment and going forward in life with a partner, sharing the future with Joanne, he was not certain. Without debate, though, he felt good about the fact that he was giving this eventuality more than passing consideration, and it was for him somewhere on a line between recognition and self-congratulation. At least, he thought, his introspection was becoming habitual, and he knew that he could no longer simply cut and run. For someone as unfamiliar as he knew he'd been with the value of self-contemplation, this was not yet a cause for a full celebration, but still it was a source of some true pleasure.

He drove home on a drizzling Friday evening having prepared a nearly full day for himself at work the following day. Weekends, without the daily structure his colleagues and clients would otherwise provide, were the worst. Aimlessness was his enemy, and he did what he could reasonably do to erect defenses between it and himself. He would spend at least half of it consumed by computer modeling drainage canals and a reservoir for a new development outside of St. Albans on the Canadian border. That would leave only Sunday.

He reached mindlessly for the day's mail and opened the door to his apartment. Out of habit, he tossed the mail on the kitchen counter, walked into the living room, and switched on the television. Dan Rather was describing the potential track of Hurricane Kermit as it arced across the Atlantic, then switched live to a reporter at the National Weather Service. Keyes changed channels to hear that one of the National League's leading pitchers was charged with cocaine possession and facing a lengthy suspension.

He walked back into the kitchen and riffled through the day's mail as he reached for the phone and pressed Memory One. It was a thin pile of mail today. A flyer from the local supermarket. And a letter. It was written on onionskin paper and postmarked Labrea, Brazil. Keyes was tearing it open and starting to read it when Joanne answered on the first ring.

"Hello, stranger."

"Guess what, Joanne? I just got a letter from Brazil." His voice didn't betray the rush of excitement as he unfolded the thin sheets of paper.

"Who from?"

"It's from Jimmy! He's visiting his family for a few days, then he's coming up here to visit." He read the words quickly and Joanne waited for him silently. "He's scheduled to arrive next Sunday. That's only eight days away."

"That's great, Matt. You really miss him, don't you?"

"I do. He's a great friend." He continued reading and Joanne smiled as she thought she could almost hear his lips move as he went on. "He's coming here first, then he's going to visit a friend in Massachusetts. He says he wants to meet you when he gets to Boston. Did I tell you about his friend who lives in Fall River?"

"The fisherman from the Azores? Uh huh. Is he staying in Fall River when he comes east?"

"He doesn't say. He says they had a party for him, and he got some free airline tickets. Here. I'll read it from the start. 'Dear Matt . . .'"

As Matt read the letter to her from start to finish, Joanne read pure joy in his voice.

***

THE SUNSET THIS evening on the island of Antigua was typically rich, changing in velvet tones from deep pink to flashes of red and then purple. Whenever Rosemary Oates saw a sunset from the balcony of her condominium on the island, she thought of Henry and how much she missed him. She truly missed him those evenings when the sky would boil in a palette of warm colors mixed with faint brush strokes of clouds across it. The sunsets were the reason he and Rosemary had selected this particular island and this particular condominium. Henry once said to her in a rare poetic moment that he would like to spend eternity here and enjoy the magic of the Caribbean sunsets with her "every night forever."

She and Henry had a peculiar marriage by many measures. Like so many wives of career military men, she had entered into their marriage with expectations of moving with her husband across the world, settling in just long enough to get comfortable before moving on to the next base. In fact, that is exactly how their lives together had begun. Henry Oates, tall, powerfully built, and very handsome looked like the definition of an officer. Rosemary, slender and blonde, had movie star good looks and a body to match.

Henry and Rosemary were childless, not by choice, but by chance. A uterine infection she contracted when they lived in Thailand rendered her unable to successfully complete a pregnancy. After three miscarriages, at the age of twenty-nine, they jointly decided to reengineer their plans for the future, and Henry underwent a vasectomy.

At about that same time, Rosemary and Henry began to drive themselves harder and more intensely into different directions. Henry had been an only child and aspired to sire a large brood of children. He felt cheated by fate and the U.S. Navy that stationed him in Thailand in the first place. He turned his attention to advancement, and set his sights on a command position. If he couldn't be the head of a large conventional family, he would lead a family on board ship, a large ship. He enrolled in every program that was expected of those seeking that career direction. He volunteered for every assignment, however miserable, with the goal of a significant command in mind. An eighteen-month stint in the outer Aleutians was the worst. His colleagues took to calling him "Ambition Oates," and he saw that as a compliment. In the highly competitive and just as highly political games of the U.S. Navy, Henry Oates didn't consider ambition a dirty word.

Gifted with a scientific mind and a facility in mathematics, Henry found his talents, ambitions, and opportunities focused in high-tech weaponry. Within six years, having served in minor commands around the globe, Henry Oates had become a prominent authority on nuclear warfare at sea. In a stroke of great fortune, his initiative and talents were brought to the attention of the Naval Chief of Staff, Admiral Bernard Sternhauer, who personally selected Oates to work at his side as his chief assistant. His office would be in the Executive Office Building in Washington, adjacent to the White House, and right next door to his new boss. Oates gladly accepted, and he saw this as the last step forward before being awarded command of a major vessel.

Oates found a willing and capable patron in Sternhauer. The admiral was a demanding boss with an insatiable ego, and Oates fulfilled his needs. Once, in a private moment after a White House dinner honoring the General Secretary of the United Nations, Sternhauer asked Oates a question. "What's your job, Oates?" Sternhauer was in a good mood. The President spent a good deal of time kibitzing casually and often with the admiral throughout the evening. Sternhauer and Oates had returned to the admiral's private office to celebrate with a few glasses of Metaxa Amphora Seven Star brandy. Oates replied, "I work for you, admiral."

The admiral took a sip and looked Oates straight in the eye. "I'm going to be more specific. Your job, Captain Oates, is to make your boss look good. To make me look so fucking good that the fucking President of the United States considers it his duty and privilege to kiss my German ass. That," he ended emphatically, "is your fucking job!"

Oates listened. His boss wasn't through. "And let me say, Oates, that you're doing a great fucking job." With that, the admiral turned, smiled, and strode purposefully from the room.

His command, Oates was certain, was a shoo-in.

***

MEANWHILE, ROSEMARY CEASED performing the role of the dutiful Navy wife. When Henry wrapped himself tightly in career ambition, she decided to go in a different direction. No more cheap apartments in far-flung ports standing by her man. Instead, Rosemary went back to school. She had already earned a Masters in finance. Now it was time for law school. She took her degrees and her drive to an investment firm in downtown Washington, where she established herself quickly. Her client list was comprised largely of the sons and daughters and grandsons and granddaughters of people who actually earned the fortunes their descendants lived on. Countless lunches were spent listening to the woes of these clients, most of them spoiled brats from ages twenty to eighty. She hated them with a passion born of jealousy and greed. And she learned.

Rosemary's reputation in taxation and investments, especially in how to help the well-to-do avoid taxes on their investments, drew attention, and her client list grew. By the age of thirty-eight, Rosemary was both respected and rich.

When Henry returned to Washington as Admiral Sternhauer's chosen one, she and Henry had not shared a single night together in five years. Henry's vigorous drive for advancement was not one she cared to feed by being recast as the supportive spouse. She was surprised and pleased that Henry was not insisting on her becoming one. Instead, she maintained her professional life, and he saw to the needs of Admiral Sternhauer. Henry and Rosemary had not been separated by acrimony, but by their own needs as individuals to excel and to achieve.

They moved to a lovely brick colonial in Fairfax County and

gradually reestablished first their friendship, then their closeness, and finally their love. They had each reconciled their sense of loss in their own ways, but until now, not with each other. Then the admiral died.

The call came at 3 o'clock in the morning. Sternhauer had suffered a stroke. By 4 o'clock, Oates was standing with the admiral's wife, supporting her by the arm, as they walked and waited in the hospital corridor. By 7 o'clock, the rugged, broad-shouldered admiral was dead.

His funeral was three days later. The President paid his respects by calling Sternhauer one of the great leaders of our time. The admiral was sent to his reward with all the pomp and pageantry one would expect for a fallen hero. Mrs. Sternhauer stood at the head of the casket under overcast skies at Arlington cemetery to receive the flag, and Oates would later recall the sad sound of taps and recognize it as the point in time when his dreams for a major command were being buried that morning with the admiral.

Within ten days, Admiral James Michael Murphy was named to fill the shoes of Sternhauer. Oates knew Murphy well and personally liked the man. Murphy was garrulous, affable, and a great storyteller. But Murphy had his own coterie, and when Oates was summoned to Murphy's office for a private chat, he knew the ending of the story he would be told. "Your genius," Murphy summed up, "will be wasted on serving the likes of me. Imagine, here you are, the world's authority on sea warfare and weaponry, pushing papers and doing the bidding of a tired old fart like James Michael Murphy. No, I need you, Oates, but not here. I need you ...America, for chrissake, needs you ...for a bigger job than this."

Oates tried twice to interrupt and put his goal of a command forward, but Murphy would have none of it. As if on cue, Murphy's intercom buzzed and he was advised that the President wanted to see him immediately. On his way out, he shook Oates' hand and congratulated him. "Take some time off, Henry. You've worked hard and you deserve it."

Rosemary Oates had seen her husband grieve before. When his

mother died five months after their wedding. When they learned that bearing children was no longer an option. When Sternhauer died. But the grief over losing the chance for a major command drove Oates into a depression deeper than she had ever seen. For a solid week, he didn't leave the house. He didn't shave. He didn't shower. She found him once in the middle of the night, sobbing and alone in their living room. She stayed with him all night trying to comfort him and to ease his pain. In the morning, she decided to consult a friend at a psychotherapy clinic in her office building where she worked. She was exhausted and knew that her husband was on the brink of blackness.

Her friend recommended a psychiatrist in Alexandria who specialized in working with adult males. In fact, she would call the doctor herself and arrange to get Oates seen on an emergency basis. That same afternoon, Rosemary drove a haggard Henry Oates to the office of Dr. Harold Furst. Oates was suffering from major clinical depression, he concluded, and recommended that he be admitted as an inpatient for closely monitored individual and group psychotherapy. When he resisted, the doctor prescribed a treatment of daily psychotherapy and desipramine, an antidepressant, to be increased gradually. This, he insisted, would also require that Rosemary stay at his side constantly.

Noting no change after the first three days, Rosemary spoke with Dr. Furst privately. To her, Henry was simply lingering in crisis; perhaps she could convince Henry to admit himself for treatment. Dr. Furst did not discourage her, but marked that Henry showed signs of extraordinary inner strength that he felt would reveal itself shortly. He urged her to be patient, and he was right. Over the next several days, she discerned remarkable changes in Henry. He was sleeping through the night, regaining his formerly prodigious appetite, and taking better care of himself. Dr. Furst suggested that shorter and less frequent sessions would be appropriate and advised Rosemary that she ought to resume going to work herself. Henry, he reassured her, was coming along famously.

One week after that conversation, Henry strode into the

Pentagon and assumed the new role that Admiral Murphy had arranged to carve out for him. His office had all the trappings, and he dove into his work with determination. His responsibilities were enormous, overseeing vast fortunes of high-tech weapons testing and acquisition. While Rosemary was pleased at the progress Henry was apparently making, she distinguished a different man than the one she had known. Henry was attacking his work with the intensity of a man possessed. But unlike those days when his drive was based on the desire to advance and achieve, he did not appear to be enjoying this. On the contrary, he bore the grim mask of someone consumed with vengeance.

She confronted him one evening as they climbed into bed, and she learned of a different Henry Oates. This was a man who was not merely angry at being passed over for the job he so desperately wanted and for which he had been preparing himself so well and for so long. Henry Oates was resolved to pursue his own agenda. Rosemary listened, awed by the complexity of his vision and the intensity of his determination. He related his plan. It would use every advantage of his position and authority. He would get even, he said, and take back "pound for pound," the blood and sweat he had spent for his once beloved Navy. He would take it out of the Navy's hide. And Rosemary bought in.

***

TONIGHT THE ANTIGUAN sunset was gradually assailed by the misty scrim of a gentle, blowing rain. Autumn was the season of changeable weather in this part of the world, and the end of this day matched the mixed melancholy of her mood perfectly. She stood on the balcony, facing into the breeze, feeling cleansed by the warm fog. The glass of wine she had poured was drained, and she set it on the rail as she absorbed the twilight dew. *Here I stand, the wealthiest woman I know, and where are you, Henry Oates? We could have done anything we wanted, Henry. There was no need for any more.*

She looked down over the edge of the rail and examined the distance to the tangled tendrils of bougainvillea on the soggy ground below, inhaled deeply, not yet at peace with the prospects of a future alone, and returned to the comfort of the living room. The air had grown cool, so she went to the armoire to find a sweater. In her haste to leave their home in Virginia, she hadn't had time to pack properly, and wondered if she even brought one with her. There was no sweater in view, so she searched the drawers. When that proved fruitless, she turned to the closet where Henry had occasionally stored clothes during past visits. Maybe she could find one of his sweaters to wear. The closet was empty save for a small, leather, carry-on satchel that Henry must have left there. She took a chance and hoped she might find a jacket rolled up inside. She opened it and emptied the contents on the bed. Yes, there was a light blue nylon windbreaker. It would do fine.

As she put her arms in the sleeves, she casually eyed the rest of the satchel's contents. A hairbrush. Several pens. A vinyl portfolio, and a micro diskette. Curious, she picked up the portfolio. Inside was a pad of ruled yellow paper on which nothing was written. She placed it back on the bed. The diskette was unmarked, and she wondered what it held. Henry used a desktop often, at home and at the Pentagon. He even carried a laptop with him on trips occasionally, and she assumed it was for the usual reasons. Notes, memoranda, schedules, budgets. She used one daily herself in her work, but relished her time away from it when she was at home.

She walked into the den where the desktop had sat idle since Henry and she had last come here together. She turned it on and sat at the keyboard. She waited for the prompt so she could search the disk. She scanned the contents and found a directory named "FINAL." *Final what?* It was for a word processing program, and she entered it. What she read in the next forty minutes stunned her. Henry had shared much of his work with her. They had jointly agreed to a scheme that could be extremely dangerous, but would definitely be absolutely, extraordinarily lucrative. But as she read, she was jolted by the depth and weight of the plot her husband had hatched. He had made several oblique references to a purchasing and distribution strategy that, he said, would be his final project in the military. As she read, she finally understood the gravity of the machinations and the reasons why his references were decidedly obscure.

She finished, benumbed by what she had read. She considered the disk's contents again and again, for it was an as yet unfinished saga. She closed her eyes and wondered whether she could write the final chapter as a testament to Henry.

***

BURLINGTON INTERNATIONAL AIRPORT was experiencing some delays, and Keyes cursed the clouds and rain. The weather had been glorious for several days in a row, and Keyes hoped it would hold for at least another day. Unfortunately, the clouds slid into position that morning, and the rain began in earnest by midafternoon. Jimmy's flight, scheduled to arrive at 6:30, was already one hour late. At last check, the gate agent told him to expect at least another half hour. Intermittent breaks were allowing some flights to land, and Keyes sat and waited impatiently.

Forty minutes later, the first passengers making their appearance exited the Jetway and entered the terminal. Keyes stood and tried to gain a position to spot Jimmy, but since this was a wide-body jet, he prepared himself for a long wait. Suddenly, among the first passengers to enter the terminal was his friend, smiling broadly as usual and in the company of a much taller and very attractive blond woman. They were talking animatedly and the woman laughed at something Jimmy said. She was lovely. Jimmy was passing Keyes and stopped abruptly. He called to the woman who was still walking towards the main terminal. "Elaine, wait a minute. I want you to meet my friend." Jimmy turned to Keyes, and they hugged each other in greeting.

When they parted, the woman put her hand out to Keyes. "You must be Matthew," she said. "I'm Elaine, and I've heard a great deal about you from Jimmy." They shook hands and she turned to Jimmy. "Here's your bag, Jimmy. I hope you have a wonderful time in the states. I'm sure you will." She bent to hug Jimmy and placed a lingering kiss on his lips. "Please call me if you have a chance. You have my number." Her smile welded Jimmy in place.

With that, she was gone, and Jimmy turned to Keyes. "What do you think, Matt? She works for the airline. Got me into first class and everything."

"And carried your bags! I am impressed." Keyes picked up the carry-on bag that Elaine had been toting for Jimmy, and together they walked and talked as they went to retrieve Jimmy's luggage in the terminal.

Jimmy was hungry, and Keyes opted to bring him to Rose's, a delicatessen in downtown Burlington. Famous for their enormous sandwiches and desserts, Rose's was the ideal spot to match Jimmy's appetite. All during their meal, they swapped stories and brought each other up-to-date on their lives since they had last been together. While it had only been a few weeks, they had a great deal of news to share. Keyes laughed loudly and often when Jimmy described the dinner in his honor and the aquavit toasting that followed.

Keyes spoke of his days in Boston upon his return and of Joanne. Jimmy could see that his friend was very much in love with Joanne and asked, "So, why do you stay here, so far away, when you want to be with Joanne so much?"

Keyes felt that he had no good answer, but tried to explain his feelings. "Several years ago, I moved away from her very quickly, and that hurt her. I love her, and I want to return to Boston and to be with her. But we both agreed that we need to move carefully." He paused and considered his own words. "Does that make sense? I mean, we want to be together, but before we make a life commitment, we need to be sure that we have both given it a lot of thought."

"I think I understand, my friend. Sometimes the best friendships get better when you both know what it means to be apart."

***

JIMMY'S VISIT WITH Keyes was only four days long. In that time, they had visited the foggy and stunning shore of Grand Isle on Lake Champlain, hiked through the forests partway up Mt.

Mansfield, which in early autumn was ablaze with magnificent shades of yellow and gold, and walked around the old section of downtown Montreal. Jimmy ate fresh salmon for the first time and decided that he would simply have to return to visit at least once every year to enjoy it. Once, Keyes brought him to his office to meet his associates, and then to the college where his project was in its early stages.

Jimmy had elected to take a bus from Burlington to Boston rather than fly, the better to get a flavor of the area, he said. When the morning arrived for Keyes to drop him off at the terminal for his ride to Boston, neither wanted their visit to end so quickly. Keyes gave him a farewell embrace, and he could feel his eyes filling up.

As soon as Keyes returned to his condo, he poured himself a cup of coffee and punched Memory One. Joanne's mother answered. "Matthew. I didn't expect you to be calling so early. Joanne's upstairs with Joshua. I'll get her."

Keyes felt very much alone. He wanted to feel Joanne in his arms, to feel her squeeze back. They talked for over an hour. He told her when to expect Jimmy, and she marked down the time. Jimmy would be arriving in the middle of the afternoon. Joanne had already arranged for the day off and was looking forward to meeting him.

***

JACK MUNROE WAS crawling beneath the sheets of his bed at the Great Falls Marriott. He was in a cold sweat and stared at the ceiling. The call had been put through to his room twenty minutes earlier. He had already showered and was relaxing, seated in his suite, wrapped in a terry cloth bathrobe and reading his notes for the next morning. He heard a knock on his door, rose, and looked through the peephole, then opened the door for his visitor. Lisa Sobolewski, his press secretary and now also one of his closest advisers, stopped by his room with the excuse of dropping off a fresh copy of his speech. In the several months that she had been on his staff, Munroe found Lisa to be brilliant, efficient, reliable, and a fierce warrior for his election to the presidency. Munroe had learned to rely on her to keep his days organized, to keep him focused, and to keep the press sharks at bay. The public and the press learned much of what they knew of Jack Munroe from Lisa Sobolewski.

In most private settings, Jack Munroe had also come to thoroughly enjoy Lisa's magnificent presence in bed. And she made it clear to him that her desire to bed him was no less strong. She once mused after an especially torrid session, neither was married, they each admired the other, and they truly enjoyed each other's company. The physical attraction for one another added a whole new and delicious dimension to their relationship. Munroe didn't disagree.

He had just unbuttoned the top button of Lisa's white silk blouse and was teasing an erect nipple through the thin fabric when the telephone rang. He ignored it at first. They kissed, hard, openmouthed, and steamy, and he began to unzip her skirt. The telephone rang again, and he whispered as if to the phone, "Go away." Lisa's hand was on his erection, squeezing him. The telephone persisted, and she pulled her hand away and stood back. "It might be Leland, Jack. You'd better answer it."

Munroe was flushed and cursed the interruption. "I'll tell him I've got a migraine and make it quick," he said.

The caller wasn't Leland Hayes. It was a woman's voice, and she spoke deliberately and steadily. Without inflection, she recited as if from a list. Dates and times. Names, places, precise, and without pause. In less than ninety seconds, she had finished and hung up. Munroe, paralyzed by the call, continued to hold the phone to his ear for several moments before his arm slowly slid to his side and the handset fell to the floor. "Jack?" Lisa asked. "What's the matter? Was it Leland? What's wrong?" Jack sat down on the edge of the bed and stared straight ahead, not hearing Lisa or seeing her. He crawled under the covers while Lisa stood, half undressed, and dazed by Munroe's bizarre behavior.

Rosemary Oates had considered various options. The information that Henry had amassed in one spot would undoubtedly prove lethal to the Munroe candidacy. She could expose the weapons-selling cabal by going public with the story, but that would most decidedly portray her husband in a most undesirable light. She did not want to damage the reputation of a man who had worked very hard to make one, even if he was dead. No, she thought, she would rather make it known to Munroe that someone else knew the intricacies of the highly illegal buying and selling of extraordinarily powerful weapons to certain nations, and even to certain individuals, exchanges in which Munroe was a key player. With that decision made, the matter became one of simply locating Munroe and then establishing communication with him. Given the fact that the daily agenda of a Presidential candidate of a major party was very public knowledge …access to any U.S. newspaper would do nicely …she then made the call.

Rosemary Oates was prepared for being stalled and put off by the hotel telephone operator, but found that to be surprisingly easy. Merely saying she was Munroe's mother and wished to be put through to his room at once was sufficient. When the candidate's voice suddenly came on the line, she froze and nearly hung up. She regained her composure after only a moment's pause and started to speak in measured tones, reading directly from the screen in front of her. They were Henry's notes:

January 8—in Chicago with Munroe. Assured funds transferred properly and on time. Advised shipment would be made by February 1 to Clive Grant Industries, Auckland, via Honolulu. Received information regarding possible need for similar shipment to Capetown. Munroe to confirm upon final approval of his Chairman.
February 27—Washington, Munroe advised Capetown approval. Shipment required by May 15 to Claridge Walton Forbes, Limited.
April 20—Washington, funds confirmed Zurich.
May 2—Munroe order for London changed to Glasgow. Board will confirm funds May 10.
There was much more on Henry's disk. Precise amounts. Weapon types. Names. Places. Early in their marriage, she had once accused Henry of being pathologically organized, and she remembered that he wasn't offended in the least. She learned to live with his obsession for systematizing his daily life, and at this moment, she toasted the memory of Henry Oates with the last sip of a fine Chardonnay.

She paused at the end of her remarks, waiting for some sort of response from Munroe. She smiled as she listened to his breathing and knew he was still on the line. Nothing. She hung up, pleased with her initial performance and determined to call again soon.

***

JIMMY'S BUS ARRIVED on time at the downtown transportation terminal near Boston Common. He had napped part of the way and was rubbing the sleep from his eyes. He looked out of the window and saw that it was a cloudless clear morning.

Joanne O'Byrne sat in the waiting area and watched the passengers enter the terminal. Since Keyes had shown her a few photographs of Jimmy, she looked for a slim young man with a dark complexion and an oversized grin. When Jimmy appeared, she recognized him at once. She approached him and said, "If your name is Jimmy, I'm the person you're looking for."

Jimmy had not seen photographs of Joanne, but Keyes described her to him. "If your name is Joanne, I will tell Matt that his description of you does not do you justice."

Joanne gave him a hug and thanked him for his kind words. They walked together and Joanne said, "Matt told me I should be very careful around you. He said you are very charming and that you were accompanied by a beautiful woman when you arrived in Burlington."

"Ah, yes. Elaine. She is very beautiful, but she is also very tall. I think we might have been awkward. You and I, on the other hand, will make a very handsome couple." Joanne laughed and Jimmy saw the warmth and openness Matt spoke of. He could see how Keyes could fall in love with her.

In Melrose, Joanne introduced Jimmy to her mother and her son. Joshua took to Jimmy right away, and it was he who showed Jimmy to his room. Later, over coffee and rolls, Joanne and Jimmy got to know each other better. Jimmy hoped to spend three days with Joanne before he went to visit his friend in Fall River. They planned the rest of the day, and Joanne made sure to include a trip to an apple orchard for tomorrow.

Sitting alone in his Jeep Grand Cherokee at the corner of tree-lined Carter Street in Melrose, an older gentleman in a trench coat watched Joanne O'Byrne pull into the driveway of her mother's home with her passenger. He noted the time and took a mental photograph of the young man in her passenger seat. *That would be Jimmy,* Trygve Jensen thought to himself. He moved the gearshift lever to drive and moved on.

***

JIMMY HAD NEVER before seen such brilliant colors of a New England autumn, and that, coupled with the smells of the leaves and fresh apples were enchanting.

Together, Joanne and Jimmy walked through the orchard in Bolton, Massachusetts, each carrying a bag for the apples they would pick. Jimmy climbed the trees with ease, grabbing only the most perfect of the apples at the top. Joanne was less eager to climb, but still managed to fill her bag with ripe and delicious apples. She promised to make an apple pie. "Actually, Jimmy, it's my mother who'll make the pie. I feel like a little kid every time she makes one, and wait until you smell it baking in the oven."

On their way back to Melrose, they talked and laughed. Joanne especially liked Jimmy's stories about his family. At one point, Jimmy glanced over his shoulder and remarked to Joanne, "Did you see that car behind us this morning?"

She looked in the rearview mirror and saw a white sedan with a man behind the wheel.

"It doesn't look familiar to me, but I wasn't paying a lot of attention."

Jimmy glanced again quickly behind him. "I think that the car behind us was also behind us this morning. I recognize the driver."

Joanne looked again in the rearview mirror. The driver of the white car appeared to be a gaunt man. He wore a green sweater or jacket. Still, she did not register anything from this morning's drive. "Are you sure, Jimmy?"

"I think so. Do you know the man driving it?"

She tried to get a better look at the driver, but the windshield glare precluded a clear view. "No. But I can't see him very well." Joanne was getting anxious. She looked over to Jimmy, who was trying to keep the white car in view through the right-hand mirror. She decided to turn right abruptly onto a side road without signaling, and the white car continued straight ahead and out of sight. She sighed with relief and pulled to the side of the road. "You had me worried for a minute, Jimmy. See, nobody's following us."

Jimmy smiled in return and replied, "Maybe it was just another white car I saw this morning. I'm sorry if I upset you." But he didn't feel relieved on the inside. Jimmy knew well Keyes' story of seeing a possible murder in the Prudential Tower and reporting it to the police. He also knew that Matt and Joanne had visited with Detective Collins, conducted a search for missing person reports, and delivered the newspaper articles to police headquarters. Matt told Jimmy that Collins never followed up and about the unsettling sense of being followed. Once by Trygve Jensen for certain.

***

THE THIN MAN with the pockmarked face reached for the phone angrily. He pressed a series of numbers and waited. No answer on the first ring. Or the second. Then he heard a click and a series of tones. He had reached the recorder, left his message, and hung up. He decided he would park in the lot of the supermarket in Melrose and wait for Joanne O'Byrne to drive by. He had been trying to remain a discreet distance from her car all day, but the trip through small towns and back roads made the tail more difficult than usual. No matter. He was a patient man.

CHAPTER FIFTEEN

B Y THE TIME Joanne and Jimmy pulled into the driveway in Melrose, they had agreed that there had been no one following them. They had also discussed at some length the murder Keyes had witnessed and reported. Joanne surprised Jimmy when she told him of her ambivalence about the investigation. "I know Matt wouldn't agree with me, but I'm a little glad that Detective Collins never called back. The only missing people Matt and I could up with were a Navy captain and a FedEx deliveryman. If I was Collins, I probably would have round-filed the whole mess before this. Like he kept telling us, he's got plenty of real dead bodies and plenty of bad guys to keep him busy without having this phantom Matt thinks he saw to occupy his time."

Jimmy asked, "What about being followed by that man in the library. Doesn't that make you worry that there's something to Matt's suspicion?"

Joanne said nothing, but wrinkled her nose.

"He was real, Joanne."

"I know, Jimmy. That was Trygve Jensen, I'm sure of it. But Jensen's a strange man to begin with. He might have seen Matt in Boston and just decided to follow him. Jensen's retired now, and maybe he got curious and has too much time on his hands." She didn't believe that herself, but she couldn't come up with anything better.

Jimmy asked if she would mind if he called Detective Collins on Matt's behalf to follow up on the newspaper reports he had dropped off. No, she wouldn't mind, but she assured him that he was just chasing geese.

Joanne looked for Collins' card when they went inside while

Joshua claimed Jimmy as his own and led him by the hand to his sandbox. Jimmy sat on the edge of the box and pushed a toy truck through the sand. Joshua was using bulldozer to make a mountain of sand. In between the sounds of engines Joshua made, he peppered Jimmy with questions. "Do you have any children? What is it like where you live? Do you live near a school? Do you like to climb trees?"

Jimmy tried to make his answers just as straight to the point as Joshua's questions. Joshua listened to each answer and evidently satisfied, shoveled sand into Jimmy's truck. "You're supposed to dump it over there." Joshua pointed to another corner, and Jimmy followed instructions.

"Joshua," it was his mother, "would you let Jimmy come in here for a minute. He needs to make a phone call."

Joshua kept up the lingual motor noises and nodded that it was fine with him. Jimmy went inside and Joanne handed him Collins' card. "Do you want to call him now?"

Jimmy nodded. Joanne dialed the number and handed the phone to Jimmy.

"Homicide, this is Fatima Cabral. Can I help you?"

Jimmy had expected a man's voice. "Yes. I am trying to reach Detective Collins."

"He's not in right now. Can I leave a message, or can someone else help you?"

"Maybe. I'm calling for Matthew Keyes. He dropped off some newspaper reports a few weeks ago. Mr. Keyes asked me to follow up."

Fatima Cabral remembered Matthew Keyes; she had studied the face when he came in. Kind face. Handsome in a way. "I remember him. I'll leave a message for Detective Collins when he comes in. Can you give me your name and number?"

"My name is Jimmy. The last name is very long, so just plain Jimmy is fine." He read the number from the phone, thanked her, and hung up.

"He's not there?" Joanne was standing near him while he called.

"No. But the woman who answered said he would call back."

"That's what Matt said. But he never did call back." She was torn between wanting Matt's case to be resolved in a way that proved he wasn't dreaming and wanting the case to dry up like the season's falling leaves and blow away. She hugged Jimmy and said, "I'm sure he'll call back, Jimmy. And if he doesn't, we'll just call him again and again until he does."

***

THE TELEPHONE RANG at 4:30. Anne Stowe, Joanne, Joshua, and Jimmy were all crowded in the kitchen while Anne stirred a pot of spaghetti. Jimmy was inhaling the aroma of Italian sausage simmering in a fry pan as Joshua drew pictures in crayon for him. He talked as he colored. Trees, a dog, a horse. Joanne was arguing with her mother about the specific meaning of "al dente." Joanne was demonstrating how to throw a strand of spaghetti against the refrigerator door to test doneness. Anne insisted that throwing food was a stupid way to test anything. It was a noisy place.

Joanne picked up the phone and stepped into the dining room to avoid some of the noise. It was Collins.

"Thank you, Detective Collins. Yes, Matt's friend, Jimmy, called you. This is Joanne O'Byrne."

"I remember you, Miss O'Byrne. The message said something about an envelope Mr. Keyes dropped off at my office."

"Yes. Copies of newspaper articles about missing persons that he thought could be connected to his case."

"Look, Miss O'Byrne," Collins undoubtedly was having a bad day, and his impatience came through the phone line clearly. "I see lots of things come across my desk, but I never got any newspaper articles from Mr. Keyes. In fact, when I never heard anything more from him, I sent his report downstairs for filing."

Joanne was angry, and her tone let Collins know it. "If you want to stuff the report and call it closed, fine. Go right ahead. But

I was with Matt when we found the articles, and I went with him to the station when he dropped them off with your secretary. If you don't have it, you must have lost it. Or she did!" Anne came into the room at Joanne's raised voice. Joanne motioned her that she was fine.

"Miss O'Byrne, I didn't lose anything here but time, lots of precious time." He caught himself getting as angry with her as she had been. "Hold on a sec, please." He covered the phone with his palm and Joanne could hear him speak to someone else in his office. She could hear a woman's voice reply, but couldn't make out the words. Collins came back on the line. "I'm sorry. Mr. Keyes apparently was here and dropped something off at my office. But, honest, I never got whatever it was."

"Well, somebody got it!"

"Miss O'Byrne, if I told anyone here that I spent more than ten minutes looking into this case, based on evidence that doesn't exist, or even a body that doesn't exist except in Matthew Keyes' mind, I'd probably be fired in the morning. But look, can you get me copies of whatever he dropped off? I promise I'll take a look and get back to you."

"You bet. You'll have copies on your desk tomorrow morning."

"Thanks, Miss O'Byrne. And, uh, if I sound a little fried, I apologize."

"No offense taken. You'll get your envelope, and I'll wait to hear from you." The phone was returned to its cradle with a slam.

When Joanne walked back in the kitchen, it was silent.

***

JIMMY ACCOMPANIED JOANNE on her drive to work the next morning. He would have the day to himself and play tourist. Before he could begin, however, he needed to complete two assignments. Joanne had recorded the dates and page numbers of the newspapers she and Matt had found at the library, and had given Jimmy directions on locating the library and finding the Microtext room. He would get two sets of copies and deliver one to Collins' office at headquarters. She wanted to keep an extra set for herself, just in case.

They drove from Melrose into the bottleneck that is sometimes called Interstate 93. Joanne weaved through the traffic while Jimmy gripped the armrest. They swerved from Storrow Drive into the narrow streets of Back Bay and parked on Stanhope Street, a short two-block walk to the Crane & Stewart offices.

Jimmy hurried to keep up with Joanne as she walked briskly along Stuart Street. Jimmy had seen traffic jams before, and the noisy, crowded streets of Sao Paolo where he attended college were threatening enough for him. He stayed close to Joanne as she darted and dared her way across Clarendon and Boylston between moving cars and buses. It was part of daily life for Joanne, but to Jimmy it was mayhem.

Armed with maps of the streets of Boston and the subway system, Jimmy returned Joanne's hug and kiss, and set off for the Boston Public Library. There he quickly found the Microtext room and asked the librarian if she would make copies of the articles Joanne had marked down for him. He was about to be told by the librarian to first go upstairs and receive a library card, but she saw that his request was clearly and completely written out, and making the copies would take only minutes. She retrieved the microfilms, made the copies, and Jimmy was on his way shortly.

The next stop was the police station building, and he found it without trouble on Berkeley. He asked the guard at the front door for the office of detective Collins, and then was directed to the stairway on the right. "It's a little early, so there might not be anybody there for a few more minutes," the guard said. Jimmy looked at his watch. It was 8:20. He found the office and knocked before entering. When he walked in, he discovered a woman, obviously startled and anxiously reaching into a bottom drawer of her desk, apparently stubbing out a cigarette. Wisps of smoke curling from her lips betrayed her. Fatima Cabral's violation of the smoking regulations had been interrupted, and she was muttering angrily. Jimmy was surprised to hear such expletives from this lady, more astonished that the words she used were Portuguese, and impressed that these crudest and vilest of words rolled so easily from her mouth. She slammed the drawer closed and snapped at Jimmy, furious that he was smiling at catching her in her transgression. "What do you want?"

Jimmy addressed Fatima Cabral in his finest and most polite Portuguese. "Please forgive me for barging in on you like this with no notice, madam. It was not my intent to trouble you." Fatima Cabral was momentarily speechless. She rose from her chair and responded with a grace that belied her previous vulgarity.

"You have not caused me trouble, sir. Please come in and sit down. May I offer you a cup of coffee."

"Yes, that would be very nice."

"Cream or sugar?"

He asked for both, and she poured the freshly made coffee into a paper cup.

"You surprised me with your beautiful Portuguese. You speak it very well."

"I am from Brazil, and it is the language in which I was raised. Please call me Jimmy. And you are …?" He sipped the hot, strong coffee awaiting her reply.

"Fatima Cabral. From Lisboa." She was almost blushing.

"Ah," said Jimmy knowingly, as if that would explain everything.

"I apologize for cursing when you first came in. I didn't expect anyone here so early."

"I am here to drop off some information for a gentleman named Collins. I have it here." He placed the envelope on the desk. Fatima read the words: To Detective Collins from Matthew Keyes.

She recognized the name. "He will be here in a few minutes. I will be sure he gets this. You are a friend of Matthew Keyes?"

Jimmy and Fatima went on for several more minutes chatting comfortably in their native tongues. Jimmy explained that Matt had dropped off a similar packet some time ago, but that Collins claimed to have never received it. This caused Fatima Cabral to scowl and explain that she herself had placed the envelope in the proper tray. She could not understand how it could have been misplaced, but she would hand this to Collins personally.

Jimmy finished his coffee and rose to leave. "You have been most gracious, Miss Cabral. Thank you for the coffee."

***

JIMMY LEFT HEADQUARTERS to begin his tour of the city. He reached into his back pocket to retrieve his map when he spotted a tall, thin man standing on the sidewalk directly across the street. When they made eye contact, the man quickly turned and walked slowly along the sidewalk. But Jimmy had held contact long enough to place the eyes as those of the man driving the white sedan that was following them the day before. From the way the man abruptly turned when Jimmy saw him, Jimmy was sure that this man was following him again.

Jimmy stayed where he was and watched the man reach the end of the block and wait to cross. He glanced once over his shoulder in Jimmy's direction, who pretended to study his map and decided that he would let this game play out for a little while. He wanted some time, but he was an outsider in this city and would be disadvantaged. He meandered slowly along the sidewalk and tried to think the situation through. He felt there was some connection here with Matt's case; after all, he was a stranger in this country, unknown to all but a few. He was certain that this was the same man who followed them yesterday. As if to confirm this, he moved his eyes to the right, trying to keep the tall man in sight. He was still there, angular, rangy, dressed in a green sports coat and walking in the same direction, glancing occasionally across the street to keep Jimmy in view.

He thought through his options and walked slowly. Call Matt. Call Joanne. Call Collins. It was a short list. Matt was out; too far away to do anything about the matter right now. Joanne was a better possibility, and he reserved that thought. Collins. If he could get to

Collins, he would accomplish what? Maybe find out who this man is tailing him. Maybe piece together something to advance Matt's case. He decided this would be his first step. If that didn't achieve anything positive, he would still have Joanne.

He reached a corner and looked at the street sign. Newbury and Berkeley. He looked around for a pay phone, and seeing none, walked up Newbury Street. He could see that the direction he had chosen had numerous restaurants and shops. The search for a telephone was promising. He looked across the street, trying to keep the follower in view. He didn't see him, and stopped, pretending to consult his map again. He looked behind him and saw that the tall man was now perhaps fifty yards to his rear, looking at a storefront display. Jimmy folded the map and continued walking, sighting a public telephone just ahead. As he approached the phone, he reached into his pocket and removed Collins' card that Joanne had given him earlier. He read the directions on the phone, deposited coins, and carefully pressed the numbers.

"Collins."

"Yes, sir. I was at your office a while ago and dropped off an envelope for you from Matthew Keyes."

"I have it here. I haven't opened it yet, but like I told Miss O'Byrne yesterday, she shouldn't expect anything to happen right away. Tell her I'll get to it as soon as I can."

Collins waited for some response, but there was nothing. He hung up. It was a puzzling the way for the call to end, but he barely gave it a thought and returned his attention to his desk and the mountain of cases he faced.

The envelope was on top, placed there by Fatima with some insistence that he not lose it this time. He opened it and slid out the photocopied articles. A small story about a missing FedEx deliveryman. The case was fairly close to Boston and he called Fatima over to his desk.

"Fatima, when you have a minute, call the Natick police and see if you can get a description of this guy."

Fatima took the article to her desk, looked up the number for Natick and dialed.

Collins looked at the second, much longer article about Henry Oates, with a photograph of the captain. He read the article with some interest and was about to slide the contents back into place when he paused in thought.

He was interrupted by Fatima, who called over to him. "This guy's five seven, African American, one fifty-five, had his head shaved bald at the time of his disappearance. What else do you want? I've got Natick on hold here."

"Nothing else. Thanks." The guy was about six inches too short and five shades too dark for Keyes' man at the Prudential Tower.

He picked up the Oates article again. He had come across that name recently, and he tried to recall where. Oates. The name was on a recent routine FBI bulletin that circulated through the department. Something about the wife of a deceased high up Navy guy, wanted for income tax evasion and related questioning. He marked the name on a slip of paper and handed it to Fatima with instructions to find a copy of that report.

Fatima Cabral liked to be sent off to other departments from time to time. It gave her the chance to occasionally sneak out for a quick cigarette while her bosses would think she was busy elsewhere. But when she saw that this errand dealt with the envelope Jimmy had just dropped off, she put aside any thoughts of smoking and headed off. It took her twenty minutes to find the report and obtain a copy. She read it on the way back to Homicide.

Pretty lady, she thought when she saw the photograph of Rosemary Oates on the bulletin. Wanted for questioning. Income tax evasion. Wife of recently deceased Navy Captain Henry Oates. Departed U.S. in July. Recently reentered U.S. through Miami. The bulletin listed several cities where she would most likely be expected to be found. Washington was listed first, with Boston as number eight. The bulletin cautioned that Mrs. Oates was as yet unaware of the search being conducted. No press releases will be made by the bureau until apprehension, it said. The bulletin was three days old.

***

JIMMY NEVER SAW the tall man approach from behind. He felt an intense pressure at a point just above the base of his spine and smelled the sour, stale breath of the tall man simultaneously. "Hang up the phone." Jimmy did as he was told and didn't consider resisting. "You're going to walk in front of me, and I'm going to have a gun in my pocket aimed at you at all times. I'll tell you where to go." Jimmy walked down Newbury Street and turned left onto Clarendon when he was told. The man spoke in a low voice. "If you try to run, I'll shoot you. But even if I miss, I'll get Joanne O'Byrne, or her mother, or the little kid. And you'll remember forever that you could have stopped it." Jimmy understood perfectly. They walked in silence until they reached a parking lot and the tall man directed him to the white sedan he and Joanne had seen yesterday. The tall man ordered him into the passenger seat. Jimmy bent over to enter, felt a sharp heavy pain in his neck, and blacked out.

The tall man pushed Jimmy's small frame onto the floor of the car and closed the door. He opened the trunk and retrieved a dirty blanket. Opening the driver's side door, he entered the car and covered Jimmy with the blanket.

***

THE SECOND CONTACT Munroe received from Rosemary Oates took the form of a gift presented to him at a dinner in Seattle. Munroe had just delivered a rousing speech on the great future of the Northwest in the twenty-first century. The audience had loved it. After dinner, in a special reception at the hotel for selected invitees only, Munroe posed for photographs with his guests, joked, and laughed with them. To any onlooker, Munroe had the manner of a relaxed but energetic future president. Leland Hayes, standing near the door, was pleased with Munroe's performance tonight. He had flown in yesterday, interrupting his scheduled meetings in Philadelphia on the upcoming debates to meet with his candidate on an "emergency basis" and calm him down. The call came from the Chairman himself, and there was mixture of anger and fear in the man's voice. "We've got a major problem on our hands, and you have to keep Jack from exploding. He's on the edge." When Hayes pressed for information, the cause of the alarm was described as "none of you're fucking business." He accepted that there would be reasons from time to time for discretion, and that there were some other incidents in this campaign that were bothersome, but he resented the fact that he felt ignored and unimportant at times, that he was being asked to operate blind. Nevertheless, he apologized profusely to the opposition's campaign chairman, obliquely citing a sudden illness, and jumped a flight to Seattle at once.

Lisa Sobolewski met Hayes at the hotel. She cautioned him that Munroe was not himself, that he had been nearly catatonic on the chartered flight from Montana. She had hastily changed flights and schedules to keep Munroe under wraps and out of public view until Hayes arrived. This meant canceling a breakfast meeting in Boise with the Idaho Potato Growers Confederation and an appearance in Olympia with Governor Forbes, one of Munroe's early supporters. These were trivial, however, compared to his upcoming scheduled appearance on *Meet the Press* and the debate preparations that were scheduled to follow.

Sobolewski's warnings didn't prepare him for the Jack Munroe Hayes saw. When he entered the candidate's suite, he saw Munroe curled up on a sofa and sobbing. Earl was seated in the chair opposite him, carefully watching over Munroe. Over the next four hours, Hayes and Sobolewski sat with him and reassured him. Occasionally, Munroe would blubber about the call that came to his room in Montana the night before. Nothing more than, "She knows everything." Or, "I'm done."

Sobolewski couldn't fill in any of the gaps, even though, Hayes learned, she was present when Munroe received the phone call. Based on the times he had been told when he was called to this mission, he surmised that this unknown female caller must have reached Munroe at about 1 o'clock in the morning, Mountain Time. That Lisa Sobolewski would be with Munroe in his room at that hour was curious to him. He would file that away for later.

The immediate challenge was getting Munroe in some kind of shape for the evening's dinner. Munroe had recited the text of his speech so often that Hayes was not worried about him stumbling. Once Jack began, he'd do fine. The problem was getting Jack to dress up and show up. They had less than five hours. In between the sobs, Hayes and Sobolewski worked magic, convincing Munroe that this woman, whoever she was, was a red herring, a plant by the opposition. The Chairman had already started working on stopping this threat, Hayes went on, and Munroe began to feel somewhat at ease.

Progress came in small steps, but by the time the dinner began, Munroe was bursting with his usual enthusiasm, shaking the hands of well-wishers with a firm grasp, and using that smile to his advantage. If Munroe was a quivering mass of frightened jelly inside, observers saw nothing but a sure and confident winner.

The reception suite began to empty, and by 11, the only ones remaining were Hayes, Sobolewski, Todd Bernard and Waylon Jump from the Secret Service, and Munroe. A table set at the side of the entry door had been set up for gifts, tokens, and especially envelopes with checks for the campaign. As usual, anything left for the candidate this late in the campaign was first checked over by Secret Service. Letter bombs hadn't been used for a long time, but that didn't deter the search. Hayes was handed the envelopes by Jump, and they moved out of the room to a service elevator. The candidate was especially buoyant tonight, and he winked at Hayes saying, "I don't know how to thank you." The explanation was unspoken in the presence of Bernard and Jump, who otherwise had become quite friendly with those closest to the candidate.

Jack asked Hayes for the envelopes. He wanted to flip through them on the way back to his room to see who had given what. "This is one we've been waiting for, eh Leland?" He held up the back of the envelope for Hayes to see the donor's name and address. George Takehito owned the largest fish-processing firm in the state of Washington and was extraordinarily wealthy. He was also one of the biggest contributors to the opposition party in prior years. Munroe had a reason to be pleased.

Hayes knew that Munroe's campaign couldn't spend all the money it had access to if it tried. Nevertheless, the Chairman pointed out, the wealthy expect to be asked for money. "It makes them feel like they have a solid connection with the candidate," he said. "Remember, Leland, to the other guys, every last buck is important, and they'll chase promises of contributions back and forth across the country. Wasting time and energy, Leland, is what they're doing. You just keep scheduling these little parties as Jack goes from state to state. The people who contribute will feel grateful, believe me."

Munroe continued flipping through the evening's stack of envelopes, commenting occasionally on the nature or personality of the donor. "Here's one with no name." Munroe peeled the white envelope open and removed a sheet of light blue stationery. He began to read and Hayes saw his mouth sag. It was a bad sign. The elevator came to a stop and the group moved as one towards the candidate's room. Munroe was staring blankly by this time, his arms dangling at his side. Sobolewski held him by the arm.

"Jack, what's wrong?" Munroe's eyes were glazed over. He didn't answer, but simply held out the blue paper for Lisa. They entered the room, the Secret Service checking each corner and closet before leaving silently.

Lisa began to read. It was a short note written in a flowing hand: "Records, transcripts, deposit slips, account numbers, receipts, types, serial numbers, shipping records, times, and dates. They will be yours. Or someone else's. For a fee. The phone call was just the beginning." It was signed "The Captain's Beloved Wife and Grieving Widow."

Lisa was puzzled. She handed the letter to Hayes and went to Munroe, who was standing where he had been when they entered. He had not moved. Lisa could see the same hypnotic stare she had seen before. A single tear ran down his cheek.

CHAPTER SIXTEEN

J IMMY'S FIRST SENSATIONS were the taste and smell of oily dirt. He tried to move, but the throbbing pain at the base of his skull was intense. He opted for staying in position and opening his right eye.

He could sense a source of artificial light overhead as soon as he opened the eye a crack. His head was pounding with pain and even the effort of opening one eye and moving it made the pain worse. He would have to take this in small steps.

He was enclosed in a small room of some kind. Musty. Damp. He could see a wooden door. Carefully he moved his eye to take note of the latch. It was a simple latch mechanism. Next to the door he saw a bamboo rake with a third of its tines either missing or broken. A light switch was adjacent to the door. Must control the source of light overhead, he considered.

He closed his eye and dared to try raising himself from the floor. Every movement caused excruciating pain in his left shoulder, his neck, and his skull. His chest ached with every intake of breath. He recalled being struck once, but that was just the first of several, he was sure. He decided that he must have been hit at least a few more times later on. He placed the palm of his right hand flat on the floor and used it as a fulcrum. Slowly he moved his left arm to a corresponding position. Carefully he applied pressure and started to force his upper body to move, bending at the waist so that he was next fixed on his hands and knees. He could feel stickiness around his collar and decided that he must have been bleeding. Maybe he was bleeding still. He remained still for several minutes to gain control of his breathing and to assess his condition.

He tried turning his head left and then right. Up, then down.

The head pain was modifying into a dull ache. His shoulder and neck were continuing to experience sharp bolts of pain, but he slowly flexed the muscles in the area and decided that nothing felt broken. He paused again to allow his body to adjust, but this time he took in more of his surroundings. He guessed the room to be approximately ten by twelve and it was used as a storage room for outdoor equipment. A bare lightbulb hung from the ceiling in the center of the room. The only way in or out was through the wooden door at the center of the short end wall. To the left of the door was an assortment of items, all reflecting years of neglect. A straw broom with just a stubble of dirty straw left at the end. Cobwebs everywhere. Two pieces of fence post, both punky, rotted at the ends. A rusting metal pail. The skeleton of an outdoor umbrella, with a few torn remnants of faded green canvass still clinging stubbornly to the frame. Layers of dirt and dust coated every surface.

Jimmy stretched his body and rose slowly from his knees to a crouch, and feeling no added pain, reached his full height. He rubbed his shoulder and felt for the source of blood. His scalp had been lacerated, but the flow of blood had stopped. He gently peeled back the collar of his shirt to help the blood dry out and allow him some greater freedom of movement.

He turned around to continue surveying his prison cell. There were no windows. In a rear corner stood the tired remnants of a lawn mower, its wheels removed and its engine frozen with rust and scale. Next to it was an opened can of motor oil, its top thick with grime. An assortment of plastic flowerpots was stacked in another corner, and next to that a small, glass, baby food jar that contained two small screws, a finish nail, and a lock washer.

Jimmy bent down to pick up the rusty pail with hopes that, when turned upside down, it would furnish his new home with a place to sit. It worked. He sat and considered his options.

He looked around the room once again and surveyed the scene. Almost immediately he rose, stepped to the door and tried the latch. Locked. Probably padlocked. He looked at the door hinges. Rusted but substantial, and he decided to give the door a push. He pressed his right shoulder against it and exerted as much force as he could. The pain from his damaged left shoulder streaked through his body, causing him to fall to the dirt floor in a sweat. The door didn't move at all. Jimmy resumed his seat on the upside-down bucket. It was warm, so he decided to turn off the light. The room was pitched into near total darkness. He squatted and peeked through a space in the door through which the latch mechanism passed and which now served as the only pinhole of light. Through the slim sliver of an aperture, Jimmy could make out the edge of a large barn, and beyond that, the corner of a white house. He guessed himself to be twenty feet from the garage and sixty feet from the house. He saw a gravel driveway, but he could see no cars. There were no noises outside, no sign of life nearby. He sat down once again and tried to organize his thoughts.

***

AT 5 O'CLOCK that afternoon, Joanne O'Byrne sat on the edge of Phyllis Rhodes' reception desk at Crane & Stewart, looking at her watch periodically, and swinging a leg back and forth with impatience. Jimmy was overdue, and Joanne was getting anxious and angry at the same time. He had assured her that he would be back no later than 4:30, and that he would call the office if there was any problem. Phyllis Rhodes encouraged Joanne to relax. "I'll be here until 5:30 anyway. Why don't you get a cup of coffee and sit down. I'm sure he'll be here soon. He probably just got distracted or maybe he's on one of those sight-seeing rides and can't call right now."

Joanne said nothing, but glared at Phyllis. She grabbed her purse and walked back to her office. She saw no reasonable way of locating Jimmy right now, and maybe she could get some work done while she waited.

She looked through a stack of time charges, but she couldn't focus and she put them down. Instead, she took a blank time charge sheet and tried to fill in where Jimmy might have gone during the day. She started at 8 o'clock and wrote 'Library' in the space. She allowed a full hour there, even though it could have been much faster. She gave him ten minutes to walk to "Police HQ" and inserted that at ten past nine. She dropped down to 4:30, inserted "Return" in that spot, and studied the huge blank space in the middle. To the side she jotted down notes: Fanueil Hall, Quincy Market, Harvard Square, Old North Church, North End. She tried to remember the names of places Jimmy had mentioned. She tapped the pencil on her desk, then reached for her phone and called Matt.

It was almost 5:30 when he picked up the phone. He sat back and smiled when he heard Joanne's voice. As quickly, he sat upright and listened. Joanne was upset. Jimmy was supposed to be there an hour ago. She sounded close to panic, and Matt tried to soothe her by coming up with possibilities.

"You sound just like Phyllis. She said the same thing. But I'm getting nervous, Matt. Was he ever unreliable when you worked with him?" Matt conceded that Jimmy was extremely prompt and reliable, but suggested that Boston, being a new city to him, perhaps he just lost track of time and didn't realize the distance back to her office.

Joanne wanted to dismiss that idea. It didn't sound like Jimmy. She agreed to wait until 6 and to call Matt later. When Phyllis left the office, Joanne sat at the reception desk and watched the phone.

***

ROSEMARY OATES STEPPED off the plane in Boston and hailed a taxi to the Four Seasons Hotel. There, her bags were attended to as she checked in, using the name on her Swiss passport, her maiden name: R. Anne Madden. Henry had insisted on that precaution two years ago, and now she was glad she indulged him. She was also delighted with the progress she had made with Munroe. She was prepared to continue the contest and was somewhat disappointed that she would not be able to enjoy dropping more names, dates, and other increasingly specific information into Munroe's lap.

She wished she could have seen Munroe's face when he read the note that she arranged to be placed at the hotel reception in Seattle.

The hotel had been so obliging. Of course, as soon as her express delivery arrived, they would see that the envelope was delivered at once. It was too easy. Her follow-up phone call was intended to relay one more incriminating list to her prey. Then she would establish a dollar amount and a drop-off point. Instead, he was ready to deal. There was no arguing about the price. He sounded shaken, but three million was agreed to with no hesitation. Later, on the flight from Baltimore to Boston, she wondered if she should have opened higher. The location caused a bit of arguing. He insisted on Boston, while she preferred New York. She had hoped to grab the Amtrak from Penn Station to Montreal and from there the Swiss Air flight to Zurich, but Boston suited her almost as well. Besides, Munroe had said the money was there already, in cash.

She agreed that a meeting place and time would be sent to her room with a bottle of champagne at precisely 7:30. But Rosemary Oates had her own plan, and she wanted to control the meeting place. She'd send a return message of her own: The meeting had to be in public and during the day. She decided South Station. In front of the main entry. Plenty of pedestrian traffic at that time. Nowhere for the senator to run and nowhere for him to hide. And tomorrow morning at 8. For Rosemary, it would be a short walk from there to the 8:15 Amtrak train to Springfield and Montreal. By tomorrow evening, she'd be in First Class on Air Canada's flight to London. Then on to Zurich. And Henry's plan would be complete.

She rode the elevator with the bellman and followed him down the hall to her room. She had asked for a suite overlooking Boston Common and was pleased when the bellman opened the drapes to see that her wishes had been accommodated. When he returned with a fresh bucket of ice, she handed him a ten-dollar bill, poured herself a Perrier from the in room bar and sat in the overstuffed armchair to relax.

***

WORD REACHED THE Farm at 7 o'clock that Matthew Keyes was ticketed on an early morning flight from Burlington to Boston. This was expected. The daily phone call from Keyes to O'Byrne came earlier than usual and was tense and brief. He would come to Boston immediately and search with Joanne for Jimmy. Keyes also agreed that Joanne should call Collins at once and advise him of Jimmy's failure to appear. The Chairman spoke with Hayes and directed him to send Earl back to Boston at once. That was the subject of some debate, with Hayes insisting that Munroe needed Earl at his side. "Munroe is paranoid enough as it is, sir. Earl gives him some stability, even if he doesn't say much. I'm afraid if we send him away, Munroe will go off the deep end. Believe me, sir, he is hanging on right now by a thread."

The Chairman agreed, but reluctantly. He would have to use Hector, the pockmarked, skinny one he called "Stretch." He would have preferred Earl's quiet muscle, but he had to agree that Hector could be as efficient. He was certainly a mean bastard when he needed to be. He had beaten the daylights out of that little Brazilian fellow in the shed. He would have at least two more assignments for Hector.

Now that Keyes would be coming to Boston, the Chairman saw the game converging into a whirling vortex, where Matthew Keyes, Joanne O'Byrne, Rosemary Oates, and the little Brazilian would disappear into a black hole. He worked out a plan in his mind that would spell permanent relief for Jack Munroe. Finally, he could get on with the business of becoming President. If only Hayes can keep him contained for even another day.

***

AT 7:30, DETECTIVE Collins received a message on his beeper and returned the call to Joanne O'Byrne. Since he had read the full account in the *New York Times* about Oates' body turning up in Connecticut, as well as the FBI bulletin about Oates' wife, he was beginning to put a great deal of stock in the events Matthew Keyes had first reported last November. The interrupted phone call from Keyes' messenger this morning didn't cause him much concern at the time, but now that the fellow was missing, there were too many curiosities to call it just another coincidence.

Collins arranged to meet Joanne at Logan when Matt arrived in the morning. Meanwhile, he would circulate Jimmy's description throughout the department and try to find him. He didn't tell Joanne that there was also a confirmation that Rosemary Oates had departed Baltimore that afternoon. Using her maiden name, she purchased three tickets. One to New York, another to Chicago, and a third to Boston. The FBI was already working with the airlines to determine which city was her true destination. From there, it would be a matter of checking with the city's hotels. If she was in or around any of those cities, Collins expected that she would be arrested and in custody before dawn.

Joanne was reassured that Matt was on his way. She also took some comfort from Collins' distinct change in attitude. She only wished that the change had come sooner. She was desperately worried about Jimmy.

Joanne's mother put Joshua to bed that evening. Joshua asked questions about Jimmy. Where is he? Why didn't he come home with Mommy? Anne Stowe explained that Jimmy had some work to do and that he would be coming back soon. She immediately switched the conversation to Halloween, which would be celebrated in a few short weeks. Joanne remained downstairs. She had been on the phone with Collins and paced the floor in thought when she hung up.

Impulsively, Joanne went into the pantry behind the kitchen, opened her mother's handbag, and removed a pack of Marlboro Lights. She took a cigarette and a book of matches and went outside to the porch. A full moon cast a gentle light across the neighborhood. She lit up and inhaled deeply. She hadn't smoked a cigarette in four years and the sensation made her momentarily dizzy. She took another drag and sat in the wicker chair she remembered being on this porch when she was Joshua's age.

There was little she could do about Jimmy that she had not already done. The police were looking for him. Matt would be flying into Boston soon. She rose from her chair and went to the steps of the porch where she put out the cigarette in an old flowerpot.

Less than fifty feet away, Hector stood hidden in the shadow of a large maple tree. He watched Joanne finish her smoke and instinctively reached for his pack in the pocket of his green sports coat. It would wait, though, at least for a few more minutes. He didn't want to bring attention to himself by lighting up right now. He checked the luminous dial of his wristwatch. 8:15. Plenty of time to get his work done and still be ready for tomorrow.

***

KEYES' ARRIVAL IN Boston was late by ten minutes, which was fortuitous for Collins, who was having a devil's time trying to get through the Callahan Tunnel to Logan Airport. When he finally reached the gate, he saw Joanne O'Byrne nervously pacing the waiting area. She saw him approaching and waved her hand, telling him that Matt's plane had just landed and was on its way to the gate.

"Any news about Jimmy?" Joanne looked tired and pale. Collins could see that the stress of the past day was taking its toll on her.

"Nothing yet. We passed the missing persons report to the State Police, and his description is in every police station in the area this morning. I asked the department to page me if they had any news at all."

"Thanks," she said.

Collins was about to add that Rosemary Oates had been traced to Boston, and that the FBI was probably interrogating her at this very moment. But he saw Joanne on tiptoe, straining to see the nose of Keyes' plane ease up to the gate. He would tell them both later.

Keyes trotted off the plane, weaving past other passengers to greet Joanne standing at the head of the Jetway. He gave her a great hug and kiss, then they walked arm in arm to where Collins was standing. Keyes shook his hand and Collins suggested that they sit down at the coffee shop and talk through the facts for a few minutes. Now that Keyes was here, he hoped to assemble some details and draw a more complete picture of the case. Collins received a copy of Oates' autopsy report from the Windham County Sheriff's Office by fax yesterday with a detailed description of the fatal wound. He also visited the Prudential Tower last night and the building manager assured him that he would pull the maintenance and other building records for last November and present Collins with a package this afternoon. Perhaps with Keyes here, he might be able to gather some additional helpful information and maybe put a few pieces together.

The three entered a cafeteria in the terminal. Each ordered coffee and sat in a booth, as far as possible from the nearest customers. Collins removed a small notebook from his jacket pocket and opened it, placing it on the table. He began by asking Keyes about the assault he witnessed last November. After a short pause, Matt answered with certitude. "The left side of the head, I'm sure. He was standing to my right, and whatever he was hit with, it was in the other guy's right hand. I remember seeing him reach behind him with his right hand."

Collins reached into his breast pocket and removed his copy of the summary findings of the autopsy of Henry Oates. "The newspaper article you found on Captain Henry Oates led me to call the Medical Examiner in Connecticut, who performed the autopsy. The sheriff's department there sent me this." Collins turned the report around so that Matt and Joanne could see it and pointed with his pen to the appropriate section.

It read: "A wound is presented on the subject's skull, a puncture wound, roughly circular in shape and twenty-four millimeters in diameter, on the left side, one and three quarter inches above and one inch forward of the glenoid fossa. Fragments of the sphenoid and temporal bone are present, with two fragments remaining affixed to the wound, bent inward. The middle cerebral artery is severed by one of the fragments. Other fragments are found embedded in the cortex. The depth of the wound is approximately three and one quarter inches. This suggests a penetration wound to the subject.

No foreign fragments or indications of a projectile wound such as a bullet were found."

Matt and Joanne read in silence.

Collins waited until they were finished. "Oates was struck by something hard and probably round, with enough force to puncture his skull and penetrate his brain. Can you think back and try to see what it was?"

Keyes shrugged. "I've tried several times since then, but it happened very quickly."

Collins used the opportunity to describe the disappearance and later reappearance of this deceased's widow, and the FBI activity in attempting to apprehend her. His audience sat in stunned silence.

"The FBI doesn't say very much, but it seems that Captain Oates was involved in a scheme where he used his Pentagon position for his own financial gain. Apparently, there was a lot of money running through this man's hands, and he set himself up quite well. His widow moved to an island in the Caribbean after he turned up dead, and the FBI has been waiting for her to make a move to come back to the states. I already spoke with the head of the Boston office and explained the possible connection her late husband had with your case. There's not a lot to go on, but there are enough unusual circumstances that the FBI agreed to let me speak with Mrs. Oates when they bring her in."

At that moment, his beeper sounded and he excused himself to find a phone.

The minutes he was away were filled with worried kisses and bits of conversation between Matt and Joanne. Matt was clearly exhausted, and so was Joanne. "I think I feel as bad as you look, Matt," Joanne said, raising the hint of a smile from him.

Collins returned to the booth, but remained standing. His brow was furrowed. "That was my partner on the phone. The FBI caught up with Rosemary Oates. She was just found dead in her suite at the Four Seasons Hotel."

Joanne gasped at the news and put her hand to her face. Matt stared at Collins, trying to make some sense of the news and wondering what the implications were for finding Jimmy. Collins took his seat and breathed deeply. "I have to head over there now. But I want you both to go home to Melrose and stay indoors and out of sight for a while. We have to operate on the assumption that whoever is responsible for killing Mrs. Oates is also somehow tied in with Jimmy's disappearance. And if I'm right, that means that both of you could also be in danger."

Joanne reached to hold Matt's hand while Collins spoke. Keyes was about to ask a question of Collins but hesitated. He looked at Joanne, whose eyes were damp with tears. Collins opened his notebook and flipped through some pages before he found what he wanted.

"I'm supposed to be at the Prudential at 3 this afternoon, but I'll be lucky to make it there by 7. They're supposed to have the building records available for me today." Collins looked at Keyes and continued, "I'll plan on calling you after I've had a chance to look them over. If you need to reach me before then, if Jimmy turns up at home, or whatever, I want you to call me right away. The department will page me if I'm not there."

When he left, Joanne put her head on Matt's shoulder and wept. They stayed in the booth for a few minutes before they wordlessly left and walked slowly to the parking garage and left the airport.

Joanne was the first to break the silence on the drive home. "Matt, what can we do about Jimmy? I can't think of a place to start."

"There's not much we can do, Joanne, except wait and hope that Jimmy's safe." They drove in silence through the narrow, busy, industrial streets of Chelsea, cutting across the crowded roads of Medford, making their way to the tree-lined residential streets of Melrose. When she and Alan O'Byrne were married, they lived in the town of Belmont, in a rambling, four-bedroom white clapboard ranch with a manicured lawn. Alan had insisted on a home in a community that would reflect some prestige. (His mother would call it "cachet.") Joanne, though, had grown up in Melrose, where older homes were closer together and neighbors still sat on their porches and called over to each other. Belmont, she told Alan, was lovely, but she found it an antiseptic life. She hardly knew any neighbors, and the ones she knew she didn't care for. So when she and Alan divorced and she moved back to Melrose to live with her mother, she welcomed the enormous trees and the narrow house lots. Someday she hoped to establish a home of her own, and she would look for one in a community more like her own.

Keyes slowed as he approached an intersection when Joanne saw a white sedan cross their path. It was driven by a young woman with a child's car seat in the rear, but it caught her eye and she pointed at it and burst out, "A white car!"

Her sudden shout startled Matt, who turned to look at the car and back to Joanne. "What is it, Joanne?"

"A white car. When Jimmy and I were coming back from picking apples the other day, he thought we were being followed. It was a white car like that one. I turned off on a side street and the car went right by, so I figured it wasn't following us, but maybe it was."

"That was a Buick that just went by. Was it a Buick you saw the other day?"

"It could have been. I'm not sure, but it just struck me. Even though it drove by, it gave me kind of a creepy feeling." She looked over at Matt, who tried to fit this bit of data into place, but who obviously found it difficult. "Not much help, huh?"

He drove on and made the turn onto Carter Street. Ahead of them, six houses up on the right and directly in front of Joanne's mother's home were two Melrose police cruisers, both with blue lights flashing. He pulled up behind them and Joanne was out the door before the car rolled to a stop. Matt ran after her. On the front porch, Joanne was listening to a police officer who put a hand on her arm as he spoke. Anne Stowe had been standing on the small deck at the side door, saw Matt, and wailed in wild distress. Another officer stood with her, obviously trying to calm her and to ask questions. She cried out to Matt in broken sobs, "Joshua," she yelled out. "My Joshua, he's gone!"

A third cruiser suddenly screeched to a halt in the middle of the road and two officers ran out. Keyes watched the scene playing out, rooted in place, unable to move in any direction, but completely aware of every sound, every voice. His head pounded with fury and fear. "Where was he when you last saw him, ma'am? What color pants was he wearing? We're going house to house now. Did you hear anything at all?"

He saw Joanne run into the house, crying for her son, and Anne being eased inside by a police officer as she shrieked in agonized cries of grief. A policeman suddenly appeared at Keyes' side, and Matt heard him ask, "Are you the boy's father?"

"No," he answered, still watching the activity in front of him, and in an even voice that surprised him for its calm.

"I'm …his father lives in California somewhere. San Diego." He suddenly turned to face the officer. "What happened? What's happened to Joshua?"

"We think he's been abducted, but we're not sure,' the officer replied. "We're trying to find out now."

"Abducted …kidnapped." Keyes wasn't asking a question. It was a statement.

The officer said nothing at first, but looked at Matt's vacant stare. "Do you know the father? I mean, was there any problem with visitation rights or child support? Anything like that?"

"No. Not at all. It's not the boy's father."

Keyes walked away from the officer and opened the door. Joanne met him, running into his arms, sobbing angry tears. "They've got Joshua, Matt. The fucking bastards took Joshua." She pounded on his chest with her fists, her face drenched from weeping, strands of hair matted to her skin.

***

WITHIN FORTY MINUTES, only one cruiser remained at 52 Carter Street in Melrose. One of the two remaining officers sat at the kitchen table with Joanne's mother asking questions and taking notes. The other was with Joanne and Matt in the living room, looking at several photographs of Joshua. Joanne pointed to a snapshot of Joshua standing in the middle of his sandbox, smiling straight into the camera's lens. "That one is the best likeness of him," Joanne said as the officer held it in his hands. He would hold onto it for now, he said.

The three looked at the front door when they heard the doorbell. The officer went over at once and opened it. He spoke a few words to whoever was there and walked back into the room, followed by a short, balding man in a rumpled gray jacket. "This is Detective Lyons," the officer said, introducing the newcomer.

Lyons explained the current situation as he knew it. At approximately 9 o'clock, Joshua went out the side door of the house to play in his sandbox. He had eaten breakfast at approximately 7:30, and Mrs. Stowe helped him get dressed before he went out. Mrs. Stowe kept the side door open when he went out so she could hear him outside. Between 9 o'clock and 9:10, she checked on him at least once and saw him playing alone. At 9:15, she looked outside and didn't see Joshua, so she went outside to the backyard. After several minutes of searching for him in the adjacent yards and across the street, she returned to the house, checked inside the house to see if he might have come in the front door. When she couldn't find him, she called 911 and reported him missing. The call came in at 9:22.

Police officers had searched every yard in the neighborhood and questioned neighbors. No one reported seeing the boy and no one reported anything unusual. There were no reports of strangers or strange cars in the area.

"I just got off the phone with the San Diego police," Lyons went on, "and they visited the boy's father at his home and found him there. He was identified as Alan O'Byrne. They checked his driver's license and his photo was a good enough match for the San Diego Police. They advised him of this morning's events, and I will call him momentarily and speak with him." He had been looking at Matt and Joanne as he spoke, but he directed this to Joanne: "I'd like you to speak with him as well, Mrs. O'Byrne." She nodded in agreement.

"This appears to be an abduction. I've contacted the FBI Office in Boston, and representatives of the bureau will be here shortly. We will work closely with them on this case. I would expect that they will want to set up a monitoring line on your telephone soon after they arrive."

Until this point, Lyons had not referred to any notes, but now he opened the thick notebook he was holding in his hand and referred to it. Inside he had the snapshot of Joshua that the uniformed officer must have given him when Lyons first arrived. "We're checking the Child Find files at the police department to see if we have prints of the boy on file."

Joanne interrupted, "I took him downtown this summer and had his fingerprints taken, so I'm sure they're on file. I just never thought anybody would ever need them."

"Then we'll have them for the FBI also, Mrs. O'Byrne." He looked back at his notes. "Your mother gave the responding officer a description of the clothes he had on when he went outside. We have him dressed in blue jeans, a yellow long-sleeved jersey, and a dark blue jacket with the words "Red Sox" on the back. Also white sneakers."

Joanne nodded when Lyons paused. Keyes could see she was blank, empty, and in excruciating pain. In the kitchen, Matt could hear occasional anguished whimpers from Anne Stowe. Except for her sobs, there was a prolonged silence inside the home. He did not want to believe that what was happening was true.

Two FBI agents arrived and spent the first fifteen minutes with Lyons on the front porch. Together, they walked around the house and scrutinized the yard, especially the area in and around the sandbox. When they entered, they introduced themselves. One had a briefcase that he set on the kitchen table and opened. Inside was an array of electronic gear and wires. The agent went to the wall telephone, removed the jack and plugged it into an outlet inside the briefcase. He then attached another jack into the handset, and hung up the phone. He then picked up the phone and held it to his ear. A soft whirring noise came from the briefcase and continued until he hung up the phone once again. He pressed several buttons inside the briefcase and held the phone to his ear once more. He signaled to his partner to come over and look at a display on a screen inside the briefcase.

"It's being tapped already," said one of the agents to the other. He looked at Keyes. "Did you know that somebody has been tapping your phone?"

Matt and Joanne looked at each other and shook their heads. Who would be listening to their conversations, they both wondered.

"It looks like someone has gained access to your line and has run leads to it. We're going to try to find out where, but first let me explain how the monitor would work. If the phone rings, answer it like you would any phone call. The recorder will activate as soon as the phone is answered. If it's the kidnapper, try to keep the person on the phone for thirty seconds. Longer if possible. This will give the computer more time to trace the number."

"Where's the computer?" Keyes asked.

"It's right in here," the agent said, pointing to the briefcase.

The other agent interjected. "Agree to whatever the caller asks for. Money. Drop-off point. It's important to let the caller know that you want to cooperate."

The first agent added, "We'll be monitoring the calls also. As soon as the caller hangs up, we will call you immediately with instructions."

***

HECTOR HATED DEALING with kids. He didn't mind doing dirty work, but messing with kids was another story. As he drove towards the Farm, he occasionally looked over his shoulder into the backseat. There, under the same blanket he had used to cover up the little Brazilian guy yesterday was a young boy trussed up with yards of duct tape. He had followed instructions, and grabbing the kid was easy. He was playing alone in a sandbox within plain sight of the street.

Still, he hated it. *It's just not fair messing with kids,* he thought.

Hector looked at his watch. Barely 10 in the morning, and he was beat. Practically no sleep when he got the call to grab the kid. He much preferred his other assignments yesterday. Yesterday was almost fun. First grab the Brazilian kid and drop him at the Farm. Make sure he's secure and then haul ass back into Boston and wait. Finally, take care of business with Rosemary Oates. That woman was one tough bitch, and she put up one helluva fight. Hector relived his meeting with Rosemary Oates as he drove.

He had been waiting for the call by sitting in his car at a parking lot at Park Square reading *True Detective* by the light of a street lamp. The call came at 7 o'clock and interrupted a story he was reading about how a small town cop in Georgia broke open a huge interstate stolen car ring. He picked up the phone and listened. Rosemary Oates had arrived. The FBI and local police will probably find out this same information in the next few hours, so speed was essential. Four Seasons, room nine hundred. Then a credit card name and number. The phone went dead, and he went to work. In the trunk of his white Oldsmobile, Hector kept a rather odd assortment of tools. He would take only one with him tonight. The four-foot length of piano wire with the loops at each end.

He closed the trunk and coiled the wire up in the pocket of his green sports coat. Then he walked in the direction of the Four Seasons and entered the hotel through the front door. He went first to the front desk where he found small wicker baskets filled with matchbooks. Hector picked one up and proceeded to the bank of telephones. There, he dialed the number from the matchbook cover and waited.

"Four Seasons Hotel, may we help you?"

"Yes. I'd like to arrange to have a bottle of champagne sent to room nine hundred, please."

"Certainly, sir. I'll connect you to the concierge, who will take your order."

Three minutes and a stolen credit card number later, Hector completed his order with the concierge. A bottle of chilled champagne would be delivered with a brief note: "Looking forward to seeing you — J". He went to the men's room after specifying that the champagne and the note should be delivered in fifteen minutes, at exactly 7:30. He washed his hands, combed his hair, and made sure his wire was ready. Then he took the elevator to the ninth floor.

He walked past room nine hundred and sought the nearest stairwell. *Less than five minutes*, he thought. He kept the door open a crack and waited for room service to arrive on the ninth floor and knock on the door to room nine hundred. He slid on a pair of surgical gloves. Hector timed his move at exactly the point when the waiter announced himself, knowing she would use the peephole and ask the waiter his purpose.

He straightened up, counted to three and began walking down the hallway, just another guest in the hotel. As he passed by the waiter in the hallway, he heard Mrs. Oates disengaging the dead bolt and begin to open the door. In one fluid move, he chopped the waiter behind the ear and threw him against the door, forcing the door to open wide. The champagne, the tray, and fluted glasses scattered across the carpet. Mrs. Oates knew exactly what was happening and ran towards her bedroom. She was dressed in a long bathrobe, the hem of which Hector snared with his left hand. He was on her and holding her down within moments of the waiter's knock.

With his right hand, he punched Mrs. Oates hard across the mouth. She was struggling and kicking. He punched her hard once more, this time her nose streaming blood. A third punch knocked two teeth from the front of her mouth. The blood in her mouth and his weight on her chest kept her from being able to scream. He bent down to her ear and said with teeth clenched, "Who else knows?" She could only gurgle, blood pouring from her wounds.

"Who knows, bitch?" She could feel his hot, foul breath on her cheek and ear.

She tried to roll over, but Hector grabbed her by the hair. "Last time. Who else knows?"

Her eyes were wide and wild. She was able to pull her right hand free and rammed her thumb into Hector's eye. He almost brayed in pain. With a low growl, he seized her hand and bent her fingers until they snapped back and broke. In an instant, he rolled her face down on to the carpet, slipped the wire around her throat and pulled tight. He released her when she stopped resisting, then used both hands to grasp her head. With a quick twist, her neck snapped.

He leaped off her body and ran quickly to the waiter, still lying inert just inside the threshold. He dragged the waiter into the room and closed the door. He was still out cold. Hector used the same quick head snap on the waiter that he'd used on Rosemary Oates. He unbuttoned the waiter's crisp white shirt, removed it, and let the young man's lifeless body fall in a twisted heap near the bathroom door.

Hector then began a quick, methodical search of the room, looking for documents, lists, anything that looked remotely like a record of transactions. His instructions had been vague, for no one but Mrs. Oates knew the precise format of the records. Fortunately for Hector, she had carried minimal luggage to Boston, and he was able to focus his attention on the area in and on top of her dresser. There he found a large purse, a Louis Vuitton, as if Hector knew or cared, and he emptied its contents on the floor. Beside the usual collection of lipstick, eye shadow, pens, and tissues, he saw what he recognized as a computer diskette. He stuffed it into the rear pocket of his trousers, deciding further that the dead woman's pocket calendar might be of some use; it was filled with telephone numbers and other jottings; Hector didn't want to leave it behind, just in case it held something of value to his employer. A careful look through her garment bag and clothing yielded nothing of consequence, then Hector decided his job was complete.

He went into the bathroom and removed the bloody gloves, then his jacket and shirt, both also red and wet with the blood of Rosemary Oates. He calmly slid on the waiter's clean shirt, stuffed the gloves and the bloody shirt in the sleeve of his jacket and draped the jacket over his arm in a way that concealed the stains. He examined himself in the mirror and broke into a wide grin arrayed with yellowed stumps. On his way out of the room, he stooped down to pick up the note that was to have been delivered with the champagne. *Didn't even break a sweat*, he mused in self-admiration.

CHAPTER SEVENTEEN

WETMAN GREETED COLLINS sourly. "Where the fuck have you been? The FBI is all over this frigging place, the commissioner's all over my ass, and I can't get a fucking investigation out of first gear because my partner is tied up with some loony toons in fucking Melrose!"

Collins let Wetman vent every drop of venom. There was no use interrupting the process. He'd just keep on going until he was done anyway.

"So I told the commissioner, I said that you were tracking down a lead on a big case, that you'd be here right away. He says he's going to send over Brock and Leininger. I asked him to cool it, told him we were the best and he didn't need to send in any second team."

Wetman was fulminating. He had Collins against the wall of the ninth floor lobby, giving him this lecture in a voice so low it wouldn't be heard ten feet away.

Collins said calmly. "Fill me in. On the phone you said there were two deaths. Who else besides Mrs. Oates? What happened?"

Wetman would have none of that. Not yet. "And the FBI says that they have to bring in some of their people from Worcester because they've got a kidnapping in where? Fucking Melrose, that's where. So I'm here trying to work the scene all alone, 'cause these assholes from the bureau, they don't give a shit who you are, 'cause their shit don't stink. And I'm getting ordered around by some thirty-year-old dickhead from Worcester."

Collins never changed expression. When there was a pause long enough to signal an end to Wetman's diatribe, he said once again, "Fill me in."

Wetman looked Collins straight in the eye from eight inches

away. His face was red with rage. He backed away and started speaking rationally. Collins had seen this behavior in Wetman before. He didn't mind that he happened to be Wetman's target this time. What he liked about Wetman was his ability to get his anger up, over, and out of the way.

From now on, they'd work professionally as if no words had been exchanged.

"Victim A is Rosemary Oates, age forty-one. Widow of Captain Henry Oates, also a homicide, whose body was found in a lake in Connecticut a few months ago. Unsolved. Victim B is Luis Alvarado, twenty-one. Worked here at the hotel. He delivered a bottle of champagne to the room last night. Never reported back. Concierge downstairs figures he bolted afterwards. It was close to the end of his shift anyway."

Collins continued listening as Wetman walked into the suite. Inside were photographers, a Scene of Crime team, and what appeared to be six or seven suits. *FBI*, Collins thought. The body of Rosemary Oates was crumpled near the doorway to the bedroom of the suite, her long, pink, terry cloth bathrobe stained with blood. Her head was turned to her left at an odd angle. Blood smeared her face. Long strands of blond hair stuck to the side of her head, and her jaw held an eternal grimace. No dignity for the dead. Especially the violently dead. No chance to close her mouth or straighten her robe. Collins heard Wetman resume explaining. To Collins' right was strewn the body of Luis Alvarado, flopped in a corner of the room, shirtless. No FBI agents anywhere near him. Not important to them.

"Estimated time of death approximately 7:30 to 8:30. Cause of death appears to be strangulation, broken neck, or both. Signs of a struggle include four broken fingers, multiple blunt trauma to the face; hair and skin of possible perpetrator appear to be under the fingernails. The kid over there went quietly. Neck snapped. Hey, Collins, you with me here?"

Collins looked at his notebook and remarked more to himself than to his partner, "So the FBI tracked her here too late. Son of a bitch."

"FBI? No way!" Wetman said. "The first call to the station came from a local. The kid's mother called the hotel this morning. The kid never showed up at home last night. He's usually home by 9. So the district sent a cruiser just to double-check. The call didn't even come in on 911. No emergency. FBI tracked her down? My ass."

Collins' beeper went off. Wetman heard it and handed Collins his flip phone. Collins stepped back into the hall and called Fatima Cabral.

The news that Joanne O'Byrne's young son had been kidnapped sent Collins reeling. Barely able to digest the killing of Rosemary Oates, he considered the toll so far in Matthew Keyes' so-called phantom case: Three dead and two missing for the bad guys. And the good guys don't even know what game is being played.

Fatima went on about the little boy, the desperation in the voice of Matthew Keyes, the shared hope that the little boy would be found safe, and that Jimmy, the charming young man who speaks beautiful Portuguese, would likewise be unharmed. Collins' ears heard, but his mind went in another direction. After he hung up, he went back into room nine hundred and motioned Wetman to come to him.

"I need your help, Jerry, and I need to tell you why I need it. And when I get finished, you might want to call the commissioner and tell him that Brock and Leininger would be perfect for this job."

Wetman stared at Collins with a puzzled look. Collins went on. "I don't mean to confuse you, Jerry, but we need to sit down for a few minutes so I can bring you up-to-date."

Wetman continued staring. Collins' eyes pleaded for a hearing. Wetman ran Collins' words through his brain, but they wouldn't compute. "You outta your mind?"

Collins tried to explain, but Wetman cut him off. "We've got a major, major case twenty feet away, and the FBI beating us up. We get ourselves a doubleheader, and you want me to walk away, turn it over to a couple of shitheads who'd stab your mother to get ahead,

and spend some quality fucking time listening to you tell me a story
…is that what you're saying, or did I mishear you?"

"I need your help, Jerry. I'm asking you."

Wetman reached into his pocket and opened his flip phone.
He pressed some numbers and held it to his ear. He stared at
Collins when he spoke. "Fatima, listen to me. I want you to call
the commissioner's office and tell him that me and Collins are
requesting that Brock and Leininger be assigned to the Rosemary
Oates murder investigation." Wetman paused and Collins could
hear Fatima's voice carry loudly. "I know, Fatima. But just do it.
And call a couple of psychiatrists for me and Collins when you have
a chance." He ended the call and put the phone back in his pocket.
"OK, Collins, talk to me."

Collins wanted to give Wetman a fat, wet kiss on the lips.

**

IN THE LINCOLN ROOM of the Washington Sheraton, six
hot Klieg lights were aimed at a podium. At a long table behind
the lights, Leland Hayes and Lisa Sobolewski sat and riffled through
thick sheaves of white paper. There was no one else present.

The Lincoln room would be the site of two full days of Jack
Munroe's practice sessions for the upcoming Presidential Candidates
Debate. Munroe had been rehearsing and sharpening his skills
with the help of his friends and colleagues, the senior senator from
California, Bob Demers, and the representative from Georgia, Cal
Pressman, but the Lincoln Room would be the "hot" venue, the place
where Munroe would be immersed into as hostile an environment
as could be. If he could feel comfortable here, he'd shatter his
competition on national television. He needed to score big to lock
up the election, and his numbers were flattening out lately.

Missing some key appearances out west didn't help. Warren
Day called earlier in some distress. "What's going on with Jack?"
he asked Hayes. Hayes did his best to explain that the rigors of the
campaign had worn down Jack's ability to fight off a nagging cold.
When Hayes advised Day that Jack was in his room resting and

couldn't speak with him momentarily, Day accepted the explanation. However, he cautioned Hayes that the press would draw its own conclusions, and rumors of a more serious illness would surface. A healthy, bright-eyed Munroe would have to surface soon.

Today, with Demers continuing his roles as surrogate opposition candidate, and with Pressman providing some valuable points of attack, Munroe would be grilled, coached, and run through a dress rehearsal. There would probably be more before the first debate next Thursday.

Hayes and Sobolewski shared some private thoughts as they waited for Munroe, Demers, and Pressman to appear. Neither had much reason to feel secure over the past few days as they watched their man dissemble before their eyes. Now, they could rest at least a bit easier, for Hayes had learned by telephone from the Chairman that the cause of Munroe's distress, a woman whose name was never revealed to Hayes, had been "taken care of." Hayes did not like the way the Chairman phrased it, but the Chairman would not elaborate. "Just tell Jack that he doesn't have to worry about any more letters or phone calls from that woman."

Sobolewski and Hayes were tightly strung competitors, and they had been engaged in a high stakes competition for Munroe's attention over the past year. They didn't often share private thoughts, lest they give any useful information to the enemy. But now, having seen the object of their competition nearly topple from his pedestal, they felt more like comrades in the same foxhole.

Sobolewski spoke about Munroe's gradual rise yesterday from stupor to enthusiasm. "He came around during the day. But he's still scared to death. I can see it in his eyes, and I can hear it in the edge to his voice."

"Lisa, we've got to hold him together today. I told Jack this morning about the Chairman's phone call, about the woman who has been causing some problems for him. I figured that was what was on his mind, but he's still going to be fragile going into the last two weeks of the campaign. Bo Day's getting nervous, too."

"What does Jack have to fear from this woman anyway? Do you have any ideas, Leland?"

"Whatever it is, it's serious enough for him to crumble at the thought of her. And it's enough to get the Chairman personally involved. I'm not sure, but my guess is that she's got some information of some sort. Maybe an old girlfriend that the public isn't supposed to know about. But shit, every candidate's got something he did that he doesn't want to be made public. In my opinion, what we witnessed when Jack opened that note in Seattle was a man being blackmailed. I just have no idea why. I'll bet she has something, though."

At that moment, the door to the Lincoln Room opened and Todd Bernard stepped in. He nodded a hello to Hayes and Sobolewski and walked the perimeter of the room quickly. When he went back to the door, Munroe entered, Pressman and Demers right behind him. Bernard and Jump would stay by the door.

The candidate looked refreshed and ready this morning, and the rehearsal went well. Munroe listened carefully to the questions. The Klieg lights were kept bright and in Munroe's eyes to intimidate him, and to give him practice in dealing with hostile or unexpected questions. The lights blinded him, and he was forced to focus on the questions and his answers. After three hours of intense grilling, Hayes called for a lunch break, which Munroe gladly agreed to. Hayes and Sobolewski smiled at Munroe's apparent command of himself. They were cautiously reassured that the next two weeks, grueling as they would be, would at least be rid of the dangerous distraction of the woman he feared.

***

WETMAN AND COLLINS sat silently facing each other in the lobby of the Four Seasons. Collins had finished relating the convoluted tale to Wetman and was awaiting his reaction. He could tell that Wetman was silently digesting and dashing through the information looking for threads. When he found one, he'd respond. Collins was patient.

Finally, Wetman looked at his watch and rose from his seat. "Let's get over to the Prudential now, even though it's a little early. There are some important things we have to learn over there."

Collins lit up at Wetman's intensity and determination and had to trot after Wetman to keep up with him.

***

WHEN THEY ARRIVED at the Prudential Center, Wetman spoke. "You go to the office and start going through any information they have that looks useful. I'll come to the office later."

Collins had worked with Wetman long enough to know not to ask questions at this moment. He did as he was told, and Wetman strode to the elevators of the fifty-two story building.

The manager of the Prudential Center was not surprised when Collins arrived earlier than planned. The materials he wanted were already stacked on a long table in the manager's conference room. Collins thanked him, sat down, and went to work.

***

JIMMY LOOKED THROUGH the crack of light above the door. He was standing on the upturned pail, using it as a stool. He had been working on a plan, carefully assembling his thoughts and ideas in precise order. Then he heard a car driving across the gravel driveway. It was the same white car that had been used to transport him here. The same one, he was certain, that had been following him and Joanne.

When Jimmy saw the tall, lanky driver step out, he uttered an old Andean curse. There was the monster in the green sports coat. Jimmy could only catch a sliver of the scene through the narrow gap, but he could see that the tall man was opening the back door of the car and removing something.

In a moment, the door was closed and the tall man was out of view. Jimmy heard the door to the house open and close.

He sat on the bucket and went back to work, carefully and methodically. If this planned worked as he hoped, he might have a fighting chance to escape. If it didn't, he would at least go to his death knowing that he tried his best.

Finding the long, rusted screw was a godsend, he considered. With it, he could make a neat hole. It was this that consumed his attention.

***

THE LATE AFTERNOON sun cast long shadows, and the broad-shouldered maple trees along Carter Street in Melrose, still holding stubbornly to the last rusty leaves of the season, threw wide, irregular strips of darkness across the pavement. Keyes sat on the steps of the front porch, his anger being built steadily by the inability to act. He could not sit still, nor could he think of any alternative. Joanne and her mother sat inside in the living room, trying to seek encouragement from each other. An FBI agent sat alone in the kitchen, reading a ballistics manual and waiting for the phone to ring. He would stay the night, he said.

An irritated Keyes rose from his seat and went inside. He told Joanne he was going to take a walk and would return in fifteen minutes. *This*, he thought, *might at least burn off some of my pent up anxiety.* Joanne was too wrung out to object and asked him to stop at the convenience store at the end of the street and buy cigarettes. He could see that she and her mother had amassed an overflowing ashtray of cigarette butts. He went out.

The convenience store was a short walk away, and he was there within five minutes. Besides the cigarettes, he bought a newspaper and two packages of gum. He paid the clerk and walked through the front door. The door had not yet closed behind him when a youngster on a bicycle wheeled in his direction calling, "Mister. Hey, mister." The boy was probably twelve years old, his jeans too short for his legs. He brought the bike to a squealing halt so close to Matt that he stepped back, then handed him a folded piece of paper. "This is for you."

The boy started to pedal away as quickly as he arrived, and Keyes called to him, "Who gave this to you? Come back here for a minute." The youngster skidded to a stop and yelled back to Matt over his shoulder, "Some old guy. He asked me to give it to you."

"What old guy? Where is he?"

"He took off in his car, mister. He just said to give it to you when you came out of the store. That's all." With that, the boy stepped hard on the pedals and sped away down the sidewalk.

Keyes looked around. There was plenty of traffic passing by, but he couldn't guess who the "old guy" might be, or where he might be by now. He opened up the folded paper and read the shaky writing. "Must meet tonight. Midnight. Come alone. (Those last two words were underlined.) Boston side of the Blue Line, where the Committee and the Court needed shoring up. Remember your first PM job, Matthew? I have much to tell you."

It was unsigned. He looked at the handwriting, and something about it struck him as familiar. He read it once again, mouthing the words to himself. "Boston Blue." What did this mean?

He crossed the street and walked back up Carter Street slowly, sifting through the cryptic words on a note from an old man. By the time he reached number fifty-two and walked up the porch steps, the note was in his pocket, and he knew where he had to be at midnight. But who would be there to meet him?

***

WETMAN STROLLED INTO the manager's conference room and slapped a list of handwritten numbers on the table. "Where's the tenant list?" Collins had been rummaging through pounds of paper looking for something, anything that would stand out as unusual. His own note pad had five items listed.

"Right here." Collins handed Wetman a file folder with several sheets of paper stapled together. "They update the list each month. This is the list for last November."

"Fine," Wetman said, stripping off his jacket and seating himself across the table. Collins looked at Wetman flipping through the tenant list and jotting notes in his note pad.

He knew better than to ask him anything right now, so he went back to the materials in front of him.

Minutes later, Wetman turned around his pad of paper so that Collins could read it. "There, my friend, is my best guess at where Matthew Keyes saw what he saw." It was a list of twenty suites of offices in the Prudential Tower.

"How do you know it's one of these?"

"What you need is a little organization, that's all. Look, these are all the tenants on the east side of the building between the fortieth and forty-ninth floors. The top floor is the observatory, and it sort of sticks out different from the rest, so that's out. The next floor below is out, because Keyes would remember if it was the topmost office floor. It would have stuck in his mind. Same reason for the next one down.

"So whatever he saw was probably on the forty-ninth floor or somewhere in the next several floors below. And you told me Keyes recalled it was somewhere on the upper floors."

Wetman sat back and smiled at Collins, a crafty smile as if there was more to come.

"The numbers are the suite numbers with space facing east, in the direction of the John Hancock building. So we're down to twenty-one possiblities." Collins scanned the list. Top drawer companies, law firms, an airline, an architect, even a U.S. senator had offices on those floors facing the John Hancock building.

Collins looked from the list to Wetman and posed a question. "Now what? There's no way of confirming who was in the building at that time. These tenants come and go as they please, and they don't sign in or out."

Wetman answered Collins with a question. "How would you know if a tenant left the premises? Footprints?"

He waited for an answer but Collins knew that Wetman already had it.

"Well, most of the tenants go home. They might go by bus, or subway, or even walk if they live around here. Or they'd drive. So I checked the list of reserved parking spaces for tenants in the

Prudential Center garage, and eleven of these twenty-one suite numbers have one or more reserved spaces. Every time a tenant with one of these reserved spaces drives in or out, he has to use a magnetic card. And that, my friend, is recorded."

"I'm with you, Jerry, and I knew about the parking spaces a long time ago. I looked at the entries of who went in and who went out. There was nothing unusual."

Wetman's smug expression turned dark when he heard Collins say that he had already checked the parking records. "Are you sure?" Wetman was certain he was on to something, and Collins was dashing his hopes.

"Look for yourself. The records are in the blue folders at the end of the table."

Wetman reached over and opened the file folder. The first sheet listed a series of parking permit numbers in the order in which the cars entered. The second listed the cars exiting. Beside each number was a time. The file folder held the records from three days before to three days after the incident in question.

The purpose of recording usage this way was to prevent a permit holder from lending his permit to another driver, effectively letting that driver park for free. If a permit was recorded on the garage computer as being used to enter the garage, that permit would reject a second car subsequently attempting to enter the garage on the same permit number. Only when that permit holder used his card to exit the garage would a subsequent entry be allowed.

Wetman was silent as he pored over the lists, occasionally jotting numbers and times. Collins continued his research, but was getting nowhere fast. He thought of Jimmy and the little boy and wondered how malformed a mind must be to consider taking them as fair game.

Wetman chuckled to himself, a sign Collins knew to be antecedent to his having something important to say. Collins looked in Wetman's direction and waited.

"You might find this interesting, Collins. Here are four cards that were used to enter the garage on the day of the incident, and which were used over the next two days to exit the garage. So the cars must have remained in the garage overnight."

"So? That could happen if someone worked late and stayed in town overnight, or if someone took a cab to the airport for a business trip and left his car at the garage."

"But on the day of the incident, one of the garage attendants overrode the system and let one of these cars out without a permit. Look at this." Collins walked over to Wetman's side of the table and looked over his shoulder.

Wetman pointed to the list as he spoke. "Whoever has permit four fifty two went in the garage at 8:50 that morning. Then, at 11:17, the parking attendant let the same permit holder out, but because he didn't have his magnetic card on him, there was no way for number four fifty two to exit without having to pay."

Collins found this of some interest, but still didn't see where Wetman was going with it.

Wetman didn't make Collins wait long. "But over here, on the next day, you can see that number four fifty two exited the garage at 6:30 in the morning. But the attendant had to override the system, because four fifty two had not yet gone back into the garage again since the previous evening at 11:17. Or at least this tells us that he didn't get back in using his magnetic card. Tell me how this could happen, Collins."

Collins considered this for a moment. "Let's say that four fifty two went to drive out, but forgot his permit in his office. The attendant, if he recognized the driver, might override the system and let him exit. Then the next day, the permit holder drives back in, but when he drives in, he takes a ticket like everybody else who doesn't have a permit. When he leaves," Collins continued, "the system sees that four fifty two isn't recorded as going back in, but the attendant recognizes the person as a tenant and a permit holder and lets him out."

Wetman waited for Collins to think his words over.

Collins considered that scenario and went on, "But how many

people would go out at 11:17 at night, come back in and still leave once more by 6:30 in the morning?"

Wetman picked it up. "Someone with a very weird schedule, or someone who was maybe driving another person's car out, but was recognized by the attendant as a permit holder, and let out by overriding the system."

Collins went back to his side of the table and started combing the file folders for the list of parking permit holders. Wetman stood up, went to the window and looked out at the expanse of pedestrian mall and the shops, and smiled.

CHAPTER EIGHTEEN

JIMMY COMPLETED HIS preparations and prayed that his plan would work. "If it doesn't, please let me die quickly."

There was nothing to do now but wait. Darkness had come, and clouds hid the moon. When Jimmy looked out through the crack above the door, he saw nothing but inky blackness.

He picked up the pail and carried it with him as he retired to the rear corner, where he had build a crude barricade. The frayed outdoor umbrella was his best hope for safety, and that didn't provide much. There, he crawled underneath the umbrella, covered his head with the rusty pail and, tired and hungry, waited and prayed.

***

JACK MUNROE WAS enjoying a cocktail with his friends. The network polls had him still in the lead, and based on the performance he expected to make at the debates, he knew that his objective would be achieved. He'd roar into office, the people's choice, and never look back.

Hayes and Sobolewski stood at the side of the room and admired how their candidate had risen from dribbling idiot to confident leader. Munroe was joking and jovial, full of the spirit and drive that made him appear larger than life and the perfect candidate.

***

"YOU CAN'T GO! You just can't!" Joanne was determined to convince Matt not to head off into Boston for a midnight meeting, at a location somewhere underground, and with some unknown person that he couldn't even be sure would meet him. "It's insane, Matt. Joshua was kidnapped from his own yard and Jimmy is still missing. What if something happens to you? I won't be able to go on, Matt," Joanne sobbed as she pleaded.

"Whoever sent this message is on our side, Joanne. Or at least, is being attacked by the same people who took Joshua and Jimmy and killed Rosemary Oates."

"But what if you're wrong, Matt? What if it's a setup? If this person wants to get to you so bad, why not just drive over and visit right here. He knows where you are."

"Because he's afraid of being seen, or he's afraid of being seen in direct contact with us. We know the phone's been tapped, so that's not safe either."

Keyes could see that Joanne was bending, relenting. Finally, she resigned herself to accepting his decision and returned, stone-faced, to the living room.

He prepared to leave. His watch read 10:30, and he wanted plenty of time to get to his destination. He looked at the message one more time, folded it into a square, and handed it to Joanne. "Hold on to this. If I'm not back by 3 o'clock, call Collins." Joanne held the paper in her hand. Her eyes were vacant. Her child was gone, and her strength was at its end. He hugged her tightly and kissed her on her lips. She held onto him and whispered, "I love you, Matt."

***

IT WAS 11 o'clock, and a lone security guard sat in the front office of the Prudential Center, waiting for Collins and Wetman to finish their tedious work. Collins found the list of garage permit holders and laid the list on the table. He flipped pages over until he found the right one. There was four fifty two. Collins and Wetman read the name and faced each other, stunned and perplexed. Neither would speak. If their scheme had any merit, the suspicion pointed directly at the likely next President of the United States.

Wetman finally broke the silence. "There's probably a very good explanation for this."

Collins looked at Wetman, disbelieving.

"We can't just say that Jack Munroe is somehow connected with Oates' death just because he has a parking permit for the damned garage. What would we say to him? 'We think you might be involved because some guy saw you …or someone who might look like you …strike and kill someone who turned up dead in Connecticut. And, by the way, the wife of the guy we think you might have killed just turned up dead in Boston.' Yeah. Right. You read the papers? Jack Munroe is in Washington right now, and it would be somewhat difficult to connect him to Rosemary Oates' death. Somewhat difficult."

Collins thought about Matt, the missing Jimmy, and the kidnapped Joshua. "We've got to get to Keyes. Someone else knows what Matt saw that night, and they're afraid of him. The closer he gets to putting the pieces together, the hotter it gets for them. That's why his friend and the little boy were grabbed. They're trying to get to Keyes."

Wetman instinctively reached for his flip phone and handed it to Collins.

***

JIMMY WAS COLD and shivering in his hiding place. He had been given no food nor water since his imprisonment, and he wondered if his captors would simply leave him there to die. Maybe his body would never be found, but just lay there and rot and turn to dust. Who would ever know?

Suddenly he heard a door to the house open, then footsteps descending the wooden stairs from the porch. He thought he could hear a child's cry, but it was far away and his focus was on the footfalls, coming nearer and making soft, rasping crunches on the gravel. He waited. The steps were closer.

He heard keys rattling, and he knew that his time had come. Whoever was out there would be unlocking the door and entering momentarily. *As long as he turned on the light*, Jimmy thought, quaking, *the rusting pail would serve as his helmet*.

Hector finally found the right key. He would take the young

man by the neck and do the same as he had done to Rosemary Oates. Quick, snap, lights out, over. No need to make noise with a pistol held to the temple. No prolonged, agonizing screams. Hold the top of his head tight with one arm, use the other arm to twist. Perfect ending.

Hector slid the key into the padlock and turned. He slid the lock out, opened the hasp, and slid the lock back onto its hook. With his right hand, he pulled at the door handle, which creaked on its rusted hinges. "Rise and shine," he called softly. "Time to rise and shine." Jimmy made no sound. The shed was dark, and Hector took a tentative step inside, his arms and hands poised to fend off what meager attack his captive might attempt. "Come out, come out wherever you are." Hector couldn't see two feet in front of him and was getting angry at this little hide and seek game.

"Listen, you little prick; you stand up and come out now, or I'm going to make this a very long and painful night for you." Still no response.

Hector kept his left arm ready to strike, and reached slowly with his right to the light switch. "It's your funeral, my friend," Hector said, and flipped the switch.

THE EXPLOSION OF gasoline and glass was not nearly as loud as Jimmy had hoped. He had removed the lightbulb and patiently worked all day at the soft metal on the base of the bulb to create a small hole. Into the bulb, Jimmy carefully poured some gasoline that remained in the rusted, unused lawnmower.

While the fuel still retained the odor of gasoline, Jimmy's fear was that moisture and other impurities over time may have rendered it useless for his task. Drop by drop, Jimmy carefully poured the gasoline through the hole and into the body of the lightbulb. When the bulb was nearly full, he patiently worked the soft metal back into the hole to seal the fuel inside. He hoped that the arc created when the electricity was turned on would ignite the fuel and perhaps stun or blind the intruder sufficiently to allow enough time for his escape.

As soon as Hector flipped the switch, he closed the circuit and allowed electricity to flow through the wires and to the base of the lightbulb, and from there to the fine filament in the central body of the bulb. An angry pop was followed by streams of flaming gasoline in every direction, bathing the interior of the shed in a bright light, and showering Hector with the fire. Using every available item in the shed, Jimmy had erected a crude but effective barrier for himself. But Hector was fully exposed.

Hector's first sensation was of intense but brief heat. His eyebrows, eyelashes and the hair at the front of his head were singed off immediately. Blinded by the flash, he covered his face with his hands and stumbled hard into the front wall.

Jimmy peered over his makeshift barricade, anxious to see what damage he had been able to inflict. With a lurch, he leaped from his crouch in the direction of the open door. His barricade collapsed noisily. Hector, with eyes still closed, reached wildly at the sound and found Jimmy's leg. Together, they crashed to the floor, with Jimmy frantically kicking, desperate to free himself from his enemy's grasp.

The only available light came from the flames licking cloth remnants of the umbrella and the shoulders of the tall man's shirt. *Why isn't this man screaming?* he wondered. So close to the fresh air of freedom, Jimmy gave one exhausting shove with his free foot, pulling away at last. Scrambling to his feet, he shoved hard at the door, sending a still blinded Hector backwards in a crash. Jimmy slid the padlock on the door, slammed the lock home and dashed from the shed. The tall man was banging against the door, and Jimmy heard him growl like an animal.

Jimmy found cover in some evergreen bushes behind the house. He needed a moment to get his bearings, and as yet, he didn't know if any others would pour from the house to aid their comrade in the burning shed. He stayed low, creeping slowly to the far side of the house, and there he heard the distinct sound of a crying child. So far, there were no other signs of motion, in spite of his vanquished captor continuing to loudly bang against the door. He waited another minute and crept to a window from which sobbing sounds could be heard. He inched himself up until his eyes peered over the sill of a window. Light came from a lamp on a table near the window. Stretching himself to his full length, Jimmy spotted a child, hands bound behind him, and taped to a wooden chair. He pulled himself up higher against the window to get a better view and slid backwards in a bush. The noise caused the child to turn towards its source, and it was then that Jimmy saw Joshua.

Tearing away to the side door, Jimmy dashed inside and grabbed Joshua, chair and all. He was racing, carrying a hysterical Joshua from the house when he saw a set of keys on the kitchen counter. Holding Joshua in one arm, he snatched the keys and ran out. The car, the white sedan, sat in the gravel drive. Jimmy opened the back door and set Joshua on the rear seat, still firmly imprisoned with thick duct tape by the chair. He got into the driver's seat, inserted the key, and smiled broadly when the engine came to life. He drove in a circle and came to the road, not knowing in which direction to turn. He looked over his shoulder to the shed and flames began to shoot through the roof's edge. Jimmy turned left, hoped he was correct, and drove on. Five minutes and perhaps three miles away, he pulled onto the road's shoulder, climbed in back and untied and untaped his young companion. Joshua hugged Jimmy tightly. And for the first time since he'd been told to hang up the phone, Jimmy's face opened in a broad grin.

***

COLLINS HELD WETMAN'S cell phone to his ear and listened with disbelief to a weeping Joanne O'Byrne. Matt had left the house alone for a clandestine midnight meeting with an unknown party. He pressed Joanne, insisting on more. "Where? Did he say *where*, Joanne?"

"He got a message on a piece of paper telling him where and when to meet. It's in some kind of code, and he told me if he didn't return by 3 in the morning to call you."

"Do you have the note, Joanne?"

"Yes. I'll read it to you. Maybe you can make some sense out of it."

Joanne read the note and Collins carefully copied the words down. "That's it? There's no more to the note?"

"I'm sorry, but that's everything." Joanne was losing all hope fast.

"Joanne, I'll call you later."

Collins folded the phone and shook his head. The note meant little to him: "...the Boston side of the Blue Line where the Committee and the Court needed shoring up ..."

Wetman looked over his partner's shoulder to read the contents of the note. In an instant, he took the flip phone from Collins' hand, slid it into his pocket, and started a slow trot from the conference room, calling for Collins to follow. "C'mon, Collins. Let's get going."

Collins raced to catch up with Wetman. "Where the hell are we going?"

"Court Street Station."

Collins had never heard of it, and he knew every stop on the MBTA lines. "Where in hell is Court Street Station?"

"Just keep running. We don't have a lot of time." When they reached their car, both were out of breath.

Collins took the passenger seat. Wetman pulled a U-turn on Huntington Avenue and drove towards Copley Square. Collins finally gained enough breath to ask, "What's with Court Street Station, Jerry?"

Wetman drove like a crazy man even when he wasn't in a hurry. Tonight, he swerved, cut, and slashed his way through traffic, blue light flashing on the dash.

"School Committee Headquarters is just above it," Wetman said. "We'll have to go in from Government Center."

Collins was puzzled, and Wetman explained, simultaneously leaning on his horn.

"My old man was a gandy dancer for the MBTA. His job was to walk the tracks, looking for loose spikes in the rails and pound them back in. He'd walk the rails every day with a sackful of spikes over one shoulder and a long sledgehammer over the other. I used to go with him sometimes. That's how I know about Court Street Station.

"It's on the Boston side of the Blue Line Tunnel to East Boston. It's been closed for years, ever since they ran the line up to Cambridge Street. Abandoned."

Collins marveled at Wetman's mastery of the unusual and the arcane. "And that's where Keyes is going to his meeting tonight?"

"Keyes knew where it was because the note said something about shoring up. It also said he should remember his first job as 'PM,' meaning he must have been the project manager for his engineering firm when they had some work underground. Keyes must have done some design work to beef up the supports for the buildings above the station."

Collins looked at his watch. 11:40.

***

IT WAS NEARING midnight, and Joanne was asleep in a living room chair when the phone rang. Her mother, seated at the kitchen table with the FBI agent, picked up the phone on the second ring. The agent slipped on earphones and Joanne ran into the kitchen.

"Hello?" was Anne Stowe's tentative greeting.

"Hello." The voice sounded far away, and there were background noises of traffic. "I've got Joshua."

"Oh my god," Anne Stowe nearly fainted. The FBI agent motioned for her to continue conversing with the caller. The computer was clicking and humming away, homing in on the caller's location.

"What do you want?" Anne Stowe had no idea what to say.

"Directions. I want directions. I'm at a pay telephone, and I don't know where I'm headed."

Anne Stowe wore a puzzled frown. She handed the phone to Joanne and whispered, "Something about directions."

Joanne took the phone. "Hello. This is Joanne O'Byrne, Joshua's mother. Tell me your directions. But please don't hurt my son."

"Look, Joshua's fine, but how am I supposed to give you directions? I'm the one who's lost, for crying out loud." Jimmy was confounded. Joshua was standing next to him in the phone booth.

Joanne heard the voice and yelled, "Jimmy! Is that you, Jimmy?" The FBI agent pulled off his earphones, his ears ringing from Joanne's sudden shouts.

"Yes. It's Jimmy. We're lost out here."

"Is Joshua with you?"

Jimmy handed the phone for Joshua. "Here. Say hello to your mother."

CHAPTER NINETEEN

MATT KEYES PARKED in the public garage near Haymarket Square and trotted towards Government Center. At 11:25, he entered the MBTA station in front of City Hall and rode the escalator down.

He passed a dollar bill through the opening at the token booth and was given one token and some coins in return. He slipped the token into its slot and passed through the turnstile.

Walking quickly, he stayed close to the wall of the underground walkway. When he reached the platform, he saw two people standing there, waiting for the next train to arrive. Two young men, maybe students, heading for home. Keyes stood behind a pillar to conceal himself. He did not want to draw undue attention.

To his right, the tracks led to a tunnel that would take him in the direction of the old Court Street Station. He remembered it well, for it represented his very first assignment as project manager. It was a small job, and it mostly amounted to installing steel beams and piers throughout the outbound platform area adjacent to the ones already there, and designing a trench with a pump to keep water from further undermining the earth beneath the piers.

But to Keyes, it was a milestone. Every engineer remembered that very first job as PM.

He eased his way in the shadows closer to the tunnel and waited to make his move. The two young men were joined by an old drunk, and Keyes guessed that they were being hit up for some spare change. He watched them try to distance themselves from the bum, and the distraction gave Keyes the opening he needed. In seconds, he was in the darkness of the tunnel and out of sight.

He made his way carefully along the tracks, staying close to the wall on his right. There were several places to hide if a subway car came along. He could simply move behind any of concrete pillars that supported the roof of the underground line and wait for the train to pass. He would just need enough time to locate the right pillar and hide to avoid being picked out by the train's headlights.

Keyes knew, though, that the shrill squeal of metal wheels scraping against metal tracks would echo throughout the tunnel and announce each train well in advance of him having to rush for cover. At this hour, service was less frequent. He registered only a distant train approaching, probably still two stations away, and from his rear. An occasional bare lightbulb served to guide him along his way.

The odor inside the tunnel was fusty, the walls damp with moisture dripping through the soil above and leeching through at weak points in the walls. Mold and dust covered every surface. Ahead he spotted a pair of red, deriding eyes reflecting whatever minimal light there was and heard the scurrying chatter and contemptible hiss of colonies of rats who called this place home. The eyes held him and ran off. Keyes shuddered at the thought of these creatures and knew that perhaps a thousand of them were within one hundred yards of his current position. He thought of the irony of having spent months in deep jungle, surrounded by creatures at least as hideous, and that he was not nearly as bothered by them as by these rats.

The main tunnel curved to the left and headed north towards Cambridge. The abandoned tunnel was blocked by a sagging chain link fence and curved gently to the right and led to the Court Street Station. He left the main track, squeezed through a gap in the fence, and walked in the center of the deserted rail bed. Based on his recollection from the time he had last been here, Keyes estimated that he would quickly reach his destination. It could not be more than five hundred feet away. He moved steadily forward. Ahead of him was a faint glow of light. Someone had obviously been here recently, for, except for this very meeting, there would be little reason for anyone else to venture into the bowels of the abandoned and forgotten station. As he continued along the rail bed, he spotted the edge of the outbound platform of the deserted station ahead of him. The light was becoming brighter. He slowed his pace, reached the platform, and stopped. It was 11:48, and Keyes was now in Court Street Station. It was someone else's move.

***

WETMAN PULLED UP onto the flowing brick plaza in front of City Hall. He turned off the ignition and yelled to Collins, "Time?"

Collins looked at his watch. "11:59."

"Let's hustle."

The blue light remained flashing on the roof of their car as they dashed into Government Center Station and down the stairs. They both ignored the turnstiles and leaped over. The noise of their rapid footsteps rattled around the hard surfaces of the underground walkway. They reached the platform, and Wetman pointed to his right towards the tunnel.

"This way," he shouted.

Collins glanced behind him as he followed Wetman and saw no one waiting on the platform. Ahead of him, Wetman was already entering the subway tunnel.

Collins checked the time. Four minutes past twelve.

***

KEYES FOUND A spot on a railing on which he could sit and from which he could take in most of the remains of the Court Street Station. The only light came from the weak glow of a bulb somewhere behind a concrete column to his right. When he turned to look behind him, all was as black as pitch. From his perch, he could make out both entrances to the station. One was ahead of him to his right, and it had been sealed years before. *There might be someone hiding there,* he acknowledged, *someone who came here ahead of me and is waiting for me now.*

The other was to his left, across the adjacent rail bed. He could barely distinguish the platform from this distance. With all the pillars and piers, anyone could be hiding there. *Fifty people could be hiding there right now, and I'd never know it*, he thought.

He slowly scanned the scene from left to right. Broken glass littered the area. Portions of a sign overhead could still be made out in the dim light. "Court Street," it read. Keyes saw that the shoring work he had managed here was still apparently doing its job. No signs of any deterioration or cave-ins that he could see. He remembered this scene when high intensity work lamps made the area as bright as high noon in Arizona. He came here frequently then to see the welders and the ironworkers turn his paper plans into reality. He was there when the water pump arrived, and when it was installed. He also remembered the comforting sound that came from the pump when it worked properly on its initial test. It was a simple design, really, but to see the whole thing come together was a giant thrill.

Far away, Keyes heard the occasional squeal of metal upon metal. Closer, he heard the unnerving chatter of the rats. The uneven sound of water seeping, dropping in loud plops into puddles, punctuated the range of his hearing. Matt waited. Impatient now. He glanced at his watch and turned it to capture a grain of the dim light. Exactly midnight. *Where are you? Come out now. Show yourself.*

The powerful beam of a flashlight caught him square in the eyes, and Keyes turned his head aside.

"Matthew Keyes." He knew that voice.

"What is it, Mr. Jensen? Where are you?"

"Are you alone?"

"Yes."

"You look well, Matthew. You look very well."

"Mr. Jensen," Keyes spoke, unwilling to tolerate politeness in these circumstances.

"Please, Matthew, call me Trig."

"Trig, then. I got your message. I came here on your terms and on time. What is it you have to tell me?"

"Oh, so much, Matthew. There's so much to tell you, and I've been thinking about this all day. I still don't know where to start."

"Start with this, Trig. Are my friend and the little boy safe?"

"You see, Matthew, I can tell you a great many things, but I really don't know where the child and your South American friend are being kept, I'm afraid. I don't believe they're harmed, though. At least, I..."

Keyes started to speak, but Jensen raised his hand as if to beg for a moment's time. Jensen could see the loathing in Keyes' eyes.

"Please, Matthew, bear with me for a few more moments. I'll fill in so many blank spaces for you, I'm sure. First, though, let me come a little closer, and I'll take this foolish light out of your eyes."

Keyes had recognized Trygve Jensen's voice at once, but it struck him as odd that the voice had softened and slowed. He sounded almost gentle. Not at all the voice of the crusty bastard he remembered. Jensen shone the light at the ceiling, where its reflection immediately softened the scenery. Keyes could see a shape holding the flashlight and could hear the shuffle of Jensen's feet as he walked across the platform. When Jensen was about ten feet away, he stopped.

"I'm waiting, Trig."

"Yes. Well, I'll start at the beginning. That would be about three years ago, but I suppose I could start seventy-three years ago as well."

"Stop playing games." Keyes could see Jensen clearly now, and he looked much older than he remembered. A bit stoop shouldered and much thinner than he remembered him. His hair was gray and combed straight back. A brown suit hung limply on his frame.

"I'll make this the short version."

"I'll agree with you on that." Matt's voice was testy. He didn't have the luxury of time. He wanted answers quickly. Now.

"The important thing is to first stop the insanity." Jensen set the flashlight on the top of an ancient wooden crate that stood on its end. He stepped to the side and continued to speak. "I was asked, Matthew, along with several business friends and acquaintances, to form a committee which would have as its ultimate purpose the election of a particular person to the Presidency. We are, I think you would say, a well-heeled group with some political influence that many people might envy. Initially, we used our contacts and our organizational skills to build a campaign fund. We also provided some seed money to get the process started.

"Our little group is called the Board of Directors. Not a particularly imaginative name, but it fairly describes our roles. Running an election campaign, especially for the highest office in the country, is a great deal like running a business. You need to establish a vision for the enterprise, amass a capital base, and choose capable executives to handle the day-to-day operations."

Keyes was unable to endure a drawn out saga, and this appeared to be the start of one. "Is there a point to your story? What does this have to do with Jimmy or Joshua?"

"Oh, a great deal, Matthew. Be patient. You know, when I first saw you on the job at Crane & Stewart, I remarked that I thought you would be an excellent engineer. Largely because of your impatience, really. You were eager to get things done, and you didn't dawdle, like some of the others. But right now, I wish you'd just bear with me."

"Go on."

"I'll tell you about our candidate. You know of him, I'm sure. Jack Munroe."

Of course Keyes knew of him. His face was in the news every day, and he was probably going to win the election.

"Jack would be a fine President. Grew up in Groton, you know, just thirty miles from here. He did a respectable job as a member of the Massachusetts House, and he's done a fair job in Washington, as well. He has a few flaws, but he's not nearly as shallow as he sometimes appears, and compared to most of the candidates I've seen run for President over the last fifty years, he'd be better than most of them."

Keyes stared at Jensen, and his eyes urged him on.

"Jack went for the plan right away. He has ambition, and this was, of course, the most ambitious race of them all. I must say he was doing quite well, too."

"Was? Last I heard, he was pulling way ahead in all the polls."

"That's correct. But over the past few weeks, he's been under a great deal of pressure, and it nearly broke the back of his campaign."

"This is all very interesting, but what does this have to do with me? And what does it have to do with kidnapping my friend and a little boy?"

"It has everything to do with you, Matthew. Because, you see, Jack Munroe became involved in a very bitter dispute. It was almost a year ago, and the argument resulted in the untimely death of the other party." Jensen could see Keyes' perplexed expression. "The argument took place in Munroe's office in the Prudential Tower, and the other party was a certain Henry Oates, captain in the United States Navy."

Keyes' eyes bore in on Jensen. "It was Munroe who killed Oates?"

"Yes, I'm afraid it was."

"And you knew all about it?" Keyes couldn't veil his disgust.

"Well, I knew that Jack had been involved in an altercation, and that Captain Oates was dead. I did not know, however, the real reasons behind the altercation. At least, not at the time."

"What was the real reason?"

"I was told that Oates was blackmailing Munroe with information he discovered while working in the Pentagon. The captain was trying to derail Jack's plan to run for office by dragging up some rather damaging information from Jack's past. Jack, you see, was in the Navy for a brief period after completing law school. He received a medical discharge after only twelve weeks."

"So what? What's so damaging about that?"

"The specific reason for the medical discharge was confidential. I was led to believe that Oates knew the reason for the discharge, and was threatening to release information that would portray Jack as having experienced, shall we say, a sexual identity crisis during his brief naval career."

"Are you telling me Munroe is gay?"

"I'm telling you what I was told, and what the captain wished to use against him. I must say that I knew Jack Munroe for some time, and I never suspected him of being anything but normal, at least in that way. But the world is full of surprises, and for all I knew, Jack Munroe wore a lace brassiere and dressed up in high heel pumps." Jensen chuckled. "But what does it matter now? I was fed lies. It wasn't true at all. I learned just recently that the reason behind Jack Munroe's discharge was a case of acute asthma. Nothing more. Harmless information, you see."

Jensen shook his head at this, collected his thoughts, and went on. "But since I was told that Oates could expose some very damaging information about Jack, and I knew that Jack was involved in the captain's death, an accidental death, by the way, I went along with the plan to keep the entire incident concealed. It made wonderful sense, Matt, until we learned that you decided to use a telescope in the Hancock Tower and happened upon the ugly scene."

"So that's why you came after me?"

"Not right away. Jack was kept under wraps for a few days as a sort of a retreat for him until we could be sure he wouldn't come unglued. It was a week or so later that I decided it would be best to keep one eye open just in case word got out about the Oates affair. I know a young fellow on the Boston police force, and I asked him to watch for any report on the incident that might be made. Perhaps someone outside Jack's office in the Prudential overheard their arguing. Or maybe someone might have seen Jack and Earl leaving with Oates' body that night. It was several weeks before your report was seen by my friend at headquarters. Then we knew there was a witness. But it was a very weak report, not worth anyone's time really, and we had no idea at the time that it was you, Matthew, who reported it."

"Who's your contact at headquarters?"

"No one you'd know, Matthew. Just an officer whose child is quite ill. Leukemia. Poor thing. Needs lots of very expensive treatment. And, frankly, I was advised that this unfortunate gentleman would not be averse to accepting some fairly substantial sums for what amounts to some quite simple activities on his part. In other words, I had an opportunity to take advantage of him and his unquestioned access to the inner offices of the police headquarters building. And I did. He told me about Collins scheduling a meeting with someone on the report. I went down to headquarters and saw you and Joanne walking into it. I was astounded, of course. I couldn't be sure if it was you who were prying into the matter, so I followed you to the library. When my friend scooped the newspaper reports you later dropped off at Collins' office at Homicide, I knew that it was you, and that you were far too close for comfort. It was your damned determination, Matthew, that I knew would drive you to see your report brought to a conclusion. I saw that in you when you worked for us. As a matter of fact, it was I who chose you to be the PM for the project to do the work on this very station we are standing in. It's why I knew you would understand my note today."

Keyes was stunned by Jensen's words and was about to ask a question when he heard the shuffling of feet from somewhere in the tunnel. They were not alone. Jensen and Keyes both tried to find the source of the noise. Jensen reached for the flashlight, and Keyes eased off the railing. Suddenly, a voice from the dark caused them to stop where they stood.

"Leave the flashlight where it is, Trygve. And Matthew, stay where you are."

Keyes recognized the voice of Marshall Banks instantly. It was brittle, though, and bitter.

"Go on Trygve, tell Matthew the rest of your story. He may as well hear it all now. He won't be doing us any more harm."

Jensen said nothing, but caught Matt's eyes. In a low, conspiratorial whisper, he said, "When I move, you get under cover."

Keyes, who never liked Jensen, found himself trusting him at this moment. Jensen then quickly started to his right in an effort to get behind one of the huge concrete piers. Keyes dropped to the floor and scrambled in the opposite direction. Two shots rang out and echoed through the cavernous space. As Keyes took cover in the inky shadow of an enormous concrete pillar, he heard Jensen groan.

He could see from his vantage point that Jensen had slumped to the floor of the platform and was still partly exposed. Keyes stayed frozen in place and watched Jensen drag himself into the darkness and protection of the huge pier.

"That was stupid, Trygve. You must know how this will end. There's no use trying for a grand escape." It was Banks once more, this time his voice clearer, perhaps closer.

Jensen said nothing, but Keyes could hear labored breathing from that direction.

"Well, Matthew, let me continue where my former associate left off." Keyes turned to the voice echoing in the tunnel, but all was darkness, and he could not determine Banks' position.

"What Trygve hasn't mentioned is the complications brought about by the entry of your young Brazilian friend. Of course, we knew he was coming to Boston, and we followed him. When he went to the police headquarters in your place, we simply had to take him out of commission."

"Where is he? Is he safe?"

"Your friend is, by my best calculations, somewhere in the netherworld. If he led a clean life, perhaps he sits now with his god. If not, I shudder to think of his fate."

"You're a bastard!"

"I'm very saddened to hear you say that, Matthew. I know that you held me in high regard until a few moments ago."

"What about the little boy?"

"Young Joshua O'Byrne? Now isn't he the product of a wonderful marriage? What Joanne ever saw in Alan O'Byrne, I will never understand." Banks snickered. "But the boy is not hurt. At least not to my knowledge. Of course, Hector does have a frightful temper, and if the lad doesn't behave ..."

"What kind of monster are you?" Matt was raging, and he wanted to find Banks and strangle him.

"Me? A monster? You consider me a monster, Matthew?

No, I'm afraid you're mistaken about that. Not that there are no monsters, Matthew, but they're not here with us. The real monsters are upstairs, just over our heads. They're walking the streets of Boston above us right at this moment, as we speak." Banks' voice retained its patrician polish.

"What kind of nonsense are you talking about?"

"Think about it, Matthew. Use your clever mind to figure it out. Look at Oklahoma City, or Phoenix, or Pretoria, and Delhi. They're in Mexico and Algeria and Afghanistan. Plenty of monsters there, wouldn't you agree? Not to mention the Twin Towers in Manhattan. Or even quaint old Boston. If you want monsters, I'll show you plenty, all within a stone's throw above our heads."

Keyes interjected, "Anyone who stoops to kidnapping a little boy is a monster, in my opinion. A gutless monster."

Marshall Banks' voice rose in angry crescendo. "Look at the world, Matthew! Be honest about it! What do you see? Do you see the chaos? Do you see that there are armies forming in our cities? I'm talking about real armies. They're well armed and well trained, and they have a mission, Matthew, just like any legitimate army would have. They're armed with assault weapons, even some larger arms, and they're willing to send this country and the rest of the world back to the goddamned Stone Age because they feel cheated or wronged. Dissed? Now that's a wonderful reason to start a war, isn't it? We be dissed. You be dissed. He, she, or it be dissed." Banks' voice was continuing to rise, shrill in its vehemence.

"Look at the world around us, Matthew. Tell me it makes sense to sit back and do nothing when some redneck sons of bitches with a pickup truck and a load of fertilizer can vaporize hundreds of innocent people and turn the country into an armed camp. Tell me it makes sense to sit back and watch a small group of deranged religious nuts commandeer a passel of airliners and use them as guided missiles. You want to speak of monsters, Matthew? They are the monsters!"

Keyes listened to Banks' diatribe, but focused on the sound. He edged around the platform and cocked his ear, gauging the source. He narrowed his focus on an area to his right. There were three pillars in a row, the faces of which were clearly illuminated by the glow from Jensen's flashlight.

Jensen was sitting up now, and Keyes could see him motioning to him. Jensen called to Banks in a cracking voice. "Marshall, go on. Tell him about Oates. Tell him about Commander Oates, Marshall."

As Banks' laugh reverberated through the darkness, Jensen continued gesturing to Keyes. "Go. Go." Jensen's whisper was weak, but Keyes understood.

Banks went on, and Keyes moved to a crouch and slid slowly to his left. He needed to get behind Banks, and for that, he needed the cover of sound.

"Certainly, Trygve. I thought you'd have the stomach for it, and I was wrong. You see, Matthew, Commander Oates presented an unusual opportunity to us. Jack knew his background well. He told me about this poor, brilliant man and how he had been passed over for promotion. Oates went on to oversee a nuclear weapons arsenal, which is an extraordinarily important position in its own right, but it seems that he was not satisfied, and Jack happened to mention this to me in passing. That intrigued me, I have to say. I sensed a weakness that might serve my purposes, and Jack saw it as well. Jack, however, tended to see things in a financial sort of way: Use Oates to make money. I, on the other hand, saw this for more than just its potential financial rewards. I saw it as part of a much grander vision, a chance to do the kind of business that would keep the world better protected from the maniacs out there."

Keyes made a move through the protection of the shadows to an adjacent pillar, searching for a way to get behind Banks. He hoped Banks would continue his angry tirade, and he was rewarded.

"Oh, there will be war, Matthew. You know that. It may not be a standing uniformed army invading our shores, or an enemy air force sending nuclear warheads overhead—although there are plenty of third world leaders who would love the chance to heave a nuke across the ocean at New York or Los Angeles. And with all the untraceable nuclear materials spilling out of the old Soviet Union, there are probably a couple of them out there right now who aren't too far from being able to do it."

Banks paused and Jensen picked up on the need to keep him talking.

"Tell Matthew about how Oates fit into your plans, Marshall. Go on."

"There will be war, Matthew. And in any war, there are winners and losers. Every time. I saw Oates as the way to accomplish another goal. It would be supremely lucrative, of course, and mounting a successful campaign requires enormous wealth. But more important, I could use Oates to arrange to put the world's finest weapons into the hands of people I knew could be trusted to respond properly when the war eventually arrives."

Keyes heard a delicious malice in Banks' voice, but his mind was intent on creeping to the next pillar, and he sensed he'd be behind Banks and within a few feet if he could make it. He tested every step to avoid making any sound. The confines and hard surfaces of the tunnel would amplify every noise. He prepared to make his move when Banks went on.

"If there have to be winners, Matthew, they may as well be us. Ironically, the complications came when we achieved both of these goals. You see, Captain Oates didn't want to stop. His greed got the better of him, Matthew. He wanted to keep up the weapons sales, and Jack couldn't get him to listen to reason. That led to a dreadful argument, but you already know the next part, don't you, Matthew? Matthew?"

Keyes had Banks' shadow in view now, not more than fifteen feet away, but could not respond without giving away his position.

Jensen tried once again to cover for him.

"Don't stop now, Marshall. We're all ears." Jensen coughed, wheezing as he spoke.

"Matthew? Say something, Matthew." Banks now knew that Keyes was presenting a danger, and he went silent.

Keyes remained motionless, but he'd lost sight of Banks. He

crouched low behind a pillar and breathed slowly. He had been able to move from the platform across the abandoned rail bed to his current location, and he needed to keep Banks distracted.

Jensen tried once again to provide valuable cover. "What's the matter, Marshall? Why the silence all of a sudden? Tell Matt about Rosemary Oates. She really fucked up your barbecue, didn't she?"

"Shut up, Trygve. Shut up."

Jensen ignored him and picked up the story. He spoke slowly, interrupted by coughing and wheezing. Keyes guessed he had been hit, probably in the chest.

"Jack Munroe killed Henry Oates." Jensen picked up the tail of Banks' saga. "And Marshall took care of the body. What Marshall didn't know was that the captain had left his lovely wife, Rosemary, with a vast inheritance of information, as well as money. It didn't take her long to see its value and devise a clever way to use it. She located Jack a few weeks ago, and the blackmail began. She ached for vengeance and lusted for money. Two very powerful motivational forces. Nearly drove Jack over the edge. Right, Marshall?"

Banks would not speak, and Keyes was sure he'd lost him. He strained to hear any sound that might give him away. Jensen was in serious trouble, but he made a valiant effort to continue.

"So you had her killed. Simple, straight, and to the point. How did Hector do it, Marshall? Knife? Gun? Come on, Marshall, tell us. Did he rape her before he did it, or did he wait until later? Tell Matthew that Hector is the same Neanderthal who nabbed his friend and the little boy. Go on, Marshall, tell him."

"Shut up!"

Keyes saw some movement ahead of him. Banks was moving away. Keyes leaned around the corner of the pillar and suddenly felt a large hand gripping his shoulder. He gasped, but a soft whisper against his ear kept him in place. "It's me, Collins." Keyes' heart had raced to warp speed in the space of a second. Adrenaline surged through his veins. Collins could sense Keyes tighten and then release. He squeezed his shoulder as if to say, "It's all right now."

"What is that?" Marshall Banks was rattled. "Who's there?"

He aimed his pistol in the direction from which Matt's gasp had come and squeezed the trigger. The bullet ricocheted loudly, but harmlessly into the tunnel. Collins held Matthew with one hand and Matt saw that he held a pistol in the other. A rat skittered across the ground and Banks fired wildly at the sound.

Collins stood, aimed his pistol, and supported his firing arm with the other. "Drop the weapon."

Banks did not answer, but the crunch of broken glass under his feet announced that he was on the move.

CHAPTER TWENTY

COLLINS KEPT HIS voice low. "Stay here," he told Keyes, and he edged back into darkness.

Alone once more in the darkness, Matt struggled to hear any sounds beyond the ambient noises of rats scurrying and water dripping. Jensen's wheezing had ceased. Matt wondered if he was dead.

Keyes silently tried to digest what he had heard from both Jensen and Banks. This was not the same Marshall Banks he knew. This man was a vile human being. Where was the genuine warmth, the gentle caring and concern he had come to expect of him?

And Jensen. Keyes remembered Trygve Jensen as permanently cross and unpleasant. But it appeared now that of the two, it was only Jensen with an ethical code that he would not cross.

Keyes was caught unaware when another voice, one he did not recognize, broke the eerie silence from an indistinguishable distance.

"Mr. Banks, this is Sergeant Jerome Wetman of the Boston Police Department." The voice was strong and sure. "I want you to give yourself up. There is no way, Mr. Banks, no way for you to escape."

Keyes guessed that Wetman's voice came from a point far on the other end of the platform. How many others were here? Keyes waited, but he could perceive nothing. He leaned around the corner from his hiding spot and searched the cavern. The batteries from Jensen's flashlight were beginning to weaken, and it painted the walls with a mustard glow. Keyes felt helpless, and any hopes he had of achieving his objective of retrieving Jimmy and Joshua were being methodically destroyed by the man he once considered his mentor and friend.

Suddenly, as if the gauze of ten years had immediately been peeled away, Keyes recollected something from his work on this station that could prove Wetman wrong. There was, in fact, a way for Banks to escape.

When Keyes worked on the Court Street project, he found that the laborers there would ascend to street level by walking across the rail beds of the station to the inbound platform on the other side. There, they used a narrow alley to reach a rusting set of steel stairs that ended at a doorway to the basement of the old City Hall Annex. From the basement, it was one flight up and outdoors to Court Street. Would it not be likely that Banks knew this same route?

Keyes tried to seek out Collins to pass him this information. He looked around him in every direction, but saw no sign of Collins. He whispered his name. No reply. Collins was probably too far away now to hear him.

Keyes rose from his crouch. If he retraced his way back down the outbound rail bed from which he entered, perhaps fifty feet and no more than seventy-five, he would search for an opening in the wall to the other side of the station. He recalled that there were several such passageways though. Once there, he could cross the inbound rail bed and reach the inbound platform.

He took a step backwards, then another, being careful to remain soundless as he placed his feet against the littered ground. He reached the partition wall separating the inbound and outbound sides of the station. Sidling against the wall, he kept one hand extended, searching for an opening. In seconds, he found what he was looking for and stepped through. He moved to his left once and then again across the rail bed, more confident with each step that he was approaching the inbound platform. The faint light afforded by a single lightbulb and a failing flashlight gave Matt sparing chance to form the outline of the platform. He would have to rely on memory.

The end of the platform should be about ten feet in front of me and thirty feet to my right, he considered. He counted his steps as he went, mentally measuring how far he would need to go. He reached out. The platform should be here. His hand struck the dusty concrete of the tunnel wall. *Could I have gone too far?* He tried to establish the location again in his mind. No. He had not gone far enough. He sidled carefully another ten feet to the right.

Slowly, he placed his right hand in front of him and felt … nothing. A good sign. He moved his hand further down and found the edge of the platform. He cautiously moved his hands across the platform surface. He would need to pull himself up the vertical distance of three feet onto the surface, and he did not want to bring noisy attention to himself by disturbing any debris. The space was clear and he put his palms on the edge of the platform. As if to confirm his initial suspicion, he heard the sound of feet moving quickly up the steel stairs. Banks did know of this egress, and he was getting away. Keyes called loudly.

"Over here! He's getting out from the outbound side."

He hoisted himself up to the platform and saw the bright white beam of a flashlight appear besides an opening in the partition wall. Keyes was bathed in its light, and Collins reached him in seconds.

"Where?"

Keyes pointed to the alley opening and Collins ran to it, pistol drawn and raised high. Wetman followed, and Keyes joined the chase, behind their lighted trail. Above him, he heard a door slam shut, and he knew that Banks was now in the basement of the Annex. Collins raced up the stairs and reached that same door, opening it tentatively with one arm extended and keeping his body protected by the concrete foundation. He did not wish to be met by bullets, and Banks had already indicated every intention to shoot.

Wetman, with Keyes on his heels, reached the same spot. Collins moved slowly into the door opening. There was no sign of Banks. Wetman followed cautiously, trailed by Keyes. The three stood silently in the basement together and listened to the labored breathing of an elderly, but still unseen Marshall Banks. Collins motioned to Wetman with his pistol. In silent agreement, Wetman edged to the left side of the foot of the staircase that led up to street level. Collins moved along the back of the basement wall until he reached the other side of the staircase. Matt remained stationery in the open doorway from the station below.

Wetman waited for Collins to reach the opposite side. On a signal, they moved the beams of their flashlights to the source of the sounds emanating from the staircase. There, near the top, lay their weary prey. Marshall Banks, dressed shabbily in worn-out clothes, torn jacket, and dirty knit cap, looked into the bright beams, squinting. Matt moved to a point behind Wetman and saw over his shoulder the bum he noticed earlier in Government Center Station looking for handouts. Banks had been waiting for Keyes to enter the tunnel so he could follow him to Court Street Station and his meeting with Trygve Jensen.

Drained and treed now like an animal, Banks looked down the flight of stairs at his captors. Collins addressed him in a low and even voice. "Mr. Banks, please put down your weapon. It's all over."

Banks could only see the two bright circles of light. Between gulps of air, a spent Marshall Banks addressed Keyes.

"Matthew, you have such dreadful timing. If you hadn't seen what you saw, perhaps none of this would have happened."

Keyes spoke in a calm tone. "That wouldn't have stopped Rosemary Oates, Mr. Banks. You would still have had her to deal with."

"You're right, of course, but we did take care of her, didn't we? I mean, one has to expect some bumps in the road. One deals with them when they arise. This is not always a gentleman's sport, you know." Banks stopped speaking and caught his breath before going on.

"But you, Matthew, you wouldn't stop your nonsense. As soon as I thought you had quit the chase, you'd come at us again." His breathing came harder. "A sign of impulsiveness, Matthew. Not a trait to which you should aspire.

"Most pitiably, you really kept us from a great achievement, one deserving your favor. And your support. Our goals, you know, are right and proper."

"No, they're not, Mr. Banks. They're not."

"Oh, Matthew, don't be childish. What do you think we should do? Shall we beat back the evil empire with copies of the Constitution? Why, imagine the paper cuts we would inflict upon the enemy." Banks alone found this amusing, his scornful chortle resonating upon the basement walls.

"You're naive, young man. Ingenuous. Take my advice, my innocent, young friend, and prepare for battle. It will come."

Collins spoke up again. "Mr. Banks, please put down your weapon."

"My weapon?" He waved the pistol. "This? You can have it in just a moment. Be patient." With that, Marshall Banks put the barrel into his mouth and squeezed the trigger.

***

THE AMBULANCES WERE called in by Wetman. He went out to Court Street after Banks' final move and used his flip phone. Banks was dead, but there was still Jensen to worry about. Wetman found Jensen alive and still conscious. The bullet had pierced his right lung. Any questions they had would have to wait; Jensen was in no condition to respond. Using flashlights, the EMTs carried Jensen on a stretcher all the way back to Government Center Station.

Police department photographers finished up their work quickly and were gone. So were the reporters and television cameras. Now, only Collins, Wetman, and three bored MBTA security guards remained underground at the long abandoned Court Street Station.

Collins discerned from Wetman's tone that he was beginning to wind down. Whenever he did, he'd be ready to go. Meanwhile, he wondered about Keyes. After Banks blew the back of his head off, the three of them watched in silence as Banks slumped forward. The gases inside the bullet cartridge exploded with such force that Banks' eyes burst from their sockets. The wall of the staircase behind him was coated with flesh, bone, blood, and brains. Keyes stared, not comprehending right away what he had witnessed. Collins holstered his pistol, went to Keyes and put an arm on his shoulders. Keyes wept.

The second call on Wetman's flip phone was made by Matthew Keyes. He called Melrose to explain to Joanne what had happened and that he was safe, but never got past the news that Jimmy and Joshua were unharmed and on their way back from an all-night diner in Framingham, eighteen miles away. That, after all, was the best news any of them had heard in a long time.

Collins asked a uniformed sergeant on the scene to drive Keyes to Melrose, and Matt gladly accepted the offer. Collins would see Keyes again in a few hours. This whole episode would take some sorting out.

***

ON THE RIDE back to Melrose, the sergeant listened quietly as Keyes described the past few days of his life. The sergeant listened attentively and nodded occasionally. He knew how therapeutic talking could be at times of stress, and he let Matt ramble on. This, in his opinion, was a most stressful time in Matthew's life.

Keyes directed the sergeant to Carter Street. In front of number fifty-two were parked two Melrose cruisers and a black Chevrolet. *FBI*, Keyes thought. Further up the street, several other cars were parked. From the lights on at number fifty-two, he knew where everyone must be.

He hopped out of the Boston cruiser and thanked his driver effusively. "No problem, young man," the sergeant said. "Take care of yourself, son. It's a great day to be alive." Keyes listened to the words, thanked the sergeant again, and ran to the house.

The kitchen was crammed with bodies. Uniformed officers. The FBI agents he met earlier. Detective Lyons across the room. Some, he guessed, were newspaper reporters. Anne Stowe wore an apron and laughed at something one of the FBI agents said. The loud conversations and the generally smiling faces gave the appearance of a party.

Keyes could see Joanne smiling and doing her best to convince Lyons to share a toast with her. "Oh, c'mon," she coaxed, "my little boy is safe, and he's going to be here any minute. Have a drink, damn you."

Lyons saw Keyes enter the kitchen before Joanne did and he winked in Matt's direction. "Get over here, Mr. Keyes. There's a lady here wants to propose a toast, and she needs a partner."

Matt met Joanne halfway into the kitchen and hugged her tightly. Tears of joy ran down her cheeks. "Matt," was all she could say, saying the name over and over in a voice barely above a whisper. She stood back and looked at him in admiration and wonderment. Then she led him by the hand into the living room, where the population density thinned out considerably.

"Jimmy and Joshua will be here in ten minutes. The Melrose police sent a cruiser out to pick them up. I spoke with Joshua, and he's fine. And Jimmy, too." She hugged him again and said into his ear, "My mother says it's a miracle. And I believe her."

Lyons walked in on the two of them. He held a bottle of Christian Brothers brandy in one hand and three cordial glasses in the other. "Saints be praised, I always say." He set the glasses down on the coffee table and poured two fingers into each glass. "To God, America, your friend, Mr. Keyes, and your son, madam." A drink never tasted so sweet.

A young Melrose police officer stepped into the room and asked, "Excuse me, but where's the bathroom?" Joanne smiled and pointed down the hallway. "Thanks, ma'am." He started off down the hall, stopped abruptly, and addressed Joanne. "I have to say, ma'am, that your kitchen smells like a kitchen ought to smell."

Keyes noticed for the first time the aroma of apples and cinnamon wafting from the kitchen. "My mom promised Jimmy some apple pie, and she's coming through."

***

COLLINS AND WETMAN stood together in the floodlit remnants of Court Street Station. It was coming up to 4 o'clock in the morning, but Wetman was wound up and ready to go another shift. "Look at this, Collins. Look at this." Wetman was giving an enthusiastic tour of the abandoned station to Collins, whether Collins wanted it or not. "This turnstile is as old as the station, and it still works like new. Damn station was built in 1900." Collins might have been awed if it had been another day, another time. Right now, he was ready to fall asleep standing up.

They both realized that there would be many more hours to go before sleep would be theirs, though. There were too many questions to be answered, too many forms to fill out, and an impatient police commissioner waiting for their return to headquarters. The death of Marshall Banks would not wait long to be explained. But Wetman enjoyed keeping the commissioner waiting, and as long as he stayed deep underground, out of radio contact, he could claim any number of reasons for being delayed.

Collins would stay with Wetman until he was ready to leave. "I told you how my old man was a gandy dancer, right?" Collins nodded. "Sometime, I'll show you some of the other abandoned stations. And there's an abandoned incline real close by on Cambridge Street; used to be set up to take trains up to Harvard Square." Collins nodded.

Collins looked around him now. One of the MBTA security guards leaned against a railing and looked at his watch. Collins heard Wetman calling him. "Are you going to stay here forever, Collins? We've got a commissioner waiting on us. Let's hustle."

CHAPTER TWENTY-ONE

COLLINS AND WETMAN waited in their office for Keyes to arrive. They had much to discuss. Fatima Cabral put on her fourth pot of coffee and it was only 11 o'clock. She had never seen Wetman or Collins as exhausted as they looked to be now.

Wetman tried to work on the *Herald* crossword, but tossed it aside in disgust. "Who really gives a shit about Enid's wife?"

Fatima Cabral thought he was talking to her. "What was that?"

"Where the hell is the creativity? Guido's high note? Does knowing that make a person enlightened? I mean, it asks for a retired tennis great. You'd think Arthur Ashe was the only retired tennis great in the world." Collins raised his head and looked at his partner. "Besides, the goddamned *Herald* is too skinny. Damned editors sitting around: 'Not enough news? Just use bigger pictures.' I never saw a paper like this. You take the racing form out, there's only three pages left. Six hundred thousand people in this goddamned city, and they find three pages to write about."

Collins said nothing.

Fatima Cabral rose from her seat and dropped a stack of paperwork on the corner of Wetman's desk. "When are you going to get to all this?" Cabral asked, indicating several tall stacks of reports and files amassed over the past several days. They remained untouched by Wetman, in the same positions where she had placed them.

"Where does it say that you should kick my ass, Fatima? Is it on my face or something?"

"No, but look at this mess." Fatima was unsympathetic. "You should be ashamed."

"Let him be, Fatima," Collins added from his side of the office. "Just let it be for now."

She looked back at Collins, who was hunched over his desk. She gave Wetman a pursed lip and returned to her desk.

"Collins," Wetman said. "What do you think of that asshole commissioner this morning?" Neither had talked about the early morning session they had had in the police commissioner's office. It was not a friendly session, and the tone was set early when the commissioner told them he was "ashamed and appalled by the actions, the attitudes, and the irresponsibility" of the pair. The commissioner had been caught unaware by a telephone call to his home from the city editor of the *Boston Globe* at two in the morning. "I was dancing a jig for this guy, trying to buy time. I'm the friggin' commissioner of police, and this reporter knew a lot more about the biggest case in the city, maybe even the whole goddamned country, than I did. I'm the *commissioner*, dammit!"

Wetman and Collins were not even offered a seat in his office. They remained standing like a couple of adolescents hearing the riot act from the school principal. After a few minutes of being harangued, Wetman took out his note pad and began scribbling. The commissioner asked him what he was doing and Wetman kept writing, ignoring him. He tore off the page, dropped it on the commissioner's desk, and headed for the door.

"What's this, Wetman?" the commissioner demanded.

"You can read it at your leisure, sir. I'm going home."

The commissioner glanced at the scribbled words and bellowed, "Get back here, Wetman. I'm not accepting your resignation."

Wetman stopped at the door and turned around, an expression of innocent surprise on his face. "I'm sorry, sir; what did you say?"

"I said get back here." He motioned to the two cushioned chairs in front of his desk. "Both of you, please sit down."

Collins took a seat and Wetman returned and joined him.

"Look, both of you, let's start over, OK? Let's just start over."

That was as close to an apology as Collins and Wetman had ever heard from their boss.

"Just tell me what's going on, because the last time I heard from you guys, Brock and Leininger were replacing you on the Four Seasons murder. That shocked me to shit, let me tell you. And did I get any reason? No way. Did I get any word as to what would be occupying your time instead? No way. I hear absolutely nothing about what you're up to until the *Globe* calls, and the guy's telling me, telling me, for chrissake, what you two have been doing."

Collins spoke up for the first time. "It was my fault that we ended up calling in Brock and Leininger. I talked Jerry into helping me on this other case. Then, we started digging and lost track of time. It was practically midnight before we had it figured that something would be going down in the old T station. So don't blame Jerry. I'm the one who dragged him into this."

The commissioner sat back in his seat and thought this over before he continued. "Look, maybe we're all just tired. Both of you have been working all day and all night, and you're both to be commended on getting to Mr. Keyes before he could be hurt. I understand that the child involved was found safely as well. Is that true?"

"Yes, sir," Collins replied. "He and Mr. Keyes' friend, who was abducted from Newbury Street two days ago, escaped last night. The Melrose police picked them up early this morning in Framingham and brought them home."

"And you seem certain that the murder of Rosemary Oates was connected to these abductions?"

Wetman cut in. "We believe so, sir. We're going to get statements from everybody, of course, but we believe that the same guy is responsible for all three crimes. First nabbing the Brazilian kid on Newbury Street, then doing Rosemary Oates in the Four Seasons, and right after that, snatching the little O'Byrne kid in Melrose. It was like the guy was running errands."

The commissioner listened to Wetman and considered his words before he said them. "Leininger tells me that he and Brock do not share your view. They tell me it is highly unlikely that the same person would have killed Mrs. Oates at the hotel at night, and then snatched the child in Melrose."

Wetman wasted no time responding. "I beg your pardon, sir, but Leininger has shit for brains, and Brock is nothing but ..."

Collins jumped in to save his friend. "What Sergeant Wetman and I believe is ..."

Wetman would have none of this. "Brock is a butt wipe. Goddamned waste of good oxygen. If you want to lose money, just put your bet on those two peckerheads."

The commissioner looked at Collins and then at Wetman. "Let's just forget them for the moment. Give me your take on the story. And don't leave out anything about Senator Munroe. The press is going to be on me like horseflies on warm manure, and I want to know what the facts are so far."

Collins started. Ninety minutes went by before he was finished. He had not referred to a single note from beginning to end. When he ended the story with Banks' suicide, the commissioner was staring at him, jaw slackened in amazement. Wetman was snoring.

The Commissioner suggested Collins go home and rest. The FBI, he knew, would be taking statements from Keyes and the others in Melrose today. He asked Collins to meet with the FBI at Mass General Hospital at 9 o'clock in the morning to interview Jensen.

Collins thanked the commissioner and rose from his seat. He was about to shake Wetman awake when the commissioner said, "Let him be for now, Collins. I'll tell him about your meeting with Jensen when he wakes up. And, Collins? Good job."

"Thank you, sir."

***

"EXCUSE ME." MATT arrived at Mass General at noon.

Collins rose from his seat and reached for Matt's hand. "How are you doing this morning, Matt?"

Wetman gave Matt a tired one-hand wave from his seat.

Collins saw that Joanne was standing behind Matt and waved her into the room as well. The dark-skinned young man behind her with the smile must be Jimmy, he reasoned.

Jimmy eagerly shook the hands of Collins and Wetman. He

wore a small bandage on his forehead. Wetman rose from his seat when he saw Jimmy and said, "I heard about what you did to escape. Man, that was creativity. Burn your head?"

"Cut it on a metal bucket," Jimmy said, the smile etched permanently on his face. "Bled like a pig."

With all five comfortably seated in a meeting room at the hospital, Collins opened the session. "I'm going to tape this, if you don't mind."

No one disagreed.

"Let's begin with you, Matt. Then Joanne, and then Jimmy. I know we've been over a lot of this already at different times, but why not start at the beginning?"

***

BY THE TIME they were finished, the time was after 2 o'clock. Wetman had ordered sandwiches, and they continued taping straight through lunch. Collins pressed the stop button and ejected the fourth cassette. Both he and Wetman had jotted pages of notes during the meeting.

Wetman asked Jimmy the first question. "Are you sure you can identify this guy who grabbed you and knocked you out?"

"Absolutely, sir. I can tell you everything about him. His height, his clothes, everything."

"And you're certain that this same individual is the one who abducted Joshua?"

"No question," Jimmy assured him. "Joshua and I talked about him a lot. The tall, skinny guy with the bad skin."

"And the last time you saw him, he was inside the burning storage building?"

"Yes, sir. He was banging on the door and the building was shooting flames in the air. It was scary, believe me."

Collins and Wetman had seen a report that the FBI had done of the remains of the storage shed. At the moment, they did not wish to share the conclusions with those present in the room. The FBI had found a pile of hot ashes and twisted metal at the remote

"Farm," based on Jimmy's description of the area. A pair of men's shoes were found in the rubble, but no signs at all of human remains. A search of the house and all of the other buildings revealed nothing. Whoever was in the burning shed when Jimmy and Joshua took off did not die in the fire.

Matt had several questions.

"How did Mr. Banks know that I would be meeting with Trygve Jensen? The only people who knew I would be there were Jensen himself and Joanne. Why would Jensen tell Banks if they had become enemies?"

"Jensen didn't tell him you'd be there," Collins explained. "Here's what we think, based on what we've learned from Jensen and the FBI. Banks sensed that Jensen had turned on him. Jensen was horrified to learn about the real story behind Captain Oates and his illegal arms shipments. Then, almost immediately, he learned about Jimmy being nabbed, and then Joshua, and finally the murder of Rosemary Oates. That's when Jensen tried to reach you. Banks was following him, hoping he'd lead him to you. He had already taken care of Rosemary Oates, so she wasn't a threat any longer. He also had Jimmy under control, and figured he'd be out of the picture soon. Joshua was taken as a means to get to you, and maybe even Joanne. We'll never know for sure. But to Marshall Banks, you were definitely a loose cannon, and here you were back in Boston again. Banks knew that Jensen was hanging around your neighborhood in Melrose, and maybe he even saw the note get passed by the kid on the bike. When Banks saw that Jensen was going into the tunnel in the direction of the old MBTA station, he knew you'd be coming in soon. So he just hung back and waited for you to appear."

Wetman picked up when Collins finished. "Banks did all kinds of work for the MBTA over the past forty or fifty years. He knew about Court Street Station, of course, and he put two and two together. There'd be no other reason for Jensen to go there."

Keyes asked, "But why was he dressed like a bum? Mr. Banks was always dressed in the best clothes."

"To blend into the background, we figure," Wetman answered.

Not many people pay attention to an old, homeless guy hanging around in the city of Boston. Mr. Banks was well-known in the city, and if he was dressed up as usual, someone would be sure to recognize him right away."

Joanne asked about Senator Jack Munroe. "Has he been arrested yet?"

Collins responded. "Not yet. And right now, there's no assurance that he'll ever be arrested. Jensen gave us a lot of information this morning, and he filled in some big gaps. We'll be meeting with the FBI later on to talk about the next step as far as Munroe is concerned."

"But Matt was an eyewitness. He saw the whole thing." Joanne wasn't ready to accept the possibility that Munroe could walk away free.

"I understand, and Matt's description of what he saw will help a great deal. Especially since he reported it the next morning. Jensen gave us a statement that will help, too. He wasn't present, but he certainly knew about Oates being killed that night. Unfortunately, his is mostly hearsay evidence. In other words, Jensen knows what someone else told him about what happened. He didn't hear anything directly from Monroe, and I wouldn't hold my breath waiting for Munroe to incriminate himself. The FBI is looking for blood and other evidence from Munroe's office at the Prudential. A trace of Oates' blood anywhere in there will help a lot. And maybe they'll even find the weapon. We don't know."

Joanne didn't accept this well. "Do you mean to tell me that you know that a murderer is running for President, and you can't do a thing about it? So I suppose you'll have to wait for this guy to get into the White House before you arrest him. That's just great."

Wetman interjected. "Exactly my sentiments, Mrs. O'Byrne. But that thorny little situation may resolve itself shortly when Senator Munroe holds a press conference later today."

"Really?" Joanne hadn't heard this news. "When did you hear this?"

"Well," said Wetman, looking at his watch, "let's just say that we have a reliable source who told us that Senator Munroe received a phone call a little while ago from the head of the FBI's Boston office. He was presented with some information about the case, and about Jensen's conversations this morning. If I were you, Mrs. O'Byrne, I would suggest you stay close to a television this evening."

Matt turned to Collins. "What about Captain Oates and all the arms he sold?"

"Well, that's not something you're going to hear about on the nightly news, Matt. Oates is dead, of course. And his wife. And now Banks. Jensen's alive, but he doesn't know much more about the arms sales than we do. Obviously, the Feds want to know who received what. Munroe probably has the most knowledge about the arms and who they went to, but I don't think that he'll be volunteering much about that right now."

Wetman added, "The FBI did find a microdisc in Mrs. Oates' room at the Four Seasons, and they're finding quite a bit of interesting information on it. Whether it's accurate or complete, they don't know. They didn't tell us much, Matt. We know that they were in touch with Interpol this morning, but that's about all we know."

"Trygve Jensen." Matt shook his head. "Is he going to be all right?"

"He'll be up and walking around tomorrow morning," Collins said. "The docs said he'll be discharged in a few days. I wouldn't even be surprised if he went back to work one of these days."

"Are you kidding? That mean-spirited man is coming back to Crane & Stewart?" Joanne didn't hide her disgust when it came to Jensen.

Collins offered, "I'm going to ask you to reserve judgment until you have a chance to talk to the man. You might be surprised, Joanne."

***

MATT AND JOANNE were permitted to visit Jensen that afternoon in his room at Mass General. A uniformed Boston police officer stood outside his room in the hall.

Laying down in a hospital bed, Trygve Jensen was not the intimidating character they remembered him to be. His left shoulder was heavily taped, and his skin was pale, but he seemed surprisingly alert and serene for a man who'd suffered a serious bullet wound only thirty-six hours earlier.

"Hello, Matthew. Hello, Joanne. Please, sit down." Jensen seemed the kind host as well. "I'd offer to shake hands, but I'm afraid one arm is temporarily out of commission, and the other has an intravenous line in it."

"You look like you're coming along well, Mr. Jensen," Matt said.

"Thank you, Matthew. But as I said to you earlier, please call me Trig. I suppose you have a few questions to ask me."

"We have a lot of questions, Trig."

"I'll wager that I know what some of them are. But I will ask you to hold them for a bit while I tell you a few things that may surprise or even shock you."

Joanne didn't yet trust the kindly, soft-spoken manner of the man she knew to be Trygve Jensen, and her tone of voice let him know it. "There's nothing you could say at this point that would shock us."

Jensen smiled as he responded. "I can't say that I'm astonished at your reaction, Joanne. After all, I know very well that I'm recognized as the most despised man at Crane & Stewart. I hope you'll pardon me for a bit of vulgarity, but does this sound familiar? 'Lo, though I walk through the valley of the shadow of death, I shall fear no evil, for I am the meanest motherfucker in the valley.'"

Joanne was stunned. Those were the very words she and her colleagues would share with new employees about Trygve Jensen when they first encountered his wrath. It was almost routine, but she never suspected that Jensen knew.

"Did you think I was unaware? I'm quite certain that you'll be surprised to learn that this acerbic disposition was by design. By Marshall Banks." He let this sink in before he continued. "It was no accident that Banks was the good-hearted partner who doled out praise and gentle encouragement, and I the agitated partner who fired and chastened. I will give Marshall credit. He knew very well the importance of having a villain in the organization. He decided that I would be it. And I accepted the role."

Joanne couldn't accept this without more explanation from Jensen. "Why would anyone intentionally set out to include a disagreeable person in an organization? It doesn't make sense."

"Ah, but it served a purpose, Joanne. At least for Marshall it did. Marshall wanted to be liked, and that's a reasonable motive. He also enjoyed manipulating people. So much so that he institutionalized the positions of bad guy and good guy. And to tell you the truth, I'm not sure that it's such a terrible concept."

"That's diabolical, if you ask me," huffed Joanne.

"I won't disagree. But it reveals a good deal about the man, don't you think? Understand, I wasn't reluctant to take on the role I assumed. I suppose that reveals a good deal about me as well.

"Marshall and I were very good friends from the beginning. He is, or was, some ten years older than I, and I knew him when I was not much more than a child. We were raised in the same neighborhood in Dorchester. I admired him, and I saw him as my role model.

"So, when I became a licensed surveyor, I was really following in his footsteps. Marshall had been with Crane & Stewart for some time by then and had married Mr. Crane's daughter, Caroline. Marshall convinced his father-in-law to take me on as an apprentice. When Crane passed on and Marshall took over the firm, he asked me to be his number two man in the company. That was pretty heady stuff for a young man like me, and I jumped at the opportunity. Marshall and I became even better friends as the years went by, and we worked quite well together. The firm flourished, and we both became rather wealthy."

"How did you and he become involved with Munroe?" Matt asked. "Was this something that Marshall Banks started?"

"Marshall was basically a manipulative human being, as I've told you. Politics, of course, is the art of manipulation, and Marshall was politically astute. Do you think that all of those government contracts came to Crane & Stewart because we were simply a fine engineering firm?" His question was rhetorical. "There are dozens of engineering firms in the city with equal talent. But Marshall understood the game of politics better than most, and I learned a great deal working at his side.

"I believe I told you that Marshall saw an opportunity to promote his own agenda on a large scale, a presidential scale, in this election year. Basically, economic conservatism. Social libertarianism. Nothing startling there. It was quite easy, really, to assemble a group of like-minded individuals and to gain support for asserting their shared opinions. His 'Board of Directors.'

"We would need a substantial amount of money, of course. By pulling such a group together, we were able to construct the foundation of a sizable campaign fund. There were twelve of us, and if you saw the roster of Munroe's backers, you would recognize many familiar names.

"We needed a candidate, as well, and that would be Munroe, without question."

"Why do you say that?"

"Why Munroe?" Jensen considered the question before going on.

"Do you recall when the whole issue of supporting a reduction in military aid to Japan surfaced? It was Marshall who spurred Jack to take the point position for his party. There were a lot of high-powered politicians in Washington who were similarly inclined, but the issue was a prototypical 'hot potato,' and none were willing to grab hold. When Jack stepped forward, his colleagues in the Senate were relieved. That was a stroke of genius, and it distinguished Jack nationally."

"So now you had money and a candidate," Joanne observed. "Matt told me about your involvement with Oates."

"When I learned of Oates and of his death, it was portrayed by Marshall in quite a different light from the truth as we know it now. It was only recently that I learned about Marshall using Jack

Munroe and Henry Oates to arrange for these horrible arms sales. Over the past several days, Marshall was becoming obsessed, terribly obsessed with you, Matthew. I confronted him about this, and it was then that Marshall described his scheme to me. I was shocked, to say the least. Treasonous. Powerful weapons to the people and the countries he selected. Vast sums of money in return. You heard him, Matthew. He was possessed. And quite insane."

Matt nodded, recalling the horror he sensed upon hearing Marshall Banks describe arming against the "real monsters." He asked Jensen, "When you found all this out, why didn't you just go to the police?"

"I nearly did, Matthew. Yesterday. But I didn't know where the young man and the child were being held, and I didn't believe Marshall would harm them, at least not right away. I did know that if Marshall suspected that I had turned against him and contacted the police, he'd simply eliminate them at once. After all, it was you he was trying to draw out; they were just tools he was using to get to you. So I decided instead to let Marshall continue believing that I still supported him. I chose to present the facts to you, privately, face-to-face; I didn't know that Marshall had already ordered them killed. It was a marvel that they managed to escape."

Joanne was focused on something Jensen had said earlier. "You didn't settle on Munroe as your candidate just because of his position on military aid to Japan. You said Munroe would be your candidate 'without question,' but I still don't see the reason why Marshall Banks had a particular interest in Jack Munroe."

Jensen inhaled deeply. He was tiring. "Marshall took an interest in Munroe from the very start. It was Marshall who financed Jack's education. Marshall who connected Jack politically. It was Marshall who arranged for Jack to be adopted by the Munroe family in Groton. A very fine couple."

"But why?" Joanne pressed for an answer.

Jensen seemed to be reluctant to answer. He took another deep breath. "You wouldn't remember Marshall's wife, Joanne, but Caroline was frail and quite ill throughout her short life. They could never have children. When she died, Marshall was still a young man. He cut a handsome figure and liked the companionship of the ladies. Marshall became, shall I say, intimate with a lovely young lady whose profession might be considered rather unsavory, especially given the times. She was a stage performer at one of the burlesque houses in Scollay Square. Marshall was quite taken by the girl, and she bore him a son."

"Jack Munroe is the son of Marshall Banks?" Joanne was stupefied. "What happened to the mother?"

"Marshall would not wed her, and I am unsure truly if she would agree to marry him, even if he had indeed asked. She went on to dance on other stages in other cities. I don't think Marshall ever tried to maintain contact with her."

"Does Munroe know that he is the son of Marshall Banks?"

"I only know what I just told you from my close association with Marshall. I doubt if Marshall ever told Jack, and I cannot speak for the Munroes. Marshall did provide the Munroes with funds from time to time, especially for Jack's education. My guess is that Jack Munroe has no reason to believe his parents to be any other than the nice couple in Groton who still reside there."

CHAPTER TWENTY-TWO

WHEN MATT AND Joanne walked out of Jensen's room an hour later, they had a great deal on their minds. Sorting through all the deceit surrounding the man they knew as Marshall Banks was difficult and painful. Both had admired the man greatly, and in spite of his evident cruelty and duplicity, his death remained a source of grief for them.

Again, Trygve Jensen was enigmatic. Whatever thoughts Joanne and Matt once shared of the man had been dismantled and reconstructed before their eyes. The man was beguiling and forthright. And the offer by Jensen of a permanent position at Crane & Stewart weighed heavily on Keyes. "I am not a young man," Jensen said, "and the firm needs a strong and bright individual who can shepherd it into the twenty-first century. I am asking you to be that person, Matthew."

Keyes felt uncomfortable at the offer and asked Jensen for some time to consider it. Jensen complied, understanding that the rigors of the past several days would test any man's ability to reach an important decision, certainly one with so many ramifications. "Time," he said to Keyes. "Take some time to heal and refresh yourself. Crane & Stewart will be there when you decide."

Keyes looked at Joanne, whose face gave no clue as to her feelings. He welcomed the opportunity for some quiet repose to examine the offer professionally, and more importantly, to assess his resolve to return to Boston and to become ...or not to become ...truly committed to Joanne.

Joanne held his hand as they walked the length of the corridor in silence.

They looked for Jimmy, who had been sitting with Collins and

Wetman when they went into Jensen's room, but he was nowhere in sight. They decided to check the cafeteria, thinking it would be as logical place to find him as any in the labyrinthine Mass General complex. What they found when they reached the cafeteria was a crowd of uniformed police officers huddled around one of the corner tables. Collins was standing with the group and saw Matt and Joanne enter. He waved them over.

As they neared the cluster, they could hear Jimmy's voice. "I found a long nail in a glass jar in the corner, and I figured, hey, this could be useful."

"Tell them what happened when the asshole switched on the light, Jimmy." It was Wetman's voice they heard now.

"Well, the tall guy, the one with the face? He's saying 'come out, come out, wherever you are', and I'm underneath all this stuff, see? And the guy gets mad, cause it's dark and he can't see me."

Matt and Joanne each took a seat among the rapt audience. They would wait for Jimmy to finish his saga before the short ride back to Melrose.

***

THE TELEPHONE IN Senator John Munroe's Washington office would not stop ringing. His secretaries and staff assistants had gone home, and only the senator and Lisa Sobolewski remained. He reached over the top of his desk to the phone and removed the jack. For now, at least, the chafing noise would be confined to the receptionist's office, two rooms away. The senator stood in shirtsleeves at the window, looking out at the street below. Bathed in a soothing twilight glow, the scene belied its gentle serenity. Munroe knew well that the moment of cruel truth lurked in the shadows, relentless, patient, and poised to overwhelm him and bring him to his knees. It would be a very public execution, he suspected.

Lisa was seated on a sofa, her shoeless feet tucked underneath her. An open bottle of Glenfiddich occupied a corner of his desk, and the pair had managed to put a dent in the contents. "When do you think it'll happen, Jack?" Lisa asked. They had been talking about

Warren Day. Munroe called him earlier and they spoke for two hours. He called Day again after returning from the Marriott downtown, where he held his press conference. The candidacy of Senator Jack Munroe was officially over. Day had watched the press conference on C-Span and responded to Munroe with abrupt certitude: He would not stay an active candidate, either. Instead, Day would hold his own press conference and distance himself from Jack Munroe as far as he possibly could.

"He said he'd do it tonight. The time is anybody's guess."

Munroe took another sip from his glass. The Scotch whiskey warmed his stomach and smoothed his nerves. He turned to Lisa. "You need to hold your own press conference, Lisa. I'd offer to help, but my help can only cause you further damage. Leland, now, he was the smart one. He jumped ship as soon as he heard the old man was dead. You should do the same."

"Leland Hayes is a mercenary," Lisa said, spite in her tone.

"Aren't we all?"

She thought for a moment and looked at Munroe. Their gaze was locked for several seconds as she considered the pathos of the man she had admired, supported, even loved. Then she stood, stepped into her shoes, and walked to the senator. She gave him a quick kiss on the cheek, turned, and was gone.

Munroe listened to the door close to his outer office. Now he was completely alone. The phones continued to ring.

The FBI would be back at 6 o'clock, he knew. It was 5:15 now. He took another sip, but his glass was empty. He walked to his desk and sat, waiting in the leather chair he had received from his mother and father when he was elected to Congress.

CHAPTER TWENTY-THREE

SIX WEEKS LATER

THE SKIES WERE as clear as crystal, dotted occasionally by puffs of white clouds. The plane banked to the right and descended as the pilot brought the craft into a swooping arc over the black water below. As he leveled off, Matt spied the dock in the distance. Getting nearer, he could see the small figure leaning against a tree where the dock met the river. A smile erupted and he turned to the passenger in the rear. "Look, Joanne. On the right. It's Jimmy."

The pontoons broke the surface, skipped, and skimmed for a few moments, and settled finally into a lazy turn toward the dock. The heat at ground level was felt instantly, and the pilot slid his window open to create a breeze. Jimmy was waiting, rope in hand, at the edge of the dock, his smile reflecting the bright rays of the tropical sun. Matt knew the drill and waited for the pilot to guide the plane and step out and on to the dock. In a moment, the plane was turned around and Matt opened his door. He stepped quickly to the dock and hugged his diminutive friend in a tight clasp. "Welcome back, Matthew."

Matt then reached for Joanne's hand and guided her to the dock where she greeted Jimmy with tears of joy. The pilot pulled their duffels from the rear and shook everyone's hand before he pushed off and made his way to the river's center for his takeoff.

Jimmy grabbed both duffels and nodded in the direction of the gleaming green Range Rover parked in the shade. Matt gave out a low whistle, expecting instead to see the mud-encrusted Blazer. "Brand-new last week," Jimmy said, "and since I got here a little early, I used the river water to wash it up for you two. After all, it's not every day we get a chance to welcome a beautiful lady to our little project."

"Thank you, Jimmy," Joanne responded, enjoying this bit of regal flattery in the remote depths of the Brazilian rain forest. She climbed into the backseat as Jimmy threw the bags into the rear hatch. "You're in back, too, Matthew. This is a limousine for today, and I'm your driver."

The drive took the route with which Matt had become familiar, and he eagerly described everything he saw to Joanne: The tall umbrella of leaves overhead, the rich neon blossoms that graced the jungle, orchids spraying their delicate petals from mossy branches in the dappled shade. Birds swooping by occasionally, showing their brightest colors. Joanne could feel the rush of Matt's kindled enthusiasm as he spoke and smiled throughout. Jimmy joined the conversation and the rapid-fire questions and answers brought frequent laughs and a steady comfort to the trio. It was a wonderful journey.

Made in the USA
Lexington, KY
19 March 2010